CALAMITY

LIBBIE HAWKER

RUNNING RABBIT PRESS

ALSO BY LIBBIE HAWKER

Tidewater

Baptism for the Dead

Writing as Olivia Hawker

The Ragged Edge of Night

One for the Blackbird, One for the Crow (2019)

In memory of my dad, who was his own kind of calamity.
And for Paul, with love.

Many people think Calamity Jane is a heated myth of the disordered brain of some penny-a-liner, but she is a reality, and the pen of a half crazy imagination is not needed to enhance her actual deeds.

– *The Cheyenne Daily Leader*, 1885

Neither of us have been angels, but let that drop. No one ever gets any consolation looking back into a shadowed past.

– *Deadwood Dick's Big Deal*, Edward Wheeler, 1883

THE GAL'S GOT HONOR LEFT WITH HER GRIT, OUT OF THE WRECK OF A YOUNG LIFE

THIS IS THE FIRST THING I CAN REMEMBER: THE CRACK OF A RIFLE IN the clear blue air, and ringing from the distant hills the shot repeated, bouncing back across the sunlit plain like a jackrabbit in flight.

I turned in the saddle when I heard the shot—an involuntary thing, for the quiet fear that had whispered at me all the way from Missouri shouted in my head all at once, and leaped up in my heart, and even though I knew it was foolish to look back, still I couldn't stop myself. I saw my Pa with both his arms wrapped tight around his body, and his face turned down to the grass where the ends of his dropped reins dragged. He looked as if he was trying to contain some sudden, terrible part of himself that he never knew existed before—the hot, bursting pain roaring through like a blast of dynamite. He leaned, then he tipped, and then, as his horse stopped walking and lowered its head to graze, he fell from the saddle. Just before he disappeared into the knee-high grass I saw the red flower blooming on his back.

I didn't know what to do. Well, what *does* a body do when that body is only twelve years old and a girl and suddenly, quick as a snap of the fingers, an orphan? I turned my own horse around and stared at the place where my Pa had fallen. There was a voice in my head—the very voice that had been whispering fear—and it told me I ought to scream and cry, but all I seemed capable of was looking. Looking at the blue shadow in the grass, the pressed-down place that concealed my father's body, waiting for him to jump up and let loose a string of cusses and shout at me to stop staring and get out of his damn sight before he knocked my fool head in. I looked, and the prairie stayed still. His horse took one slow step, then another, intent on its forage. The sound of tearing as it ripped grass from the earth came loud across the space between us.

Then hooves beating fast against thick earth. I looked up toward the rise—the little hill Pa and I had ridden up just moments before—and saw the crown of a black sugarloaf hat bob up and vanish again behind the crest. Then it rose again, and rose yet more as the horse carried its rider up and over and into the line of my sight. He was an ugly man—or I remember him that way, with a hard, hateful scowl half-shadowed by the brim of his hat. A dirty green scarf hung loose around his neck and his shoulders were thin and wiry.

He never took his eyes off me as he reined in beside my Pa's mount. For a long while we sat watching one another. He was waiting for me to scream, maybe, though the little town outside Fort Kearney was two miles off at least, and even my strident voice would never carry that far. The wagon train we'd been following was an hour's ride to the west—and there my five little brothers and sisters rode, tucked in the back of an old prairie schooner amid barrels of oats and jars of pickled eggs. They were too far off to help me, but they weren't near big or strong enough to lend a hand, anyhow.

After a spell, the rider in the black hat broke my wide-eyed gaze and looked down into the grass where my father lay. The smooth-worn stock of his rifle glinted beside his saddle horn—the rifle that had killed my Pa. The rider's mouth moved quietly on a cuss I couldn't hear. Then he spat into the grass.

"Get out!" I shouted at him, because I had to do something.

The man crossed his wrists on the saddle horn and slouched a little, the very picture of unconcern. He laughed at me, slow and easy. "Or what? What are you going to do about it, girl?"

Tears stung my eyes then. I felt I was drifting a mile above my saddle, floating away from this terrible scene, from the shadow in the grass and the rider's hard, flashing smile. I became aware, with slow, prickling horror, that the skirt of my faded brown linsey-woolsey dress was pushed far up my leg, baring my knee and even the cuff of my drawers. I tried to pull the cloth down to cover myself.

That only made the man laugh harder. "Easy, filly. I got no interest in you. Look like you been clobbered in the face by the ugly stick."

He tapped his horse with his gads and the big gelding danced sideways, nearer to Pa's mount. The rider slid his hand into my father's saddle bag and pulled out a small leather pouch—his money bag, and all I or anyone with the Canary name had left in the world. "This is all I come for," the man said. "Now I've got it, I'll be leaving you in peace."

"Wait!" I cried. "No, you can't!" Reaching out my hand toward him as if I could stop him somehow, take the purse back or knock him from his saddle, or twist his green scarf till it choked off his breath. "We need that money, Mister. I got five brothers and sisters—just little ones. I got to pay for their space in the wagon or the driver will kick them off!"

"I'm afraid that's not *my* trouble to sort out, little missy."

"I'll be left in the wide-open prairie with five babies to look after."

"Your daddy should'a thought of that before he cheated me at faro. There's honest ways for a man to earn a buck and provide for his get."

"Ain't you a Christian man?"

The rider dropped my money into his saddle bag and made a hawking sound, as if my story—or maybe my question—left a bad taste in his mouth. He said, "Fuck off outta here before I shoot you, too. And I'd be doing you a favor if I did. Turn that nag around and ride; I'll give you a count of fifty before I start firing in your direction. You hear me?"

I heard him. My heart leaped all at once in my throat, just as my horse leaped and reeled away, and I clung to its coarse, dry mane and beat its ribs with my heels, and sent it flying off across the prairie, as far as I could get from my father and the vengeful gambler who'd felled him. The whole time I was braced for the impact of his bullet, and my head was ready to crack open with the sound of his shot. The thunder never came.

———

IT WASN'T QUITE TRUE, Short Pants—what I told you just now. That is to say, every word about my Pa's death and the rider in the black hat—that's all true as the gospel, down to the last word. But it ain't so, that it was the first thing I can remember.

I was twelve years old then, just on the verge of thirteen. Of course I remember loads about my life from before my father was killed—before I was left alone in the world. But ever since that day, I have felt that *I* truly began, for better or worse, with that first calamity. Still and all, since I'm coming clean—since you want to know the real truth of me, all of it without no legends or fantasies—I suppose it can't hurt to sketch out my early life in brief.

I was born Martha Canary, in the town of Princeton, Missouri. You know some folks call it Misery, and by my accounting that's not far from the truth. For my Ma it was surely a pit of despair, though the Lord knows we all did our best to make life go easy on her. I suppose a woman can't enjoy any ease in life when she has six children to care for. I was the oldest of them all—her first, and therefore the source of all her troubles. I've always felt guilty over being first, the shackle on her ankle and the weight she was made to drag, though by God it was no choice of mine to come along when and how I did.

This is the way it happened. Pa—that is, Robert Canary by name—was a young man of around twenty years. He was heading with his own pa and ma and his brothers and their wives from Ohio to Misery via Iowa, the place of fair fields and sunny days, and there he spotted the sunlight falling on my Ma's black hair. She was called Charlotte Burch at that point in time, and she was fifteen, a sleek, glossy blackbird of the prairie. That was the way Pa liked to tell the tale.

Whenever he'd recount the story, we little ones all whooped and clapped when he got to the part where he saw Ma for the first time. She was starry and bright in our imaginations, a pretty slip of a girl, a hero's reward in some grand adventure tale. But whenever Pa told it, Ma's smile got tight and her eyes looked small and narrow, as if she peered through the walls of our little cabin toward a thing impossibly far off. Another life that might have been, if she'd spurned Robert's charms, if the blackbird of the prairie had been left to fly free. Instead, she tumbled in some haystack with Robert Canary and when she stood up with the hay still clinging to her long black hair, she had me already planted in her belly.

She married my pa at fifteen, because that's the way good girls do, and though Charlotte had never been very good, she had ambitions back then to make right and live a respectable life. Her own family wouldn't consent to look at her, let alone speak to her —even married now to make good on her grave mistake. So she left Iowa with the husband she hardly knew and settled with him in Missouri.

She was only sixteen when I came into this world. She said I screamed like the dickens and was an ugly baby besides, and those features combined made me impossible to love. But she never loved the other children much, either—even the pretty ones and the quiet ones. She made as if she despised my pa—most of the time, anyway, far as I can recall. Still, she must have counted him tolerable enough, for she kept having babies, one after another, and that only happens by miracle if your name is The Virgin Mary.

By the time Ma was in her grave and Pa was yearning for the gold fields, I came to believe that maybe my mother hadn't always amused herself with her lawfully wedded husband. She was fond of drinking, and as soon as I was old enough to feed and change a child on my own, she left me to tend the brood and spent most of her days at one of Princeton's two dance halls, kicking it up with the railroad men and the bawdy girls who entertained them. For all I know, she took to playing hostess-of-the-hour herself, and that accounts for my five brothers and sisters.

Understand, I don't say these things to disparage her or to smirch up her memory. The prairie is a lonesome place, and life is a cruel, sad thing. If I'd'a been in her shoes, I'd likely do the same.

Since we are talking of recollection, of my life before the rifle's blast, let me tell you what I remember of my childhood. It wasn't all my mother's sadness or the hopelessness of poverty.

I remember vast blue storms building like castle ramparts over the fresh green of the prairie, their upper parts sharply defined, their lower edges swept and blurred by distant veils of rain. I remember the smell of wet sage and dust turned to mud, and gusting across the river on a cool wind, the biting scent of animal herds with rain-soaked hides—cattle, buffalo, pronghorn, the wild horses that sometimes roamed through.

I remember in the mornings the rooster with the scraggly yellow tail chasing a string of hens around and around the cabin, how Lije and I would laugh to watch them scramble, the proud way that rooster stretched his spiky neck and glared as his little clucking wives ran in fear of him.

In the summer when the grass was just turning yellow, I would lean all day on the pasture fence and talk to the horses, listen as they moved together, their warm, full, patient hoofbeats on the hot earth, each of them taking one slow step and pausing, each of them swishing their tails to clear away the flies, and when they all together had moved and picked out a mouthful of grass they would move again, another slow step, as if they shared a single, round-sided, sun-warmed body and one sweet and gentle mind. I named them all, though Pa never saw much point in naming horses since they came and went with his gambling habits. Bess and Button and Sharlamain, Zee and Indian and Red Cat with spots on his hind end like a leopard's hide. If I stood quiet enough for a long enough spell, they'd graze around me and allow me to braid flowers in their hair.

I remember every spring, just as the rivers began to slacken, the wagon trains would form up and creep along the edge of the earth. They were a long, white, endless rope stretched where the prairie met the sky. Their canvas canopies were alike from one wagon to the next, and from a distance I couldn't tell their oxen apart by color. The beasts were all the same, all one shade of umber shadow, the same blocky forms tossing their thick heads in unison, their flat backs bobbing to a common rhythm. How I longed to be among the wagons! I imagined myself riding Red Cat or Bess down that line, listening to the creak of axles and the breathing of the beasts. Heading west—West—to Oregon Territory, or to Wyoming, or Salt Lake City where the Mormons would give you fresh fruit and fry bread and where the sun shone like gold on the flat expanse of their inland sea. Sometimes storm clouds would rise up above the wagons, and like teeth in a singing mouth they stood out bold and white against the rain that obscured everything beyond. And a fork of lightning would flash down from the heavens, and I would imagine a saddle rocking beneath me, a horse tossing its head in alarm, and the pop of thunder put me in mind of all those great teeth gnashing.

Being poor was a great adventure to me, back when I was young. When you have no obligations to society and no one has any expectations of you, either, then the world opens up and flowers with possibility. I could, you see, ride off and join one of those wagon trains any time I pleased. It wasn't just a daydream; I could have done it truly, whenever I made up my mind to go, and not much of anyone would miss me—not for long. That's why I loved to watch the prairie schooners go by, why I loved the company of horses who could carry me off in any direction, off to any Western horizon I might set within my sights. The world was a beauty and a mystery, because even at a tender age I was free to seize it all.

I wish I could say my Ma ever got such enjoyment out of being poor, of having no expectations to meet. But the only pleasure she ever found was in a bottle. I was only a small thing when it dawned on me that our nearest neighbors looked away when any Canary—man, woman, or child—passed by their gate. And not much older when I figured out that my aunts and uncles lived in Princeton, too—also my grandfather, a red-faced, stoop-shoul-dered old man—but it was a rare day I saw their faces, and then the meetings were rushed and tense, and they cast glances over their shoulders as if fearful of who might see them consorting with Robert and his pack of questionable get. I never could puzzle out whether they all stayed away because my Pa preferred gambling to farming, or whether it was my Ma's drinking and dancing that put them off so. I don't suppose it matters, in the end.

Once I recall my Pa drove a cart back from town, an old rocky thing which I thought the pinnacle of magnificence because its two wheels reached so high up its sides and made such a grand growling sound as they rolled along the hard-packed road. I sat atop an empty crate, upturned, for it had held the harvest of our small potato patch and Pa'd had good luck to sell the whole crop in one go. This was a rare combination of occurrences. He had money in his pocket which he hadn't thought to bet at faro—not yet—and had bought me a twist of molasses candy which I sucked as fast as I could, so it'd be mostly gone by the time we got home and the little ones clamored around begging for a taste. Our cabin was in sight around the road's final bend, and as we passed in front of the neighbor's yard—Sowders was their name—Mrs. Sowders came storming out from her clapboard house shaking her fist with her angry teeth showing. She shouted at my father so loud I nearly dropped my candy in the dirt, and the little naked boy who followed her across the yard gripped onto her skirt and screamed in fear of her howling voice.

"Robert Canary," she said, "the Devil has a place all prepared for gamblers. You'll go to Hell and take your pack of misbehaving brats with you if you don't do right by the Lord. This town won't stand no more of your miscreant ways, nor the sins of your wife, who just yesterday was trying to get my own husband to buy her a drink and a dance at Curdy's. And he wasn't even in the saloon neither, just walking by, for he knows how to be a proper man. If you don't tame that strumpet Charlotte—"

At that very moment, the strumpet herself came riding by. Neither Pa nor I knew she'd been in town, nor could we say how long she'd been there, whether an hour or since sunup. Nor did we know just where exactly she had spent her time. She was riding a strange horse we'd never seen before, galloping hard with the wind pulling her hair out of its knot, and her cheeks were hot as embers. When she rode, she never bothered going sidesaddle. Her skirt was pushed up over her knees. The wind rippled the cloth of her bloomers and the little satin bows at the cuffs shivered and bounced in time with the horse's stride. For some reason I never have puzzled out, she carried a long piece of scarlet cloth balled up under one arm. Perhaps she'd intended to make a dress with it, or work it into the only quilt she ever made, a patchwork she never did manage to finish. But Mrs. Sowders watched her thunder up, and stood there slack-jawed and afraid, as my Ma pulled the horse in so hard it rose up on its lathered haunches.

"Here, you old cat," my Ma said. She took the red cloth from under her arm and tossed it over the fence; it hit Mrs. Sowders in the face and draped over her shoulder like a winter scarf while she stared at my Ma in stunned silence. Even the naked boy shut up his yowling and goggled at her.

Ma said, "Take that cloth and make a dress for that bastard of yours."

Then she yipped like a bullwhacker on the trail, and the horse sprang away. I sucked in a breath—it was dry and gritty with the dust of her mount's hooves—and my heart about busted with pride at the sight of her upright back, her knees sharp and flagrant in their satin and lace, the locks of her black hair bouncing. She was like the heroine of some grand tale, all fire and devilry. I never loved my mother more than in that moment, when I saw her soaring free.

Three months later they found her at the bottom of a river gulch. Pa said she must have fallen from a horse, all that long way to the flat red rocks below—an accident, Pa said. He never let me see her body, but I imagine when they found her, her arms were outspread like a black bird flying.

ALL THAT LONG winter while I stayed inside, cooking and cleaning for the little ones—more than I ever had done before—my Pa talked about the gold fields. "Martha," he told me, "in Montana when the sun rises you can't look at the foothills for the way they sparkle with gold. The shiningness will blind you, but it'll make you rich, so you can buy a new set of eyes. A man can walk through a crick bed there, and when he gets out the other side, he can tap his boots and collect the resultant pile of gold dust and sell it and live like a king."

Of course, I didn't believe him. I doubt he believed himself. But he needed something to hitch to, some star to set a course by, or he'd go crazy from looking at all six of his children's faces— each of us needing something, food or shoes that fit and didn't have holes in the sides, or enough candles to keep the feared dark at bay, or a man we could rely on to provide for us proper. All six of us with Ma's features, her dark eyes and her wide, flat mouth, her high cheekbones, her pale skin. But only me with a lick of his own influence.

Well, that spring, just as the castles of thunder built themselves in the sky brick by purple brick, Pa came home from town and stood in the doorway of our cabin and announced in a big, hopeful voice that we was all setting out for Montana, to become a family of prospectors and make ourselves rich as King Midas. He said we would set out that very day. We must all pack up our few belongings, and catch the hens and put them in crates, and sell the horses we didn't need because by that night we'd be sleeping under a blanket of stars. Then he stepped aside like a showman and gestured grandly out into the yard, and I looked past him at the canvas-topped wagon that stood waiting out there in the afternoon light. A pair of red steers with heavy necks and mournful eyes was yoked to the hitch, and it looked so like the wagons I'd watched creep along the horizon every spring and summer that I clapped my hands and skipped from foot to foot just like the little ones.

Although he hadn't given any more warning than chattering about the gold fields all winter long, still I wasn't surprised by this turn of events. I'd sensed it coming, I think, ever since Ma's funeral. As the few good souls who attended her service sang out a hymn that was far more sweet and serene than my mother had been, I'd felt my father tremble beside me, and felt something rattle inside him. Ma's death cut my father loose. Like a wild pony, he wanted to run. That was fine by me; I was ready for adventure, too. Or I thought myself ready.

It didn't take more than a few hours to roll up and tie our bits of property in blankets and flour sacks. While we children worked, Pa explained how he'd sold the forty mostly-barren acres of the farm and used the money to buy the wagon, and a couple of shovels and picks for us to dig with when we got to the golden foothills. We had enough food in the cabin to last us for a few days, plus the hens were still laying eggs, and when they stopped we could butcher them and turn them into soup, cooked over a chip fire on the prairie, just like the Indians did. And when we ran out of food, Pa said, he would ride to the nearest town and strike up a game of faro and use his winnings to buy flour and sugar and onions and smoked meat for our soup kettle.

It seemed like a grand idea to me—the very adventure I'd been dreaming of all my young life. With Pa's help, I bundled the little ones into the wagon and saddled two horses—one for me, one for my brother Cilus, who was almost two years my junior. Well before the sun set, the Canary tribe was making tracks out across the prairie, following the river's gentle bend, searching for the place where the grass was pounded down into a wide, dry road and the ruts of countless wheels and heavy hooves had worn deep down into the earth.

I turned a couple of times in the saddle, looking back at the cabin where I'd spent the whole of my life. But after a while it was just a little dark thing among the sage, sharp-cornered but insignificant, like a bit of knapped flint dropped and forgotten. I turned my back to the cabin for the last time and felt its hold let go. Somewhere ahead lay Montana and gold, and a new life was calling.

WE DIDN'T MAKE it very far before the wagon broke down. I esti-mate it was three days, maybe four, before an axle gave out. Pa hadn't reckoned with that possibility. True, he'd traveled by wagon nearly fourteen years before, the time he found my Ma in the fields of Iowa. But his own father had been at the helm, as it were, and Pa had ridden about carefree, and left the driving and the upkeep of the prairie schooner to others.

We waited at the side of the trail more than two days before help arrived. During that time, we slept away the day's heat in the dirt beneath the wagon bed. The wagon settled down against its busted part like an old man leaning quiet and near-broken on a cane. The cattle was tethered nearby and grazed till they grew fat and lazy, and every night, once the mosquitoes had all gone to sleep, we walked the cattle and the horses down to a hidden crick for water.

Pa kept a restless eye on the trail. His face in the blue shadow of the wagon was pale and strained, and he squinted continually to the south and east. At the time, I thought he was fearful of Indians. I think now he was looking for soldiers—rebels or unionists, it made no difference, for the few times either kind of soldier came through Princeton they raised Hell and were prone to anger and violence.

"If I give the word," Pa told us (more times than I could count over those two long days), "you pick up the baby, Martha, and all of you kids run like Hell for the crick bed. Stick your finger in Sara's mouth so she don't cry. Stay quiet and hide till you hear me call you back, or if you never hear me call, stay out of sight of the trail till nightfall."

On the third morning of our stranding, just as I used the last bit of flour to cook plain cakes on a flat rock beside a weak, smokeless fire, six or seven wagons came up through the prairie, rising from the distant line of grasses like clouds gathering on a horizon. Pa gave a long sigh and leaned on the wagon box, as if fear had been all that had held him upright, and now, with fear draining away, he wilted and sagged. He had Cilus and me rustle the little ones out of our wagon's shadow and spit on a kerchief to clean their faces, and we all lined up beside the trail's tracks in order of height, to make a good presentation to the newcomers.

The sound of their wagons rumbling reached out along the prairie and overtook all our senses long before the party was in shouting range. That jarring, never-ending, bone-rough malaise the little ones had complained of all the days since leaving our cabin—just hearing the rattle again set them to fidgeting and whining in anticipation of more tiring hours spent in a wagon's bed. But Pa snapped at them to stand still and I boosted baby Sara on my hip and watched the wagons slow through the glittering haze of trail dust. The lead schooner stopped level with us and the driver, a fat man with a long black beard, looked us all over in silence.

"Had a little trouble," my Pa said. "Axle broke and I don't have 'nother."

A woman's long, lean face appeared below the drawn-up canvas of the canopy. She wore a blue ruffle bonnet over her hair and she had raking, sharp pale eyes. She squinted at me with the baby on my hip, then she hid her mouth behind a hand and whispered in the fat man's ear. He made an abrupt motion like shooing flies. The woman disappeared again into the depths of the wagon.

"Got no axle to spare," the man said, "but if you can pay your way, you and the children may ride with us."

Pa patted his trouser pockets vaguely, searching for something he knew he wouldn't find. Finally he said, "All's I got to pay with is some chickens in these crates."

"And the oxen," the man said. "Your horses and saddles, too."

I got fearful at that, the prospect of no longer riding free but having to endure the jolting and jarring of the wagons, and I picked at Pa's sleeve with nervous fingers.

"Only one horse and saddle," Pa insisted. "I'll need one of my own for coming and going, and one to keep fresh."

"Coming and going where?" The fat man laughed, wheezing trail dust.

"And," Pa added, "my biggest boy here can chop fire wood when we stop at nights. He has an axe and he keeps it sharp."

"Not a lot of trees between here and Montana."

"Plenty of broken-down wagons, though, I bet. And chopping's work you'd rather not do at the end of a long day of driving."

Such a fat man certainly isn't fond of exertion, was my ungracious thought.

"Got no milk for the baby," the woman's voice called shrilly from inside the wagon. "Unless that slip of a thing beside you is your wife and can nurse it herself, in which case she is too young for you, mister, and you're bound for Hellfire."

Even though Pa wanted us all to keep quiet and look as good as we could manage, and allow him to do the bargaining, I couldn't help but speak up. "I'm not her mother but her sister, Missuz. Our ma's dead, but Baby Sara eats all right without any milk. She's got most of her teeth and I chew up her food for her, so there!"

Pa cast me a dark glance. My *so there* was unnecessary, I knew, but still I felt it was warranted.

"My daughter Martha here is fourteen." Pa lied, but I was big and strong enough to look it. "She can do the washing real good."

I stifled a groan. There was no task on God's green earth I hated more than washing clothes. I imagined the fat man's trousers stank of that awful, musty sweat you get between the cheeks. You know the kind, when you've been sitting in the sun too long and washing too little. But there wasn't much for it. We might wait another week for more wagons to come by, and we had run out of flour. Our few scrawny hens wouldn't see us through many more days. If I had to work to feed my brothers and sisters, I'd do it. But I wouldn't do it with a smile on my face.

The fat man finally nodded, and Pa approached, hand outstretched to shake. When the deal was done, a few tall, strapping boys emerged from the wagon to tie the oxen to the back of their box and take Cilus's horse. Cilus blinked back the tears he wasn't willing to shed before these tall stranger-boys with their harsh laughter and darting eyes, their wiry arms hard and angled from months spent working on the trail.

Pa tried to pull his shaking-hand away from the fat man, but he gripped him tighter and said with half a laugh, "The oxen and the horse, and your chickens, and labor from your two kids—that gets you a ride and a share of our food for a week. After that, we leave you wherever we are unless you can come up with more."

"That's mighty un-Christian of you," Pa told him.

"Be grateful, Mister. In a week we'll be out of the range of the soldiers and your children will be safer than they are here."

"In a week we'll be in Indian country."

"Rather face reds than rebs." The fat man laughed real loud at his own wit.

Pa jerked his hand away and turned back to us. He gave a quick nod; Cilus, Lena, and Lije pulled the chicken crates from the shade and slung their bundles on their backs, while I handed Baby Sara to the squint-eyed woman in the wagon and boosted little Isabelle up inside, too. I was about to climb up to tend my smallest sisters, but Pa restrained me with a hand on my shoulder.

"On your horse, Martha."

"You sure?"

"I won't have one of these young jacks making off with your horse and never giving it back."

When I was mounted, and the fat man called to his oxen to get a move on—when the train started moving again, creaking toward a far, faint suggestion of blue mountains—I sat still on my horse as Pa maneuvered close beside me. He watched the wagons roll along for a time in silence.

Then I said, "One week, and we gave them all we had. Will we reach Montana in a week?"

"Not even close."

"What'll we do, then?"

"We'll ride to every town we pass and scare up a game of faro."

I grinned at him then and felt the sun hot on my cheeks. My Pa didn't impress when it came to farming, or fathering, or being a quality husband to my poor dead mother, but no one could fault his luck at faro. He patted his horse's neck and nodded significantly. With two mounts of our own, we could zip to and fro and make out all right, as long as Pa could find a saloon. He was a born winner, made by the Lord with a lucky hand. Or that's what I thought at the time.

He conjured enough money at faro to keep us rolling along with that wagon train for three whole weeks. Then his luck ran out, and I came to understand that he never possessed a bit of luck to begin with. It was all trickery and fraud with him; I guess it always had been so. Pa's cheating ways caught up to him that day outside of Kearney.

Well, that's how my Pa came to be in the predicament of being shot to death on the prairie. And that's how I came to be in the predicament of being an orphan, not quite thirteen years old and in hostile company, with five children in my care. And you can see that's why I've always considered it my beginning, the start of my life. The first in a long string of sorrows.

No one has ever put it in a book before—all the books they've writ about me, they all start with grand adventure and the wind in my hair like the wind was in my mother's hair. But it's never an adventure that starts a true tale. It's loss and blood and wanting. It's a shadow in the grass and a child's knees uncovered. And life for me—as it is for you—was just a string of calamities.

IT TOOK two hours at least for me to catch up to that wagon train. I rode as fast as my horse would consent to go; I urged that poor beast on with my heels and desperate shouts, and sometimes with the flat of my hand on his rump, till he was lathered up and blowing. I never looked behind me, though I can't tell you now whether I was more afraid I'd see the man in the black hat, hot on my tail with his rifle trained towards me, or the ghost of my father risen up and coming after, calling me a coward for running and a fool for thinking I might ever get back alive.

After a time, when my horse slowed and wouldn't move faster than a walk, no matter how I flailed at his sides or whipped his neck with the reins, I lost the prickle between my shoulder blades. Death didn't seem so close anymore, though I had just witnessed it not long ago. I allowed my horse to plod. Terror drained out of me; I filled up instead with something far worse. Practical considerations overtook my thoughts—even overtook my sorrow at losing my pa. I was left in charge (in the blink of an eye, or as it were, the click of a rifle's hammer) of a gaggle of skinny little goslings. That weight of responsibility dragged at my soul and sat there, hot and crushing inside my guts, as if some mean-spirited angel had pried my jaws apart and dumped molten lead right down my tender young throat. The gambler wasn't behind me now. I no longer needed to fear him. Something much worse lay ahead.

With time, I found a high bluff and rode up its side. At the top I let my horse drop his head to graze. Far below, the plain had gone blue with the onset of dusk, and away to the east I could see the wagons of our party moving slow across the land. In my haste to save my hide I had overtaken them, though I was somewhat north of the trail.

"All right," I told my horse, "this is it. Back we go empty-handed, and God have mercy on us all."

I rode down onto the grassy flats and waited in the middle of the trail for the wagons to come to me. I was aching by then from the long, hard ride, and worried my horse might go lame. So I dismounted and held his reins and flipped the ends against my hand so they smack-smacked in the quiet prairie evening. The only other sounds was an endless churring of bugs in the grass, and the sleepy notes of meadowlarks.

Finally the fat man's wagon came near. His piggy eyes watched me with suspicion, but he didn't speak a word. I pulled my horse out of his way, then fell in walking beside the wagon.

His wife with the blue bonnet raised one side of the canvas canopy and looked down at me. I could read the reproach in her eyes. In the fading light, her face looked longer and sharper than ever, and there was no color about her gaze, no flush of passion or feeling.

"Where's your daddy?" she said crossly.

I tried to make out just who was in that wagon, whether my brothers and sisters was awake and listening. But I couldn't see a thing, save for the solid black shapes of barrels and boxes, and the rhythmic sway of a brick of hard-packed cane sugar, swinging from a rope high in the canopy's hoops.

There was no getting around her question, so I answered. "Dead."

One half of her tight mouth smiled. "That's no surprise to me. Your daddy wasn't a good man, and now no doubt he's gone down to Hell."

"You sure know how to comfort a body, Missuz."

It was impudence and I knew it. I also knew that I had neither mother nor father to smack me or scold me for it. My stomach felt light and fluttering, like a caged bird set free. I could say most anything, I reasoned, and get away with it. Who could stop me?

"He wasn't a good man," the wife repeated. "But we're about to stop for the night and your pack of brats is paid up through today. You'll sleep with us, but in the morning you're all out on your own."

I stared at her hard, trying to discern how serious she was. I thought perhaps I'd find some soft place at her edges, somewhere I could see pity and Christian charity crumbling the meanness of her soul. Some place I might work in my fingers and pry at her, and pick loose a little compassion. But there was nothing to her—

only a flat, cold, uncaring glower, an impatience to be rid of the whole Canary mess.

"You ain't concerned at all with the plight of six orphan children alone in the world, exposed to wolves and Indians and God knows what else on the wide-open plain?"

The woman shrugged.

"Reckon that makes *you* the one lacking in goodness, mam. Not my pa."

The fat man who drove the wagon heard my retort and he bellowed that he'd skin me alive himself, and by God no savior ever said good honest people had to care for the whelps of gamblers and thieves, and he'd stay awake all night to be sure I didn't pinch any food or clothes or guns from his family. He said in the morning he would be glad to leave us all in his dust, for I was a poor hand at laundry and no use to him a-tall.

When he pulled the wagon to a stop and the others in the party circled up and all the women set to making a cook fire, I tugged open the canvas to find my five brothers and sisters huddled close together, clinging with grubby hands to thin bodies, the lot of them tangled up into one mass like a ball of frayed, dirty rope. Tears streaked their cheeks and their eyes were red and swollen, but they wept without making a sound, even the baby.

———

I WOKE the children when dawn was only a gray whisper, when the biggest and brightest of the stars was still clear in the bow-curve of the sky—before the camp began to stir. When the fat man and his hard-hearted wife and their stupid, laughing sons woke—when the whole uncaring family readied their wagons for the day's long haul—I wanted them to see the Canary lot standing tall and proud, as tall as we could stand, six children that we were.

We still had my horse and one saddle to our name, and that was something. Cilus also had a pocket knife among his belongings and little Lije had a length of fishing line with a metal hook, which he'd won off one of the wagon boys in a game of dares. I figured if we could scare up a piece of flint, we would have the means to make a fire, and we might leave the wagon trail and follow a stream down to a river, and fish for our sustenance as we crept along its bank. We'd follow the river wherever it flowed, and sooner or later we would come across a town, maybe even a city. Then all our troubles would be over.

As a spot of pink light blushed the horizon, I told the children how it would be. Isabelle and Sara, being smallest, must ride all the time on the horse. Lena and Lije could take it in turns to sit up behind them and make sure Sara didn't fall from the saddle. Cilus and I would walk the whole way, but that would give us plenty of opportunity to look for flints as well as snakes and prairie dogs, which maybe we could kill if we was fast enough and chucked rocks hard enough at their little heads. They all agreed it was a suitable plan, and I was proud that none of them cried as I hoisted the three girls up into the saddle and lined up the boys beside me.

The Canarys stood arrayed in that stoic tableau as the wagon party packed up, as the fat man's sons kicked out the ashes of the fire and collared the protesting oxen. None of those devils glanced at us once while they went about their business, and I swear I even heard that hatchet-faced blue-bonnet bitch singing when the first wagon bumped back onto the trail, just as if a burden had been lifted from her soul.

My stomach was so empty, the pain of it made me sick, and as I watched the wagons depart all my bravery vanished like stars behind a cold, black cloud. A deep shiver of fear rattled inside me. It shook my feet loose from where I'd resolutely planted them in the earth.

I forgot Canary pride and my show of stubbornness. I ran a few steps toward the wagons. The horse, unprepared for my sudden movement, threw up its head and the reins clutched in my fist arrested me. Tethered, I kicked at tufts of grass and cried out with rising desperation. "Wait! You can't leave us. Wait!" But no one stopped, or even looked around.

Cilus sucked on his lip a minute, and then he said real slow and thoughtful, "We—ll." I looked at my brother and saw in his determined black eyes what we must do.

"Come on," I said to them all, including the horse, and set off in the wake of the wagons

---

UNLESS THERE'S REAL DANGER—INDIANS or a flash flood or robbers on the road—a wagon train don't move fast. Oxen are plodding creatures, and a few children on foot can keep pace with laden prairie schooners.

Of course, none of us was used to so much walking. We must have covered twenty miles every day, and by the time the wagons pulled off the trail and their cook fires flared within the rampart of their circle, my whole body ached like an old woman's—hips, knees, ankles, back, even my neck and shoulders felt worn away by fatigue.

I had found a small flint half-buried in a wagon rut, and Lena had collected some dried dung which she kept tied up in her pinafore. We had a small cook fire of our own, over which we roasted the two bull snakes Cilus had ambushed and dispatched with his pocket knife, as well as a few fat, yellow grubs Lije dug out of the earth and skewered on long stems of grass. It wasn't a filling supper, but we had scared it up on our own and it made me feel as if we could surely make do—providing I woke at all the next day and didn't expire in my sleep from pure exhaustion.

Again I arrayed the children well before dawn, resolved to show those heartless pioneers just who was strong and hardy. And again we followed the wagon train on foot, trailing some hundred yards to its rear. We barely spoke all that second day; even the baby Sara was too tired to fuss, though she did cough now and again. When merciful night came, we collapsed on the ground together, far beyond the circle of the wagon train, too footsore and weary to build a fire even though Lena had plenty of buffalo chips in her apron. We ate our supper of grubs and roots raw, and drank from a crick with our bare hands, and fell asleep in one another's arms.

I felt sure we would die that night. The two smallest, at least, for their eyes was so dull and their bodies drooping; their souls seemed already to have fled. Sara's cough troubled me greatly; it was persistent and rattled some, and though I knew nothing of illness, still I didn't like the sound of it. But wouldn't you know, the smallest Canarys was the first to wake—up before the larks began to sing—and by the time our third day had well and truly begun, I felt a touch stronger.

At mid-day, Cilus ran down a hawk that was struggling to rise with its prey, and he came bouncing back through the grass holding a kicking, bleeding jackrabbit up by one long hind leg. We ate like kings that night. The smell of our roasted rabbit drifted over to the wagon camp, where they supped on onion broth and gritty bread. Once their bellies was full, the boys occupied themselves with fleshing the rabbit skin in the purple twilight, and I could hear them laughing quietly over some private joke. The familiar sound mingled with the smoke of our fire and stung my eyes, and soon I was teary, recalling the warm hearth of our cabin back in Missouri, thinking how many miles our old home lay to the east.

In the midst of my sorrowing reverie, Lena tapped my wrist and whispered, "Look, Martha. Who's that coming?"

Three long, thin shadows had broken from the ring of wagons. They made their way across't the empty space toward us. Lije stood up with the rabbit skin in his hand, stared at the approaching figures, then retreated into the swaying grass like some small and skittish critter going to ground. Long before those shadows reached our circle of firelight, I recognized them by their wiry frames and their dusty, mocking laughter. They was the sons of the fat man and the blue-bonnet bitch. One of them carried a flour sack in his hands; it swung around his knees as if it had some real weight to it. I tried to imagine what might be in that bag, but all I could think of was the brick of pressed sugar their mother kept tied up in her canopy, and my mouth filled suddenly with water.

The boys stopped at the edge of the light and stared at me. I rose from my crouch and folded my arms, considering them, pleased my body was not near as tired as it had been, and feeling I must look something like a real woman after days of travail—strong and steady-eyed, not like a kid at all.

"You been following us," the tallest boy said.

"We can go wherever we please. You ain't got no claim to the trail. We're heading to Montana to prospect for gold, so tend to your own party and leave us be."

The boy held out the flour sack. The weight of whatever it contained swung, tantalizing, above the fire. "Brought you something."

I stepped forward and reached for the sack, but he pulled it back again and his brothers gave an ugly unison snicker.

"Ain't a gift," he said. "It's for barter."

"You know we ain't got nothing to trade. And you ain't getting my horse, so..." I recalled the man with the rifle, his dangerous grin below the brim of his sugarloaf hat. "So fuck off out of here," I finished, and Lena gasped.

"*You* got something to trade all right, missy. Think about it; don't be so stupid."

I paused, considering. There was no telling what might be in that sack, but whatever it was—flour, bacon fat, wool socks, even salt for curing the rabbit skin—we had sore need of it. I kicked my feet in the dust for a minute, more concerned with what my brothers and sisters might think than with any question of sin or morality. Finally I shrugged my shoulders and told the little girls to go off and find Lije in the grass and sit with him till I called.

Cilus edged closer to me. I could see the tip of his pocket knife poking out between his knuckles. He held it low, along his leg, doing his best to conceal it. "Martha," he began, but I pointed towards the wagons.

"Stand over there and keep watch. If Fat Head comes looking for his dumb little whelps, he'll scald us for sure if he sees what's up."

Cilus hesitated. His eyes darted to the flour sack, then back to me, but they returned to the mysterious barter and lingered there. Then he nodded. "All right, if you think it's best." He strode off into the darkness.

I drove a hard bargain that night. I knew what those boys wanted—no girl could grow to the age of almost-thirteen with Charlotte Burch Canary for a mother, and not get some inkling of what those boys wanted—what all men want. But recent events had made me patient and calculating, and I wasn't fool enough to give up my best goods for an unknown trade. They had been on the trail a long time, under the eye of their stiff-necked parents, with little time to dart off for a fiddle alone in the grass. I had the upper hand, and I knew it. I resolved to use every speck of my advantage.

It took only a moment to unbutton my dress from collar to waist. I slid my bony shoulders out of my sleeves and let them get a good long look at my chest. I didn't have much in the way of taddies—not ever, but especially not then. Still, whatever meager charms I possessed enchanted those boys like no pretty face by moonlight ever could. One of them set to grabbing himself right then and there, and made a sound that was half grunt, half laugh, *uh-huh-huh-huh*, while he toiled away with his eyes popping. The other two stepped close and touched me—each one laid a hand on a side of my chest, and for a moment I had the dizzy feeling they was fixing to push me over, backwards, into the fire. My heart beat hard; I could feel it pounding against one boy's palm. Then with a long, indrawn breath he stepped away, and so did his brother, and without a word he placed the flour sack at my feet.

I was quick to snatch it up. I gripped it hard against my naked chest, and stood watching as the three of them hurried off into the night. They didn't go back towards the wagons; I figured they would in time, when their personal business was concluded. I smiled to myself, right pleased that I'd outwitted those fools and got my trade for so little work. I pulled up my dress and worked the buttons with one hand, still unwilling to let that flour sack go. Then I called the children back to the fire with a note of glee in my voice that none of us had heard since the day our father was killed.

Oh, the treasures that bag contained! I showed them all when they huddled around the flames, with the red light turning their faces to hungry, harried masks. Most of it was flour—a few measures left inside the sack. But sitting right on top was two chunks of smoked venison, each the size of my fist, and six pickled eggs sticky and clotted with flour.

The wagon boys had gleaned a few scraps from their parents' stores—no doubt pinched at great peril when the fat man's back was turned, or his shrewish wife was napping. With such unchari-table parents, I figured the wagon boys ran a great risk by putting together their trade. They must be near enough desperate for what I had to barter.

I passed out the eggs right then and there. After our feast of roasted rabbit, we would have been wiser to save the eggs for a hungrier night, but I sensed I had gained a great advantage over the wagon train, and I felt a celebration was in order. What satis-faction it gave me to watch as my brothers and sisters licked the flour from the eggs, from their thin, dirty fingers. And oh, the taste when I bit into my egg—they were beet-pickled, bright pink and pretty as Christmas. Vinegar-sharp, biting back with spice. Never in all my life had I tasted anything so good.

THAT'S how we got by for three more weeks. Every few nights, one or two of the boys—sometimes all three—slipped away from the encampment and brought the provisions they had skimmed. At first, it was enough to undo my buttons and let them feel my chest. But soon they declared the top half of me old news and threatened to cut off the supply unless I offered more enticing wares.

I figured they would tire of my chest soon enough, but I had already made up my mind to price every inch of my bare skin sky-high. Before too long, I made some demands of my own. We fell into a habit of trade—one that suited both parties so well that our partnership continued amiably enough.

I got two extra sleeping mats and a ripped old blanket for a look at the backs of my knees. For the price of a slingshot—which Cilus used quite handily to kill us a bird or a rabbit almost every night—I let each of the wagon boys rub his little stick against my lower thigh. And for the sight and one touch apiece of my anatomy under my drawers—front and back—I got a slab of bacon so big it lasted five days, as well as a rag dolly for the girls to play with.

My best victory of all came when I told them I wanted a horse and saddle—and not a lame horse, either; one capable of carrying weight for a full day, and gentle enough for the little ones to ride. I made the demand the way one asks for a castle in the sky or a pot of fairy gold. I didn't think the boys would ever come through— how in Hell could they expect to get a horse away from the wagon train? But in the purpling dusk, I watched them lead a gray mare toward our tiny fire, and its stride was good and sound, and when they stood it for my inspection, I saw that its eye was soft and kind. The mare had no saddle, but it did have a bridle with a metal bit. I figured that was good enough.

"How'd you get this horse away from your pa?" I asked.

"Doesn't matter," the oldest boy said. "None of your business anyway."

I could tell by the way he shifted his feet and glanced down at the ground, then over his shoulder, that somebody in the wagon train knew exactly what those boys was up to. Maybe it was their fat pa, or maybe one of the uncles or cousins who inhabited the other schooners. Whoever it was, they consented to turn a blind eye to our bartering, and they surely thought me the cheapest of harlots. I got a knot in my stomach, wondering how long it'd be till grown men came in the night, too, bearing goods I'd be hard-pressed to resist.

But that was a problem for another day. The wagon boys had come through on the deal; Martha Canary was an honest girl, and not one to skitter out of an agreement. I sent the little ones off into the grass so I could pay the price for our new horse. It wasn't anything to me. I had certainly worked much harder in my young life, and had handled tasks far more disagreeable. While the boys went about their business, I looked up at the stars, at their sharp points and cold light, and I thought about the foothills of Montana where my dead pa said the earth gleamed so bright with gold you couldn't look at it for fear of going blind.

Many a person would call what I did then whoredom of the basest degree. I am guilty of that sin, more times over than I can ever count. But still to this day, I insist I was never a whore on the wagon trail. Whoring is an act done for one's own gain. But all the shameful things I did on the edge of my thirteenth year of life, I did for the sake of the children. I'll account myself no harlot for saving the lives of my brothers and sisters. And if God thinks otherwise, then God is a damn blind food, and you can quote me on that.

THE NOTORIOUS FREE-AND-EASY WAIF OF THE ROCKY WESTERN COUNTRY

FROM THE NEXT DAY ON, THE WORLD GREW HOTTER AND DRIER around us, and after a time the land turned from pale gold to red. Grassland gave way to bare earth between islands of sage, rough and dry with gnarled branches. The land smelled old and exposed; the scent of it left a tingle on your tongue like bicarbonate of soda. We followed the wagons for three days into the red waste, and I said very little to the children, for I could sense that something was wrong, but I didn't know what, nor how to explain the wrongness to my brothers and sisters. I had done a passable job of keeping them alive; I had begun to feel somewhat accomplished—maybe even clever. I didn't want to face the doubt that dragged at my spirit. But here's what gnawed at me as the plains turned to desert: in all his talk of Montana and the glorious fields of gold, Pa had never mentioned no baked-dry land like this. I knew we wasn't in Montana. We wasn't even close.

On our third night in the red wasteland, one of the boys came over for his trade. He had made some wire snares—which wouldn't be much use on the trail, since you have to leave a snare alone and go back to check it, time and again. On the trail, you're never in the same place twice, and riding back to check a snare means hours and miles wasted. Still, the workmanship was neat, and I thought maybe the snares would come in handy when we all settled down in the gold fields, so I took them in good faith.

When our business was concluded, and we occupied ourselves with putting our clothes to rights, I said, "Where are we now, anyway? This place ain't Montana; I know that much." I said it as if I was some world-wise traveler, like I could speak with real authority on the topic.

The boy didn't fall for my put-on. "Jee-zus," he said, "you are a dumb little bitch sometimes, Martha Canary. Of course this ain't Montana. This is Utah Territory. Tomorrow we'll be in Salt Lake City."

I went cold at his words, and didn't know what to say in response. I'd never looked at a map before, but I was sure Salt Lake must be far from our destination. "Well," I said, trying to make like I wasn't terrified all of a sudden, "what's the gold like in Salt Lake City?"

The boy hooted while he did up his trousers. "By God, girl, there ain't a bit of gold in Salt Lake. Nothin' but Mormons there. We're bound for California. My pa has a claim on some good farm land. If you got a brain in that ugly head, you'll stay in Salt Lake 'stead of following us west. The Mormons will find a place for you quick enough."

I'd heard all about Mormons and what kind of places they had for girls like me. I wasn't fixing to be any man's wife just yet, and I sure didn't aim to be one wife out of a hundred. I gave that boy such a stare as to tell him exactly what I thought about him.

"Don't follow us," he said. "The desert might not kill you, but it'll kill those little girls sure enough, and probably your brothers, too. My pa's too hard to relent and let you back in the wagon. Besides, we're all getting bored with your mangle and there won't be no more trades soon. You best think hard before you try the desert with nothing to sustain you."

That night I lay awake for a long time in my bedroll. I could hear the little ones sleeping all around me, their breath and their dream-murmurs. I thought of what lay ahead of us, what I might do to make good for my brothers and sisters. Prospecting for gold was out of the question, but I understood by then that we would have made piss-poor prospectors anyhow, with most of us too small to wield a shovel or pan in the streams. Besides, Pa had given our prospecting tools to the wagon train as payment for our passage, and thus far the boys hadn't traded them back.

Children have a way of being confident in the face of the unknown. It don't occur to a child that she might be overmatched or out of luck or even headed right over the precipice of disaster. Children just keep on doing, with might good cheer. That's the blessing of the young: to blind yourself to the doom that's coming, to go on as if nothing in the world is wrong. Humans are resilient creatures when we're young. We don't learn how to be brittle till age creeps up—till life has knocked us around some, and cheated us dirty, and taught us to doubt and to harbor suspicions.

So, young and confident as I was, I lined up my options and examined them, as if any was just as likely to work out as all the others. Taking up as a wife to some Mormon fella was right out of the question. Wifing hadn't agreed with my mother; I was determined not to make the same mistake. I reasoned I'd find some place to work, and just like that, I'd get a little house for the children and me, and send Cilus and Lije off to school. That was how adults did it, when they had children to care for—or that was how respectable adults did it, I was given to understand. My parents had been somewhat less than respectable, so reason told me that if I wanted to care for my brothers and sisters properly, all I had to do was whatever my ma and pa wouldn't have done themselves.

The only difficult part would be finding work. I was a big, strong girl, but I was still young, and I suspected I might have a trial, trying to convince some boss to let me tend tables at a restaurant or wash in a laundry. Certainly, I would need to find myself a dress that went all the way down to my ankles, if anyone was to take me seriously and believe I could do a grown woman's work. I couldn't sew and had no money for cloth, besides—but dresses could be borrowed from those Christianly sorts of ladies, the ones who take pity on struggling orphans.

I was damn sure I wouldn't work as a hostess in a saloon or as a dance-hall girl. The boys from the wagon train was one thing, but full-grown men, drunk and stinking of whiskey—maybe mean into the bargain—was another thing altogether. Besides, once I reached Salt Lake City, such carryings-on would be unforgivable in a girl of my age. I was dead set on giving my brothers and sisters a regular life, a chance for respect and dignity some far-off day when we was all grown up. God might have taken our parents for reasons only He knew, but that didn't mean the Canary children had to consign themselves to perfect waifdom.

I lay beside the dying embers of our fire, staring up at the night sky. The stars shone pale silver, crowded into every patch of blackness. I imagined the city would be like that: people everywhere you looked, packed in tighter than the stars. In those uncountable thousands of women and men, there must be someone who would offer me honest work. *With my luck*, I told myself, *it'll be laundry for sure*. But the prospect didn't trouble me over-much. I hated laundry, but if it was a path that would allow all us Canarys to forge ahead together, I was determined to wash and wring and scrub till my hands was chapped bloody, and never mind the pain.

NEXT MORNING, some time before noon, we followed the wagon train up to the crest of a long, gradual rise. As we climbed, three of us to a horse, we could see nothing beyond the top of that hill save for blue sky, cloudless and stretching on forever, its belly tickled by the tops of the thin, wiry grass that grew in desert sand.

But by the time we reached the crest, it seemed all the world lay spread out before us.

I reined my horse to a stop. Cilus did the same, on the gray mare with Lije and Isabelle sitting a-front and behind him. We set and stared down at the valley in silence, and my mouth fell open far enough that I could have caught gnats for my supper. The sun dazzled on a great body of water, a hundred times wider than any river I had seen. It stretched almost to the horizon, and where it should have met the sky in a hard line, there was only the softness of haze, a shimmer blending water and earth and air into one rippling band of blue. The far-off peaks of mountains rose from that mobile blueness, and they was blue, too, but darker than the sky and the haze, and their jagged tops shone pale with snow.

Cilus said, "Is that the ocean?"

I shook my head. We hadn't gone all the way to California, and besides, the ocean was big enough that you couldn't see any mountains across't it. I didn't know much about travel, or the world at large, but I knew that much, at least. The water we stared at, though—close in and well advanced of the blue shimmer—was as golden as any thief could please. Against that near-endless plain of perfect smoothness, the sunlight was so bright it made my eyes ache. I had to squint to look down at the water. It made me long for the gold fields Pa had promised us in Montana.

"This is as good as we'll get," I told the children. "That's the only field of gold we'll ever see."

Salt Lake City lay below us, arrayed on the nearest shore. It was big, with great stone-and-brick buildings that seemed almost white against the brown-gray of desert. From our vantage we could see green patches of garden and farm, like patches on a quilt amid the buildings. After our long and weary travels, and the deprivations of the trail, those gardens gave me a mighty upwelling of hope. A real craving for carrots, too, pulled straight from the ground, still tasting of damp soil. From up high, the city made me feel properly calm and collected, for it was laid out in perfect squares, neat and broad with no funny angles or roads running askew. The whole place seemed to speak of order and comfort—everything was well in hand. Salt Lake City seemed to promise an end to all weariness and despair—and I had brought us to that welcome all on my own, without any disaster falling, unless you count Pa's death.

The wagon train was already snaking down the hill toward the city, rocking along the deep-rutted road. The oxen tossed their heads and shortened their strides almost to a stagger, and leaned back to brace the weight of the burdens they bore. The Canarys would find slow going if we stayed behind the fat man's wagon. A thinner path, not much more than a deer trail, broke away from the main road.

"Come on," I said to Cilus.

I kicked my horse and turned his head toward that narrow trail. Cilus followed close behind. I didn't even glance at the wagon train as we took our leave. Not one of the children raised their hands in farewell, neither. We was all glad to be done with that pack of heartless bastards. Glad never to see those boys again, never to work another trade. A better future lay ahead. We could see it now, golden as the promise of Montana, shining and warm in the sun.

ALL THIS TALK has made my throat dry. Pour us another whiskey, Short Pants. I always liked whiskey best of all the spiteful spirits.

I heard a preacher say that once: spiteful spirits. He told me I oughtn't to drink, and maybe he was right, but I've done a powerful lot of things I oughtn't to have done, including what I did with that preacher. He paid me with silver, and with another sermon about how I oughtn't to fornicate for money. I wonder if anybody ever sermoned him over his own sins.

Understand, I don't mean to make light of my wrongs. I do feel them still. They drag at me; they hold me here, when I should have left this place long ago. The trading with the boys from the wagon train—that was no sin. But once we reached Salt Lake City, that was the moment when I fell from the narrow ledge of grace.

Another whiskey. Then I'll talk on.

———

IT TOOK near an hour to descend the hill and find our way to the heart of the city. The roads was so broad that each one seemed like a plain itself, a vastness long and intimidating to cross. And the buildings! I'd never seen any structures so fine or new back in Princeton, Missouri. Everything made out of brick or wood was fresh and pure. Everything made from stone was pale, clean as a scraped bone. But bones are left over when something is long dead, and Salt Lake City was new, thriving—growing up fast as dandy-lions in a field.

I had been right enough about the stars. There was at least as many folks in that city as points of light in the nighttime sky, but unlike stars, the people never held still. Crowds flowed around us like water—men with great beards spilling down their chests and women in long dresses of joyless colors with high collars and sleeves near down to their fingertips. Not a one of them looked at us. We was six children packed like panniers onto the backs of two tired old horses; one child an infant not old enough to speak her first words, and coughing something terrible, besides. And not one person looked. They simply parted and moved around us. They gave us berth, but couldn't be troubled to see our need. That was when the truth first struck me: It would prove harder than I had supposed to find a long dress or a job, or even a crust of bread for the little ones to eat. In the maze, in the canyons of the city, we were of as much consequence as twigs swept along on a river's current.

We wandered up one great street and down another, crossing

and re-crossing the neat squares of the town. We passed a restaurant with gentlemen and ladies seated behind its rippled glass window, talking over the pretty white plates that held their food, so clean and shiny and small. A rich, warm smell of something baking drifted from the restaurant's door, and all at once the children began to complain of their hunger. We still had some provisions left in our flour sack, enough to pinch by for a few more days. But we had found our destination—the place we must accept as our new home, or so I thought at the time—and I thought a kind of celebration was in order.

I slid down from my horse's saddle and passed his reins to Cilus. "Ride up and down this street," I told him, "and don't cross over into any other road. You'll see me again when I'm ready."

Then I set off on foot. Salt Lake was grand in its newness, but I reasoned it must operate about the same as Princeton did. I was right. Without much trouble, I found the alley that led to the back of the restaurant, and there beside a green-painted door stood several tin pails, exactly the type pig farmers set out for eateries to drop their slops into. It was the work of a few moments, to pick through the discarded bits and find a few half-eaten rolls. The bread had soaked up the foul-smelling juice of the slops, but only here and there. I pulled the soggy parts away, leaving whatever was soft and sweet intact, then stuffed the rolls in my dirty pockets and made off with my prize before I could be spotted and hollered at. In those days I feared a hollering as only a thirteen-year-old girl can do.

I waited outside the restaurant till Cilus re-appeared, walking the horses slowly along the road and encouraging Lena to sing in her high, sweet voice, which was sometimes the only way to keep Isabelle and Sarah from fussing. Lena sang, "Tramp, tramp, tramp, the boys are marching!" and it made a funny counterpoint to the slow, head-down plodding of the horses and my two young brothers looking so worn out and tired. But when they saw me, they all perked up some, even the horses.

"I got us something special," I told them.

Cilus said, "I found a green place down yonder, at the end of the street. A field or maybe a graze, but there ain't no fence around it."

"If there's no fence, then it's public property." I spoke as if I knew exactly what I was talking about, even though at just-barely-thirteen I was ill-versed in law—even worse than I am now.

I walked alongside the horses; my legs was grateful for a stretch. We found Cilus's field, a grassy lot between two fenced gardens. No one had yet built upon the lot, and it was tangled up with all kinds of weedy growth. The weeds made an acceptable screen. We sat down together in the welcoming coolness of long grass. It was powerful good not to feel the steady rock of a horse beneath you for a time. Gratefully, we rolled among the thick growing things, the tender leaves and soft clover, while the horses grazed and seemed content. Everyone felt we had come to a good place—everyone except me, but I didn't let on about my doubts. I didn't want to trouble the little ones till I knew I had no other choice—till I had proof that all hope was lost.

I took the bread from my pockets. The children exclaimed over their surprise. Lena, who hadn't yet learned to be hard and mean, pinched off bits to feed the horses and whispered praises as they ate. The horses nodded their heads, as if to say, "Yes mam, that bread is mighty good." We all savored the rolls in rapturous silence. None of us had tasted bread in weeks, you see, except the poor flatcakes I made out of plain flour and crick water along the trail. Those flatcakes don't count because they hadn't any leavening, and tasted like mud besides. But those slop-bucket rolls was about as delicious as a bride's wedding cake. I hadn't the nerve to tell my brothers and sisters I had fished them out of pails meant for pigs' feed. Privately, I thought it didn't matter. If pigs ate like kings in Salt Lake City, then once I found a bit of work, the Canarys would be living high as hogs, too.

That overgrown lot went deep, stretching back between gardens and houses till it snugged up against the steep foot of a sage-covered hill. When our bread was all gone, I clambered up on my weary legs and waded back into the tangle of grass. There was a few cottonwoods below the hill, just at the edge of our lot, and we made our camp there, far from the road. I ground-tied the horses and let them graze while Cilus rolled out our flat, dirty beds beneath the trees. Lije found a trickle of a crick and filled our skins with water, and for the first time since leaving home, we went without a fire as the sun set and evening came on. What did we have to fear, now that we was surrounded by people instead of the great arching cage of loneliness, the emptiness of prairie sky?

Next morning, I rose early and stood still beneath the cottonwoods, listening to the city waking. I could hear roosters calling from the yards of distant homes, and the ringing of a hammer, repetitive and sharp, echoing down the long empty stretch of cobblestones. A faint rattle of cart wheels sounded from some unseen lane. I heard it over the swish of our horses' tails and the wind moving gently through the leaves. In the bedroll next to Lena, Baby Sara coughed in her sleep. Her cough had picked up a fearful rasp with a sort of gurgle at the end. I didn't like the sound of it, not one bit.

I made my way through the grassy lot to the edge of the street. A horse would have got me around faster, but I figured a horse would make me look more prosperous than I was, too, and would somewhat diminish my useful air of patheticness. Without a horse, I might expect a Christian soul to be moved by my sad state of affairs—assuming I could find a soul to look right at me, rather than turning a blind eye, as they all had done the day before.

I came across a laundry shop first thing, right on the edge of town. Laundries used to be on the edge of town in those days, Short Pants—the lye smelled fearful, and high-living folks didn't take to it well. This laundry was just opening its doors for the day.

It was run by a little Chinese lady who didn't look especially old in the face, but all the same, she had the air of a grandmother about her. Maybe her small stature gave me that impression, or maybe it was the slight bend to her back. It's terribly hard work, you know, washing day in and day out, from sun to sun. You're stooped over the tubs all the time, and if you have occasion to straighten your spine and take a stretch, it's a miracle worthy of celebration.

This Chinese lady didn't speak the language too good, but she made her meaning clear without any trouble. She had been propping open her shop door with a wedge of wood, but when she saw me coming up the sidewalk with a hopeful smile on my face she said, "You get away, you dirty girl!"

I looked down at my dress, my ankles showing plain beneath the short hem. Both hem and boots was grimy, more grayish-brown than whatever color they had originally been. My boots was in a dreadful poor state, too, even if you didn't account for the dirt. Scuffs had paled the toes and worn almost clear through the leather. My soles had ground away, uneven from walking countless miles along that rutted trail. I must have looked a pure fright.

She said, "I got nothing! I want no beggars here. Got nothing to give you, so go away! Go away!"

I said, "Mam, I am not looking for a handout—only a job. I'm stronger than I look, and I can work real hard, and I got experience doing laundry. Please take me on. I need the job real bad."

"You are too dirty," she said.

"I'll get clean if I stick my arms in a tub of hot water while I'm washing up the shirts."

I guess she took my answer for sauce, though I never intended it. That little old laundress grabbed something from inside her shop's door and came at me like a whirlwind, so fast she might have been an arrow shot from a bow. I saw that she held a stout, smooth-worn bat in her hands, the kind you use to smack a ball of wet cloth and beat all the grime out of it. She raised it up over her head as she flew toward me.

"I only want a job!" I hollered, backing away.

"Get out, you dirty girl, get out!"

I felt my only course was to run away as fast as my legs would take me. I darted across the street, and by a twist of luck a wagon rumbled past at that moment, which put a barrier between the laundress and me. I'm certain to this very day that she would have bludgeoned my brains right out of my head if she'd-a caught me.

On the other side of the road I found a bakery opening its door and rolling up the shutter of its paned window, and the wholesome, clean smell of fresh-baked bread drifted out like a cloud of glory. But the baker didn't need to scowl at me twice. After I saw the forbidding squint of his eyes, I thought better of asking for work and kept on walking, brisk as I could, pretending I had no designs to speak with him, except for a "Morning, sir," which was only polite.

Next I found a dry goods store with bins of nails and seed and fabrics of all kinds lining the walls high up where dirty children couldn't touch, and a great big jar of bright-colored hard candies on the counter, sparkling like a king's crown. How I wished I had a few pennies to my name, so I could have brought some candies back for the kids. The shopkeeper was a fat, white-haired fella with a beard like a hill of snow and a smart pair of specs over his sharp little eyes. He looked at me, silent and skeptical, when I stepped through his door. I have no doubt that he could tell just by looking that I was penniless. But I spoke up at once and stated my need, so he wouldn't suspect me of trying to pinch his goods.

"I'm in real sore need of work. Can you give me a job, sir?"

He told me in no uncertain terms that minding shop wasn't a fit occupation for anybody who had never kept books, nor a body who didn't know how to make change nor run fractions in their head. I didn't even know what the hell a fraction was. There was no need for me to admit I wasn't qualified for the work; the shop-keep could tell by the way my face fell.

But he was a kindly sort of man, despite his suspicious glances upon my appearance inside his store. He took a grandfatherly pity on me, and advised me to inquire at the eateries down the way and at the hotel, which was near the big white half-built temple standing at the heart of town. He said the hotel sometimes hired girls my age to wait at tables, and he heard they paid fifteen dollars a month.

"But," he said, "you really ought to clean yourself up before you go a-calling in any more shops, young lady. No one will like the idea of letting a ball of mud such as yourself roll through their establishment, tumbleweed-fashion."

I said, "Mister, thank you kindly for the advice, but I got no place to clean myself up in. My ma and pa are both dead, and I got five little ones to look after all by myself, and we only just arrived in Salt Lake City."

The shopkeep looked real sorry then. "Lord God," he said, "but it's a cruel world, and no mercy for the little children."

He led me around out back of his shop, into an alley not unlike the one where I found the buckets of pig slops. A tin spout ran up the side of the brick building, clear to the roof, and below it was a rain barrel with a tight-fitted lid. Utah Territory didn't look to me as if it received much rain, but somehow this man had collected whatever drips and drops fell in days long past. He pushed aside the spout and pried the lid off the barrel. The barrel was almost as high as my shoulders. It was full near to the top with rain. The water smelled of mold and moss.

"It's no good for drinking," he said, "but all the dirt and bugs settle to the bottom. I scoop some out as needed, to clean the tools folks bring me to sell or trade. You can wash your face and hands here, and clean up your boots as best you can. There's not much you can do about your dress, I suppose." Then, before he went back inside his shop, he pulled a tortoiseshell comb from his pocket and laid it on the edge of the barrel so I could neaten the black rat's nest of my hair.

It took me a long while to sluice weeks of grime from my body. First I did my legs, pulling off my boots and my drawers, hiking my stiff, torn skirt up to throw it over my shoulder. There was no one in the alley but me; however, at that point I was beyond caring if anybody saw my bare behind. The old rain water stank, but it was pleasantly cool against my skin and oh, the feel of weeks' worth of dirt and toil and shame and sorrow running off my hide! I cupped handful after handful of water and rubbed and splashed and watched the brown rivulets race away through the cracks between cobblestones. When my legs was as clean as I thought they was ever like to be, I unbuttoned the top of my dress, just as I had done when trading with the wagon boys, and reveled in the washing of my arms and chest and face.

I had nothing to wash my hair with, but I wetted it down with rainwater and worked out all the tangles with the shopkeeper's comb. I had no mirror to see my handiwork. The barrel was too dark, its water too ripply to offer up a serviceable reflection. I patted my head with my hands and satisfied myself that my hair was passably smooth.

Then I went back inside to return the kindly man's comb. I told him, "I put the top back on your barrel, Mister, and returned the spout so you needn't worry that you won't catch the next rain that comes through."

He said, "Young miss, I am no Mormon—but perhaps it's fortunate you've found yourself in Mormon country. The womenfolk of these parts have a certain organization. They call it the Female Relief Society, and they make it a special mission to look out for the downtrodden. I have heard tell that they take particular pains over orphans. You might seek them out. I think they may be of some use in your predicament."

I don't know why, but something rebellious rose up inside me when I heard the shopkeeper's words. Maybe it was only because I was washed and combed and feeling more like myself. Or maybe something in me didn't like the thought of turning the remnants of the Canary clan over to the keeping of religious women. I had only ever known religious women to be like Mrs. Sowders back in Princeton—that sour neighbor with the screeching naked child clinging to her skirt. I had contrived to bring us this far on my own, without the meddling of any religious types. Now I was set and determined to pull us back up to our feet—all six of us, whatever it might cost me to do it. I didn't like being called downtrodden, neither, when I had trod all across the plain and survived.

I thanked the man sincerely for his kindness, but I left that shop bound and determined to avoid the Female Relief Society at all costs. Now that my body was clean, if not my dress, I would find a job waiting tables. I knew I could keep the family in passable comfort for fifteen dollars a month. Pa had often made less than that, between his skimpy crops and slow weeks at the faro table.

Of course, I didn't even get a chance to ask at the first two eateries I approached. The owner of one chased me off with shouts and curses, though not with a laundry bat like the Chinese lady had done, thank God. He was a speedy fella, and could have clubbed me a good one behind the ear if he'd had any sort of weapon to hand. At the other eatery, it was a waiting girl who drove me away, and she did it with nothing worse than a withering look. She had a guant, harried look about her face, and something hard and mean in her eyes that seemed to say, *There ain't but one job here, and I already got it, so get away before I make you wish you'd scooted sooner.*

By the time I reached the hotel near the temple, I was feeling despondent—exactly what the Female Relief Society would call downtrodden. I don't know if you've ever seen the Mormon temple but it is a real spectacle, great towers with spires up top and its sides shining white so they almost glow in the sun. There's no cross atop it, as you'd find elsewhere in the Christian world.

Instead, you'll find a golden statue of a man up there on the highest spire, standing tall with a trumpet raised to his lips. That's what the temple looks like now, but back then—the year must have been 1865—the temple wasn't finished yet. It rose two stories into the air, and the flat tops of its towers was crowned by black scaffolds. But the stone was white and beautiful, the windows high and arched. I could tell it would be a fine place someday; it already was the grandest building I had ever seen, and it wasn't near being finished.

I thought of all the money that must have gone into the construction. The purchase and transport of pure white stone, the labor of countless men to raise the temple higher, and ever higher still. Surely the Mormons could have spared a little money to build at least one poor-house, one place where my brothers and sisters and I could find a proper meal and a soft place to lay our heads. The longer I looked at the temple and all those tiny men moving like ants along its pure-white surface, the more it seemed as if God Himself was mocking me. *Martha Canary*, He seemed to say, *you are one dumb little bitch, and no mistake. I took all the gold in Montana and gave it to the Mormons, and there it all is, bound up in stone where you can't get to it, and now there's nothing left for you or the little ones. Nothing at all.*

I think you're a real rotten scoundrel, I said back to God. Then I got scared, because I figured He'd best like to hit me with a lightning bolt for sassing him back. And if there was one thing I didn't need right then—one thing that would surely compound my troubles—it was swift and decisive judgment from On High.

After a time, I figured I wouldn't improve my odds of finding work by setting around outside the hotel—and anyhow, my eyes was watery and sore from staring up at the temple. So I stood and went on inside the hotel, mud-stained dress and all.

The inside of that hotel was about as beautiful as the outside of the temple. Thick rugs with bright patterns of red and gold covered the floors, and everywhere was the gleam of polished wood, a mellow red-brown that made me feel sleepy and content. I knew there wasn't a powerful lot of trees for miles around—I had seen the land with my own eyes on that long and dreary trek —so I figured whoever owned the place must have carted the wood in at great expense. If he had so much money, surely he could spare a little for me, if I worked hard at cleaning up his rented rooms or serving fancy ladies their coffee and tea. But the man behind the hotel desk wanted nothing to do with me. He shooed me off before I'd got two words out of my mouth.

Three more bakeries sent me packing, and another laundry, which I found clear out on the opposite edge of town from the laundry where the Chinese lady waited with her cudgel. Two hands at two different livery stables laughed right in my face when I tried to tell them I had a way with horses. And no less than seven mistresses of boarding houses scolded me till I hauled my bedraggled carcass off their front steps.

It was long past noon by the time I made it back to our little camp under the cottonwoods. I was hungry as a springtime bear, and growled at the children till they fed me on the small scraps of provisions we had left. There was a bit of stringy meat—Lije had snared some ground squirrels earlier that day and roasted them over the coals—and some hard pieces of the unleavened, flour- and-water bread I'd made out in the high, red plain two nights before we'd come down to the city. Everything else, the children had eaten in my absence. All of the Canarys had felt so much for-certain that I would find work straight away; they didn't see the point of saving our provisions. Truth to tell, I'd been certain I would find work, too.

After I gulped down my food, I was so well tuckered that I fell into my bedroll and slept the afternoon away. I slept most of the night, too, only waking long enough to see Lije dispatch another couple of ground squirrels among the tall grass. Baby Sara's cough was a misery to us all. She choked and spit and hacked up till her little face was red and flustered, and after each coughing fit she had so little strength left, she could only whimper and squeeze out one small tear, maybe two. An awful despair settled into my heart as blue twilight closed around our tiny field, shutting out sight of the city. The world shrank down around us. In the half-dark, all that seemed real to me was the little ones and our two horses, the flat emptiness of the flour sack and my mud-gray dress. All I could hear was the churr of insects in between the baby's fits of coughing. The city was gone, vanished to my dulled senses, and I was vanished to the city—transparent as a ghost, so invisible I might never have existed at all.

I said to myself, *It's the gold fields or nothing. The Canarys wasn't made for city life.* I resolved that in the morning I would devise some plan to round up enough food—by pillaging more slop buckets or from outright theft, if need be—to get us up to Montana. All I needed was a few crumbs of gold dust, and I could by a good sensible dress that wouldn't mark me out as a dirty, worthless orphan. With a long dress of respectable cut and color, I could find work in a laundry or an eatery, I knew it; and surely Montana was packed full of eateries and hotels. Where else did the prospectors spend all their gold? All I needed was the means to clothe myself proper, and the world would open like a rose before me.

Well, the very thought of setting out on the trail again wearied me something awful. I tried to fall sleep once more, but the baby gave an awful rasp and my blood turned to ice with one quick beat of my heart. Then Sara stopped breathing altogether. I felt the moment when her breathing stopped; my baby sister's terrible fear seemed to pulse along my own veins, flooding me with panic. All desire to sleep fled me in an instant. I jumped up from my bedroll like I'd been stung by a scorpion, and Lena, who was tucked in beside the baby, was just as quick to rouse. Sara's face was dark red—even in the night-time, with only a sliver of moon, I could see her color—and her poor eyes was wide, blind with terror.

"She'll choke to death, Martha," Lena screamed. I didn't know what to do, but Lena moved by some instinct I never possessed, and walloped the baby on the back, right between her shoulders.

Baby Sara spit out a great lump of something and began to cry. Lena relaxed a little, for now at least she knew Sara was breathing —but the baby's voice was weak, and her wailing wasn't especially defiant. I took one look at the poor little scrap and knew she was bound to die if I took her on the trail again.

Lena's scream had waked the whole Canary camp. All of us huddled around the baby, fearful and sober. We took turns rocking Sara till at last she fell asleep again, and her breathing was as clear and steady as it ever was in those days. In silence, we passed Sara around the circle, none of us saying a word, each one holding our baby sister close and kissing her dear soft thin little cheeks.

The mood was grim as a funeral. I believe each of my brothers and sisters thought Baby Sara would die—if not that very night, then soon, for something had changed in her. A dullness had come over her, clouding her eyes as if she could only look inward now, could only see the last battle her tiny soul must fight.

But I was powerful set on Baby Sara's survival. It wasn't only for her sake, though God knows that was motivation enough. I couldn't stand the thought of having brought her all this way only for her to perish. I had kept the mite alive out there on the trail— trading for the food she needed, chewing up roasted rabbits and the raw, stringy meat of bullsnakes and spitting that slim nourishment right into her mouth. It was a shame too immense to contemplate, that Sara should falter and fade away now, when I had carried her out of the wilderness and returned her to civilization. If she died, I would have failed my whole family—most especially my ma and pa, who never did think much of me, but even so, I was the strongest and most capable child they had.

There was no money for a doctor. I knew that; Hell, there was no money for a dress. But Salt Lake City had something no other place could claim: tender-hearted Mormon ladies with a special fondness for the downtrodden. And I had never met a tender-hearted lady who could resist a baby in peril.

We got precious little sleep that night, saying our farewells to Sara—so when the morning dawned red over the high mountains, most of the little ones was still sound asleep. Only Cilus saw me rise, for he was up having a piss in the long grass. He watched me head off across the unbuilt lot toward the city. When he was done pissing, he bounded after me and said, "Where you going off to today, Martha? I'm awful scared for the baby. I don't know what to do for her if she chokes again."

"Keep her close to Lena; she'll smack Baby Sara on the back again if she chokes. But I'm off to get help for the baby, so you can see I can't stay. Besides, I'm no use to help a choking baby anyhow."

"Please don't be gone long," Cilus said. The poor boy was awful weary and frightened; I could see that plainly in his eyes, which was pinched and tired, more like the eyes of a haggard old man than an eleven-year-old boy. I knew Cilus harbored a fear of Baby Sara dying, and him not being able to do a damn thing to stop it. God knows, I struggled with the same terrible vision many times throughout that long night. So I hugged my brother and told him how brave and good and sensible he was, and when he seemed mollified, he let me go on my way.

Wouldn't you know, the first creature I came across was the Chinese lady from the laundry. She was up with the birds, too—God knows why. When she saw me coming, she started up to yelling again, but I stood well back, so she wouldn't think I'd come begging again.

"Missuz," I shouted from halfway down the block, "Can you tell me where the Female Relief Society meets?"

"I know nothing about them. Nothing to steal here! You leave me alone!"

"But can't you tell me where the Mormon ladies congregate?

You live in this city; you must know something about the Mormons."

She pressed her lips together for a minute and looked me up and down. I made no move to come any closer than I already was, and certainly did not raise the question of work. Because I waited patiently, she finally relented.

"Relief ladies meet all over the city. They like garden parties best. You go walking past the houses, you'll find them, soon enough."

I thanked her with such wild abandon I think I made her wary all over again. She edged toward the door of her shop. I turned and scurried away before she could reach for her cudgel.

It took nigh on half an hour to find my way out to the grand, fine homes along the finest avenue in all the city—all flower gardens and tidy white fences. I whiled away most of the morning tramping up and down, peering over every gate in search of a congregation of charitable-looking women. I'd begun to despair well before I covered the first block, for every yard was empty, but the laundress's suggestion was the only thread of hope to which I could cling. So I marched past every home I saw, and went twice past a few of them, peering over hedges and pickets with haunted, desperate eyes.

The sun climbed ever higher in the sky. Noon had almost arrived, and I was as famished as I'd ever been, for I'd eaten nothing that morning. I had just made up my mind to return to the slop buckets when I turned up a cobblestone lane and there, two houses down, I spotted a gathering of Mormon women in their peculiar, drab dresses, with their hair slicked back in severe and joyless styles. Each wore a straw hat to keep the sun off her face. I pressed myself into the shadow of a lilac tree, which over-hung a neighboring fence, and watched the women flit about the garden. They flocked to a small table in the shade of a cottonwood tree. Even at my distance, I could see that the table was heaped with fine things to eat: sandwiches and apples, cold cuts of meat, a great wheel of yellow cheese with a fancy little knife for carving off delicate pieces. My stomach was past the point of rumbling; I yearned after that food so desperately that I felt properly sick, like I might have to heave up nothing right there under the lilac bush.

All too many encounters with unfriendly city-goers had made me cautious. I didn't like the notion of strolling right into that garden—*Hello ladies, fine morning, ain't it; I am an orphan and an especially downtrodden one at that.* I felt I'd be prudent to get a feel for the society before I approached. I wanted to discern exactly the right angle from which to pitch my tale of woe. A paling fence wrapped around the garden, and the fence was backed by a thick stand of flowers and berry bushes. I casually strolled around the block till I circled all the way back towards that house, but from a different approach, just in case any of the ladies had spotted me huddled under the lilac. Then I crouched down and crept along the line of the fence till I could hear their voices, plain as day.

One of the women seemed to preach a sermon of sorts. She spoke in a very melodious voice, one that put me in mind of an elegant queen or an operatic singer. "One cannot attain exaltation without bearing children, for that is why Woman was made. She with a large family is most blessed, for that happy Sister has done her duty by the Lord thoroughly, and with a full heart."

Another lady spoke up and said, "Sister, what do you tell a woman who can't have a baby of her own?"

Another lady, who must have been seated very near where I crouched, answered with a laugh. "Is she trying hard enough?"

The first woman—the one who preached—replied in a withering tone. "Sister, we all know how babies are created. Let us not make light of a sacred process."

Another woman said, "I would like to know, too, Sister. My neighbor, Sister Shupe, has been trying for a child for three years now. The Lord hasn't blessed her yet. I fear she's becoming rather sad over her failure. There must be some way to help her."

A sober silence fell under the cottonwood. Then the preaching lady said, "We must pray for Sister Shupe, and a few of us—those with the most children—should offer ourselves for her consultation. Perhaps after all she isn't aware—"

The laughing woman blurted out, "Oh, she is aware, believe you me!"

"Perhaps she needs better counsel," the preaching woman insisted. "Perhaps we can aid her in this time of darkness. If there is some sin on her, we must help her see it, and repent of it. The Lord will provide a way, if Sister Shupe's heart is free of sin."

I had seen a house with the name SHUPE carved above the door. I wasn't an accomplished reader, but I could make out simple words, and that particular word had stuck in my head because it sounded so odd. *The light green house*, I told myself, *three blocks down from here, right on the corner.* An idea had come to me—one that wouldn't require me to approach the Female Relief Society after all—for now I feared that if I did approach the whole society, they might split up all us children and separate me from my family. I didn't like the thought of Baby Sara departing the Canary clan, but I liked the thought of her dying even less.

I made it back to our encampment just past noon. The day was hot, the air full of biting flies; sweat ran down my back and my front by the time I found the children again. The sweat had coaxed the embedded dirt out of my dress, ruining the clean state I'd achieved at the shopkeeper's rain barrel the day before. Now I could feel the grime scraping against my skin. I longed for another washing-up, but I had a more urgent task at hand.

Cilus came running to meet me as I waded through the lot's waist-high grass. He didn't look sorrowful—only tired—so I reasoned Baby Sara had held onto life.

"Go bundle up the baby and bring her to me," I told my brother.

Cilus waited, watching me in silence as if he expected some explanation. I didn't give him one. I knew if he realized what I was about to do, he would be dead-set against me. He would rile up the other children, too. I could out-wait and out-stare Cilus; we both knew it was true. After a minute or two, he turned away and disappeared into the cottonwood shade. When he returned to me, he held Baby Sara in his arms, wrapped in the threadbare scrap of her blanket.

Cilus stopped a few paces away. He looked up at me, pained and silent, and his scrawny little arms tightened around the baby, holding her close against his heart. Then he kissed Sara on the forehead and passed her over to me.

Sara hardly stirred in my arms as I bundled her up against my shoulder. She was quiet, but her breath rattled a little in her chest. She felt weightless as a new-hatched chick. I turned and headed back towards the green house on the corner, moving briskly with my jaw clenched hard so my courage wouldn't fail.

When I reached the Shupe house, I pounded hard on the door, praying to the savior that Mrs. Shupe would answer, not her husband. I had no bead on whether menfolk were susceptible to suffering babies; I suspected darkly that they were not.

Luck was on my side for once. A thin woman came to the door. Her dark hair was curled and pulled back severely, so I could see the streaks of silver that had formed at her temples. But despite her gray hair, Mrs. Shupe didn't look old—only harried and tired, like I was. She stared at me in confusion, her face blank and baffled. Then she looked at the baby in my arms.

"Sister Shupe," I said.

"Yes, what is it?"

I held my baby sister out toward her. Sara was thin as a twig, and just as brittle. "This is a gift from the Mormon Lord. A gift for you."

"Land sakes," she said to me, "what are you talking about, girl?"

I thought back on the high-flown words the preaching woman had used. "You can't get exalted without having a baby. That's why Woman was made."

Mrs. Shupe squinted at me. Something hard and hurt crimped

the corners of her eyes. She pinched up her mouth as if she thought to spit on me, but I stepped forward and pressed Baby Sara toward her again. The woman skittered back, afraid to touch the baby or me.

"This is a gift," I said again, "for you. God has provided." Still the woman hung back, so I added, "Please, mam. She'll die if you don't care for her."

I pulled back the corner of the grimy blanket that covered the baby's face. Mrs. Shupe gasped, for Baby Sara was a pathetic sight. Now, seeing my sister in this new light, on the tidy step of the Shupe home—seeing her through the other woman's eyes—I could tell exactly how sick and half-dead the baby appeared.

"Heavenly Father have mercy," Mrs. Shupe said. "The poor little thing!" Then she looked up at me, hard and spiteful again. "Why on Earth haven't you cared for her properly?"

Even hungry and filthy from head to toe, I was still a big, strapping girl. I looked somewhat older than my years. I think Mrs. Shupe believed I was the baby's mother. I didn't care what she thought at that moment, for she reached out and snatched Baby Sara from my arms, cradling her against that small, narrow breast despite the dirt and the smell that clung to the baby and to me.

"Her name is Sara Canary," I said. "I hope you'll remember that, and tell her when she's old enough to know."

The woman fixed me with her bitter eyes for a moment longer. I shivered under her stare, afraid she would push Sara back at me and tell us both to get off her doorstep. Then something softened in her face—not by much, but it was enough for me. I nodded; the deal was done. Then, without another word, Mrs. Shupe closed the door in my face.

I wept all the long walk back to the cottonwood trees, but I did it quietly. I never wailed, nor wrung my hands like tragic figures in stories do. But though I was silent, my grief was a great and fearful burden. My young body could scarce bear to drag it. I knew I'd done right by Baby Sara—the rightest I could do. Still I felt like a traitor, like I'd stuck a knife into the backs of all my brothers and sisters, into the family name itself. The Canarys had no claim to riches or class or breeding, but we had one another, sure enough. I had parceled out one of our own, broken the bond between us all—given away a portion of our only treasure. I couldn't rid myself of the suspicion that this was a fearful turning point, a moment from which there could be no going back. Now I could never expect to hold to what I once had been—what any of us had been. All of us would be forever changed, from that moment forward. And me most of all. Me especially.

Cilus was the first one I saw when I made it back to our camp. He stood almost where I'd left him, there in the tall grass apart from the others, watching out for my return with hungry, avid eyes and a pale face. He looked down at my arms and saw that they held nothing. Slowly, he turned his back to me and walked off into the low glow of sunset, his head hung low, his steps like those of a grown-up man, weary and reluctant.

The other children squatted around our little fire, roasting the skimpy meat of ground squirrels trussed up on cottonwood twigs. They looked up at me, each wide-eyed and hollow, but none of them said a word about Sara. I took my place in the circle. Lije passed me a bit of squirrel meat, and though something thick and heavy set low in my chest, I also felt a certain clarity in the air, a freshness and lightness, just like when a wind comes down from the hills and blows away wildfire smoke or oppressive thunder. I had separated Sara from our family. She was likely lost to us forever. But Sara was also safe. The same couldn't be said for the rest of the Canarys. Every one of us knew—even little Isabelle, I think—that Sara wouldn't have held on much longer. The poor mite had used up all her strength to make it this far. I looked at my brothers and sisters, at their thin shoulders pressing through dirty shirts, the swell of their knobby knees on skinny legs. I wondered how much deeper their wells of strength ran. I wondered how much longer I could keep going.

There ain't much more to say about that night. After we picked the squirrels' bones clean and tossed them into the fire, I told the children that come the morning we would set off again, headed north, for there wasn't any work to be had in Salt Lake City. I might have parceled out the rest of the children to the Female Relief Society, but there was still some strength left in each of them, and I was determined to keep what remained of our clan bound tightly together for as long as I could manage.

I said, "They're building the railroad straight through Wyoming. I heard some men talking all about it yesterday, when I was out searching for work. I guess there'll be new towns growing up along the rail line. It ain't like prospecting for gold, I know—but in a town that's still growing, we'll find work for sure."

"I'll work, too," Cilus said. He didn't seem happy about the prospect, but he did seem awful set on keeping the rest of us united. "I'll learn how to drive a spike and I'll join some of the work gangs on the rails."

"And I'll work," Lije said, though he was but nine years old.

That night I slept heavily. I wish I could tell you that I dreamed no dreams. A hundred dreadful visions haunted me, but I was too exhausted by toil and sorrow to pull myself out of sleep. Worst of all my dreams was a dark nightmare: gangs of men with blank and featureless faces, spiking railroad ties to the hot red earth. The ties was made of thin little bones, white and clean—the bones of boys like Lije and Cilus, the bones of twelve-year-old whores.

THE VERY NEXT MORNING, slim and fickle Fortune smiled on me, however briefly. I found a wagon train that was headed north, to the rail camps outside Piedmont, Wyoming. I was obliged to hand over our two horses and the one saddle we owned, but that sacrifice did make a small place for all of us in the back of one wagon, among barrels of apples and pickles and the flat, hard sacks of flour.

I pledged myself to laundry work, too, and every night before I had my supper, I washed and beat and wrung clothing for the whole wagon train. It was hard and dreary labor; washing left me so worn out that I slept all day on the trail, propped up and wedged between two crates in the back of a jouncy wagon, with my legs pulled up against my chest. But I was determined to make our way fairly and honorably, without any of the trading I done on the way from Missouri. After all, the men of the wagon train were men in truth, not boys. Somehow it seemed extra sinful to me, to contemplate fooling around with grown-up types instead of other children like me.

There was plenty of men on that wagon train, hard-working types with dirt and sweat and the body grime of horses and cattle ground deep into their clothes. After a couple nights spent washing, my hands was chapped so red they was near-about bloody. The skin of my knuckles and around my fingernails cracked open, and hurt so bad I could scarce stand to pick at my cold supper when the last of the clothes was hung up to dry beside the fire.

One night of that trek to Piedmont I can recall with especial clarity. The light of the campfires glowed red, pushing back the sober, cold, blue-black shadows of night. I huddled on the ground, leaning back against a wagon wheel, too bone-weary to lift myself and go to my bedroll. Lena climbed into my lap and tucked her black curls right beneath my chin. I rested against her, grateful for her warmth, full of a timid, fragile gladness that we was still together. Dear little Lena held my hand in her own. She turned it over so she could study my cracked palm, the red angry blooms from the lye, the abrasions marring my knuckles. She contemplated my hand in silence. After a space she said, very quietly, "When we get to Wyoming, Martha, will you find a place for me, too—like you did for Baby Sara?"

I said, "Ain't you afraid of never seeing us again?"

Lena was always a good Bible girl, even if she didn't go to church much, being a Canary and all. God alone knows where she got her religious tendencies. She said, "The Lord will bring us back together someday. Don't fear on that count."

But I did fear. I feared down to the depths of my soul, to the bottom of my well of strength, which was rapidly running dry. I didn't know how to answer, so I pulled Lena tighter against my chest. I rocked her gently, side to side, and sang softly in her ear.

I never possessed a suitable voice for singing—not even as a child, and a child's voice is supposed to be high and sweet. But I sang anyway. I sang to drive away the hate I felt for myself; I despised myself passionately for giving Baby Sara away. And I sang to drive away the relief I felt at the mere thought of finding a place for Lena—and for Isabelle, and Cilus and Lije. Oh, how I wanted to free the little ones from that life of privation and failure. And how I wanted—more desperately than I can say—to hold our family together.

Dear Lena, I tried. You never forgave me for all the ways I failed, but when I held you close in the firelight, when I sang to you in my cracked, unsatisfactory voice—and sang from the middle of my very soul—I hope you knew then that I tried.

THE HEROINE OF WHOOP-UP

WHAT WORDS CAN I FIND TO EXPRESS THE RELIEF I FELT WHEN AT last we reached the rail camp outside Piedmont, Wyoming? The camp was about the ugliest place I'd ever seen, an orderless assemblage of canvas tents with roofs that flapped slowly in a lazy wind. Here and there, shacks made of old wood—busted up wagons, I suspect—crouched among the tents. The ground was flattened from the tramping of countless feet, all the grass worn away, so a haze of dust hung above the hot, dry earth. The camp didn't seem like any type of home—an unlikely place to cultivate hope. But for me and my brothers and the two sisters who remained, it meant the end of the trail—and so my first sight of that camp was a blessing, a balm to my aching heart.

We clambered down from the wagon and stood huddled together in the drifting dust while the rail workers came out of their tents and laughed with the men from the wagon train, pounding them on their backs and smacking their lips over the provisions within the carts. No one paid a speck of heed to the five bedraggled children who stood blinking and disoriented in their midst. I wasn't yet certain where to go or what I ought to do, but I was dead set on one thing: I would never take to the trail with my brothers and sisters again. It was the trail that tore us up and sickened us, the smallest first—the trail that weakened us till we had no choice but to cast ourselves apart.

The town of Piedmont stood about a mile away across a blowing stretch of prairie. Piedmont seemed a rosier prospect by far, with its new-built houses—none as fine as the homes in Salt Lake City, but a damn sight better to look at than the rail-camp tents. I could make out a couple of churches, too, white steeples stark and beckoning among slanted rooftops. It seems there's always a church close at hand; folks can't set up anywhere in this world without some minister or nun following close behind, wagging a finger and doling out God's meddling admonishments. That's my opinion of religion now, but back then, my eyes fixed to one of those steeples and I led the children toward it as fast as their little legs could march. I intended to walk right into the nearest church and throw us all on God's mercy, for I still believed in a merciful God then.

I reasoned it all out in my head while I made for that white church: *Once God can see us down here suffering, He'll put things to right. I can leave it all in His hands, and trust that we'll end up safe, and end up together.* You see, it was the hardest thing I ever done, giving Baby Sara to her new ma. I was certain I never could make myself commit such a painful deed again—nor even face the devil of that terrible choice. But that's the way of all difficult things, ain't it? And Lord, wouldn't I know. The first time you face a Devil's bargain, and make your reluctant decision, you feel you're the rottenest scoundrel alive, even if you had no real choice a-tall. But after the deed sets on your conscience for a spell, all hesitation disappears, and you find it's a fair and easy thing to do it again— or to do something worse.

We reached the town and found its main street, a broad dirt track that seemed freshly made. The church I'd been eyeing from the rail camp stood near the center of Piedmont. I never took my eyes from its steeple till I led the children through its door and straight up the center aisle of the chapel. New-made benches stood in rows, fashioned from simple planks of bright wood. The benches still looked rough in places, having not been properly broken in. Looking at the little-used benches, I thought Piedmont must have more sinners among its population than pious types. That didn't matter much to me. Sinners or saints, I intended to find one good home all us children, myself included—just as long as we could remain together.

It wasn't a Sunday. I don't remember the day now, and can't be sure I knew it then, but it surely was not a Sunday, for there was almost no one in that church except the Canarys. Our footsteps echoed among the unsat benches, a small and weary sound, like the feet of a small army marching toward an inescapable doom. The only other soul in the place was the man bent over the pulpit. He wasn't the first black man I'd seen, but he was the first I'd seen in a long while. He had a gray mustache and a shiny, high-domed pate that rose up around the tight curls of his nearly-white hair. He was busy with the stub of a pencil, scrawling notations over a few papers, which he kept riffling through and sorting into new order. As we approached the pulpit, he laid down his pencil in the groove of his opened Bible and straightened to look at us. I believe he expected to find familiar members of his congregation, for he wore a mild, welcoming smile. When he set eyes on our ragged and desperate selves, the smile vanished. He had shining, silver-wire spectacles, and very kind eyes, but the kind eyes was all that marked him out as a minister—that, and the fact that he dared to hang around the pulpit and use it as a writing desk. I reckoned no one but a minister would presume so much in the sight of God. He was dressed in an ordinary shirt and trousers (not the black robe or suit I was used to seeing on men of the church.) But I felt certain that he was the boss of the place.

"Please, sir," I said, "we're in sore need of help. Help and charity."

He came around to the front of his pulpit without saying a

word. I found I could speak no more, myself; the inescapable fact of my failure had risen up to my throat, where it blocked off my voice. I could only stare up at that man, and when his soft and gentle eyes met mine, I lost all sight of him in a blur of tears.

He stepped down from the platform where his pulpit stood. He laid a hand on my head, never hesitating to touch me though I was covered in filth from head to foot. For the first and last time in my life, I felt the peace of a blessing fall across me, body and soul. It was a great tide of terrible, suffocating warmth, as if the Almighty Himself acknowledged that I had fallen far short of everything I'd striven for, as if He knew my weakness and brokenness—and forgave me, all the same.

The minister said, "Young miss, you do look in need of assistance."

I still couldn't speak, so I clung hard to Lena's hand and nodded.

"Are your parents dead?"

It was Lije who spoke up then. "Yessir, Mister, our ma died back in Missouri and our pa was shot to death on the trail. We come an awful long way."

Lena added, "I don't want to go back on the trail again. Don't make us go."

"You haven't got anyone here in Piedmont who might care for you?" the preacher asked.

I shook my head. The shaking seemed to free my voice, but it was smaller and weaker than it had ever been before. "I done all I could do, sir, to get my brothers and sisters here safe. Please, can you find us a place? Any place will do, as long as we have food and a roof over our heads. As long as we don't have to take to the trail no more, I promise we'll be content."

The minister took my hand and set himself on the frontmost bench. Gently, he drew me down to set beside him. The moment my weight came off my feet, I felt as if my bones began to sing hallelujah. I wanted to melt into that bench like butter in the sun;

I wanted to never shift from that spot again till the Judgment Day came. The church was silent, peaceful—and the sorrowful comfort of the minister's blessing still rang inside my soul.

"Child," he said, "what fortitude and bravery you have shown. You are a signal of Christ's love to the world."

I didn't know exactly what he meant, especially the word fortitude, which was beyond me then, though I understand it now. At the time, sitting and suffering beside that man, all I could think was, *I was a coward for giving up Sara.* But even thinking it, I knew it wasn't true. It was a mystery to me then—still is to this day, all these long years later—how I could feel both shamed and proud about what I'd done back in Salt Lake City. How I could know myself for a coward and a brave girl, all in one go.

The minister went on speaking. "You may all stay here—all of you. I'll make a place for you until we can find proper families to take you in. Christ said, 'Whoever has this world's good, and sees his brother in need, and shuts up his bowels of compassion from him, how can the love of God dwell in him?'"

I said, "Are you a Mormon, sir—like in Salt Lake City?"

The minister laughed then, a big booming sound, which I took for a no.

We had no more need of our grimy, flat, dew-dampened bedrolls. That night the minister made us one great, soft bed right on the platform at the foot of the pulpit. He wrestled in a feather tick that was wide enough for all of us to bundle up on together. The tick was very old and had lost most of its softness, but after months on the trail, it seemed more comfortable than the clouds of Heaven. He brought in warm quilts stitched with bright colors, too, and cushions for our heads that smelled of a real home— wood smoke and bread and a space long lived-in.

Once our bed was laid, the minister saw to it that we had baths in a real wash tub with water he heated and carried himself—and after each of us was clean and fresh, he carried out the gray, stinking water and dumped it in the church yard, so not one of us had to suffer grimy wash-water. He was patient and tireless in caring for us, and he smiled all the time.

While Lena reveled in the miracle of her bath, I set beside the minister on the front bench, waiting my turn. "What's your name, anyhow, Mister?"

"You can call me Reverend Wilkes, young lady. What am I to call you?"

"Martha Canary. Ain't you got a wife and little ones of your own?"

"In this church," he said, "the shepherd doesn't marry. That leaves me free to care for folks like you. But I always thought, if God had chosen differently, I would have liked to be a father."

I said, "You could leave, I guess, and go be someone else. I think you'd make an awful good pa. You're nicer than my pa ever was, by far."

The Reverend's smile never slipped, but he shook his head, and it had something of severity in it. "No, Miss Martha, I'm afraid that would never do. Once God has called us and told us who we must be, we can't change the patterns of our lives. A man may try to be someone else, but it's the Lord who decides, and He will always pull us back to our proper place."

It made me a little sad to think of this kindly old man never being a father to anyone. He certainly had a knack for caring. Reverend Wilkes fed us heartily and saw to it that we had all the sleep we could stand. New clothes, too, which he sourced from the women of Piedmont, whose children were growing like weeds, he said, in the healthy sunshine of summer, nurtured by the sweet Wyoming wind. I didn't think wind was to be held accountable for any nurturing, whether it was sweet or not, and I knew only plants relied on sunshine for growing. But I liked the Reverend and I wanted him to like me, so I kept my smart opinions to myself.

Word spread around Piedmont that a passel of orphans had holed up at the little white church, and once we was clean and rested and properly dressed, word spread again. This circulation of rumor claimed that the orphans was remarkably pretty and sturdy little things—the younger ones, at least. I knew well that there wasn't much hope any of the Piedmont ladies would find me winning, but they came in small groups and gave Lena and Isabelle dollies to play with, or they gave Lije and Cilus nuts and apples for treats, which the boys always shared with us girls straight away. Then the ladies stood about, whispering together, watching us all with a speculative air.

Before Sunday came again and the church filled up, two women of the congregation approached the minister and said they would take Isabelle and Lena. Both ladies' husbands worked on the rails, and as the track spread farther west their menfolk stayed away for weeks at a time. They was powerful lonely, they said—and neither one of them had much hope of getting babies of their own, at least as long as the rail line kept their husbands so thoroughly engaged.

Reverend Wilkes turned to me with a questioning look. My heart felt ready to split in two at the thought of separating the girls from each other—from any of us. But I had discerned (from the way the women of Piedmont watched us and whispered) that my hope of all the Canary kids living together under one roof was a slim and sickly hope at best.

So I said, "Seeing as how they're both members of your church, I suppose it would be all right. The girls can still see each other on Sundays."

The lady who took Isabelle was a real pretty one with nice golden curls in her hair. She had a kind, soft voice, too, but Isabelle kicked and screamed and wailed like all the light had gone out of the world when her new ma picked her up to carry her away.

I shouted, "You be good now, Isabelle Canary! Don't make no fuss!"

But the sound of her stricken screams was like a spike driven into my heart. I thanked God in that moment that Sara had been too young to understand what I had done to her when I pushed her into that Mormon woman's arms.

Lena went along with her new mother considerably more peaceful. She walked by the woman's side, holding her dainty, smooth hand, as if this was her just reward after a long trial of suffering. I stood at the church's picket fence with the boys beside me. We watched in silence as Lena and her new mother took their leave. Now and then, as they made off into the heart of Piedmont, the woman turned her face down and, smiling the whole while, made some remark to Lena. And Lena nodded vigorously in reply, so her tumble of black curls shook and shivered in the good Wyoming sun.

She only glanced back once, taking in the sight of the church and her brothers and me—me most of all, leaning over the fence, yearning to have her back again. Me with my hot tears and snot running down my face, because I knew I would never see Lena again.

Lena's one look back at her family and her past was all too brief. Then she turned away again, and went on eagerly toward her future.

On Saturday, a man and a woman came to the church, driving a wagon pulled by a pair of bays. They were long in the tooth—the man and woman, I mean, not the horses. The minister went out to greet them with handshakes for each. He helped the woman clamber down from the wagon seat. Then he introduced the newcomers.

"Boys," he said, "here are Mr. and Mrs. Richardson. They own a cattle ranch a few miles outside Piedmont, and they need a pair of smart, strong boys to help look after the place, for they only had daughters, who are all grown up now with families of their own. What do you say? Do you think you'd like to be cowboys, and learn how to bullwhack and ride horses like the gents in the stories do?"

I felt a terrible flush of panic then, a bone-deep chill of fear that penetrated all the way down past the dullness of my grief and the bluntness of my failure. Still to this day, I can't tell you what exactly frightened me. Was it the thought of the boys going off to work for their living, young as they was, instead of going off to be pampered and adored, like the girls? Or was it simply the fact that now I would be on my own—alone in a heartless world, the last Canary without a flock to call her own.

Cilus said, "We're young and scrawny yet."

Mr. Richardson gave a tolerant chuckle. He said, "You'll feed up, and when you're grown to young men, you'll be a real help around the ranch. We'll see to it that you learn to read and do sums, if you don't already know how. And if you like horses and steers, there's plenty of 'em on the ranch. You'll never want for fun."

The boys made a silent consultation, a negotiation conducted entirely by lifts of their black eyebrows and twisting of their mouths. Finally Cilus said, "We'll go with you, but only if you take our sister Martha, too."

The Mr. and Mrs. both looked at me then. I could see by the careful stillness of their features that they didn't much care for the idea.

"We've already raised a whole herd of girls," the Mrs. said. "I think we've got no use for another."

"Martha rides better'n either of us," Lije said. "She's real knacky with horses and I bet she can make cows like her, too."

The Mrs. sniffed. "It isn't good for a girl to ride. I won't have any girl in my house who rides like a boy. Besides, she's too old to bring up properly."

"I ain't too old," I said. I didn't like the idea of living with the stodgy old Richardsons, but I liked the idea of parting with my brothers far less. "I'm only just past twelve, Missuz, and I can do laundry real good."

Mrs. Richardson turned away as if I had offended her greatly, though for the life of me I couldn't figure how I'd done it.

Her husband said, "I'm sorry, Miss Martha. We can only take two children."

"Then you won't take none of us," Lije said. "We won't go nowhere without Martha."

I clapped my hand over his mouth to shut him up. I blinked back my tears and got down real close, so I could look him in the eye. Lije had always been shrewd and sharp, and had a damn bright mind of his own. I said real quiet, "Listen, kid. You and Cilus got to go with them and learn how to be bullwhackers. Once you're growed up some and got yourself a good, solid skill, we can meet again and really make something of ourselves, and be together forever and never have to part ways again. Understand? But we can't get nowhere till you and Cilus learn how to make your way in the world."

I took my hand off his mouth and waited for him to yell out a protest again. But he squinted at me for a long while, thoughtful and weighing my words. Then he nodded. "All right, I'll do it. But only so's we can meet up again later."

I kissed Lije on his forehead, right below the black shag of his hair. "I promise I won't go far from Piedmont, so when you're big men you can find me again, or I can find you."

"And we'll get Isabelle and Lena, too," Cilus added.

And I said—because my soul felt so wild with grief that I figured it might as well fly on the wings of impossibility— "We'll all of us ride back down to Salt Lake and get Baby Sara, too. Then all together, we'll go off anywhere we please."

"To the gold fields," Lije said.

"Or," I said, "back to Missouri."

Cilus snorted at that idea. "We'll go to the end of the railroad tracks and build a fine fancy house and live like kings and queens out in California!" Then he wrapped his arms around me and squeezed me so hard I could scarcely breathe.

All too soon, Cilus pulled himself away and took Lije by the hand, and together they climbed up into the back of the wagon. "We love you, Martha," my brothers shouted as the wagon jolted and rolled and headed away from the white church. "We'll be back for you someday."

But when they was gone, they was gone. It was just me alone in the church yard, with the sweet Wyoming air and the sunshine and the dark spots in the dust between my feet where my tears had fallen down.

I HAVE no doubt that the kindly Reverend Wilkes would have let me stay in the little white church till the end of my days, if I'd asked him. But to tell you the truth, church life never was for me. I always found it oppressive to sit still and listen to talk about God in Heaven, when Heaven was so far away. A soul may have some use for Heaven, but a body had none, near as I could tell. And the world was solid and real around me, and I was in it, feeling every painful beat of my hollowed-out heart. What my body needed seemed of much greater consequence than the needs of my soul. I reckon I was just about right in those days, too. Look at me now, Short Pants, and tell me what good Heaven is to body or to spirit.

I did learn one surprising fact about myself in those days. The toils I'd performed in service to my family—all those months along the trail—left me hungry for work. Lord knows I had earned my rest, but I didn't want to take it. My hands had grown used to staying occupied. I wanted nothing of quiet contempla-tion, for it only allowed my most heart-rending thoughts to come crowding in. The church was too quiet, too serene to hold me. I had to leave it behind—get out on my own, make my way in the world. What else was a girl like me to do?

As a growing town with a bustling rail camp not far away, Piedmont had a few boarding houses lining its dirt roads. The roads themselves were still rather soft and new, and turned to trenches of mud whenever a thunder shower swept overhead. But the town was growing so fast that the boarding houses thrived despite the mud and the rusticity. I thought to take up work in one of those houses—some grand and important work, like cooking suppers, or maybe singing for guests in the evenings, though my voice wasn't much to begin with, and had gone kind of dry and flat since the little ones had left. But even though Piedmont seemed a world apart from Salt Lake City, the two towns bore a most unfortunate similarity. I found no work to speak of— none for a girl like me, just thirteen years old with a sharp spark of pain in her eye.

By and by, Reverend Wilkes secured a place for me in Piedmont society. He understood, I think, that I wasn't long for the church life. He knew if he didn't locate a branch for me to light on, I would fly about restlessly till I dropped right out of the sky. There was a married couple who came to his services sometimes, by the names of Emma and Edward Alton. They was only parttimers at the little white church, for they spent most Sundays at another church across town—a larger and finer one, with better benches. The minister at the other church wasn't as satisfactory with his gospel (or so the gossips of Piedmont held) but he was white-skinned, which some foolish folks reckoned gave him a more substantial quality than my good, kind friend Reverend Wilkes.

The third Sunday after Cilus and Lije departed, the Altons happened to appear at Reverend Wilkes' church. Both of the Altons looked like real dandies, fine and upright in their carefully made clothes. Mrs. Emma Alton wore a smart hat of dark beaver fur pinned to her golden hair, and she carried herself with a stiff pride, which I thought made her the queenliest woman in all of Wyoming.

After service, Reverend Wilkes took the Altons aside and spoke to them most earnestly. The Reverend never looked at me, but both the Altons sent frequent glances to the back pew where I sat staring fixedly at the empty pulpit, and by their sudden interest, I reasoned they was all discussing what to do about me. I listened more sharply to the Reverend's voice.

"Martha is a good, strong girl," Reverend Wilkes said quietly. "She has a laudable heart."

I didn't know that word—laudable. But I knew my own heart well enough to surmise his meaning. My heart was broke and aching, but it felt strong, too—strong and certain that it had guided me right, that the children would be well and safe, even if I wouldn't. That was all that mattered to my heart and to me. *Laudable*, that was his word.

He said, "This child has lived through horrors that would kill a grown woman—kill her dead with grief. She has the grace of Jesus Christ inside her. All she lacks in this world is the love of good Christians, guardians to teach her proper ways, to bring her up smartly. Are you followers of the Savior? Can you offer your hearts to that needy child?"

Edward Alton looked at me for a long while—I didn't take my eyes off the pulpit, for I was still musing over my laudable heart, but I could feel him staring. Finally he said, "Come over here, girl."

I went and stood before them. I felt myself drifting, like a stick or a leaf blowed into a river, surrendered to the current.

Emma said, "She's a homely thing—poor girl."

Poor girl. And Emma Alton was so lovely, with her shining hair neatly curled, and her pointed nose, and her eyes like two bright sapphires. What can a beautiful woman know of pity—of understanding? There ain't no poorer soul in all the world than an ugly girl, an ugly woman. Take it from me, Short Pants. If you ain't like Emma Alton, doors slam in your face, and your face gets blunter and sadder and your mouth more downturned with every door that closes.

Mr. Alton said, "But she's big and strapping—big as any boy."

"Can you do laundry?" the missuz asked.

"Yes mam," I said, "I do believe that laundry is my God-given purpose in this world."

She sniffed and cast the minister a disapproving look, as if I'd made a joke against the Lord, but I was in earnest.

I believe Emma Alton was set to turn me down. I believe she was on the point of walking out of that church and never coming back again, having decided after all that a white preacher who confuses the points of gospel was infinitely preferable to a black one who foists homely orphans on his part-time flock. But before she could voice her preference, her husband said, "We could use a laundress at the boarding house, since Ellie Mae got herself married off. And with time—if you're good and work hard, young Martha—you may learn how to clean the rooms and serve the boarders."

Like a leaf or a twig blowed into a river. Going where the Lord directed, or if not the Lord—if Heaven had no use for a body, only for a soul—then wherever Reverend Wilkes saw fit to send me. He was the only person in the world I trusted by then, the only one who'd shown me a lick of kindness.

I said, "I'd be very pleased to learn how to serve boarders, Mister, if you'll give me a chance." What I thought was, *I don't give a damn about your boarders, nor their laundry, neither*. But I needed a place to lay my head at night, and I knew I couldn't stay in the church eternally.

Emma Alton wasn't keen on this turn of events. But the husband is the head of the wife, as Christ is the head of the church —that was one bit of gospel I'm sure the white preacher always got down rightly. Men do love to quote it at women, whenever the occasion allows. So I stepped past Mrs. Alton and took the Reverend's hands in mine. Or he took my hands. To this day I can't remember; to this very day, I ain't sure who reached first for the other. But he held my hands warmly in his own, and smiled down at me, and for a moment I felt as if he could see right into my laudable heart.

LAUNDRY, of course, was deadly dull work—as dull in a boarding house as it was on the trail. I have no doubt that's true to this very day, though I haven't needed to wash any clothes in a powerful long time. If anything, the work was made even more wearisome by the unrelenting sameness of my surroundings. At least on the wagon trails, I set up my kettle in a new location each evening, with new vistas turning rosy before me in the setting sun, and a new world of mountains and buttes and folded plains stretching out beneath the slow-wheeling stars. But in Piedmont I had only the back side of the Altons' home to look at, or if I turned the other way, the short snub of a half-hill, flat along its top, blocking off all sight of anything beyond it—anything except an expanse of sky, which was always the same pale, cloudless blue.

Maybe there wouldn't have been much to see, even if that hill hadn't stood in my way. The land around Piedmont was much the same as it was everywhere in Wyoming: sere and unchanging, except when cloud-shadows chased each other across the prairie. But the penned-in nature of the Altons' yard made me feel restless. There had to be more to life than what I'd found in my Piedmont predicament; surely my destiny wasn't as bleak and colorless as the prairie I couldn't even see. I guess I had no real reason to believe that was so, for I hadn't yet found cause to hope for a better future, to dream of something grand—unless it was the storms I used to watch from the cabin in Missouri. Those towers of purple rising, moving free across the plains.

Emma Alton never came to trust me, nor even to like me, in all the time I lived beneath her roof. She would just as soon have sent me away—perhaps she sensed what was to come, what I would soon make of myself, and she didn't approve of my trajectory. But she was a righteous, proper woman who obeyed her husband's will, and Mr. Alton was appreciative of the work I did, so Emma couldn't speak a word against him. But countless were the times I looked up from the old wooden stool on which I used to beat wet clothing, only to find Emma watching me, narrow-eyed and suspicious, from the window of a room where she'd been making a boarder's bed, or from the screen door that led to her spotless kitchen. I do believe she thought I was likely to make off with boarders' soiled shirts or their sopping-wet underthings, just for the pleasure of thievery.

High expectations soared all around me, till I felt I lived behind a palisade. I was to come to the supper table with my hands and face freshly washed, even if I'd been at my laundry kettle all day and hadn't had the least opportunity to get dirty. I was to sit up straight, but keep my eyes lowered at all times. I was seen, but never heard, unless one of the Altons spoke to me directly, and then I was only to speak long enough to answer their questions. After supper was finished, I was to shut myself away in my tiny bedroom—where Emma expected me to occupy myself with needlework or some other girlish nonsense, I suppose. But since she never came inquiring after my evening activities, I most often laid flat on my bed (too weary to move a muscle) and dreamed up a hundred impossible plans to reunite my family.

Emma's propriety extended to my language, as I guess you've already surmised. She had no toleration for a blue tongue, nor even slangy speech. Emma Alton's high ideals—to say nothing of her sharp stare—very nearly broke my habit of talking like a Missouri farmer, but I do believe even God himself couldn't proper me up that much. However, I did my best to make her happy, for she was an awful fright when she was upset. She had a cold, hard anger. Not the sort that fired up into shouting or wild slaps—but the sort of anger that knew how to hurt, all the same. And she was ever on the lookout for opportunities to drive home a lesson in the most memorable fashion.

Once I got careless as I pulled my laundry kettle off the fire; my hand missed the wool pad I used to wrangle the kettle's handle, and the burn across my palm made me yelp out a cuss loud as a clap of thunder. Emma was out the kitchen door so fast I felt sure she must have been poised, wiggling with anticipation like a cat stalking birds, waiting for me to break one of her rules. She had a switch in her hand—a thin, whippy one—and she stood before me as I licked my palm and blinked back tears. She looked down at me with her stern, beautiful eyes and said not a word. I didn't try to explain myself. She didn't ask me to. She took my hand and extended it, turned it palm up. Then the switch cracked down across my palm, square along the track of the burn. It hurt so bad I couldn't cry, couldn't even breathe. Everything seemed to lurch in toward me, the Altons' clapboard house and the dry hill that cut off the land and the unending blueness of the sky all shuddering and toppling upon me at once, as if the pain in my hand was a sinkhole that pulled the whole world down. After a minute, I gasped a big breath and stammered out an apology for cussing, and Emma turned and walked away like it was all in a day's work. She was a beautiful woman, to be sure, but she never was motherly.

To tell the truth, Emma's lack of maternal impulse didn't trouble me much. My own ma had never carried a motherly notion in her heart. Cold cruelty was all I knew of a woman's world. What little kindness I had encountered had come from men, and it was to men I was drawn, while anything in a long skirt might as well have spit venom at me.

Despite the cussing and the switching and Emma Alton's hard blue eyes, I worked hard and did every task as well as I could manage. I dropped myself deep into the routine of washing: stoking the fire, boiling the water, measuring out the lye. The chapping of my hands and the burning of my fingers served as a useful distraction, keeping me well away from the precipice of sorrow and lonesomeness. At night I lay down in my hard, narrow bed in a room behind the stairs—not much more than a closet, really. I felt the familiar ache in my shoulders from swinging the laundry bat. I thought about my brothers and sisters every night, while the stiffness in my shoulders and back ebbed away and sleep sang a welcome song in my ear. In those hours, without Emma to watch me, it was safe to muse on the Canary predicament. I was so worn out from the work that I didn't have any spark left for crying. Calmed by exhaustion, I tried to think up clever ways to get messages to the boys at the ranch, or to Lena and Isabelle somewhere in the town with their pretty, soft new mamas. But no matter how I turned the problem in my head, I never could find any useful way a-tall. You see, I didn't know exactly where they lived—any of them, except for Baby Sara, who was too young to read a post card. Anyhow, I didn't know much about writing in those days; I could barely scratch out a M and a C to represent my own name.

Sometimes I worked myself into such a state of exhaustion that sleep would cruelly evade me. Then I laid still with only my imagination for company—but oh, the sweet visions those imaginings brought! I pictured the children, each well-fed and scrubbed clean, wearing bright, new-made clothes. I visioned up what their lives must be like now—now that they had kindly new caretakers of their own. In those imaginings, Cilus and Lije was already handsome young men on the verge of twenty, brave and competent cowpunchers who rode magnificent, tall horses with saddle that gleamed with silver. I pictured them galloping along the flat-topped hill behind the boarding house, shouting and racing free. I saw Lena and Isabelle as beautiful brides, decked in silken gowns of sky-blue or rose-pink with lace spilling from their collars and sleeves. They always married grand men in my fantasies—sheriffs or doctors or railroad magnates—and Baby Sara was their bridesmaid, growed up to a girl of thirteen just like me, but far prettier than I had ever been, with a dimpled smile and cascades of sleek, dark hair.

After a time—some three weeks or more—even Emma couldn't deny that I was a hard worker and valuable around the place. There came a morning when she set my porridge down in front of me and said, just as the bowl hit the table, "It's time you learned how to tend the rooms, Martha. You're getting so fast with the laundry, anyhow; soon you'll find yourself idle in the afternoons, and idle hands are the Devil's playthings."

I was so pleased for a change of scenery—even if the scene was only the upper floor of the boarding house—that I behaved perfect as an angel as I followed Emma through the routine of cleaning the rooms. She could strip the sheets off a bed and replace them in the blink of an eye, with a great white billow of linen floating up in the air and landing precise as you please on the mattress. Her technique never left so much as one wrinkle for her dainty white hands to smooth away.

The beds that filled the boarding rooms was serviceable, but not pretty (this was Piedmont, after all)—narrow affairs, framed with simple wooden planks, and their ticks filled with more pinfeathers than any bed ought to have, and entirely more horse-hair and straw than was comfortable. But good feathers were a luxury that didn't often find their way to Piedmont, and so (as Emma was fond of saying, if ever a boarder dared to criticize the spartan nature of her accommodations) beggars couldn't be choosers.

At least the rooms remained orderly and clean, with never a hint of dust to darken the bubbled window panes, nor cobwebs in the corners of the walls. With few words but plenty of sharp looks and pointed demonstrations, Emma taught me the right way to dust the chests-of-drawers and wash-stands: Pick up each item the boarders had set out while they went about their business in town for the day. Clean beneath with a damp cloth. Set the gewgaws and bits and pieces back, in exactly the same position as I'd found them.

"You must never give the impression of having rooted through a boarder's belongings," Emma told me. "You must always be trustworthy and commendable in all things, for once a reputation is lost, it can never be regained. And everything you do in life will depend upon your reputation. That is true for any person, but especially for a girl. Do you understand me, Martha?"

I said, "Yes mam, I surely do."

But I wasn't certain I did understand. Or rather, I wasn't certain Emma Alton truly understood me. It was clear she knew by then that I was no thief. Otherwise, she never would have allowed me in the upstairs rooms, where all the Altons' livelihood resided along with their precious reputation. Emma never forgot ignominious beginnings, and I am damn sure she never fully trusted me—though in those days, I was careful to be the very picture of a good, obedient girl. I endeavored to fix a permanent halo to my dark, unlovely head, but Emma always looked askance at its light. I think there was a part of her that sensed my past— that saw, somehow, deep into my soul and read the memories that had imprinted themselves forever. Memories of the things I'd done behind the wagon train in the dark of a prairie night. I believe she knew my reputation was shot already, though I didn't know it yet, myself.

IGNOMINIOUS. I learned that word from the papers, years after I worked at the Alton place. I was a grown woman by then—grown and tired, with the pluck all drained out of me, a transparent husk of a hell-cat like the shed skin you find discarded in the dust below a spider's web. Amber, thin, dry legs curled up, forgotten and unmoving in the darkness.

Calamity Jane has come to such a poor pass in her old age that she has been compelled to apply for admission to the poor-house in Gallatin County. That's what the paper said. Though I wasn't old then. I wasn't old ever, except in my bruised heart. I was forty-three, perhaps forty-four. But God's honest truth, I looked twenty years beyond that. It's a mistake that's easy to forgive.

She is likely to end her melodramatic career in the almshouse, the paper said. *She has outlived a dozen husbands, killed as many Injuns as the next man, and it was doubtful that she ever had a skirt on in her life, but now poor old Calamity Jane has at last turned her back on her old-time glory and gone over the hills to the poor-house.*

Somewhere all these wild-eyed scribblers got the notion that I had trailed glories in my youth. I think they truly believed I'd been the very bride of adventure, a dazzler whose life had been one crack-bang romance after another. For reasons I'll never know, they hung their dreams on me. I was the West they wanted—the dream they never stopped dreaming. And whenever one happened to meet me face-to-face, I couldn't help but disappoint.

AS PIEDMONT GREW, so did business at the Alton place, and soon enough Emma was reluctantly glad her husband had insisted on taking me in. She was often so occupied in her speckless kitchen that I was obliged to turn all the rooms myself, and I was determined to do it so well that not even Emma could fault my work. I still did the washing in the back yard, of course, but my daily climb up the stairs to the second floor was like a holiday, and a new array of inspirations waited behind every closed door.

I was endlessly fascinated by the trinkets and scraps people left out while they went about their business in Piedmont. Every object was a relic from another life—proof that the world was greater than the one I knew. In the bone handle of a razor, left on a dresser half-folded, in the tender carefulness of pretty writing on an opened envelope, I came to recognize the endless variety of human experience. With my dust cloth in one hand, I would pick up each novel, pretty thing and turn it in my palm, feel the weight of a boar-bristle hairbrush or the smoothness of a brass button. I would breathe in the sweetness of a perfumed kerchief with threads of pink or Turkey red stitched around its hem, and hold against my lips the dry soft crackle of a letter I could scarcely read.

I did know a few words. Now and then, when the mood struck him, my had pa taught me a little reading. Not that he was very good at it, neither. I read what I could of those letters with an effort that left me in a dream-like state—misty, wondering over far-away places and lives much grander than my own.

How I loved the words I read—the sound and shape of them. *Dear. Alone. Long. Western. The sky is so very blue.*

I wondered, Back East were the skies some other color? Did they live all their lives without sunshine? Still, the life of a grown man, or even a grown woman, must be impossibly grand, filled as it was with smooth shiny things, with the fineness of good combs and dainty-sewed kerchiefs and boot hooks with tortoise-shell handles.

I thought as I placed each object back exactly where I'd found it, *I must get into the grown-up world myself, for it's a far better life than anything an orphaned girl can aspire to.* I'd had plenty of grown-up experiences by that time; despite what Emma Alton believed, my reputation hadn't been soiled (not enough, at least, that anyone could tell just to look at me.) I thought I had earned a piece of the grown world. I thought I was well and truly owed.

CILUS AND LIJE and the little girls never left my thoughts, in all the months I worked for the Altons. I'd long since made up my mind to find my way to the Richardson ranch and check up on the boys. I intended to see to it that they was treated kindly. If they wasn't, I had a half-formed idea that I would spirit them away under cover of darkness, and together we would all live as bandits on the open plains. Or maybe I'd teach them how to make beds and use a dust rag.

The Altons was stiffly Biblical folks, so I did no work on

Sundays—though more often than not, they took me along to the church across town, where the white minister preached his mixed-up gospel. Then I wore a dove-gray pinafore and collar over a somber, dark-blue dress that Emma had found for me somewheres. The dress was short, in the girls' style—as was appropriate for my age, I guess, even though I was tall as a grown woman by then and looked perfectly ridiculous with my hems near up to my knees.

The longer I lived in their company, the less the Altons attended the services of Reverend Wilkes, who had taken me in when I hadn't a place to go in all the world. I reasoned that I might beg Emma to allow me to spend the next Sunday at the Reverend's church, so's I could thank him again for his kindness. And then, when she had granted permission, I would use the time away from her watchful eye to find out exactly where the Richardson ranch lay. But I soon discarded that idea, for Piedmont was a perniciously tiny town. Gossip had legs in that place. I knew word would make it back to the Altons that I had shirked my duty to the Lord and was making suspicious inquiries. I quickly came to understand that if I ever hoped to learn where my brothers had gone, I must commit an even greater act of deceit.

I committed that act on the very same day I made up my mind to do it—or rather, I did it that night. I lay awake for hours on my hard mattress in the tiny room behind the stairs, pinching my arms and my stomach to keep myself awake. When the house had fallen silent, and had remained silent for so long that I was certain everybody in it must be fast asleep—I slid out of my bed and dressed in the dark. I put on my Sunday dress, for I thought it would be wise to look as presentable as ever I could, though I left the pinafore and collar behind, for they seemed more than the occasion demanded. Then I picked up my shoes and carried them through the kitchen to its back door, the one where Emma would sometimes stand and watch me working at the laundry, her hard stare unwavering as she waited for me to slip up and sin.

The door squeaked when I opened it. The sound of it rattled all down my spine; it seemed the loudest, most awful thing I had ever heard, though in truth it wasn't noisy enough to wake the lightest sleeper, for Emma always kept its hinges oiled with goose fat or slicked up with beeswax when she could get any. I paused on the threshold, straining to catch the faintest sound of a groaning bed frame or a rustle of sheets kicked aside. But the house remained unstirring, and when my breath was a little less raggedy, I stepped outside and let the door shut softly behind me. I was terrible scared of what Emma would do if she caught me in the act, but I was scared worse of never finding my brothers again —never living up to the promise I had made.

Outside the kitchen door, I stooped and got my feet into my shoes, quick as I could. Moonlight muted the world, draining all color from it, and the dark ring of ash where I burned buffalo chips to boil my laundry kettle looked like the pit of a well sunk deep into the earth. I skirted it nervously and hurried around the corner of the house.

When I reached the front of the Altons' property, the road through Piedmont was like a river in the night—broad, flat and silver. I followed it into the heart of town. I could see lights burning low and cozy against the towering sweep of a star-covered sky. Now and then the light grew and stretched out into the street, molten gold flowing over black velvet, as the doors to the few saloons at the center of town opened and allowed lantern-glow and the distant sound of laughter and music to escape into the darkness.

I passed a dry-goods store and the blacksmith shop, shut up for the night, windows dark as punched eyes. I passed the livery, and heard horses stirring and snorting in their corrals. A few of the ponies whickered at me, hesitant, but knowing I was a friendly soul and always good to their kind. I would have liked to stop and visit with those horses—stroke their long warm faces and smell their grass-sweet breath against my cheek—but my errand was too urgent. The faster I achieved my aim and got back into bed, the less sore Emma would be with me when she learned about my sneaking. Or so I hoped.

The noise of the saloons got louder and more distinct as I approached. Now I could pick out the high, harsh notes of a jangling piano, and below it the droning wooden buzz of a hurdy-gurdy. Men laughed, loud and strong. The sound broke out over the softer presence of the night, the shush of wind through prairie grass and the snick of horses' tails swinging beside the hitching posts.

I stopped dead in the middle of the road, staring into the heart of Piedmont. Two saloons watched one another other from opposite sides of the street. I kept my eyes on those saloons, fixed by a grim enchantment. Already I could feel those two patches of light pulling at me—oases in the desert of my personal dark, my isolation. I found the draw of singing and laughter damn near impossible to resist, for it had been unaccountably long since I had last heard such sweet music. Now and then, the men who came and went chanced to open their doors at exactly the same time, and then the lantern glow came together in the center of the street. What a beautiful sight those bands of light made when they met. Warmth and cheer called to me—*Martha, come and have a taste of what you always hungered for, deep down. Come and find the joy your life has withheld.* My mouth watered, just as if I'd been hungry, but it wasn't my belly that wanted filling. It was my spirit. I hadn't had a spot of joy in my life, long as I could recall—unless you count the times in Princeton when, as a little girl, I stood among the horses in the field and watched the wagon trains creep slow along the distant foothills.

I stood in the Piedmont road feeling the tickle of laughter and music run through me. I watched men come and go along the planks of the sidewalks—how long I stood and watched, I cannot say. Then I recalled Cilus and Lije, and took a deep breath to break the spell, and continued on my mission.

I had to pick which saloon to visit first, so I chose the one on the left, for no reason I could name. As I stepped up onto the boardwalk, the piano was like a hand closing around me, holding me tight. The air seemed to thicken, and I felt as if I swam along the boardwalk rather than strolling. The saloon I chose had a red door with a big square of wire screen set into it, and the sounds from within gushed out through that opening like water from an upturned bucket. With a trembling hand, I pushed the door open and stepped inside.

The moment I was in, all apprehension fled. A spirit of joy pulled up strong beneath my heart, so overwhelming that I laughed aloud at nothing in particular. Emma didn't allow for whooping-up anywhere near her property—not even from her boarders—but I was a young thing, frolicky as young things are, despite my many months of toil and deprivation. The piano's music was as bright and saucy as the girl who danced beside it. She had rows of red sausage curls in her hair, and they bounced like loose springs while she bobbed with hands on hips. Her fine, tiny feet bore velvet slippers set with glass gems. Those beautiful slippers tapped out a quick, clever rhythm. The dancing girl wore a flounced skirt of blue velvet, too, with a tight bodice and no collar a-tall, just bare skin across the top of her bosom. I thought that girl the finest, happiest, prettiest thing in all the world. I wanted to be her—free to jig to my heart's content, possessed of a happiness well worth jigging about. And how I did envy the tribute of appreciative hoots the dancer collected from all those men. *The life of a dancing girl surely beats the life of a laundry girl*, I told myself as I watched her stamp and spin and set her blue velvet skirt to flying. I guessed a girl that happy must own a hundred tortoise-shell boot hooks and more embroidered kerchiefs than she could ever count.

"The Hell you doing in here, girl," a man said close beside me, shouting over the noise of the bar.

I looked up in alarm, thinking perhaps he recognized me as

the Altons' orphan, and was set to march me straight home and expose me to Emma and her whipping stick. He wore a stained apron and carried a towel slung over one shoulder. His was no face I recognized from the church or from town. He was only the proprietor, I realized—and my short skirts had given me away as being sinfully young for saloon life.

"I'm looking for somebody," I said.

"Who—your daddy?"

"No," I answered more sharply than I should have, "my pa's dead."

That was a mistake, and I knew it the second the words left my mouth. How many orphans could there be in Piedmont? I was only cracking the whip behind the team of rumor, ensuring it would speed all the faster to the Altons' door.

I said, "I'm looking for anyone who can tell me where the Richardson ranch it. I got some business there, and I must go to the ranch tomorrow."

The proprietor's face kind of jumped, in surprise or in amusement, and he blew out harshly through his lips, so his mustache rippled in his self-made breeze. "Girl, you got no business anywhere. Go back to wherever you belong and don't come back in my saloon till you're old enough to associate with mixed company."

Mixed company. I know what that means now—the roughs and unpredictables of the Western landscape. And I mean the West as it was then—not as it is now. In those early years—my early years—this was a different world entirely. How quickly things change. Much faster than we're ever prepared to believe.

"It's real important, Mister," I said. "Can you tell me where the Richardson ranch is? Please, and then I'll be on my way."

He pulled the towel off his shoulder and flicked it toward me, like driving off an especially pesky mosquito. I jumped back, but not towards the door. I stumbled deeper into the crowd, the men milling about or lounging in simple cane-back chairs around the tables. And as I stepped away from him, the proprietor was pulled off in some other direction by business more urgent than me. He shouted over his shoulder, "Out with you, girl!"

I ignored him. I had my mission, and aside from that, my fascination with the place was growing by the moment, my heart beating faster and more insistent with every bar the piano played. I moved from table to table, interrupting men at their card games and conversations. Such presumption is nothing I could get away with now. (You were the exception, Short Pants, having set down alone at this bar.) Even a few years after that night, while I was still accounted young, I couldn't have justified such rudeness. But there's something about a pert young girl-child that amuses men and inspires their favor, even if she ain't especially pretty.

"Excuse me, sir," I said at every table I came to, and I put my hands on my hips in imitation of the red-haired dancing girl, and I smiled my biggest. "Do you know where to find the Richardson ranch, and how long it would take a body to walk there?"

Nobody knew—or if they did, they wasn't telling unless I got friendlier. A few men grinned up at me with their glasses half-drunk, or with beer spilled across their tables. They said, "Set down on my lap and I'll tell you," or, "Give me a kiss and I'll tell." But I sensed they didn't know any better than the rest, and the wagon trail had made me too canny to fall for such simple tricks.

After I'd made thorough rounds of the first bar, I reluctantly turned my back on the pretty, jewel-bright dancing woman and crossed the road to the other saloon. My luck to the right was just as slim as it had been to the left, but the music in that place was nicer, with a man who cranked the hurdy-gurdy so it hummed like a great fat bumblebee. Three ladies danced at that saloon, instead of just one. Those dancers were more sedate— not as bouncy—but their grace and prettiness captivated me, so that after I asked every man in the place about the Richardson ranch I stood with my back against the wall and watched the ladies twirl and sway, wide-eyed and open-mouthed till the barkeeper grabbed me by the shoulder and shoved me out the door.

"Buy a drink or move along," he shouted. "Looking ain't free!"

WELL. Now that I had learned first-hand what a grand and joyous place the world could be, how could I hope to stay shut up inside the Altons' home? When I lay awake at night, I just about believed I could hear the dry-throated moan of the hurdy-gurdy singing along my bones, with every creak of my tired joints—much too tired for a girl of thirteen. Despite how ragged I was run by my chores around the boarding house, the minute I bedded down in my narrow cot under the kitchen stairs my mind boiled with excitement. I saw all over again the scenes I'd witnessed at those two saloons—the dancer's red curls bouncing, her hands so jaunty on her hips—the men with their cards bright as sunbursts in their hands—the lamplight shining like spots of sun on glasses half-filled with liquor or beer. Everything I'd seen behind the saloon doors was warm, glowing, smiling. And it was a brighter world than the one I knew under the Alton roof.

It took those saloons to make me realize I had come to view the whole damn world as a dark and disappointing place. A heavy shadow had stolen over my spirit—sometime back along the wagon trail, or maybe when I held my baby sister in my arms and gave her to a stranger to raise. Somehow, everything within my purview had deadened and grayed. But color and laughter could be found. And in the saloons, music played, flowing out into the night, out into the cold and dark, a beacon to guide me to a sweeter life.

I'm ashamed to tell you this, but it is God's honest truth. I forgot about the ranch and Cilus and Lije. I intended to remember, and in the daytime when I was drooping and shivering from tiredness, I thought of nothing but my brothers. Then I resolved all over again to find their ranch, come Hell or high water. I swore to myself that when night came, I would give in to no more distractions. But after sunset and supper, the house fell silent, and my loneliness rose up like a snake making ready to strike, and all I could think of was the jangling piano in the golden saloon.

There came a day when Emma sent down some of her oldest dresses for me to clean. "These are to be packed away till next spring," she told me, "so once they're dry and pressed, you must see that they are folded neatly with lavender to keep the moths away."

"Yes mam," I told her, and set to work. But as I hung Emma's dresses to dry in the autumn breeze, I looked carefully at their long hems, their serious and womanish style. I counted the dresses with a speculative eye. No fewer than a dozen dripped and swayed heavily above the bare earth. Emma Alton surely did own an awful lot of dresses. I suspected she wouldn't miss one if I borrowed it for a spell. And I only meant to borrow it, not take it for keeps. I've never been any kind of thief.

That evening I pulled the dresses down and pressed them, then took them to my tiny room for folding. And when I presented the stack of neatly folded, freshly washed, lavender-scented things to Emma, tied up securely with twine so she could smash the whole lot down in her trunk till springtime came again, she nodded briskly and didn't bother to count. My elation knew no limits, though I succeeded in keeping my face neutral, entirely unblushed, till she had gone back up to the second floor.

As soon as I heard Emma's bedroom door shut, I scampered to my little cell and pulled the dress I'd hidden out from under my cot. It was a pink calico with a high collar and a white bib ruffle, prettier than anything I'd ever worn. I got a sick little shiver in my stomach as I stroked the cloth by the light of my tallow candle. That twist of guilt never relented, even through supper. In fact, it grew stronger while I set in my hard chair, with my eyes properly cast down to my boiled potatoes and chicken stew, listening to the

Altons talking over the details of their day. I held myself so still and made myself so unobtrusive, the Altons didn't even notice that I barely picked at my food. I was much too nervous to eat heartily. I told Emma I would do the washing up, and she seemed mighty pleased at my eagerness for the job, never suspecting it was only an attempt to ease my heavy conscience of its burden.

But though guilt sickened me, not once did I consider staying in my bed where I belonged. I had yearned for the joyful atmosphere of the saloons for many long days. Now, at last, in my grown-woman's dress, I could slip through the saloon door without a second glance. There was no need to pinch myself awake that night. I shivered under my blanket as I listened to the house bedding down, anxious as a flea on a wet cat. When the house fell silent, I dressed by feel, doing up the pink calico's buttons in darkness, hoping I had lined up all my buttons straight.

The first time you do a rotten deed, it goes hard on the soul. You can feel the Lord watching, and you make your apologies and hope you'll be forgiven in the end. But the next time, iniquity goes down easier—and a time or two after that, you find that you've taken to rotten deeds like a duck to water. I guess that's why preachers always say never to commit a sin in the first place: they know sin only stings but once. By the time I'd put the borrowed dress on and drifted silently out the kitchen door with boots in hand, all that dreadful shivering was done. I put on my boots and fairly flew down the road to the heart of town. My mind and my immortal soul was both light as cottonwood puffs drifting on an easy wind. I reached the saloons in no time at all, following the honey trail of their distant music through the coal-black night.

As before, I entered the saloon on the left. I felt puffed up on my own cleverness; I wanted to flaunt my wits before the proprietor who had questioned me sharply about my ma and pa. I pushed open the door with its fly-screen square, just as bold as you please, and sauntered in like I owned the place. But the man with the towel was busy behind his long oak bar. He took no notice of me. It's possible that, disguised by a grown woman's long skirt, I was entirely invisible to him.

Unseen and accepted, my heart pounded and the blood rushed loud in my ears, for I realized I had entered the grown-up world. I moved through that saloon rather slowly, dreamy with disbelief, sluggish and dazed in all my movements. I found an empty table near the piano—the player was busy talking to a pair of dancing girls, neither of whom was the redhead with the bouncing curls. I sat with my back to the bar, for it occurred to me that I had no money, and long skirt or no, I'd be tossed out the moment the bar man realized I wasn't a paying customer.

"Hi, honey." A man stepped up close beside me. "Looks like you could use some company."

I looked up, alarmed, thinking for a moment that it was the proprietor, and my good time would be over before it had really begun. But it was only a fella with a patchy mustache. He wasn't a whole lot older than me, and he had a big smile with a gap between his teeth, and black eyes that sparkled with mischief. I guessed him to be Mexican or maybe part Indian, though I had no way of knowing for sure.

He said, "Mind if I join you?"

"Guess not," I said.

He pulled out a chair and set so close our shoulders almost touched. I could smell sweat and horse on him, but the smell wasn't a bit unpleasant.

"I ain't never seen you here before," he said.

"No, reckon not. I ain't from here. I come up to Piedmont on business."

"Where you from, then?"

"Salt Lake City." I figured it was wise to throw him off my trail, to stop word from traveling back to the Altons.

"Salt Lake? You a Mormon, then? Got a whole passel of sister-wives and a husband with a beard clear down to his over-used balls?"

For a second I thought maybe I'd blush at his language, but then I figured it was all part of being in the grown-up world, so I laughed instead. "I ain't married to no one," I said, "and I ain't a Mormon neither, though one of my sisters is. I'm on business for my pa. I keep his books for him." As I said it, I remembered the kindly shop keeper who had let me wash up in his rain barrel, and I pretended to myself that he was my own dear father. "My pa keeps a store," I said, before the fella could ask.

"Don't you have brothers? Strange of your pa, to send a girl your age to do his business for him."

"My brothers are occupied on a ranch," I said, and then leaned toward him urgently. "Say, Mister, do you know where the Richardson ranch is? I have... I have an errand to run there, on my pa's behalf."

He didn't know the location. He said, "How old are you, anyway, sweetheart?"

I thought there might be an official age for staying on in saloons, but I didn't know what it was, so I answered evasively: "Old enough."

He laughed at that, like it was the closing line to a joke he'd been waiting his whole life to hear. He dropped one heavy arm around my shoulders. "I bet you are at that," he said. "I bet you are." His fingers moved along my collarbone through the worn calico of Mrs. Alton's dress. His touch didn't disturb me; I'd had rougher treatment from the wagon boys. "Let me buy you a drink, honey."

"I'll have a sarsaparilla."

My pa had once let me try sarsaparilla, on a day when I accompanied him to town to sell a paltry load of corn ears. That day had been so hot, you could have sizzled bacon on the ground —but the thick, throbbing heat had fallen away the moment the invigorating spice of that drink hit my tongue. I was eager to taste it again.

My companion seemed to think I'd made another joke. He

laughed even louder than before, and his touch below my neck got a little firmer—more insistent. Then his fingers slid down a little lower. "Jake," he called back into the bar, "bring this filly a whiskey. I'm paying."

At that moment, the dancing girls took their places beside the piano, all smiling red lips and sweeps of cream-colored skin. And then the music began to play.

———

THAT FIRST TASTE OF WHISKEY. I remember it well, even to this day. A sudden woody bite upon my tongue, a reflexive swallow—and then that queer, tingling warmth running all down my throat into the pit of my stomach, to the bottom of my very soul. The fire of it spreading, perking up my senses; the hot vapor rising to the back of my throat, burning my nostrils when I exhaled.

And the rush of glee to my head, the wild wicked glory, the knowledge that however the world might try to hurt me, it could never hurt me enough. Not enough to keep me down. Not enough to break me.

Drink it the first time, and it makes you giddy and light.

Drink it a thousand times, and you're already broken. The world has already won.

But you'll keep coming back, no matter how you try to stay away. You will return time and again, thirsty for that first sip, desperate to relive the moment when you thought yourself invincible. The more you hurt—the harder the world kicks you—the more you crave it. The more your heart aches for the round, mellow comfort, its fulsome taste. The more you need the fire in your breath, and the will to go on laughing, and the blank, dark peace of forgetting.

Order up another whiskey, Short Pants. This story ain't half over yet.

I NEVER DID nothing with that Mexican fella, God's honest truth. I managed to convince him I truly was the daughter of a merchant and too respectable for cavorting, and when he disappeared for a few minutes—to piss out back, maybe, or to find another girl to woo—I retreated into the night. The sharp, woody taste of whiskey was still warm and full in my mouth. That was all I wanted for one night—all I could manage just then.

Somehow, I found my way back to my bed, even with the liquor clouding my senses. It may have been the resilience of youth, or maybe I just wasn't as skunked as I thought. In any case, I managed to slide into my cot as quietly as I slid out of it some two or three hours before, and with the burn of liquor in my belly, I fell asleep before my head hit the pillow.

I was plenty tired out next morning, tuckered as I'd ever been on the wagon trail, but as I sleep-walked through the day's work, I knew I had to get back to the saloon that very night, and all nights to come. It wasn't the man who drew me back. His fondling had meant nothing to me, for even at my tender age I was already jaded where *that* was concerned. Nor had the liquor set its hook in my soul—not yet. It was the possibility of the place that called to me. All those folks passing in and out of that red swinging door, all the people I might meet, the stories I might hear. The saloon was a world apart from the quiet routine and daily lonesomeness of the boarding house. As long as I was busy recalling the fun I had at the saloon, and pondering on what types of folks I might meet next, I had no room in my head to worry about my brothers and sisters, and no chance to berate myself for failing to round them up again and make good on my promises. The saloon was my secret salvation. I knew already that I'd never be able to let the place alone.

As I bent over the laundry kettle with hot water pinking my arms, I felt shame and guilt heat me from the inside, too. I recalled the kindly face of Reverend Wilkes, who had taken us in and done his best to bring me properly close to God. I knew the Reverend would disapprove of my sneaking and fibbing. And I knew I ought to find some way to get the pink calico dress back to Emma Alton—make some plausible excuse for its absence and hand it over, folded and neat and pressed with lavender. For as long as I kept that dress, I had the means to enter another world—a world which was still rightly forbidden to a girl of my age. The moment the dress was out of my hands, I would be helpless. I would be forced to give saloons up for good—at least till I aged up proper.

I will give it back, I told myself as I worked. I imagined I was talking to Reverend Wilkes, and maybe to Jesus Christ Himself, too, whose kindly sad eyes I sometimes felt peering down on me from the sky, or from wherever it is He's thought to dwell. (I never have been able to locate Him, from that day to this.) I thought, *I'll give the dress back after two more visits. Or three.* I only wanted another handful of nights at the saloon, a few more sweet memories to suck and savor like a good, rare candy before I gave myself over to morals and made myself into the fine upstanding lady I was supposed to grow up and be.

But the more often I went, the harder it became to abandon my secret new life. I slept only a few hours each night, but my dreams were sweet and scored by the grand, gravelly purr of the hurdy-gurdy. I was slow and clumsy at my work; I yawned over breakfast and supper alike. Sometimes my thoughts were so slow that I never was able to talk myself out of saucing Emma Alton before it was too late, and I tasted the sting of her birch stick more often than ever before.

Once I spilled a whole kettle of laundry into the dirt, and Emma, with stick raised, paused and blinked at me, startled-like. She said, "Mother of mercy, child. I believe you've got the bottle-ache."

"No mam," I said quickly, and tried to straighten up and look lively. "I don't even know what bottle-ache is, but I can assure

you, I ain't got that. It's just a head cold, I swear. Must have got it
from one of the boarders. It's making me ache something awful,
right here." I touched the place next to my nose, where you get
that dull pounding pain whenever a cold settles in. Then I simu-
lated a sneeze for good measure, and groaned good enough make
any stage actress turn green with envy.

Emma lowered her stick without striking me once, but she
stood there staring at me—a hard, level, icy-cold stare from those
pretty blue eyes. She watched me so long, I felt as if she could see
right through my chest and into my cowering, shriveled little soul.
How I ever held her gaze without busting into tears and begging
for forgiveness is a mystery to me. But at last, Emma turned away
and said, "Clean up that mess and don't be so clumsy, girl. And if
you have a head cold, tell me so I can remedy you, instead of
bumbling around making a wreckage of my home."

Well, I hardly need to tell you that the promise I'd made to
myself—to only go back to the saloon two or three more times—
was a promise I broke good and hard, just like all the rest. A week
flew by, then two, and I snuck out to the saloon every night except
Sundays, for the good people of Piedmont wouldn't suffer any
saloon to operate on the Lord's Day. Otherwise I would have been
there Sunday nights, too, sure as you're born. It wasn't the fact
that I went back again and again that shames me now, these many
years later. It's the fact that I gave up all thought of finding the
Richardson ranch and the boys, and seldom thought about the
little girls anymore, either. Between the great enjoyment of music
and the excitement of the stories I heard from the gambling men,
there was no more room in my heart for sadness. You might
account that a good thing, but I do not. If I've come to learn one
truth in all my sad and sorry existence, it's this: our sorrows drive
us. All work—all good—grows from a deep bed of longing. And in
my life, I have come to believe that longing is just another shade
of sorrow.

The men who roamed those two saloons seemed grand creatures to me. They was all quick with a laugh, and they trailed the glamour of the frontier behind them—a wake of adventure and dry dust, of flecks of gold and the broken fletchings of Indian arrows. I liked to talk to those men, for they never minded my unrefined speech. They didn't even mind when I swore. They laughed all the harder, in fact, and slapped me on the bottom in a friendly sort of way, and offered up yet more tales of their boldest deeds—and expected me to believe them, too. When they paid me any kindness, I thought myself a pretty girl, even though none of them ever said I was. I felt just as splendid and fair as Emma Alton —felt it right down to my big Missouri bones.

It was in a moment exactly like that—setting on a man's knee, with the glass of whiskey he'd bought me half-drunk already, feeling lovely as a queen—that I got the first big idea of my life. I don't remember anything about the man today—not his name nor his age, not the sound of his voice nor the quality of his smile (but they all had slow hunting grins and eyes that measured me with knowing confidence.) All I remember about that man was his words.

"I come from the railroad camp, you know. It's only two miles from the edge of town by now. Maybe three miles."

"A railroad camp must be pretty grand." I had seen the camp when we'd first arrived in Piedmont, of course. I knew it wasn't grand. But I didn't want to hurt his feelings.

"No," he said truthfully, "not at all. It's damn muddy and hard, and that's why I'm here tonight, to get a handful of something soft." He squeezed my hip, and usually that made me giggle and squirm, but for some reason I'd fastened onto his talk of the camp and I couldn't be persuaded into giggling.

I said, "Why do you do the work if it's hard and muddy?"

I don't know what I expected him to say. *For the money*, maybe. Or, *What the Hell else am I supposed to do?* But he got quiet for a minute and sipped at his liquor, and seemed to stare right through the piano and the dancing girls to a place far beyond Piedmont, a place I couldn't see. Finally he said, "Have you ever seen a train up close? Ever seen a train in motion?"

"No sir," I said, sort of quiet because I could sense his awe, his church-like reverence.

"Trains are the kind of thing only Man could make," he said. "Even God could never create something so powerful."

That shocked me, for it seemed improper, even though I had never been an especially pious girl. I drank down the rest of my whiskey and considered giggling just to get him off the subject.

He said, "There's a motion to trains that is so complete, it's almost holy. They always go somewhere, you see. They're never stuck, never stalled, never grounded. Or if they do get stuck, it ain't for long. They keep moving, and everywhere they go, they move with purpose and power. That's the kind of man I want to be: like a train. So I guess I'm in service to the trains, working for their purpose."

"Like a preacher works for God's purpose?"

"No. Like a slave works for his master." Then he looked at me funny and barked out a big, loud laugh. "Jesus, girl, you getting churchy on me?"

I wasn't getting churchy; all danger of that was long past. But that night, as I set upon his knee and let him squeeze handfuls of my softness—and later, as I walked home with the throb already building behind my eyes—I thought of purpose and power. I thought of motion, of the holiness of going somewhere, of never being grounded. And far in the back of my head, under the dwindling music of the saloons, I could hear the crying of a train's whistle.

YEARS LATER, I had occasion to watch a train go by—to really see it, I mean, and feel the thunder of its passing shudder through my body. It ain't like watching from a distance while a train creeps low along the horizon with a black fog of breath trailing behind. I didn't think of the man in the saloon when I saw that train, but I think of him now, as I remember.

I rode out to a new length of track soon after it was dedicated. I rode as close to the track as I dared, as near as I knew my horse would stand, and gazed far along its cold black length, noting how it reached deep into the heart of the West, the relentless symmetry of its rails and ties, hard as a knife-cut through the soft virgin hills. I left my horse ground-tied and grazing, and moved closer on foot. Away in the distance, from the East where civilized men and fine ladies lived, I heard the faint, hoarse cry of its whistle. Then I laid down.

Not on the tracks, as I guess you first supposed. I never once thought of doing myself in—not even when my spark was at its dimmest. That startles me now, to think back on it. I can't explain why I kept on living, except to say that I was always eager for life, always ready to feel in my heart the fullness of anything that came my way, be it sorrow or joy.

No, I laid down alongside the tracks. The grass was short there, dry and crackly, grazed by cattle and the thin brown shadows of antelopes. There, the prairie gave way to sun-scorched earth flooring the lines and ties. I laid down on my back; I closed my eyes.

It took some long while for the train to reach me. As I waited with the afternoon sun hot on my cheeks and forehead, I heard my horse where I'd left him, tearing grass with his teeth and lashing his tail at lazy flies. I heard the hollow rush of his breath and felt the faint vibration of his hooves as he moved slow across the land, one step and then another. And I heard meadowlarks singing on the sage flats, their calls rising and falling from where they perched on the high yellow spikes of silver-leaved mullein.

Then the rumble of the train's wheels started low beneath my spine, and reached up through the earth, into my body and my blood. It overtook all my other senses, though it had yet to draw near, but I could feel its power growing, feel the inevitability of its weight and its speed, the black blindness of its onward rush. My breath came short. I told myself to get up and run, yet I knew full well there was nowhere to go. Nowhere left, where the tracks wouldn't reach me sooner or later. I smelled a hot metal stink and the oily dust of coal. The train's breath, like the panting of a sick man who can't help but spread his disease.

And then the train was upon me. I opened my mouth in shock as the engineer opened the throat of his train, and it seemed that vast, piercing, howling cry came from me, right up out of my soul. The train pounded; it thrashed; it beat to death reality around my splayed body. And in the thunder of its passing, I felt the world splinter and break.

I opened my eyes. I tipped my head back to see. Bars of blue sky flashed rhythmically through a rush of metal black. The rapid change from light to dark, to light, to dark again sent all my wits spinning clean away, till I felt untethered from myself—from the whole world, severed from life as sure as if I'd thrown myself beneath the train's screaming wheels, after all.

And then it was gone. The roar of its passing seemed to fade away faster than it had come. In moments I was alone, lying on the earth, with tears of fear and wonder cutting tracks through the dirt on my face, from the corners of my eyes to my temples. The train cried again, but it was already distant, and I was already forgotten in its wake.

THE FIRST NIGHT I tip-toed off to the railroad camp was also my last night of sneaking. I left as early as I dared and followed the saloon man's directions, taking a wagon road out past the eastern edge of town, walking one foot in front of the other along a narrow, moonlit rut. It took me well over and hour to get there, but long before I arrived, I could see the rail camp nestled against the foot of a dark hill. The small, angular chips of canvas tents stood out plain in the night, like shavings from a soap bar scattered across't the ground. The air was chilly, for autumn had come, but there was still a few crickets singing in the sagebrush. I had a black shawl which Emma had given me, having no further need of it herself—and the shawl, combined with the way my muscles never stopped shivering with excitement, kept me passably warm till I reached the camp.

I smelled the camp before I heard anything of note—any song or laughter or masculine shouts cutting over the buzz of the crickets. Frontier camps always have a thick, heavy fug. It hangs like a cloak around every camp—the stink of the latrine pits and the sweat of men's bodies. I went right through the first row of tents, half expecting someone to stop me and question me, but no one ever did. As in the saloons, no one of consequence took note of me a-tall. That was exactly the way I liked it. Only when I entered the camp did I hear the sounds of drinking and dancing and music—the sounds of life.

The tent that served for a gathering place—a liquor dispensary of sorts—stood at the center of the encampment. That place was a-light with stubs of candles burning in dozens of leaded glass lanterns, all stuck up on posts and hung wherever a light could hang. The lanterns was all dented, their glass cracked and bubbled, and as they swung in the autumn wind, bars of yellow light slid and crossed and angled over the earth. It was as if the light was dancing to the music—fiddle, mouth-harp, banjaw—and in the center of all that warmth and movement, the ladies danced just as brightly.

I held still beside a lantern post and watched. Watched men coming in from the perimeter with mud still on their boots and their bracers dropped down to trail at their sides. Most of the men had stains under their arms from a long day of work, and a smell hung all about the liquor tent that was just as rank as the camp-smell, thick like the burning of tallow, but somehow far sweeter to me, compelling as cinnamon or vanilla cream. The night cracked and split with the clapping of the women's hands. They all clapped in the same rhythm, timed to the music, and soon my feet began tapping of their own accord. I laughed with pure delight whenever one of the men raised up a whoop, whenever the fiddle whined up high and the fiddler's bow darted like lightning.

Two men stood near me, watching the dancers, talking just loud enough so I could hear them.

"Heard you ain't long for this camp," one said to the other.

"That's true," the man replied. "Sioux getting fiercer by the day, it seems."

"Getting desperate," said the first.

"Maybe so. But I figure a man's got a duty to stand against them."

"So you'll go off and get yourself killed in the name of duty? Sounds damn foolish to me. You best reconsider."

"If we don't do something to stop the devils, they'll stamp us out sooner or later."

"They won't," the first man said. "They ain't smart enough to stamp us out. Besides, I heard they're sending Custer out to handle 'em."

"Custer? Of Appomattox, Custer?"

"Do you know of another one?"

"Horse shit. Where'd you hear that?"

"Somewheres or other."

"Custer's got better things to do than wallow around in the sagebrush hunting Indians."

"'Fyou say so, friend."

At that moment, one of them took note of me. "Hello there," he said in that way men have—a sudden turn to the solicitous, warming all at once to a girl. "Haven't seen you around before."

"No sir," I said, "I'm new here. I heard this camp has the best whoop-up on offer, in the whole of the territory."

"You a girl who likes a wild time?" the fellow said, looking me up and down. I thought he might size up a heifer the same way, if he was thinking he might buy it.

"She likes to dance, all right," his friend said. "See how her toes is a-tappin'."

"I like to see a girl dance."

It seemed the two men could agree on that much, if they found no common ground on the matter of Custer.

"Go on," the first fella said. "The rest of the girls will let you dance along with them. They're proper friendly."

"Oh no, I couldn't," I said. "I never danced before."

But it was already too late for my protestations. The men cupped their hands around their mouths and shouted over my head, "Hey Rosie! Hey Pearl! Here's another dancer for you, let's see how she trots!"

The girls surrounded me a moment later. Laughing, bouncing, smiling at me, their painted eyes beamed with gladness. Never had I smelled such flowery perfume or seen skin so ivory-smooth, though every girl was flushed warm from the dance. Beneath their perfume I could make out a muskier scent, primal and sharp like the smell that hangs over the prairie in the season of rut. It thrilled me to smell it. The girls took my hands, one to each side, and pulled me into their circle, close to the fiddle with its lightning bow and its high, scratching sing-song voice.

"It's easy," one of the girls said, for she saw my wide eyes, my hesitation. She laughed and tossed her tight yellow rag-curls. "There ain't nothin' but music tonight. Feel it, and do whatever it tells you to do."

That's exactly what I did. I loosened up all my fear and shame, casting away the last of what held me in check, held me tied to the moral world. My heart leaped; my feet pounded, but when I could catch my breath and see—really see what I was doing—I noted with great satisfaction that I moved in perfect time to the song.

EMMA WAS WAITING up for me when I dragged myself home with a joyous ache in my feet and elsewhere in me, too. Sunrise was still an hour off, but there was enough of dawn's gray along the flank of the land that she could see me coming down the road, could see the pink calico dress with the white ruffle on my pounding breast. I saw her standing in the yard of the boarding house, right at the front gate in her nightgown, wrapped in her fine new shawl. Her body was stiff with grim confirmation.

I walked right up to her. Where else was I to go?

"Well," she said. "I was right after all. This is what comes of trying to do good in the world."

"I'm sorry," I said, knowing full well that I wasn't.

"Not half as sorry as you'll soon be, Martha Canary."

Emma did not allow me to re-enter her house. It made no difference; everything I had was what the Altons had given me, trying to do good in the world.

She did allow me to keep that long dress, though. There was no point pretending I was still a girl—not anymore.

CAN DRINK WHISKEY, SHOOT, PLAY CARDS, OR SWEAR, IF IT COMES TO IT

I TOOK IT IN MY HEAD TO RETURN TO SALT LAKE CITY. I CAN'T SAY what drew me back to that strange, cold-shouldered place. Maybe it was the fact that it *was* a city, not a town like Piedmont or Princeton. Maybe the orderly grid of its streets called to me, promising something stable and predictable in a world that was, I was fast learning, liable to be shaken up at a moment's notice. It could also be that I had some notion of finding Baby Sara and taking her back—today I can't tell you exactly what motivated my return. My thoughts in those days was one great tangle inside my head.

However I came by the notion, I found a place for myself in a wagon party bound for Utah Territory. As before, I worked for my passage south, for I had no money to pay my way. But I didn't make it to Salt Lake before the snows set in. The wagons reached their destination, a town called Corinne, and there I was obliged to stay till I could arrange another passage south. At least I had procured warm clothing and a new bedroll from the wagon men, trading as I'd done in older days. Judge me if you like, but there was times that autumn when I thanked God for making me a girl, for at least He had equipped me with a natural means of providing for myself when there was no decent charity to be found. I felt sorry for orphan boys cast adrift in the world—I haven't often met men who prefer a boy's charms to a girl's. Even a homely girl's.

In Corinne I perceived that I'd be real lucky to find a route to Salt Lake before springtime came, for the town was off the beaten track, as the saying goes. It had sprung up some few years before near a place called Promontory, which was a high bluff overlooking all the vast dry valley and the shining expanse of the Great Salt Lake below. In those days, just before my arrival in Corinne, there was nothing at Promontory save the view. But everyone in the railroad business had known all along that Promontory was the chosen site: the holy land where the tracks going east would meet up with the tracks going west, and so connect the whole continent by rail, from Boston clear to California. The much-anticipated moment of connection had occurred some five or six months before my arrival; the last railroad tie at Promontory's summit had been fixed in its place with a golden spike. Corinne was still in a stupor of righteousness, like what I imagined the redeemed would feel when Christ returned to cleanse the world of sin. An air of unimaginable good luck hung over Corinne's snow-choked streets, a certain smug glee at having made the right choice.

For my part, I didn't see what there was to feel so proud about. It was a tiny town, hardly more than a village. Far as I could see, nobody was clamoring to get there and revel in Corinne's high society, no matter their vaunted proximity to that golden spike. Maybe the newly completed Transcontinental line would indeed bring riches undreamed-of to Corinne, and make every last man a baron and every woman a queen. But it hadn't happened yet. Corinne was like Piedmont, to my eye—but considerably less enjoyable, what with its lack of saloons and taverns where a body might enjoy a little dancing now and then.

The people of Corinne was also spiteful toward the Mormons.

They took great pride in being All Gentile (the Mormons, you know, called anybody who was not of their ranks by that name.) I couldn't imagine why a people who despised Mormons so thoroughly would stake out a claim in Utah Territory; far as I was concerned, the place had nothing to recommend it *but* Mormons, and that is a slim endorsement if you ask me. But such was the magic of the railroad. Promises lay all along its cold black lines. Folks routinely sacrificed all common sense—and more besides—on the altar of the iron horse.

The very day I arrived, I set about finding work. I had some thought of keeping up a boarding house, for I had learned plenty in Piedmont and felt certain of my skills as a duster and a laundress. But no one found me promising, and anyway, there was only two boarding houses in all of Corinne, and neither was half as big as the Altons' place. No one wanted me to wait at tables, neither; Corinne possessed but one eatery, and it was staffed by the owner's grown-up daughters. I didn't have the nerve to ask any of the women if they needed a hand caring for their children. It seemed too obscene a joke, even to try. I had done a piss-poor job by the five children left to my keeping, and they had been my own flesh and blood.

By that time, I had no qualms about working on my back. In fact, after the fun I'd witnessed at the rail camp, whoring seemed a downright pleasant prospect. But even with its lack of Mormons, Corinne was the squeaky-cleanest town I ever laid eyes on—then or since. If anyone was whoring, they was doing it in the strictest secrecy. I couldn't locate a cat house even though my life depended on it.

After two days searching for employment without any luck—and two nights spent in the half-empty hay loft of a very cold and drafty barn—I finally resolved to take myself door to door. I knocked on every last door in Corinne, asking for work or charity, whichever fickle circumstance saw fit to strew across my path. I was resolved to take on any sort of work—anything a-tall—up to and including digging latrine pits in the frozen earth, though Corinne seemed to have its latrine needs amply seen to, along with its laundering and housekeeping. Word flew around town faster than I could, so by the end of the day no one in Corinne would answer their doors when I knocked, even though I could hear footsteps inside as they crept from window to window, trying to skim a look at the mysterious, unattached girl who had appeared in their railroad sanctuary as if from thin air.

I determined to try my luck beyond the town, where a few ranch houses could be seen far and gray in the snow, huddled down low beneath a vast, oppressive weight of cloud-covered sky. I headed for the one that seemed closest, and as I left Corinne, I turned on my heel and shouted loud as I could, so all the people could hear, "You ain't got a stick of charity among you! I hope you're invaded by Mormons and I hope they pull your golden spike out of the ground and fuck every last one of you with the damnable thing!" Then I blushed terrible and hurried away, for I'd never said such a startling, unholy thing before, though I'd thought the like often enough. It's one thing to let fly a cute little cuss or two to earn your whiskey, and quite another to give a whole town at once the bluest side of your tongue.

The nearest ranch lay much farther away than it had originally seemed. Snow has that effect, I've found—as do certain other atmospheres, like spring haze or impending thunder. By the time I stumbled to the ranch house, my boots was soaked, my feet so frozen I couldn't feel the pain anymore. The bottom of my pink calico dress was gray and draggled from the snow, but I had trousers on beneath that kept my legs from suffering overmuch. Still, I was worried about my feet. I'd left a trail of footprints across the rancher's fields, stretching in a broken blue line all the way back to inhospitable Corinne. The town seemed to mock me from afar, and I swear to this day that I could still feel the eyes of all its people on my back, watching me, judging me, and not liking what they saw.

Dusk had all but settled as I approached the ranch house, nestled in the center of a ring of barns and sheds. There was an orange glow in one window, a fire inside—the only spot of color in all the lonesome, blue-gray world. I knocked hard on the door and heard some surprised cussing inside. After a minute, a man of about fifty years opened up, but only just a crack, so that one steely eye peered out at me over the half I could see of his graying mustache.

"Please, mister," I said. "I'm in real bad shape. I need to get my feet warm and dry. Can't you let me stay here for the night? I got my own bedroll. I can sleep on the floor. I won't make any noise or even ask for any food."

"The Hell you come from, girl?"

"From Corinne, but no one would take me in there, so I had to tramp all this way over the snow. And before that I was from Piedmont. I'm trying to make my way down to Salt Lake City, for my brother is going to meet me there. He's through with the Army and he has a voucher to settle some land in Utah Territory, signed by Custer himself." I was spouting nonsense now. Truth was, I had no idea whether Army men ever got vouchers, and it seemed damn silly to claim a body might possess one signed by the great hero Custer. But I reasoned that folks in Corinne probably didn't know any more about the greater state of affairs than I did. "Only I didn't make it to Salt Lake before the snows overtook me," I went on desperately. "And now I'm sore in need of a place to stay, at least for tonight. You got a wife in there? I can help her out, and I'm glad to do it, to repay your kindness. I can do laundry real good."

"Ain't got no wife," the man said. He did swing the door open a little wider, though, and I counted that reason for hope. "What's your name?"

As he opened up the door, I could feel the warmth of his wood fire roll out to greet me. I shut my eyes for a second, giving in to a shiver of fear and despair. I had never wanted anything like I wanted the safety of that rancher's hearth. I was ready to tell him anything to get it—even the truth.

"My name's Martha Canary. I got no one in all the world, sir, and I need help. Please. I'm willing to work—whatever work you have for me. I'll stay all winter and work for you, if that's what you want. I just need to wait out the snow so's I can get myself down to Salt Lake City."

I thought maybe he would take my meaning, being a man with no wife and all. But the offer flew right past his head. He said, "Ain't no kind of work on this place except driving mules."

I perked right up at that. "I can ride," I said eagerly. "I'm a real good rider, in fact."

He narrowed his eyes at my pink dress, with no attempt to hide his skepticality.

"Look," I said, and lifted up the skirt some, so he could see I wore trousers. "I *can* ride, and everybody says I'm knacky with horses."

"Mules ain't like horses."

"I know," I said. "I worked with mules, too." That wasn't true, but I reasoned mules and horses looked so much alike, they couldn't be vastly different in their natures.

There was a long pause, during which I could feel the icy ache from my feet spreading up to my ankles. The cold sought to claim me piece by piece.

Finally, he opened the door a little wider. "Well," he said slowly, "my old hand runned off two weeks ago with some girl from town, and I'm no good lately." He stepped back, the movement revealing a heavy limp. "Fell in a prairie dog hole," he said. "Damn fool accident to have, for a fella of my age. But I won't be much good till my knee's healed up, and ain't nobody come out here anyway, so I got no hope of finding a man to do whatever work needs doing. I might as well take on a girl. At least you're big. You look strong enough."

I let out an explosive breath, half sigh of relief, half laughter. "Thank you, mister! Thank you. I won't let you down."

"You ain't Mormon, I hope."

"No, sir."

"No," he said in that slow drawl, "reckon you ain't, after all. 'Fyou was, you'd be married off to some old bull with his beard and his balls hanging clear down to his knees—you and a dozen other girls besides."

I smiled. I liked the way he talked.

"Come in," he said, "and get your feet warm. I'll show you around the place in the morning."

THE MAN'S name was Braddick, and we was as much alike as any two folks may be who haven't a drop of blood in common. His fire saved my feet, though the burning as they thawed out and came back to life was about the worst pain I ever endured. I sat with my bare feet stretched out before his cheerful fire while Mr. Braddick distracted me from that searing, prickling ordeal by telling me all about his operation. He trained up teams of mules, which would haul wagon-loads of supplies from one rail camp to the next. In the years before the golden spike—when rail camps was still boiling with activity, and urgency to complete the Transcontinental still motivated every white soul in the West—Mr. Braddick's business had been strong.

"Now that the Trans is finished," he said, "ain't near as much need for the mule teams. Funny, the way it's all worked out. That damn railway made a new way of life for the men who worked to lay its tracks—and for men like me, who see to all the needs of the camps. But soon as the track is finished, it's the trains themselves that destroy those new ways of life. Yes, they do. Crush men's occupations. Crush our very identities, in fact—our whole reason for living. What's a man to live for, if not his work?"

I didn't know how to answer that question—what's a man to live for—so I held my tongue.

"Still," Braddick said, brightening up a little, "mules can go where trains can't. They can even go where horses can't. There's a few places here and there, places and men in need of my teams and my wagons. I ain't finished yet—not yet."

I could read in Braddick's eyes what he had left unspoken: *I'll be finished soon, though. Sooner or later, the rails will finish us all.*

Mr. Braddick fed me on thick, stale-tasting porridge, which I gulped down as if it was manna from Heaven. The next day, he showed me around his ranch. A corral stood behind his house, all its snow trampled down flat and pocked by muddy hoofprints. A sloped wooden awning slanted over the rear portion of the corral, and beneath that simple shelter, I found his herd of mules. It had been an awful long time since I'd been near anything resembling a horse, so I pricked up at sight of them. The mules seemed to sense my gladness to see them, too, for they all raised their big, bow-shaped heads at once, gazing at me with a curiosity and intelligence I couldn't help but love.

Braddick could get around on his injured knee just well enough to teach me everything I needed to know. At his instruction, I ducked between the rails of the corral fence and walked out into the center of the enclosure. Hardly had I ceased to move but the mules approached me of their own accord. I raised a loop of soft rope, which Braddick had given me to carry, and slipped it quietly over the neck of the first mule who came to greet me.

"You're a natural, Martha," Braddick declared. "A real whacker in the making."

All that day, Braddick instructed me in the art of mulewhacking. He taught me the parts of a harness—how it fits together around an animal's body, how a clever driver can use a creature's weight to pull and stop a wagon or sled, no matter how heavy the load. By the end of the day, Braddick had me up in the seat of a small wagon, driving six spunky mules in a tight circle inside the muddy corral.

He leaned on the fence, watching. "I'll be damned. I admit I didn't think a girl could do the job, but you got hands and a head perfectly suited for driving, Miss Martha."

I glowed with pride, and looking back, I think it was the first time I ever felt that grand, warm emotion in all my life.

Within a few days, I was working a team of six out across the snowy range, pulling an old buckboard wagon which Braddick had fitted out with sleigh runners for winter-time use.

Mules have an unfavorable reputation, but from the start I found them to be the pleasantest of creatures. It is true that they won't tolerate a lick of nonsense from a handler, but in order to gain their cooperation—even their loyalty—all a body has to do is show them a little respect. Beat a mule or cuss him out, and he'll plant his feet and throw up his head, and give you an unmistakable stare from his small, dark, infinitely peevish eye. That stare says, *Just try and move me if you think you can—you who's hardly bigger than a gnat, far as I'm concerned.* Neither lash nor spur impresses a mule; they'll tolerate an astonishing amount of pain in the interest of teaching you a lesson in courtesy. But coax a mule along with gentle words, tell her how pretty she is, how silky her ears, how brave her heart, and by God she'll march right through any hazard for your sake.

I suppose I am like a mule in that regard, and while some folks would account that a grave insult, I have enough sense to take it as a compliment. A mule never puts her feet wrong—unless she means to, for purposes of her own. She may seem graceless or even malformed when stood up beside a well-bred horse with its mane all braided and its neck arched proud. But the mule can keep working long after the horse has dropped from exhaustion. Just try to tell me there ain't something to be proud of in mulish fortitude.

Though I was but a young thing, I dare say my head was nailed

on straight, and from the first moment in the driver's seat, I
delighted in handling Braddick's mule team. There's something
marvelously natural about driving a team; any half-wit can do it if
they only pay attention to the animals' moods. All you have to do
is look where the mules is looking, and listen in the direction of
their swiveling ears, and imagine your own self in the traces. With
a little sympathy for your animals, you can feel in your own body
the bite and tug of the harness, the weight dragging along behind,
the cadence of your fellow team-mates' hooves and the warm
sway of their laboring bodies. You can hear their breath rushing
and puffing in unison. You can feel the subtle rhythm of all those
great, strong, inelegant bodies pulling together, working as one
creature toward a common good. Driving was like a dance to me
—like the bouncy, gleeful rhythm of the saloon girls, kicking and
twirling in time. Only this dance was slower and softer, and far
more intimate, for it was just me with the reins in my hands and
the cold against my face. Just me, and the sweet breath of my
animals steaming and pooling in the air around my head as we
crossed the snow-covered hills.

Once I'd got the hang of driving, I took up other work around
Braddick's ranch. Several of his fences had gone to pot, with wet
boards sagging and nails rusted and bent. There was puddles of
ice-rimmed mud inside the corrals, which I fixed easy enough by
shoveling earth over the wet places. But the longer I stayed and
toiled, the worse his ranch looked. I suspected the old man had
something amiss with his body, beyond his hurt leg—or maybe
something amiss with his head—for the ranch had surely fallen
into disrepair long before Braddick twisted his knee, long before I
arrived. But Braddick was a close-lipped fellow. He never talked
much about himself, nor anything else for that matter. I knew no
one could make a man like him confess to any bodily weakness, so
I never bothered to ask. Old men are often that way—proud and
sad in their aging, clinging to the strength they once had as if they
can get it all back again if they just suffer long and silent enough.

As I worked to improve the fences and grounds, I wondered how I might convince Braddick to let me stay on forever. By that time, he surely knew I could work as hard as any ranch hand, even if I was a girl. I liked him. He taught me card games and shuffling tricks each night while we warmed ourselves at the hearth. I had come to love that ranch as if it was my own, too. You can't work a plot of land without feeling some bond with the soil and the sky. Every spadeful of earth you dig, the land itself digs deeper into your heart, till you've become the land—and the whole muddy, snow-choked, shit-stinking breadth of it trembles with the beat of your pulse.

Sometime just after Christmas—Braddick gave me two oranges and a new pair of warm woolen stockings as a present— he sent me out on my first delivery. The route ran out to a rail- road camp, away back toward Piedmont, where the railway men still worked to connect two offshoot branches of the Transcon- tinental.

"You sure you can make this drive on your own?" he asked me as I finished tightening up the traces.

"Shit, sir," I said (he never did mind my cussing), "you said yourself I can do the run."

"But do you feel *ready* for it, girl? It's a long and lonesome trail, and the winter's dark and cold."

I smiled at him, for I knew he'd grown some scraggly kind of affection for me. That was a kindness I hadn't oft enjoyed in my short lifetime. "I'm ready, sir; I know it. Don't you worry none about me. Got the mules for company, and your rifle in case any wolves come after me."

"I do believe you find those mules real good company, too," Braddick said, kind of slow and meditative, as if he still couldn't quite believe anybody actually enjoyed the presence of mules— especially a girl, who was supposed to be delicate and frilly and fonder of park ponies than great kicking screamers with peevish little eyes.

Braddick gave me his hand to steady me as I climbed up into the wagon, though I could feel a terrible shaking in his arm and shoulder, and I knew it was he who needed steadying. "Take this along with you," he said, handing up a thick, flat packet wrapped in oil cloth and tied with soot-blackened twine. It was food, surely —though I'd already stowed a little crate under the driving seat, which held salt pork and softened apples from the root cellar, along with a couple loaves of bread, which I had made myself and burned all along the bottom. I tucked his package in with the rest of my provisions.

I tapped the brim of the big black sombrero I'd donned to cut back the glare of winter sky. "Better be off, I guess, if I want to reach the depot on time."

"Well—" Braddick said. Just that, nothing more. Then he turned and headed back toward his little, dark-sided ranch house, limping on his bad knee and trembling with every step.

When I get back, I told myself, *I'll set him down by the fire and make him see that he's got to take me on as his permanent hand. Who else will help him? He's got no one in all the world, and I can do the work of two men.*

That probably was not true—I was bigger than a girl of my age had any right to be, but I was still a girl, after all. It made me feel better to think it, though. I slapped the reins against my mules' flanks and the wagon-sledge took off smartly toward the town depot.

Soon as I was underway, a great joy surged up in my middle. Now I was off on my own, making the world mine, carving out a place for myself in the grown-up world of respectable, Christianly toil. My thrill was dampened a little as I entered the town of Corinne, which I hadn't returned to since I'd cussed the whole place out in one shot. I didn't know whether any of those upstanding citizens might recall me and wish me ill. I made my way to the train depot with an old plaid scarf pulled up high around my face, just my eyes showing below my sombrero, and in that way passed through Corinne without incident.

When the depot hands had loaded up my wagon, I set off in the direction of Piedmont. The mules grumbled and tossed their heads in protest at the weight of their burden, but I talked pretty to them, and soon enough my voice reconciled them to the task. Together we made tracks over old but unmarked snow, which cracked and crisped beneath my team's hooves, hissing loud under the runners.

I loved the snow-covered hills with a deepness and trembling that startled me, for it came upon me so damn sudden, and I felt it so strong. The world was all of one color—silver-gray, with here and there the dark recesses of shadow where some tenacious patch of sage stood up tall against the blowing of winter storms. The world's beauty held a certain fragility, a readiness to crack and shatter, as if the season meant to remind me that all things are impermanent, all things pass away. I guess most folks find such thoughts distressing. We love to tell ourselves—don't we, Short Pants—that we'll go on existing forever, that death will never come—not for us, not for us. But though I never learned much of the Bible, I do recall this much: To every thing there is a season, and a time to every purpose. He hath made everything beautiful in His time.

I rejoiced on that long, cold drive, for I was doing good—making myself useful, after a long and dreary season of failure and shame. Even the ice and the flatness and the persistent pale-gray state of the world couldn't drag my spirits down. What did I care if the sage branches shivered and snapped beneath my wagon's skids? What did I care if I, some distant day, would fall into a cold gray winter and, like the sage and the hills lying muffled under snow, shatter and break and fade? I had no need to learn the world from beginning to end. My place was simply to have a place—to be there, at the back of my team, with my sorrows standing up in the trail of mules' hoofprints and snow-slicked ruts. My sorrows standing up to follow me into the foothills, but never again to catch me.

AT NIGHT I built a little fire beside my wagon, in its lee side, where I could hear the bitter wind howling, but it couldn't reach me with its claws. My mules gathered close to shelter from the cold. One by one I lifted their feet, picking balls of ice from the hair that fringed their heels. I did it till my fingers went numb, and kept at my work till all the mules' feet was clear of ice and they relaxed with contented sighs.

When it was time to sleep, I made my bed under thick wool blankets among the stacks of provisions. And there I lay, splendidly alone, and watched the stars turn slow overhead till sleep overtook me.

THE SUN HAD ALREADY SET by the time I found the rail camp halfway between Piedmont and Corinne. Twilight sagged heavy and gray across the land. I stood up in the wagon, bracing myself against its sway, against the occasional jolt as it ran over a hidden stone. I called out to the camp: "Halloo!"

I already knew I had made an impression when I stopped my team in the heart of the camp. I guess my high-pitched holler must have given me away, so the men had already gathered, watching the approach of my mule team with curiosity plain on their faces. I swept off my sombrero and let my long black hair tumble down behind me, confirming their suspicions. The men, bundled up in wool and leather, laughed and pounded each other's backs at the sight of a girl mulewhacker. For my part, I was glad to have the company of folks again. I do find mules especially agreeable, but they leave something wanting in the realm of conversation.

"Hell if you ain't a surprise," one of the men said to me. "We got girls in this camp, sure enough, but none of them knows how to drive."

"Bet they do have some useful skills, though," I said slyly.

At that, the men all roared with laughter.

"Come on and join us for a drink and a round of cards," somebody said.

"All right if I will," I replied. I think none of them could tell my true age, so it seemed natural enough to offer me a whiskey. I craved the liquor's warming effect, for winter had sunk deep into my bones. "I'll stay the night here," I told the men, "and in the morning when you've taken everything out of my wagon, I'll be on my way."

I had only just arrived, but already I dreaded my departure. The camp was aglow with fires and the welcoming light of candle lanterns; the night hummed softly with a murmur of friendly talk. From somewhere on the edge of the camp came the aimless, tuneless, wandering sound of a mouth-harp, and it made me feel lonesome, but in a comfortable way—in a way that said, *Stay on, stay on—stay and laugh and play games. Live your life well, while it's here and ripe for the living.*

A few men got up, making space for me at a great, blazing fire. The smoke smelled of burning chips and roasted meat. I stretched out my boots before me, warming at the coals. And in another moment, as if it was magicked there, a cup of whiskey appeared in my hand, heavy and inviting. I sipped it—smooth, sweet, woody. I felt the warmth of belonging, of life, spread and slide all down my throat into my belly.

"Takes right to whiskey," somebody laughed appreciatively. "What's your name, miss?"

"Jane," I said. I don't know why I gave them my middle name instead of my first, for I didn't feel as if I had any cause to hide from these men. It was just the name that came to me out there in the night, in the comfortable society of the railroad camp.

They raised their cups in salute. "To Jane, the girl mule-whacker! To Jane, who likes her whiskey!"

And then we all drank, every last one of us, till our cups ran dry.

IN THE MORNING my head ached from liquor, for it had been many long weeks since I last wetted my tongue. But the ache wasn't so fierce that I couldn't tend to my mules. They was all glad to see me, nuzzling my hands to search for the pieces of apple I saved just for them, blowing their warm breath across't my skin.

"Got to get back," I told them. "Got to get back even though we none of us want to go."

The mules nodded in agreement, so I led them to the wagon and began harnessing up.

Cards—faro and brag and three card monte. And laughter and warmth besides. Some people might call it whooping up, but it wasn't nothing more than friendly interaction, the reaching of a few lonesome souls toward one another in the damp cold of winter, in the isolation of a vast, quiet darkness. Cards and whiskey, and under it all, the gentle singing of a mouth-harp, away off somewheres in the night.

I loved that camp, as I loved the camps I had visited before. I loved the fellas; the girls who preferred a tent to a house, and wild, open sage to mud-packed roads or the orderly walls of a city. This was life; this was living. I never wanted it to end. Still, I couldn't help but recall (with a shiver of quiet dread) what Brad-dick had told me. The rails brought change along their slick black lines. Even as we made the West, we unmade it with fire and coal, with the thunder of wheels and the scream of a whistle. I pressed my face against a mule's neck and breathed in her clear, icy scent, and heard from afar the mauls begin to ring, the rhythm of spikes driven into the ground—of ties being laid, of sleepers scoring deep into the earth.

My life—what brief time I had to live—existed in a place that both was, and was not. The West had just been born, but already it was dying, and me along with it, thirteen years old, cold-scalded, with the fire of the whiskey still smoldering inside and the lonesome cry of a harp in the darkness, echoing faint in my heart.

WINTER GAVE WAY TO SPRING. Braddick's ranch bloomed with fresh green points of sage, with drifts of yellow-and-purple flowers piled up against the feet of hills out across the range. I'd done well with the mules and deliveries all winter long, but by the time the snow melted away, I could no longer deny the truth. Braddick's business was dying—and quickly, too. Winter should have been the slowest season, with fewer camps operating out along the railway lines. But come spring, Braddick found even less demand for his mule team. By then the rails was joining up, like trickles of water that flow into each other and grow into one rushing stream. Soon the trickles would become a flood. Progress was more than Braddick's business could withstand. I knew it was so, and so did my friend.

On a bright, clear morning, the kind that should have filled a girlish heart with hope (due to an abundance of flowers and birdsong) I came in from the corrals to find Braddick sitting slumped and dreary beside his fire.

"Come here, Martha-girl," he said to me.

I didn't like the tone of his voice. I knew hard words was coming—hard for him to say, but harder for me to hear. So I spoke up, kind of pre-emptive, as I shuffled reluctantly toward him. "Let me stay on the ranch. You know I work hard. You won't have to do no more work if you don't want to. You can take it easy now, with me here. Guess you've earned that much, after a long life of hard toil."

"Hush, Martha."

I hushed, for there was a sting of tears in my eyes and I didn't trust myself to talk without bawling.

"There won't be a ranch to work no more," Braddick said. "I got to sell off my mules. Ain't enough work to justify keeping 'em."

"No, you can't!"

"Got to sell off the land, too," he went on ruthlessly, staring into the low, weak flames. "Move back to town, I guess, and board somewheres."

I shook my head, mute with pain. My heart felt crushed and severed—aching not only for the animals, who I'd come to love so dear, but for Braddick, too, who must lose the only way of life he had known. *Let me never grow so old that I see the world move on without me,* I silently prayed. But even as I prayed it, I thought I could hear God up beyond the clouds, snickering.

Braddick looked up at me then, solemn and sad. "I can't pay you for the work you done. I wish I could, for you sure worked hard and loyal. But I got no money to spare."

"I don't want money," I told him. "You gave me kindness. I guess that's payment enough."

"One thing I can give you," he said. "You take a mule of your own—any mule you like. And a good saddle and bridle from the barn. I guess that'll be enough to see you on your way safely to… wherever it is you'll go next."

Wherever it was I'd go next. I tried not to imagine it—another place like the Altons', with another Emma to scorn me and beat me. Another kettle of laundry, another stick to sting my burned palm. I'd far rather chap my hands on a team's reins than in a soup of hot lye and stinking underthings.

"Go on out," Braddick said, with his head turned so he didn't have to look at me. "Find you a good mule."

"It'll be a hard choice. I love them all."

There was a pause. It hung heavy between us, waiting for one or the other to break the silence. Then I ran to him and threw my arms around him, and kissed him on his wrinkled old cheek.

"Go on now," Braddick said. "Better if you get it done fast. It hurts somewhat less that way."

I SPENT hours considering the herd before I finally chose my mule. She was one I called Rainbow, for her coat was spotted with great, round patches of black and brown and a grayish color like the feathers of a dove, all on a background of snowy white that reminded me of that first delivery, my first drive out in the world as a lone and grown-up thing. She was flashy and memorable, and I thought a memorable mule might convey some advantage as I struck out into the world again, searching for a place to belong. But Rainbow was sensible, too, and easy to ride.

Next morning, I cried as I clung to Braddick's shoulders. I knew my face must be scrunched up all ugly, but I couldn't smooth my sorrow away. He laid his hand on my head, briefly, just as Reverend Wilkes had done to bless me—but I felt no peace with Braddick's blessing, only the hollowness of longing, a sharp pain of loss.

"Go on," he said to me, and gave me a leg up into Rainbow's saddle, though I hated to lean on him, hated the way he shook and quivered.

I looked down at Mr. Braddick from my saddle, but I couldn't think of anything to say. So after a minute I just clicked my tongue, and Rainbow and me, we headed off northward, toward Montana and the gold fields, toward the black crisscross net of the rail lines. And somewhere beyond, I desperately prayed, I would find a new way of life—one the trains could never destroy.

One that would go on forever, as unchanged, as unchangeable as the West was not.

———

I BRAIDED WHILE I RODE. I pulled long hairs from Rainbow's mane, and from her tail, too, when we stopped for water or to make camp at night. I got pretty clever at twisting and knotting those many-colored hairs into bracelets and hat bands, and whenever we passed through a town I would glide casually past a hitching post and yank a few hairs from horses' tails so I could have more colors to work with. Hour by hour, I rocked to the steady rhythm of Rainbow's gait, and braided till my fingers ached, and sang whatever songs I could think of to pass the time.

Here and there, on the edges of towns or in travelers' camps, I sold my horsehair bracelets for a penny or two apiece. Folks bought them for their daughters, for little girls always like fancy braids and pretty colors. With those few meager pennies, I managed to keep myself fed all the way to a road ranch north and east of Piedmont. I had some mind to continue on to Fort Bridger, and there find work as a mule driver again, though I knew the odds was slim that anybody in Fort Bridger would be impressed by a girl driver. But the road ranch promised a bite to eat and maybe a sip of whiskey, if I could make my pennies stretch that far. Better yet, it promised talk. Talk might guide a body to work —that much I knew—so I was plenty eager to see what rumor had in store.

Don't know if you've ever seen a road ranch in your time, but let me tell you what they was like back then. Most often, they consisted of boarding rooms up above, with a big, open space for drinking and gambling and general milling-about on the ground floor. They always featured a kitchen, though mostly the grub was pretty dismal. Now and then, you'd find a road ranch with a real cook at the helm—somebody who actually knew what to do with a potato and an onion, who could turn most any cast-off butcher's bone into a good, rich soup. Those was the places that always filled up, packed to the walls—and such places had the liveliest talk, too, and the best faro games for miles around. Nothing draws folks in like a good, hearty supper.

Of course, food and cards wasn't all a road ranch offered. For a fella who'd been out driving cattle for a week or two straight—or a boy from the rail camps who'd seen nothing but his maul and the ties since his last payday—road ranches was havens of the most precious commodity known to mankind: girls. I dare say those girls made for more appealing armfuls than the type you found out among the rail camps, too, for ranch girls found it easier to stay clean and perfumed and dressed in the finest of clothing. Many a road ranch boasted of ladies who could sing almost as good as the great stars of the stage Back East (though I confess, I never did hear a true-blue stage star sing, so I can't say one way or t'other.) But if you wanted an eyeful of ruffles and lace and shiny, curled locks—and a handful of something else—there was no place better to find it than in a frontier road ranch.

I don't recall the name of the place where I stopped that day, nor just exactly where it was. I remember the sky was blue and cloudless. The air smelled sweetly of new-blooming flowers, but despite the pleasant weather, Rainbow had started to sweat from the warmth and toil. I determined that a few hours' stay would do both of us some good. I tied my mule in the stippled shade of a cottonwood and went inside, with my much-too-thin and light-weight purse swinging from the belt of my trousers.

That road ranch, like most others I had seen, was heavily populated by men smelling of the outdoors: dust and distant rain, cattle dung on their boots. The place fairly shook with the sound of all those voices, for they all talked at once in little groups of three and four, gathered around tables with cards spread before them or huddled together at a long oak bar-counter spanning the back of the room. I edged into the crowd a little skittish-like, but no one remarked on my presence. Evidently, girls wearing britches and carrying great big sombreros in their hands was a commonplace sight along this particular road.

At the bar, I inquired after the price of a bowl of stew. I could smell it away back in the stone kitchen, which hung off the end of the road ranch like a bum leg. It didn't smell especially rich or remarkable, but my stomach rumbled loud, all the same.

"Fifteen cents," the bartender said.

I counted out my pennies and found that I had fifteen exactly. The knowledge that I would have nothing left over for whiskey—and nothing left to see me through the next day—curdled my stomach. But my gut wasn't curdled enough to stamp out the hunger. I handed the coins over.

As I stood waiting for my stew to materialize, I wished bitterly for a snare, like the kind I traded for back on the wagon trail—though truth was, I didn't know how to use a snare anyhow. Would have been better by far to have Cilus or Lije with me, to catch rabbits or prairie dogs or even the little ground squirrels that didn't give more than a mouthful of meat at best. But a mouthful was better than nothing, and out on the trails and the long, lonesome roads, nothing could mean the death of you.

To distract myself from my plight, I listened in on the conversation between two fellas set beside me.

"I tell you, Buck," one said to the other, "Robert E. Lee surrendered. The war is all over now."

"That war ain't never gonna end," the other man grumbled.

"But it did, so you owe me a dollar."

"Fuck your dollar! I'll believe it when I see it."

"What the Hell you gotta see to know it's true? General Lee paraded in chains across't the prairie?"

"For a start."

"The papers'll carry it soon enough. Maybe even tomorrow."

I turned to the men. "The war's over, you say?" I had never been much bothered by the war—far as I was concerned, it was something that happened in a place called Back East, so far away and so far removed from my own toils and troubles, it may as well have been the Queen's Palace in England or darkest Africa or Timbuk-fucking-tu. All I wanted was a way to slide myself into the talk. Conversation was what I needed just then.

The two men blinked at me, as if trying to figure out what exactly I was supposed to be—girl or boy, or a strange and mystifying spirit from a fairy story. Then one of them laughed. "Look at you!" he said, in an approving sort of way. "Under a disguise, girl? Like running away from a bad marriage?"

I smiled in what I hoped was a playful manner. "Somethin' like that."

"Well, yes Miss," the fellow said. "The war's good and over now. I heard it this morning at the newspaper office in Fort Bridger. They got a telegraph wire."

His friend waved a hand, as if to brush away some pernicious stinging fly. "Ain't no damn telegraph wire at Fort Bridger."

"There is so. They put it in for the railroad."

"Railroad don't need no telegraphs."

I listened to the two men argue away till my stew arrived. Then I spooned it into my mouth faster than it could cool, gulping it down like a starved dog ripping scraps from a bone. The men ignored me the whole time; they prattled on like housewives.

"Custer was there to witness the surrender," the first man said —the one from Fort Bridger.

"Shit," said the other, dry and ironic. "Custer appears just about everywhere, it seems. Like some goddamn ghost haunting every idiotic rumor I hear."

"They plan to send him out here to take care of the Sioux," Fort Bridger said.

At this, his friend guffawed. "That so? Custer ain't got nothing better to do?"

"Not now the war's ended."

"Suppose he'll come like Jesus Christ, with a sword for a tongue and 'Fuck The Sioux' written all down his thigh."

"Didn't your ma ever teach you not to blaspheme?" Fort Bridger said stiffly.

His friend, the blasphemer—who I liked best of the two—jerked his thumb toward me as I scraped the last of the stew from my bowl and licked the spoon clean. "Maybe this little scrap here is running from Custer, that it? Maybe her daddy wanted her to marry Old Ringlets but she didn't like the curl of his mustache."

I raised my brows, waiting to hear what Fort Bridger would say next. Some folks counted it as grave a sin to take Custer's name in vain as the Lord's.

Bridger gave a tired old sigh and looked away, as if Blasphemy's talk was more than any mortal soul could bear. "Oh, come on now," he muttered.

Blasphemy gave me a grin and a wink that said he had scored a victory. His personable ways made me sense that maybe the time was right. I reached into the pocket of my trousers and pulled out one of my horsehair bracelets.

"Want to buy this, Mister?"

He took it in his hand and eyed it carefully, but then passed it back with a shake of his head. "What would I do with a little string of hair? I look like some damn Indian to you?"

"Ain't you got a daughter somewhere who likes to play dress-up?"

Blasphemy laughed, coarse as gravel. "Fuck no, or at least I hope not. God preserve me from being a pappy. Fate worse than death!"

"I'm selling these to get by," I said. "Trying to make my way to Fort Bridger. How far is it? Have I got much longer to ride?" I looked hopefully over at Bridger himself. "You was there this morning, right? To hear them read the telegram?"

Blasphemy rolled his eyes. "He's a liar, Miss. Don't put any stock in what he says."

"You can get to Fort Bridger by nightfall, if you ride hard," Bridger said. "What you trying to do there, anyway?"

"Yeah," Blasphemy said under his breath. "If you go East you'll run right into Custer."

"Only looking for work," I said. "I can do laundry real good, and keep rooms in a boarding house, too."

"Better go on to Fort Laramie," Bridger said. "It's booming, so I hear. Good prospects for anybody who wants steady work. The Overland Stage Line just ran a route through Fort Laramie; it's as lively a place as you could hope to find."

"How far is Fort Laramie?"

"More than a day's ride," Blasphemy said, then whistled softly through his teeth. "That's for damn sure."

Bridger laid it out for me: the weeks of riding, the passes and rivers I must cross, the long empty stretches of nothingness out there in the high sage country.

"Shit," I said when he was finished.

Those two fellas grinned at each other, charmed as some men were by my coarse tongue. But I couldn't use their approval to my advantage. My mood was too dark just then. The last of my money was gone, and the Lord alone knew what prospects I could find within a day's ride. Even Fort Bridger might not be enough to sustain me.

Just then the jangling, glad music of the piano rattled out across the long hall. The men of the road ranch set up a unison whoop as, in a flurry of bright colors and a flash of gay smiles, the dancing girls came bouncing into the room. Even Bridger and Blasphemy forgot their momentary enmity; they clapped and whistled and slugged each other's shoulders as the girls took up their cue and began to dance. The ladies wove through the room, kicking their legs up over the faro tables and leaning low to reveal the tops of their plump bosoms.

The two men beside me fished coins and notes from their pockets, and watched the women with eager, speculative stares.

I watched the women, too—watched the ease with which they danced, their confidence as they tumbled down into a man's lap, then skittered away again with a flirty shake of their hips.

Laundry. Or keeping up boarding rooms. It was all just a cover; I knew that, even in my own mind, even as I tried to tell myself that I only wanted honest and respectable work. But what honest, respectable occupation could stand up to the onslaught of the rail lines?

None. That's what I knew right then. There was one sure way for a girl to make her living. And by God I would do it, or starve in the trying.

IT TOOK me almost two weeks to reach Fort Laramie. Rainbow was lucky on the trek, for the spring grass was lush and sweet, and she had her fill to eat every time I stopped to graze her. The journey went a damn sight harder on me. In Fort Bridger, I sold what assets I had for mean little bargains—for I had competition, as any girl does in an established town. I was obliged to take whatever pay I could get, and if I felt cheated, I quickly learned to swallow my complaints. But despite the tight-fisted cheats who inhabited that town, I rustled up enough hard tack and salt pork for one meal a day. Then I set out east, toward Fort Laramie, riding as hard as I dared push my mule—or myself, for my body ached and protested after days of busy work.

Every hour I spent on that trail was marked by hunger. Lord, what a trial it was to restrict myself to just one biscuit and a couple mouthfuls of that chewy, salty pork each morning when I rolled from my hard, cold bed. Way out there, alone in the open prairie, the wind would sometimes sound like a chorus of voices, all of them singing together: *Eat it all up, Martha. Fill up your belly for once in your life. If you're to die out here alone, at least die full and satisfied.*

In those desperate moments, I kept my eyes fixed to Rainbow's bobbing head, the sway of her long patchwork ears, and I answered that voice back, my thoughts treading along to the rhythm of my she-mule's walk. *No, no, never. No, no, never. Laramie is waiting for me. Laramie and money and dreams come true. Never, never, never.*

For all my desperation, the journey wasn't entirely one of dread. Moments of great beauty drew close and walked beside me for a spell, then departed as quiet as they came, leaving memory that has stayed with me all these many years. I remember a storm sweeping down from a distant line of mountains, the coal-gray underbelly of clouds breaking and spreading, bleeding a dense blue haze of rain, and a bright flick of lightning, white against dark. I listened for the thunder, but it never came. I remember how I looked up from my saddle horn and found a herd of pronghorns walking with me, peaceable, unafraid, their slim, tawny shapes emerging from the long grass and vanishing again, their black antlers stark against a hot, pale world, like the words of a letter I couldn't read. The pronghorns traveled with me for more than an hour, and by time they finally left, I was half convinced I had dreamed them up—that I had fallen into the grip of a starvation dream. Once, at the top of a gentle rise—it couldn't hardly be called a hill—I spotted three Indian women foraging near a stand of juniper trees. When they saw me, they put their children up onto their ponies' backs and ran, vanishing behind the shoulder of their slope. At night I heard wolves howling out across the prairie, and I howled along in chorus. I thought I might bring the wolves down to kill me, but in that moment, I didn't care. I was raw and bony like a wolf myself, and the song made me feel less lonesome.

Despite my privations, I did have one strange and gracious bit of luck on that long ride. Somewhere east of a mountain pass, which took me two days to cross, I smelled wood smoke on the air, too thick and acrid to be the smoke of a camp's cook fire. At first, I thought I imagined the smell. But after a mile or two, I could see a smudge of brown-gray haze hanging trapped among the cottonwoods alongside a shadowy crick. I rode toward that haze, heedless of Indians—and maybe thinking, in my stupor of hunger and lonesomeness, that if it was Indians I would throw myself on their mercy and beg them to take me in as one of their own.

As soon as I reached the source of the smoke, I realized what a fool I'd been—and realized, too, that I was far luckier than any fool deserved to be. It *was* Indians—or it had been, at least. In a recent clearing below the cottonwoods there stood the sad remains of a cabin, built all of wood with its walls charred black and its roof fallen in, and threads of smoke still rising from inside. I sat silent on my mule, staring at the wreckage. Rainbow seemed to sense the danger, too; she never twitched a muscle, but raised her head and strained her ears toward the burned house, tense and waiting. Suddenly I felt more alert than I had for days. I wanted to turn Rainbow and ride away, but I was too frightened to move, to make the slightest sound. After a long spell of fear, I realized the clearing lay dead still, except for a buzzing of flies somewhere off in the brush. I knew what those flies must be buzzing over. I didn't want to see. But I reasoned the clearing was empty now, save for me and my mule and the thing upon which all those flies was feasting. If any Sioux had remained, I would have already found myself stuck full of arrows. So I dismounted with the slowness and care that always come over a person in the presence of death. Then I crept across the trampled yard toward the cabin.

The smell of fire was sharp—choking. It raised in me the same instinctive fear and awe that it brings to the hearts of all creatures. The house was dead-black on the inside, and just about hot as the fires of Hell. A few pale squares of light showed in the walls where window shutters had once hung. The shutters was gone now, torn away or burned. My mouth was dry, bitter with the taste of ash.

My heart pounded loud in my ears. But my eyes adjusted to the dimness.

There wasn't much left inside the cabin. The Indians took it all —or else there hadn't been much to begin with. A small table and two chairs was blackened and overturned; white shards of plates and bowls lay smashed upon the hard-packed earthen floor. The roof had fallen in on one side, obscuring everything but the foot of a bed-stead, which held the smoldering timbers of the roof up in a grotesque peak, as if the house itself was still trying, of its own conscious will, to remain standing.

Near the foot of the ruined bed, I spied a small trunk and approached cautiously, as if it might conceal a nest of vipers. The trunk's lid was charred, still hot to the touch; I wrapped my kerchief around one hand to pry it loose without burning my fingers.

Inside, folded atop a couple of patchwork blankets, I found a lady's dress—finely made from a calico of tiny white flowers against a background of mulberry red. Thin strips of lace decorated the ends of the sleeves and the collar, too. Right beside the dress, perched atop the blankets, was a little felt hat in a shade of purply-red that almost matched the calico. A pearl hat pin was stabbed through the felt, right beside a curved feather of snowy white.

"Christ in Hell," I swore, staring down at the unexpected treasure. Then I felt miserably sorry for letting out such an awful cuss when people in the vicinity was freshly dead. If their spirits still hung around the place, I didn't want them latching onto me and haunting me to madness—particularly since I intended to steal from those very same spirits.

So, "Pardon me," I called out the nearest window, in the general direction of the flies, and then, "Rest in peace, poor souls." Then, before I could shiver myself out of doing it, I scooped the dress and hat up in my arms and ran from the burned-out house.

The dress fit in the top of my saddle bag, though I had to push it down hard and wrinkle it up something awful to get it inside. The hat I tied to my saddle horn, which was the only place I could think to put it where its plume wouldn't be crushed. I looked down at that bouncing, waving feather most of the way to Fort Laramie. Countless times I told that hat, *All my hopes depend on you now. Don't let me down, or I'll throw you in the river, and let the ghosts drown trying to get to you back.*

A cold wind seemed to follow me all the way from the cabin to my destination, and I sang while I rode, and talked out loud to Rainbow to distract myself from the eerie chill. Whenever I fell quiet, I could all but feel icy fingers reaching for me, seeking to tear me out of my saddle. I knew it was only my imagination, but still I couldn't rid myself of the shivers.

When at last I saw Fort Laramie on the horizon—a flat, red town nestled around the feet of low, coppery hills—my voice was hoarse and dry. But the feeling of ghosts left me all at once, as if the sight of a town was enough to drive vengeful spirits clean away. My own spirit felt considerably lightened. I rode down to a crick bed and let Rainbow suck noisily at the red water while I (screened by a bunch of scraggly willows) changed into the mulberry dress.

It was too tight in the shoulders, so I could hardly lift my arms without fear of tearing the calico, and it was a few inches shorter than it should have been. But it fit me good around the waist and bust, and looking down at my chest, I liked the look of the intricate pintucks that fanned across its bib. The lace tickled my neck. I had never worn a fancy lady's hat before and didn't quite know how to do it, but after some experimentation, I wrestled my hair up into a bird's-nest of a bun and tied it with a piece of twine from my saddle bag, and managed to stab the pearl hat pin through the felt and into my hair without spiking the thing through my skull. I counted that a major accomplishment, considering I had neither skill nor mirror.

I washed every bit of skin that showed with pure, clean crick water, hoping I didn't look like I'd just spent two weeks riding through the wilderness and howling with wolves. Then, when I was ready as I ever could be, I swung up onto Rainbow's back and arranged myself side-saddle so my knees wouldn't show, and headed straight for the town.

Almost as soon as I came out of the willow grove, I saw a man riding my way, driving a few cattle before him. He noted my dress and my ladylike posture on my mule, and lifted his hat in greeting, though he was still some way off. I waited for him to catch up. His cattle passed me, plodding toward town, heads down as if they knew what was in store for them.

"Good day to you, sir," I said in a way I thought might sound kind of formal and ladylike.

"Mam," he said.

I blushed. It was the first time anybody had ever called me mam, and I didn't quite know how to take it. I said, "I come over from Fort Bridger to look for work. Do you know anyone who's hiring girls?"

"Hiring girls," he said. "To do what, exactly?"

For answer, I tossed my head so the white plume danced. "This and that."

"In that case, you want Madam Robair. Can't say what she's like to work for, seeing as how I'm not a girl myself. But I've sampled her wares many times, and she has the best girls and the nicest cat-house in all of Fort Laramie. She's a real Frenchie, and I don't know but the French know how to sell it better than anybody else in the world."

Certainly, plenty of tents and rough shacks stood in the vicinity of Fort Laramie, but the man I'd met at the road ranch hadn't lied. The Overland Stage Line seemed a conduit for wealth and activity as much as it was a means of delivering goods. Quite a few proper buildings lined the town's main street, though all of them was newly built, as evidenced by the bright, unfaded paint and the smell of sawdust hanging on the air. More buildings remained under construction, skeletons of beam and brick rising along the town's central route. Real houses sprouted along the side streets, too, replacing shabby lean-tos and canvas tents, their growth accompanied by the relentless ring of hammers against wood. Soon enough I located Madam Robair's place, following the tell-tale sign of the clattering piano and the suggestive moan of the hurdy-gurdy.

I walked right in like I owned the place, and though none of the gentlemen who lounged about the parlor took much notice of me (their attention being otherwise engaged), there wasn't one pair of feminine eyes that failed to slit in my direction. No doubt the girls in Laramie all knew each other by sight, so I was marked out at once for an interloper. Laramie may be booming, as the fellows back at the road ranch promised—but in a boom, it was all the more crucial to grab up as much money as a body could make while the grabbing was good. Competition was never welcome anywhere. How much faster that truth held when purses was fat with money and bank notes fell from men's hands like rain.

Sensing the girls' hostility, I determined to stand my ground and carve out a sizeable chunk of Fort Laramie for myself. I braced my fists on my hips and said aloud, demanding of nobody in particular, "Where's Madam Robair? I come a real long way to speak with her, and I won't leave till I do."

The closest girl, whose hair was a forceful, unconvincing shade of red, tossed me a glare over her exposed shoulder, even as her friend of the hour covered that same shoulder in kisses. "You ain't got no business here. Better for you if you shove off now."

"I won't shove nowheres," I said. "Point me in the direction of Madam Robair and I'll thank you kindly, though."

"Oh joy," she said. A few of the other girls laughed.

The red one stood up, leading her fella by the hand. She sauntered toward a carved staircase with fancy gilding all down its newel-post and rail. One of the girls still left in the parlor said, "Just tell her, Nancy. She's too doggy to work here, anyhow. It won't make any difference; Madam'll send her packing once she gets a look at her mug."

Red Nancy laughed sort of cruelly and said, "Madam's in the back room, down that hallway there. Good luck, Missy. You're going to need it."

———

THE HALL WAS long and dark, for it was lined in fine wood paneling, as polished and slick as any that might be found in a queen's palace. At the end of the hall there stood a door, just as dark and shiny as the paneling, carved in pierce-work scrolls with bits of red glass winking in all its intricate, patterned holes. I went as slow down that hall as I'd gone toward the burned-out cabin under the cottonwoods. The feeling I got from that door, with its glaring red glass, was almost the same—dark and forbidding, a distinct sensation that I didn't belong, that I wasn't wanted.

But I had nowhere else to turn, so I rapped on the door just below the pane of scarlet glass. A second later a woman's voice called, "We!"

I didn't know what she meant by it, so I stood there like a stunned heifer till she said (impatiently this time), "Who is it! Come in!" Her accent was thick and exotic. I thought, *That's how the Queen of England must sound*, even though I reckoned the Queen of England most certainly was not French.

Accordingly, I opened the door. Then, I'm sorry to report, I stood on the threshold, staring, gape-mouthed, at the woman who sat behind the desk. She was as tiny as they come, like a little sparrow bird, with hair like a sparrow's feathers, too—a color somewhere between brown and gray and golden, impossible to name but pretty in a naturely way. The hair was fixed simply, in a great round poof atop her head, held in place by a tortoiseshell comb. She wore a dress of a modest, blue-gray color, cut in a style that could never be called showy. Her collar came up high, almost to her chin, and her sleeves was long. The buttons was covered in plain cloth, not made of silver or pearls. But though I was no great judge of finery, still I could tell at a glance that the woman was richly attired. Her dress may have been plain in color, but the fabric held a beguiling sheen, so lovely and inviting and smooth, my hands itched to feel the sleeves. The woman's face wasn't painted, either, like the girls in the front parlor—and that was well, for she must have been forty years old at least. But her skin was clear, and her mouth was naturally pink, and her bright blue eyes needed no blacking of the lashes to shine with stern command. She was as perfectly fine a woman as I had ever seen.

"Who are you?" she asked, with that strange, lilting slant to her words.

"My name is Jane," I said, again finding no inclination to supply my real name, for no reason I could think of. Maybe by that time, lying about my identity had become a matter of simple habit. "Jane Burch, out of Fort Bridger. I heard tell that Laramie is the best place in all of Wyoming Territory for a girl to find some work. I also heard tell that Madam Robair is the very best to work for. Are you the madam herself?"

"Indeed I am herself," she said, lifting one sparrow-colored brow, looking me over slowly. Her lips tensed and pressed smaller, and I knew straight away that she wasn't too impressed with what she saw. But I was determined to make the madam take me in.

"I have lots of experience with the work," I said—and that was true, though I doubted whether Madam Robair would have counted trail-trading, nor bartering for whiskey in a railroad camp, as legitimate experience.

"Do you?" she asked coolly. "How old are you, girl?"

"Seventeen."

In truth I was just about fourteen—maybe a week or two shy of that age—but I knew my bigness worked in my favor, at least where fibbing about age was concerned. I turned my head a little, inciting my fancy feather plume to shake. I hoped it made me look sophisticated and experienced.

But it only made Madam Robair sniff in a thoroughly unimpressed way. "You look a proper mess," she said.

I blushed. Maybe after all I hadn't done as good a job with my hair and hat as I had formerly thought. Primping wasn't an easy feat, without a mirror to check. I said, by way of excusing myself, "I had to ride an awful long time to get here, and I had nowhere to freshen up. But I can clean up real good, if I'm given half a chance."

Now both of her brows raised and arched in a way that said, *I doubt that very much.*

"I haven't any use for you," the madam said shortly, turning her attention back to the great book that lay open before her. She picked up a black feather pen and made a few marks in a column. She didn't so much as look at me again; it was a plain dismissal.

I couldn't accept a dismissal. I had ridden too far for this opportunity, risked too much out there in the hills and the cold mountain passes.

"I don't want to beg," I said, more sharply than I'd intended, "but I will if you make me. I won't be turned away, mam. Not at all. It's best if you find a place for me—any place, even doing laundry for your girls—"

"I have all the washer-women I need."

"But you ain't got a girl who can do card tricks, I bet."

She looked up from her book with her black feather pen quivering in her hand. This time her pink lips trembled, as if she was thinking seriously about laughing. "Card tricks? What need have I for that? It's not *card* tricks you must turn here, Jane Burch."

"I know," I said, faltering. "I know what kind of tricks. And I can do 'em better than any other girl."

"Nonsense. I've the finest girls in the West under this roof, and a collection of other girls elsewhere—in my pool hall, at my road ranch. Every one of them is far more skilled than you."

"How do you know that if you ain't willing to give me a try?"

"Your speech is appalling, for one thing." (Only she pronounced it as, *sing*.) "My girls are refined, a breath of fresh air for hard-working clients. Any common clod of mud may be found out there on the prairie. Companions of refinement are more difficult to come by."

"It don't take refinement to hike your skirt up to your waist, and that's all anybody here's after."

She narrowed her eyes at me. For a minute I thought she might shout me out of the room, or call in some big old bully to haul me away. I said quickly, "Sorry, mam—I meant to say, it *doesn't* take refinement."

A silence fell between us, and for a few shaky heartbeats I could read no expression whatsoever in Madam Robair's face. Then her sharp blue eyes widened; she burst out with a bright, chiming laugh.

As soon as her laughter died, my stomach rumbled so loud it made the madam blink. A cramp of hunger pinched me, and against my will I clamped a hand to my stomach, trying to press the pain away.

The amusement faded from the madam's face. Something rather close to pity replaced it. "Hungry?" she asked softly.

"Very much so, mam. But I ain't about to ask for charity. I'll work for my keep, and work hard—harder than any of your other girls do. I'll make you more money than you ever thought possible."

She sighed, looked at my face; her glance flitted about, taking in my sallow skin, my flat nose, my thin lips and my small, dark eyes.

"I think you will not bring much money, Jane Burch, though I am sorry to say it, for you have a certain spark that I do like very much—very much indeed. I fear you will find it a hard road to tread here in Fort Laramie. The prettiest girls have come from many hundreds of miles to try their luck here."

I sensed I was gaining some ground with her. I straightened up my spine, doing my best to look plucky. "My ma used to say, 'pretty is as pretty does.'" That wasn't true at all; I had never heard my dead mother say anything of the sort. But I heard the expression somewhere else and liked it. I hoped it was true—hoped I could be accounted pretty someday, if I only dedicated myself to kindly behavior and good works.

Madam Robair shrugged. "I do not agree with your mare, but I am a Christian woman, no matter what you might hear from my detractors. I cannot turn away a young woman in need."

I didn't know what any mare had to do with it; I hadn't spoke a word about no horse, and anyway, I rode a mule. But I did understand that Madam Robair was willing to give me a chance. I scurried forward and reached over her great carved-wooden desk to grab her delicate little hand. I shook it, vigorous in my thanks. The madam squeaked in surprise at the strength of my grip—a tiny, fragile sound.

"Oh, thank you, Madam! Thank you. I won't allow you to regret this. Where shall I go to get ready? When do you want me to start?"

"Not here," she said, extracting herself from my grip. "This house is too fine for you, I fear. But I shall tell you where to find my pool hall, out on the edge of town, and there you'll find a room of your own and food enough to fill your belly."

I didn't permit myself any disappointment. A pool hall was just as good as a fancy visiting-house. And it was a damn sight better than the raggedy tents the girls in the rail camps was obliged to use. "I'll go there straight away," I said. "Straight away."

"God have mercy. Take this hand mirror and fix your hair first. You look like an unmade bed."

FEW THERE WERE IN DEATH NOTCH WHO HAD NOT HEARD OF THE NOTORIOUS GIRL

AT MADAM ROBAIR'S POOL HALL, I FED ON PORRIDGE AND BACON and as much strong cider as I liked to drink till the hunger no longer haunted me and the hollows in my cheeks leveled out. Then, when I was healthy enough to pinch a convincing blush into my cheeks, I ventured out of the narrow crib that was my own private room, and debuted myself to the rough, raggy world of the pool hall.

Working Madam Robair's pool hall was no simple task—not at first. Many was the hour when, below the grinning bravado I showed to all the fellas in the place, I secretly nursed despair. I had convinced myself that Madam was right, that I never would find my feet among the Laramie girls, and I was doomed to fail no matter how hard I tried—no matter how desperately I needed to succeed. My struggle was simple, you see: I wasn't as pretty as the other girls. In fact, I wasn't pretty a-tall, no matter what pains I took with my appearance. I tried to give myself a little more appeal by practicing the latest ways to fix my hair, and painting my lips and my eyes in shades I hoped might read as beguiling. But once, while I worked earnestly before a round, crackled wall-mirror, twisting my unruly locks this way and that and biting my lower lip to make it flush brighter, I overheard two of the pool girls giggling, and one whispered to the other, "Now that's what I call polishing a turd."

Compared to my early days following the wagon train, the pool hall was altogether a different scene. On the trail, girls was scarce enough that I looked properly tempting. But now I thumped and rattled around the place like a dull stone kicked through a garden of lilies. Every other girl was bright and delicate, pretty as you please in a fine, well-made dress—while I offered precious little appeal in the cast-off calicoes Madam Robair found for me. Big and blocky, flat-faced, with a voice harsh and loud as a crow's. The men simply didn't want to pick me, and who could expect otherwise? They had a selection of willing beauties at their fingertips. I was poor fare if you took me on looks alone. Those first few days in the pool hall was shadowed by despair, for it seemed my career was well and truly sunk before it had even begun.

One especially difficult day—when a man had actually brayed in my face like a donkey while his friends sat around the table laughing—I found myself on the verge of giving up. I was ready to admit defeat and ride out of Laramie forever. Maybe, I thought, I'd go back to that burned-out house by the river and wait for the Indians to return and skewer me with their arrows and chop off the top of my head for a scalp. I skulked off to my crib and hid there, behind my closed door, fighting back tears and kicking the legs of my bed-stead till my toes stubbed and ached inside my boots.

But then I recalled the way Madam Robair had laughed upon our first meeting. I had made her laugh, pulled the humor right out of her guts against her steely will. I had made her like me, even when she'd been dead set against taking me on. She had seen a spark in me—and if the madam could see it, then I reasoned I could make men see it, too. After all, pretty, willing girls was a penny a dozen in Laramie. I had no hope of ever being pretty, but

I could be something far better: unique. And in that moment, I resolved to make myself the uniquest girl in all of Wyoming Territory.

I stormed down the stairs and swung into the pool hall, bold as if I was the madam myself, and all the girls in the place owed their success to me. Upheaded, working my considerable height for all it was worth, I strutted between the pool tables where the men sat intent on their games and their conversations. There wasn't no point in trying to make my hips sway. The men had learned the sound of my mannish stride; they would never glance up from their cards merely because I had passed by their tables. It would take more than prancing about to catch their attention now.

I stopped beside the pool tables.

"By shit!" I hollered at the top of my voice. "John Farley, that was the worst shot I ever seen, and I seen a half-dead, one-armed, all-the-way blind man shoot at a bale of hay 'cause he thought it was a deer."

I yelled so loud, everybody in the place stopped what they was doing and looked at me—even the girls clear across the room, working up sweet to the men at the bar.

John Farley, a regular at the hall, straightened from his table with a stare that lingered somewhere between befuddlement and rage. I laughed right in his face and turned on my heel, flouncing the skirt of my too-short mulberry dress in such an exaggerated way that nobody present could take it for anything other than a crass imitation of the flirts the prettier girls always made.

Some man or other called after me, "John's pretty bad at pool, but no way he's worse than that!"

"The hell he ain't," I hollered back. "The one-armed man actually hit that bale of hay, and it fell over dead. Made a terrible venison roast, though. Tasted like shit, and you don't want to know how I know it!"

Laughter crashed all around me like cymbals in a grand parade. I climbed up onto the biggest table, even though such acrobatics had been expressly forbidden by the madam, and strutted all down its length.

Another regular, Tom Porter, had no great liking for me. I still believe to this day that he had put the donkey-brayer up to that particular bit of mischief. Tom was the kind of sour old prick who liked to make girls feel bad about themselves. He did it to everyone, even some of the prettiest. Rumor among the girls was that he could only get hard if a girl was crying, or at least trembling and scared. Well, Tom wasn't the sort of man who could tolerate a woman preening and holding herself up, high above the crowd as I was just then. He called out to me, "Ain't no mystery to me why you know what shit tastes like. Bet it's about all you can afford to eat, with how much money you must earn."

I was ready for him. In fact, I'd been counting on Tom Porter opening his spiteful mouth. "Now, Tommy," I said. "You don't want me to tell our little secret, do you?"

"The fuck you talking about, girl?"

I leaned down, cupping a hand around my mouth, as if I was whispering to the nearest boys. But I talked loud enough for the whole hall to hear. "I'm Tom's favorite. He can't get enough of me. And boys, the things he likes to do! The Devil himself wouldn't believe it."

"That's a damn lie," Tom roared. "I got better things to waste my money on than some plug-ugly bitch like you."

"Oh, is it a lie? Then how's-a-come I know you got a red birthmark, right—here?" And I lifted my skirts up all the way, and showed the whole room that I hadn't a thing on underneath.

They hooted and hollered and stamped their feet over the laugh, but best of all in my reckoning was the look of helpless fury on Tom Porter's face. For it was true that he had a birthmark, right beside his little pecker. I'd never seen it myself, but plenty of the other girls had. Even an unpopular resident like myself still got an earful of gossip now and then.

I dropped my skirts and turned around, and shook my bottom

at Tom Porter. He shouted a few cusses in my direction, but by the time I faced him again, he was marching out the door. For a moment I thought Madam Robair would be sore with me for chasing off a loyal customer. But raucous laughter filled the hall, and I reasoned I'd done more good than harm.

"What's your name?" a fellow called out from the crowd. He was a newcomer, I guessed, for everybody else knew me by sight. I was a hard one to miss.

"Jane," I shouted back. "The cussin'est, filthiest, most daring dame in all the West! And the funnest one, too! Go ask old Tom Porter if you don't believe me!"

"Tom runned off like his ass was scorched," somebody hollered. "Like a regular calamity was 'bout to overtake him!"

"I *will* overtake him, and make him drop every last bit of silver he's got into my purse. I'm the calamity your ma warned you about, boys!"

"Calamity Jane!" somebody cried. They all took up the cry, chanting my name in unison.

I picked a big, strong fellow out of the crowd and winked at him. He seemed to know what I was thinking. I jumped off that pool table and he caught me in his arms, like I wasn't nothing more than a feather, or a dolly made of rags.

"All right," I said to him, laughing and breathless while the shouts still rang all around me. "You can put me down now."

"Not a chance," said he. "I'm taking you up to your room. And Miss Calamity Jane, I got a pocket full of silver just for you, if you think you'll like me better than old Tom Porter."

YOU'VE HEARD many tales of how I got my name, I suppose. 'Course you have, Short Pants, or else you wouldn't be here talking to me right now—or listening to me talk, as it were. I've heard all the legends, too. Let me see if I can still reel them off, list every one from my long, long memory.

I had gone up into the Black Hills with a contingent of Indian hunters, under one Captain Egan (I never knew a man by that name). The Sioux caught us out bad and dropped six of our men from their saddles, shot seven more, Captain Egan included. When I turned in my saddle to look back at our fleeing troops, I saw the Captain reeling, ready to topple off his horse, where the hooves of our company would surely trample him to dust. I galloped back and pulled him from his saddle just as he slipped to the side. Then I raced back to the safety of our camp with the Captain bleeding in my arms. His life was saved by my quick action, and in his gratitude and awe he dubbed me Calamity Jane, Heroine of the Plains.

A less flattering tale goes like this: I was born under an unlucky star, so all manner of calamities followed me from the first day my poor ma laid me in my cradle. If I rented a team from a livery, I was bound to drive them straight into a collision, through no fault of my own—an oncoming team gone wild from deer flies, or spooked by a thunder storm way up on a mountain pass, charging toward me out of control, with no room to swerve and avoid the disaster. Or if I rented a tired old plug of a horse, it would suddenly find its spirit— sensing, perhaps, the spate of bad luck that hung over me like a cloak of wet wool—and dump me in the mud. If I got up on a fence rail—so the story goes—the durned thing would get up and buck. I think I like that story best of all. You know by now that I ain't never shrank from admitting my own faults, and Lord knows I got plenty. I do believe that humility (where my faults is concerned) allows me enough leeway to brag a little on my good points. I always been good with horses—and mules—even while thoroughly drunk. There is no truth to the claim that I racked up astounding fees from the liveries, but I do still get a chuckle from the mere thought of a fence rail working up the gumption to throw me off its back.

There are some who disparage me, claiming the nickname originated in my crib. Any man who was fool enough to lay with me—so this scurrilous falsehood goes—rose up from my bed with a calamity of the venereal type. Well, that may be somewhat true, for all I can say. Many a time I had to take a cure, but that's the nature of the work, and I maintain to this day that I wasn't any dirtier than any other whore. In fact, I was a damn sight cleaner than most. Why is it always the whores who's blamed for such misfortunes, anyway, when the men who scamper from one bed to another bear an equal share of guilt—if not more?

There's more tales, I'm sure of it—there must be. How long have folks been talking about Calamity Jane, and none of them bothering to ask me for the truth—none till you came along, Short Pants. At one point, I knew every tale about my name, and every other tale that concerned my legendary doings. I still know those stories, I suppose, but I've grown weary of recalling. None of them is true. And all sound nobler than the truth—well, except for the tale about the fellas who lay with me.

Every story but one, more thrilling than the truth. Still, I wouldn't trade the truth for a dozen fantasies. The day I drove off Tom Porter and won the hearts of every man in that pool hall was the first day I knew myself to be a real force in the world—strong and capable, confident when I needed to be—perhaps with more confidence than a girl with my looks should rightly claim. That day, I knew myself for exactly what I was: a force upon the land, a power as great as a whirlwind or a thunder storm, great as any calamity should be.

FROM THAT MOMENT ON, I never lacked for work. Oh, I won't claim I had as many admirers as the other girls. Those days was yet to come. But I found myself so steadily occupied that I knew I was secure. I had made my place in the world. I had a roof above my head and enough food to fill my belly; I was content as a girl can be.

Now, my contentment didn't last overlong. All too soon, the other girls came to see me as real competition. After the Tom Porter incident, I was tolerated better by the other ladies, and even viewed with affectionate pride (as a pet might be, or a favorite saint in a church-house.) They still thought me too homely to threaten their livelihoods, but what harm was there in my conjuring up a laugh now and then? I only ever siphoned off one or two randy boys with my antics, and left the rest for the pretty girls to sweet up on.

But the other girls didn't know I had made a promise to our madam. I have faults aplenty—God knows I do—but breaking my word once I've given it is no fault you can lay at my feet. I made a vow to turn a healthy profit for Madam Robair, and by God, I was determined to see my promise through.

In time, I learned to use my ugliness as a cover, like a hunter shooting down ducks from a blind. Because the other girls saw my blunt, coarse face and curveless body as no real threat, I was able to work my way in close to the men, moving among them easily, learning their names, their ways, what made them laugh—and what made them tick. If one of the dainty, fancy ladies moved in too close to another girl's favorite fella, she was liable to get her hair pulled or her face slapped—later, of course, when there was no boys around to see the fight. But nobody suspected old Calamity Jane of poaching in claimed territory. The mere thought was downright ridiculous. I played that advantage as careful as I ever played faro at old Mr. Braddick's fireside.

I might have gone on playing my secret hand for weeks longer, too, if Red Nancy hadn't come along to spoil it. One Saturday afternoon, she appeared in the pool hall—all furious swirling skirt and terse stamp of boots, face near as scarlet as her hair. Seemed Madam Robair had found some truck with Nancy and sent her from the visiting-house to the pool hall as a kind of punishment, a busting-down. The minute Nancy entered the place, her stare locked with mine. I could see my own startlement reflected in her features, in the jerk of her slender frame and the widening of her eyes. But we both shook off our surprise, for by that time I was a girl who had seen enough to know that nothing in this life is ever much of a shock. I nodded at her, kind of cool-like, in a detached way I hoped would do Madam Robair proud. Nancy pursed her lips and glared at me through her black-caked lashes.

From her first day among the pool-hall set, it was clear to all of us that Nancy bubbled over with spite. If she was to spend her days in a mere pool hall, she was bound and determined to become the boss of the place, a sort of Madam in miniature. She harried the other girls with commands, frightening them with cold, hateful stares. Nancy even began doling out slaps, once she figured she could get away with it.

I did my best to stay out of Nancy's way, but it seemed whenever I looked up from my own business, there she was, a-glaring at me with mean promise in her eyes. I didn't want to find out whether Nancy was as keen to make good on her promises as I was. I figured she must hate me for finding a place among the Madam's girls despite my disappointing face and figure—for proving her wrong when she had been so certain Madam Robair would kick me out on my ass to wallow in the Laramie dust. I thought, *Nancy will really hate me once she sees how the fellas have taken a shine. Then it'll all be over, unless I make damn sure my path never crosses hers.*

The fellas really had taken a shine to me by then. I'm pleased to say that I became a real favorite in short order. The men was all charmed—as fellas had been before—by my habits of cussing and telling shocking tales. I guess it was still a novel thing back then, to hear a girl of tender years let loose an avalanche of words so blue they'd drop a sailor dead from shock. And I was even tenderer than they suspected, for none of them knew my genuine age.

But I had more charms than my intricate and fanciful swearing. I took every chance I got to show those boys my card tricks—all the tricks Braddick taught me, and a few more I invented besides. And of course, once I convinced the boys to let me get my hands on a deck of cards, it was the most natural thing in the world to join in their games. I was a good faro player—the only legacy my pa bequeathed me—and I impressed them all by beating them so soundly, some men began cringing in anticipation of a loss whenever they saw me coming.

Now and then, after I cleaned out the kitty with an especially wicked hand, one of the fellas would say to me, "You ain't playing fair, Calamity Jane. Everybody knows you got a way with card tricks. You're cheating; you must be."

I would wink and reply, "If you want to see my best tricks, you're going to have to pay to take me upstairs."

Every week, every day, more fellas took me up on that offer. And once I had them in my crib, I made damn sure every man who did gamble on me won big—and had a time he wouldn't soon forget.

It wasn't long before I earned as robust a take as the prettiest little things in the pool hall. I was pleased, having made good on my vow to Madam. But I was anxious, too, for the other girls had begun to note my popularity. And Red Nancy's eyes was as keen and hard as ever.

BY AND BY, the madam came around to the pool hall to check on her business, to take stock of her girls and see to the workings of her establishment. She rolled up to the front door in a sleek black carriage pulled by a couple of snow-white horses, surely the finest rig in Fort Laramie. I watched through the rippled window as her driver helped her down. She stood there on the board sidewalk, smoothing the creases from her green skirt. The color and delicate poise of the madam contrasted so vividly with red, blocky Laramie that it seemed as if Robair was the only thing that truly existed in all the world.

"Look sharp, girls," I shouted. "Madam's here!"

Every girl who wasn't upstairs and occupied with an admirer hustled into a line. We stood waiting to greet her. I took my place at the end of the line, doing my strenuous best to look like a flower instead of a slug.

Madam Robair stepped inside the pool hall with her usual brisk efficiency. She peeled white gloves from her small, delicate hands. Then she walked down the line of girls, looking each of us over, nodding in approval at the state of our dresses, our hair—or giving a quiet order to put on a different color tomorrow, or find something with a lower neckline, as her taste dictated.

When the madam got to me, away at the end of her line of fine and fancy playthings, she stared up at me and sniffed. "Your dress ees atrocious, Jane," she said in that funny accent. "Somehow eet manages to feet you like a grain sack and a death shroud all at once."

"Yes mam, that is so," I said. There was no sense denying what was plain for everyone to see.

"I will send over a seamstress to make you another. Perhaps two or three."

"That's mighty generous of you, mam."

She paused, as if wondering whether she ought to say what was on her mind. I could just about feel all the pool-hall girls holding their breath, the better to listen. No doubt Red Nancy was waiting for me to get a real good scalding, right there in front of everybody.

Madam Robair said, "You have done well, Jane. I did not think eet possible, but you proved me wrong. You have made yourself a great favorite with the men, and for that I commend you."

My cheeks burned with pleasure. It was true that I had gained quite a following. Word had spread around Fort Laramie—tales of my amusing language, my wild and raucous ways—my wild ways upstairs, too, in the privacy of my crib. I kept busy every night I worked, and I liked the job just fine, for I found the men good company. The whiskey they bought me was even better. The working girl's life had surpassed my expectations—and I had surpassed Madam Robair's.

When she had finished inspecting the pool hall, the madam took her leave, and all us girls was left murmuring in her wake. Those who had been complimented glowed with pride, displaying an air of superiority well suited to cats on a fence. Those who'd been dressed down stomped or fluttered, and generally stared knives at the rest.

I didn't need to catch Nancy's eye to know she was throwing her very sharpest daggers at me. I could feel her rage piercing me from across't the room, so I kept my head down and hurried to the back of the hall where the card games was underway. In that way I avoided a slap from Nancy's quick and peevish hand.

Nancy hadn't any real reason to hate me; I was sure of that. Some girls just couldn't let themselves love the profession. It got under their skin and iced them over, one tumble after another, till they was bitter as witches and twice as mean. I wanted to go to Nancy and tell her, "I know this life don't suit you, so you shouldn't do it no more. Let me help you find a place in the boarding houses; I'll teach you everything I know, and it'll be a more agreeable life for you, I can promise you that." But by then, I knew Nancy well enough to understand this: she would have considered my offer no kindness. It was better to let dogs lie, as the saying goes—and I guess it goes double for cats.

SKILLS of the bed wasn't the only ones I sharpened in Madam Robair's hall. I got damn good at playing cards in short order, for I practiced often enough, playing more hands every night than my old dead pa had played in his whole lifetime. Word spread that Calamity Jane was real sharp at the faro table. Fellas began to bet on me—outrageous sums for a win, or sometimes for a loss, seeing as how I was only a girl. I never took it sore when the boys bet against me. I didn't blame them for their incredulity. And if money was at stake, I collected it as my honest due—for sharping the cards was work well done, just like all the other tasks I performed for my admirers.

Money was fair pay, but I made a habit of never keeping personal property when it was at stake. Well did I remember all the precious things my family lost to my father's gambling habit— the good picture frames, a fine horse or two, my mother's silver spoons. Those losses hurt us worse than the loss of any money, for once a memory is gone it can't be bought again, no matter how many hands of faro a man may win—no matter how wealthy his vagabond luck may one day make him.

There was one night at the hall I remember well, with the autumn newly come and a grand, hissing rain storm scouring the world outside. Summer cattle had just been driven in from the ranges to the slaughter pens. The town was full of cowboys speckled with dust and raindrops, eager for some fun after weeks riding herd. The rain kept them all confined inside, but after so long away from girls, they would have been indoors with us even if the weather was sunshiney as the day after the Flood.

I held court at one of the card tables, leaning way back in my chair with my boots kicked up on the table. I looked as if I hadn't a care in the world. The skirt of a new dress was rumpled up around my knees. It was a pretty, dark-green brocade, the finest thing I ever had worn, freshly made to fit and flatter me (as much as I could be flattered) by the madam's own, very skilled seam-stress. I had paid for the dress, of course, with my earnings. But I didn't mind spending money on something so impossibly dandy.

There was a whole mess of boys gathered around me—and around my three opponents. I loved the feel of the crowd, the graceless stomp and sway of those men's bodies, the smell coming off them—earth and water and dying sage. They was like the cattle they had tended, big and warm, companionable. They watched, all rapt and attentive, as I rained down hurt on the boys who dared challenge me to a hand.

When I won my third hand, I swept up a pile of silver coins toward with a triumphant laugh, and gathered the whole lot into my purse—a new green purse that matched my dress. Then I downed what was left of my whiskey.

"I told you all," I crowed, "I can't be beat, and you're damn fools for tryin'!"

"No one can beat Calamity," one of the boys affirmed. I had never seen him at the pool hall before, so I took his praise as a signal that even out on the range, men had learned my name.

The fellow sitting across from me—not much more than a boy, really, perhaps eighteen or nineteen—started forward in his chair. For a second, I thought he would spit a curse at me, or maybe try to slug me from where he sat. When I saw him draw his pistol, my heart leaped up into my throat. I never had considered that a man might be so angry with me that he'd actually try to kill me. But before I could get up and run, or even let fly with a scream, he set the gun on the table and pushed it to the center.

"One more hand," he said.

I looked down at the gun with some relief. The panicked roar in my ears subsided with every beat of my heart. "You betting your piece?" I said.

He didn't reply, except to push the gun with one finger, a little closer to me. Some of the crowd jeered at him. Some laughed and pounded each other on their shoulders, gleeful at the promise of a good show.

"What's your name?" I asked him.

He had a shine to his eyes, a spark of something I couldn't quite read, but I knew he wasn't angry. Not exactly. He leaned toward me, shivering, and I could sense a great intensity hanging all about him. But there was nothing of anger in it. He seemed sort of hungry, sort of longing for something only I could give. A card game, I guessed—I hoped—though I had already given him three.

Whatever feeling haunted the boy evidently had stopped up his mouth. He wouldn't answer, so somebody else in the crowd spoke for him. "That's Billy Voss."

"All right, Billy Voss," said I. "If you want to bet your pistol, that's nobody's business but yours and God's." I didn't know what God might care about a gun gambled away, but I liked the saying.

The watching men set up a hoot of approval. A few tossed in coins to buy their way into the game. The money piled up around the gun, but no coins could shine as pretty as that pistol. I could tell Billy Voss took great pride in his gun and cared for it well. It had fancy engraving around the barrel and a big, mother-of-pearl star set into the handle. It was too fine a piece for a man so young. It must have been a gift—a treasure. Maybe he inherited that gun from a dead relation.

Well, I don't need to tell you that I won that hand of faro, as I did most hands. I collected my winnings, and Billy looked crumpled, yet somehow all the hungrier. I slid his pretty gun into the beaded belt that held my purse. Then I rose from the card table.

"You headed up to your room, Calamity?" one of the men asked.

"I am, but not with you. I'll only go up there with Billy."

Billy's face turned an awful shade of red. I knew he didn't have nothing to pay me with—not anymore. The crowd knew it, too, and derided him. But I went around the table and took his arm as if he was the finest, richest gentleman in Fort Laramie.

"Come on," I said. "This one's on the house."

He brightened up then and followed me up the stairs. The cheers of his fellas rang down below.

Inside my room, I lit the stub of my candle and shut the door. I watched the silent Billy for a minute. He stood shivering and wide-eyed, uncertain what to do next, though surely he had been with whores plenty of times before. Every man in Laramie had. The rain was falling hard, pounding on the roof, beating against the four square panes of my tiny window. The light from the candle, stirred by a draft, wobbled and slid over pitted walls.

I took the gun from my belt, extended it to Billy. "Here," I said. "Take it."

He shook his head slowly. "No mam. You won it fair and square. And you surely earned it, good as you are at cards. I heard you was good, but I guess I didn't believe a girl could be so skillful. I guess you might have cheated, but I can't see how. I was a fool to bet against you, Calam."

I crossed to him—didn't take more than a couple of steps—and pressed that shiny, mother-of-pearl handle against his palm. He tensed up at my nearness.

"I can tell this gun is special to you," I said. "I won't have it off you, no matter how fair I won it. But when you go back down, keep it under your vest so none of the other boys can see."

Billy took the gun. He held it for a moment, caressing it with both hands, trailing his fingers along the curves of its engravings. For a second, I thought I saw his face darken with the start of tears, but it could have been the candle light tricking me. Then he put it back in his holster and raised his eyes to mine. That strange, hungry longing had returned to his gaze—the hot, desperate intensity.

"You know I admire you an awful lot, Miss Jane."

"I don't know," I said, laughing a little, full surprised. "Don't think I ever met you before tonight."

"We haven't met, but still I think you're an awful good woman."

I didn't know what to say. Not many people in the world would call me a good woman in the first place, let alone an awful good one. I just stood there, still and silent, with the rain roaring overhead.

Billy went on with a rush. "You're so very clever, but you're also *good*, Calam, there in your heart."

Just for a moment, so brief I wasn't quite sure it happened, he reached out as if he wanted to lay his hand against the green brocade of my low-cut bodice. Not to squeeze me, but to feel my heart beating underneath. Then he dropped his hand to his side, and I remained untouched.

"You'll make a fine wife," Billy Voss said. His voice had gone dry and soft.

"Ha," said I. "If only I wasn't a whore, right?" I wasn't angry at him; just amused.

After a moment he said, "Do you suppose you'll ever give it up? Whoring, I mean."

"What," I said, incredulous, "for you?"

"Well," Billy Voss said slowly, choosing his words with great care, "I'm a nice enough fella. I wouldn't never treat you unkind. And I'm making good money now. I could be a real good husband —I know it. And we're of an age, so why not?"

I smiled and shook my head. My heart fluttered at his words— I won't lie to you and say it didn't, for every girl likes to hear that she's wanted, that a man wants to treat her sweet and kind. And oh, doesn't an ugly girl long to hear it a hundred times more than the rest? But I knew, even as my heart soared, that it never could be. "You're real nice and respectable, Billy. I know that for sure. But I won't marry you."

"Why not?"

Why not—what could I tell him? What would he believe in that moment, in the candle light, with just the two of us alone? He would deny the truth if I set it before him: that even a very nice boy would soon grow tired of a thing like me, big as an ox in the traces, with a face like a broken platter. He would abandon me someday for a prettier thing. He wanted—as all men want—a woman who was light on her feet and sweet-tempered, pretty as a springtime flower. What good was cleverness in the end? How far would my good heart take me? I knew better than to gamble when the deck was stacked against my favor.

Besides, I reckoned it was dangerous to be a wife. True, there was the risk of abandonment in a wide, lonesome world—and for a girl like me, it was a certainty I'd be left alone sooner or later. Wifing never had seemed to set well with my mother, nor with Emma Alton, and they was the only wives I ever had a chance to observe at close quarters. Wives was miserable, sad creatures, far as I could tell. But whores at least was free.

I never gave Billy Voss his answer—why not, why not? Instead I reached around to the back of my dress and undid the knot in my strings with practiced fingers. My bodice loosened and slid down my shift with a whisper I could barely hear over the rain, over the raspy, choked sound of Billy's breath.

"Come on," I said to him. "Get it while the gettin's good. My candle won't burn much longer."

I DON'T RECALL how many weeks it was after the Billy Voss incident before the pool hall gig went to shit. I do remember it was still raining. Those storms had swept the foothills nearly every day, and Fort Laramie was all red mud up to the ankles. Rain and fearful-close thunder had pressed the whole town down under its thumb, making everybody feel cooped up and restless. I blame the rain for bringing my sad affair about so quick, but it would've happened sooner or later, storms or no. Nancy had set her bitter heart on putting Calamity Jane in her place from the moment she was busted down to the pool hall.

It was morning, and I had just risen and splashed my face in my wash-basin, and rinsed out my mouth, and dressed. The usual crowd of boys wouldn't show up for some hours yet, so the pool hall was quiet down below—no piano, no stamp of dancing feet. I did what I could to pull my hair up into a semblance of style—I never could manage more than a simple bun—and then stood at my window, watching the gray clouds pile up over the hills. Under the dimness of stormy weather, the hills' reddish hides seemed more colorful than ever, blazing in shades of copper and flame with deep cracks of violet-blue shadow, bright as if they'd been lit by a setting sun, but without the sun's attendant glow. I thought the scene real pretty and peaceful; I didn't want to stop looking. But I heard voices outside my door—whispers, a few low laughs, the rustling of dresses. I didn't like the sounds a-tall.

I thought to poke my head out into the hall and find out what had caused so much fuss, but when I tried the door knob, the thing would hardly budge. Somebody was holding it from the other side.

"Come on now," I said, real properly annoyed. "Who's over there?"

The girls laughed louder this time. The laughter held a nasty note, as if a current of wild glee flowed through them all, whipping them up to a frenzy.

"Let me out," I said, pulling and pushing on the door. "T'ain't funny."

"Why don't you bust through like the big dumb bull you are?"

Oh, Nancy. The moment I heard her wicked little sneer, all my surprise vanished.

"What's the point, Nance?" I said. "You're acting like a jackass and it'll only make you look bad in the end."

"Stuff it up your cun', Calamity Jane."

The girls all hooted over that. Typically, I was the only one who used such colorful language.

"Enough now," I said, and pulled hard on the door again, wrenching the knob with all the energy I could muster.

Nancy let go suddenly; I staggered back as the door flew open, stumbled against my bed so hard that I sat down upon it. The girls leered at me through the door, grinning like feral dogs.

Nancy leaned into my crib and mooed like a cow, which set

the other girls to screaming with amusement. I lumbered up and
started toward them. I only meant to push my way through and
go about my business—ignore them all for the rest of the day—
but as I came toward them, the girls shrieked and scattered as if
I'd drawn a gun.

They went clattering down the stairs in a frantic pack, with
Nancy at the back, hollering down into the pool hall, "Help, help!
Jane's 'bout to kill every one of us!" She sounded properly
panicked, as if I posed a real imminent threat to life and limb, but
she kept looking back at me as she went, and there was no
mistaking the glitter of mischief in her eyes.

The girls spilled right out the hall and into the street, holding
up their skirts so they wouldn't get muddy. I walked slowly after
them, kind of stunned, though goodness knows I should have
stayed inside and let them flap about like the silly hens they was. I
don't know what drew me out into the street. Maybe it was the
sheer force of Nancy's will. It was considerably powerful.

Rain had tapered off for the morning, but the ground was still
plenty wet. The girls flocked into a ring with Nancy and me right
in the center. They was all laughing, grinning at each other with
their cheeks flushed pink and their eyes a-glowing, cheerful as if
we was all about to set off for a nice, friendly picnic.

Nancy strutted right up to me, the mud splashing under her
neat little boots. She jabbed a sharp-nailed finger into my chest.
"You're cheating us out of a living, Calamity. Every one of us."

I squinted down at her, plum unable to believe what I was
hearing. "The fuck you talking about, anyway, Nance?"

"You heard me. You're taking more than your fair share of the
men."

I spat into the mud to show her what I thought of that. "More
than my share?" I said. "I don't take nothing but my share. If you
want a bigger share, you'd best start working as hard as I do."

"We work plenty hard."

"None of you's willing to do the things I'll do for the boys.

That's why they like me so much. If you want more action, you'll have to work for it!"

Nancy shoved my chest again. I stumbled back a few steps, but I didn't fall. I knew she was trying to rile me; I was resolved not to take the first swing. Let her throw the first punch, I told myself—and then when I knock her to the ground, everyone will be obliged to declare that I acted in self-defense.

"Come on, you big ugly cow." Nancy advanced again. I didn't like the thought of skittering back any farther; it would only make me look weak and afraid. So I planted my feet in the mud and waited for her. She pushed right into me, nose to nose, jabbing me again with that damnable nail, lacquered and bright in the light of day. "Nobody wants you here," she said. "Nobody likes you and none of us wants you hanging around any longer, taking money from our purses."

I darted a quick glance at the sidewalk. Men walked by, going about their business. I worried that a man might hear Nancy's accusation and mistake me for a thief. I had worked hard, and with considerable care, building a good reputation in the town of Fort Laramie. One stray rumor that Calamity Jane had thieving tendencies could ruin my livelihood in a matter of hours. So I spoke up real loud, making damn sure every passing gentleman heard me. "I ain't taken a thing from anybody, except what the men give me of their own free will. I don't steal, Nancy, and you know it. Just 'cause I'm better at business than you, that's no cause to get nasty. Jealousy don't become you, anyhow. Green's as ugly on you as that bunkum shade of red you slapped all over your hair."

"You want to see 'slapped all over,' you half-baked bitch? I'll show you!"

Nancy flew at me, clawed hands whirling like a tornado. She was everywhere at once, yanking my hair, kicking my shins, slugging away at my arms and my middle—and worst of all, flailing with those deadly nails, trying to scratch up my face or maybe gouge out an eye. I took her blows easily enough, for thought she was mighty energetic, she wasn't terribly strong. But I didn't want to see my face scored and scarred by that cat's talons. I was already saddled with the handicap of ugliness; red welts across my cheeks and forehead wouldn't have done a lick of good to improve my situation. I threw my arms up to protect my face while I tried to evade Nancy's fury. My boots slipped and skidded in the mud.

"You better get away from me," I shouted through my arms. "I don't want to hurt you!"

"You couldn't hurt me if you tried!" Her attacks never ceased, even while she spoke. She was an inexhaustible well of hatred. "I'll beat you to a pulp, you damn bloody clout! I'll shove your head up your own rotten hole! God knows it's loose enough to take it, what with all the men you've been luring up to your room. What are you doing to trick the men into sleeping with you, huh? That's what we all want to know. 'Cause it's a sure thing they ain't doing it of their own accord! Just look at you! The only man who'd pick you out of a crowd is the kind of who's got a secret hope of finding a prick hiding under your petticoats."

Nancy had really begun to shriek by then, letting her vile accusations fly right up to the new-made rooftops. As I ducked behind my upraised arms and cringed away from her onslaught, I could see fellas cutting their eyes toward the fight, or hurrying along the sidewalk to put themselves clear of the commotion. If I didn't stop Nancy's madness in short order, she would grind my good reputation into the mud.

So I swung out hard, nice and sudden, with my big, square, work-roughened fist. It caught Nancy smack in the jaw. She turned halfway around, eyes wide and staring but blank as undyed cotton. Then she swayed on her feet for a moment and pitched forward, face-first, into the mud.

The circle of girls fell deathly silent. Half of them gaped down at Nancy, who was now sprawled most ungracefully in the street.

The other half stared at me with a kind of half-frightened, half-thrilled sparkle in their eyes. No one said a word.

"Better flip her over," I told the girls casually, "'less you intend to let her drown in a puddle. It's all one to me."

I made my way back into the pool hall, but I could hear them scrambling and murmuring behind me, rolling Nancy onto her back. Somebody called for smelling salts. One of the girls ran past me into the hall and up the stairs, no doubt to fetch the salts and bring Red Nancy around. I was sore—not from Nancy's beating, which hadn't troubled me much more than a few gnat stings—but sick at heart and angry. I had made a place for myself in Fort Laramie. For the first time in my life, I was mistress of my own fate, with enough jingle in my purse to give me hope for a good future. Nancy and her friends had thrown my hope out into the street like a bucket of slops, and all because they coveted what I had worked so hard to build.

I didn't feel like working that day, or that night, for after what had transpired in the street, I knew I'd never be able to drive the scowl from my face and make the gentlemen smile. To this day, I've never had the knack some whores possess, the ability to wear a mask of false emotion. I lament that particular failing, for in my trade, there's no skill more valuable than making a man believe you're having the time of your life—or tricking him into thinking he can't frighten you, that you're cool as winter in the face of his violent rages. I've always worn my heart on my sleeve—or on my unlovely face, as it were—and at the age of fourteen I certainly had no hope of keeping a smile fixed firmly in its place. Now I knew the whole damned pool hall to be a nest of vipers, and every one just itching to bite my heel. So I begged off work with a head cold for an excuse, and spent the day laying in my bed, glowering through the window when the rain returned.

As a brief and feeble sunset colored the sky outside, I could hear the hall below coming to life. The music grew livelier, and the rhythm of girls dancing—their feet stamping in time to the fiddle and piano—pounded all through the building. Now and then gusts of laughter made their way upstairs, the big, booming laughs of men intertwined with women's soft giggles. I strained to listen every time, trying to discern from the confines of my crib whether Nancy's voice was among them.

I had clocked her pretty good, I knew, for she'd gone out cold right there in the muddy street. She must have a hell of a bruise by now, I reckoned—maybe even a swollen face. I didn't feel a speck of pity for her, nor the least bit of remorse. A good, sound beating was no more than what she deserved. I was merely trying to discern whether it was worth venturing downstairs and trying my luck with the gentlemen, for I had begun to feel a little less sour by then, and some of my confidence was returning.

In that very moment, however, I heard a hesitant step outside my door. "Jane?" The voice called so softly I could scarce hear above the noise downstairs. But I recognized its source: Delia, a blonde girl not much older than me. She hadn't been among the crowd in the street that morning.

I opened my door. Delia was waiting on the threshold, twisting her fingers together in an anxious sort of way. She glanced over her shoulder to be sure no one was coming up the stairs.

"You can come in, if you want to talk," I told her.

"That's not a good idea. If I were seen coming out of your crib afterwards, Nancy would light into me next. I just came up to warn you, now that the night's getting good and lively and nobody is likely to tell that I'm missing just yet."

"Warn me—what do you mean?"

"Nancy's awful chapped at you."

I laughed. "'Course she is. I knocked her clean out. Did she show her face down there among the men?"

"She did. She's got a shiner, and she's been telling everyone who'll listen that you attacked her."

"What a load of horse shit," I said in disgust. "Everybody knows it ain't true. She attacked me first, the bitch."

"We all know the truth, but no one will say boo to Nancy. She just about runs this place now, as long as Madam isn't here."

I felt a chill way down deep in my stomach. Nancy could tarnish my good name with this rumor, almost as fast as she could do it with her lies about me stealing money from the girls' purses.

Delia understood my grim expression. She reached across the threshold, took me by the arm. There was such trembling of urgency in her touch that I went colder still. "Jane," she whispered, "Nancy is dangerous. She already hated you before, but now— after you knocked her down in front of everybody and gave her a big ugly bruise, besides—she's ready to do you in."

"She can't do me in," I said, not at all confident that I was right.

"She can, and she will. She's awful mean, Jane, and she has it out for you now. She's been telling the other girls she intends to take a knife to you."

"A knife? Do you think she's serious?"

"I know she is. Nancy's crazy; she'll do anything, anything at all that comes into her head. She's dead set on seeing you out of this pool hall for good—and probably out of Laramie, too. One way or another, she intends to be rid of you. I came to warn you."

I stood in silence for a long while, listening to the music and the stamping of feet, the innocent laughter below. If Delia was right, and Nancy was so damnably determined to put me out for good, then I would only get her off my back by fighting all the harder. I must do some real damage to Nancy, beyond a mere clocking on the jaw. If I hoped to frighten her out of her hate, I would have to hurt her badly. It was either that, or I must allow her to hurt me badly—maybe even kill me. There wasn't any other way to placate a fiend of Nancy's sort.

"I can't fight Nancy again," I said quietly. "If I do, I'll have to really let her have it. Otherwise, she'll never leave me be. What should I do, Delia?"

Even as I asked the question, I knew the answer. Delia knew it, too. She pulled me into a rough hug, then held me firmly by the shoulders, at arm's length, as if she had already reconciled herself to my going.

"I got to leave," I said, defeated. "Leave the hall, leave town… there's no other way out of this mess."

"I know it," she said. "I'll miss you, Calam. If you pack up your things now, you can be off before Nancy comes looking for you. She won't come until most of the boys have gone away for the night, so you've got a couple hours yet. I'd help you pack, but if I'm away too long somebody might come looking for me. Nancy can't know that I warned you."

Miserable, I nodded. "I don't have much to pack. That's one good thing, at least."

"There's a good boarding house on the next street over, right next to the livery stable where you keep your mule. Take a room there for the night. Nancy won't think to look for you in a boarding house; she'll never suspect you've decided to skip town. Then you can ride at first light."

"Thanks for the advice," I said as Delia turned away—already headed back to the hall below, to the world of fun and admiration that were hers by right, seeing as she was a pretty girl and all.

It took me no more than a few minutes to dress in my old riding trousers and shirt. Then I bundled up my three pretty dresses and the few small possessions I owned. I wrapped the whole lot in a wool blanket from my bed—a gal could always do with an extra blanket on the trail—and paused for one last look at my little crib. Cramped though it was, and despite the nature of the work that went on there, that lone, narrow room had been my home for months—and the best home I'd ever had, too, a place entirely my own, obtained through my own cleverness and commitment. I didn't like to leave it, for that crib was a signal to me that I could do the impossible, if I just set my mind to it. I was clever enough to carve out a place for myself, even in a world that was never meant for me—even when the deck was stacked against me.

I waited till the music kicked up lively below and the walls of the pool hall shivered to the rhythm of stamping feet. The hoots and whistles of eager men sounded piercing and sharp above the rapid clang of the piano. That was my cue to go, for even Nancy would be too distracted by the fun to look for me. I hurried downstairs without a backward glance at my abandoned crib. Then I pushed through the crowd, out into a cold, deep-blue night.

Delia's suggestion that I board for the night near the livery stable was a good one. If I'd been in a sounder frame of mind, I might have taken it. But having made up my mind to vacate Fort Laramie altogether, I was already subject to the lure of the trail— and by the time that crisp night air struck my face and filled my lungs with the smell of dust and sage, I was hankering for the wilderness again. That's not to say I'd forgotten the hardships of the trail—nor the fright of being a woman alone in the wilderness. I was merely confident that I could face those dangers and come out on top; I had licked Red Nancy, after all. I could lick her again if I wanted to stick around and face her knives. Whatever I lacked in good looks, I made up for with grit and cleverness—the pool hall had taught me that much. I felt equal to the challenge of the trail, and the sooner I put Laramie at my back, the sooner I would reach my new destination… whatever it may be.

The town was still lively, for though darkness came earlier each day, commerce hadn't slowed. That was one of the perks of situating a town along the Overland Stage Line, I suppose: there was always new freight coming in, always work for the idle, and most of all, always some excuse for money to change hands. After months spent working for Madam Robair, I had more money than I'd ever dreamed of—though to be sure, it wasn't exactly a fortune—and I thought if I meant to hit the trail again, I might as well do the job properly. So I headed first thing to the livery and the general store that stood next door.

The fellow that kept the livery tipped his hat when he saw me enter the yard. He was a sharp young man by the name of Juan, a Mexican with a heavy accent, always dressed real smart and turned out like every day was Sunday, which I accounted some kind of miracle, since he spent all his time shoveling horse shit.

Juan leaned on his pitchfork under the glare of a lantern, burning high up on a pole. "Miss Jane," he said, "good to see you again. What brings you out tonight?" Juan knew me well, for I had dropped by at least twice a week to take Rainbow out for a ride, and I always paid her board fee on time.

"I come for my mule." I shifted my bundle, for it had grown heavy across my shoulders. I was eager to fill my saddle bags and head out of town. "But this time, I'm taking her for good. I aim to hit the trail again, and I don't expect to be back in Laramie for an awful long time."

Juan stroked his mustache, looking around the livery yard almost as if something had frightened him. I couldn't imagine why my declaration had put up his hackles, unless he was sore over losing his best boarder. Then he said, real slow and cautious, "I don't understand, Miss Jane. I sold your mule two days ago, just like you asked."

My bundle hit the dirt with a thud. I stood there gawping at the man while he swayed from one foot to the other, looking like he planned to take off running.

"I got a note from you," Juan said. "A note, Miss Jane, telling me to sell off that mule. I got the money. Of course I kept it for you."

"I… I never sent no note." I didn't like the way my voice sounded, high and wavering like maybe I was about to cry. And in that moment, I saw Nancy's hand in the affair. Every girl in the pool hall knew how much I loved my mule, and cherished the time I spent riding. One of those bitter old cats had sent a note in my stead, just to pull one over on me—and I would have wagered all the gold in Montana that Nancy had done the deed.

I pressed my hands to my face so Juan couldn't see my tears fall. Rainbow had been my only friend in the world, my true companion. Worse, she was my last tie to Mr. Braddick, a reminder of the happy days I'd spent working on his ranch, driving alone out into the great wide open. I never got to say good-bye to that mule—my dearest friend. I couldn't help but feel that Rainbow would resent me forever, believing I had sent her off all uncaring, leaving her to toil in the traces for some hard-handed master without even one last pat on the neck from me. It about shattered my heart, to know that Rainbow and I was parted forever—and worse, that she would assume I had done it on purpose. It cost me all my strength to remain on my feet. I wanted nothing more than to fall to my knees beside my bundle and weep out all the inconsolable grief of my heart.

The initial shock passed, leaving anger in its wake. I stood there for a long time, my face still hidden behind my quaking hands, weighing the merits of returning to the pool hall and calling Nancy out into the street for a real fight. If she was spoiling to get at me, then let her do her worst. I could bend that bitch around my knee, easy as a blacksmith shaping iron. But no —if I showed Nancy how deep she had hurt me, she would only take it for a victory, and crow about it from her bed while every bone I'd broken in her miserable body knit back together, making her stronger and meaner than ever before. I had no choice but to concede the fight, and put Fort Laramie behind me all the faster, before I talked myself into doing something truly stupid.

When I looked up, Juan stood beside me, holding out a few banknotes—the money from Rainbow's sale, less his commission. I nodded mutely and slipped the notes into my purse. Then I swallowed hard a few times till I felt strong enough to talk.

"I'll need a horse," I said. "And a saddle, I guess, for I bet that note said to sell my tack, too. Show me whatever horses you got

for sale. I'll take the best out of the lot." At least I had enough
money to afford a decent mount—I was sure of that.

Before much longer, I was cinching a fine saddle around the
belly of a black mare. She was young, something of a spitfire, and
I didn't know her well enough yet to like her. Nevertheless, something had drawn me to her the moment Juan pointed her out in
the corral. She was big and rough around the edges, with a steep
goose rump and a head like a half-sawn log, heavy and coarse. But
she had a keen, clever eye and she looked inexhaustible, and when
Juan slipped between the rails and kissed out loud to make the
herd move, I could see how free and easy the black mare ran.
Maybe that's what drew me to her—maybe she put me in mind of
my own self. Nothing pretty to look at, but boy, could she get the
job done.

I bid Juan a heartbroken farewell and led my new horse to the
general store. The old man and woman who ran it was making
ready to close up for the night, but they held the door open for
me. I purchased a new bed roll and a couple more blankets, a good
flint and steel for sparking my camp fires, and various other
sundries I thought might sustain me on a trek of indeterminate
length. Winter wasn't far off, so I added a good pair of fleece-lined
gloves, three pairs of thick wool stockings, and a fur-lined jacket
with a scarf long enough to wrap around my head and my neck at
the same time.

As the old woman tallied up my purchase, I watched her
husband put the final buff on a pistol he'd been cleaning behind
the counter. Something about that gun held my attention. I
stared at the piece while the oil-stained rag ran across its surface
—the scrollwork etched into the barrel, the pearl-white star set
into the handle. Then I remembered where I'd seen that pistol
last.

"Billy Voss," I blurted out.

The man stopped polishing the gun. He looked up at me, kind
of slow and mournful like.

"That's Billy Voss's gun," I said. "I'd recognize it anywhere. How did you come to have it, sir? Did he gamble it away again?"

"No, miss," the shopkeeper said. "If you were a friend of Billy Voss, then I'm sorry to be the one to give you bad news. Billy was killed about a week ago running steers out on the range. Fell from his horse and broke his neck. Sure is an awful shame; he was a good fellow."

I hung my head. I hadn't known Billy Voss for more than one night, but I remembered him well. He said I would make a fine wife. He had asked me to marry him, and I laughed at the offer. How I regretted it now.

"Billy's friends brought in all his worldly goods," the shopkeeper said, "and sold them to pay for his funeral expenses. He hadn't any family, the poor boy. He was an orphan, all alone in the world."

An orphan—just like me.

"How much for the gun?" I asked.

"Thirty-five, with the holster."

I took the money from my purse—it had lightened considerably since I'd left the pool hall—plus a dollar for two boxes of cartridges.

Solemnly, the shopkeep passed me the gun. "Do you know how to use it?"

"Sure," I said. "I know the general idea."

"I'm awful glad a friend of Billy's will keep his gun. I think he'd be glad to know it, too."

I buckled the holster around my waist and slipped the pearl-handled gun into its cradle. Then I gathered up my goods, nodded my thanks to the shopkeep and his wife, and left the store. With every step I took, the pistol bounced against my thigh —a sensation unfamiliar, yet infinitely comforting. By the time I secured my goods in my saddle bags and swung up onto the black mare's back, the pistol had already begun to feel like a part of me. I rested my hand on the gun, palm pressed tight against that pearl star, as I rode east into the darkness. East towards the dawn.

I'LL SPARE you the details of my ride from Laramie to Cheyenne, for if truth be told, one stretch of trail is very much like another. A few weary days after my departure from Laramie, I rode up Cheyenne's broad main street considerably more familiar with my new horse and my new pistol, for I had put both through their paces out on the gray Wyoming plains. I'd never intended Cheyenne to be my destination. I had only meant to replenish some of my supplies, for each night on the trail had been colder than the last and I knew winter would come on harsh, brutal, and early. If I was to make it farther east—pushing toward an unknown goal, driven by the loneliness and anger that still haunted me—I would need more provisions and a warmer set of clothes.

But as the black mare loped easily up the street, I looked at Cheyenne with a new set of eyes. Though it had stood only three or four years at most, still Cheyenne reminded me of Piedmont, with its tidy new houses and brightly painted shops—and most of all, the little white church that recalled the sanctuary and blessing I received at the hands of Reverend Wilkes. And quite naturally, when I thought of the Piedmont church I remembered my brothers and sisters, and I asked myself what I was doing riding off into the tarnation east instead of back toward the place where I had left them. I have no defense for such foolishness. I'd only been caught up in the wild flights of fancy to which most girls of fourteen are susceptible. But then and there, I made up my mind to overwinter in Cheyenne, working all the while, and to take my earnings back to Piedmont as soon as the spring thaw came, and reunite the Canarys for good and all.

I spent a few days boarding in a noisy, crowded house—dusty

and thick with the stench of bullwhackers and the animals they drove, but the cheapest place a body could hope to lay its head in all of Cheyenne. Every night, I patrolled the cat houses and pool halls, paying close heed to each one. I watched the girls coming and going, and the gentlemen, too, assessing the caliber of each establishment with the greatest care. I knew what I must look for: a house that boasted more fun than refinement, for the tricks I'd used to make myself popular at Robair's pool hall would fall flat in too dandy a place.

That was how I found myself at McDaniel's one brisk autumn morning, dressed in my green brocade with my matching purse hung on one hip and my star-handled pistol on the other. I had taken pains with my hair and hat before I'd left the boarding house, and I thought I looked as smart as I was ever like to do, with my long black hair braided and twisted all around my crown and a few love-locks pulled free to curl around my face. I wasn't pretty, exactly, but at least I looked more girlish than I ever did in my trousers and shirt, with my hair a tangled nest, dull and gritty from the dirt of the trail.

McDaniel's was as raucous a hurdy-gurdy house as you'd ever like to see. Day and night, the music never stopped playing, and the stage that ran the full length of the hall featured a new performer every hour. McDaniel's was more like a circus than the standard run of dance hall, for the girls who took to the stage could perform such feats of contortion and acrobatics as the West had never seen before. I presented myself to James McDaniel, the stout, balding proprietor, with no small amount of trepidation. All the while as I spoke to him at the back of the hall, the hurdy-gurdy moaned a lively tune and three red-haired girls dressed in pantaloons and lacy camisoles folded themselves up like Chinese paper cranes. Those girls bent their slender bodies into such impossible positions that I felt rather sick to my stomach at the sight. I couldn't help but imagine myself cricked backwards that way, or trying to roll across the stage as those girls did, with their ankles pulled up over their heads and their backs round as wheels. Not a one of them so much as dropped her smile while she twisted and cavorted before those cheering, stamping men.

"You can see, Miss Jane," said James McDaniels, "that I run a unique establishment. My girls don't only perform great feats in the cribs upstairs. They must prove exceptional talents in other ways, too."

He gestured at the stage, where the three girls had formed a pantaloon-clad pyramid. I said, "Yes sir, I can see as much."

"What exceptional talents would you bring to my hall, if I were to take you on?"

I pulled my pistol from its holster and spun it fast around my finger, so many revolutions it'd make you dizzy to try and count them. Then I caught it smartly and tossed it to my left hand, where I spun it again, just as agilely. "I can tell good jokes, too," I said, "While I sling my gun around. And I can trick-shoot real good."

That last part was an outright lie. I had only fired my pistol in my unsuccessful attempts to bring down small critters along the trail. But I figured it couldn't be so terribly hard to learn how to trick-shoot. All I needed was a little practice.

James McDaniels looked rather doubtful. He even shook his head and seemed on the point of dismissing me, but I said quickly, "Madam Robair of Fort Laramie took me in and put me to work. You can write her and ask whether I was any good. She didn't believe in me at first, neither, but I showed a real knack with men. I can make them like me, sir, I swear it—make them like me better than any other girl you got. I did the job so thoroughly over in Laramie that I left town in fear for my life. The other girls was ready to come after me with knives because of my success. Why do you think a little slip like me carries a gun?"

McDaniels laughed aloud at that, in spite of his reservations— just as I'd hoped he would. The thought of a big, blocky creature like myself living in fear of a gang of girlish whores was too absurd. Once he laughed, I knew I had him—and I knew I could captivate any of his customers just as readily.

"How old are you?" he asked when he was done with his chuckle.

"Eighteen."

"Girl, you are not."

I shrugged. "Sixteen. Which is old enough, in Wyoming Territory." Of course I was but fourteen years of age, but what James McDaniels didn't know wouldn't hurt me.

He seemed to accept the proffered age. "You can start tomorrow, but only with comedy. It'll take me some time to figure out how to make use of a trick shooter indoors."

I said that was fine by me. Inwardly, I breathed a sigh of relief. If he had wanted me to dazzle the crowd with my shooting from day one, the jig would have been up before it had really begun, and I would have found myself back in the saddle, riding for the next town.

It turned out that James McDaniels couldn't work out the problem of trick shooting indoors for some months. By that time, my brash antics on stage had already earned me a pack of admirers, and the money began to trickle in once more. I was careful now not to make myself too popular; I had learned that lesson well from Red Nancy. So my gains was modest, but still sufficient to bring me bobbing back up to the surface of hope. By the time I'd taught myself how to trick-shoot—riding out into the plains on my days off so no one would see me trying and failing to hit my targets—I had a crowd of gentlemen callers eager to see me put that gun to good use. McDaniels had one of his girls pass out cotton balls whenever I took to the stage, so no one would be deafened by the roar of my pistol. He built a wall of straw bales off the right-hand side of the stage, so I could fire at my targets without blowing holes in the wall. And when spring arrived—first in a trickle, then in a bright, cold gush of melting snow—Calamity Jane had made a new name for herself: the struttin'est, cussin'est girl in all the West, who could shoot an apple off a wooden mannequin's head at twelve paces and strip a fella of his spare cash at no paces, upstairs.

The novelty of my act drew so much attention that I soon began to plead with McDaniels to send me elsewhere—for he owned similar establishments throughout the Territory, and I didn't like to make myself too popular in any one spot. That was how I came to tour from one hurdy-gurdy house to the next, working no more than six or seven weeks in any one place before I moved on again. The balance suited me fine, for after a few weeks had passed, I found myself craving the open wilderness again, the solitude of the trail, and the self-reliance long travel required. And the break from my other duties, of course—those I performed in the cribs.

In fact, I found the touring life so thoroughly agreeable that it plum caught me in its snare. I still entertained the old fantasy of returning to Piedmont and reuniting the clan. But the more money I made and the more I came to savor those days and weeks spent alone on the trail, the more my plans for Piedmont became an abstraction rather than a concrete set of plans. Oh, I wrote to my brothers—for by the time I reached the age of fifteen, I had decided to make of myself a properly and truly literate woman, as worldly and sophisticated as a girl like me could ever hope to be. But if my letters reached the Richardson ranch, I never knew. Neither Cilus nor Lije ever wrote me back.

I told myself I hadn't given up on my brothers and sisters. I told them the same, when I scrawled my inelegant missives and carried them off to the post, hoping the letters would find their intended recipients. But I liked the weight of money in my purse too much to give up the touring life. And before I knew it, a year had passed—then two—and I was no closer to storming Piedmont and rounding up the widely scattered Canary children. In fact, I had settled into a new dream—one entirely my own. I had never forgotten what I'd learned at Braddick's ranch. Nor had the strange weight of melancholy left me from the night of my first delivery with the mule team. I knew the West wouldn't last forever—not as it was then, wild and alive, a creature of its own reckless determination. The rails would tame it soon enough, domesticate the land and shape it into a beast unrecognizable. I intended to see my world before the West fell to its sad and inevitable fate.

LEST THE YEARNING, HUNGRY LOOK
IN HER WILDLY BEAUTIFUL EYES
SHOULD PAIN HIM

I NEVER WAS BIT BY A RATTLER; THAT'S ONE SMALL MERCY FOR which I may sincerely thank the Lord. I saw plenty of men who was, though, for by God in my day I saw everything.

I remember one man in particular who showed me the place on his leg where he'd been bit, just above the bone of his ankle, which was unexpectedly delicate, a pale white roundness with skin soft as flour. And marring the ladylike perfection of his ankle, two angry red holes with black at their center and thin veins of scarlet and old-bruise blue, running off in all directions like the rays of a star, like the reaching arms of a sunburst high up on a church wall.

"Rattler bit me," he said as we got dressed. Our transaction was all over, and the day was cold, so neither of us was much inclined to linger in the ivory. "Some two years gone, out along the Platte River."

I said, "Two years is an awful long time to leave holes like that in your skin. Didn't you ever see a doctor?"

"Course I did. I seen every doctor in Nebraska, and probably half of them what's in Wyoming, besides. But no one can heal it."

He said a rattler pumps poison from its fangs, and once that poison's in you, it stays—no matter what cure you seek, no matter what any doctor may try. Assuming you don't die or cut off the bitten limb, you will carry the snake's hot venom everywhere you go, through every clime. The venom throbs along your veins; it sets your blood afire. At night you get no relief. In coolness and in stillness, the ache of the poison fills your soul and affords you little rest. All your thoughts are consumed by the snake. You wonder if it got away, if it ever bit another man. Or if you shot it, or spiked its head in vengeance, then a serpentine ghost will haunt you, curling 'round your heart so you feel it—the cold loops of its body and the ridges of its scales—pressing down upon your soul. The snake never lets you be.

He said to me: "Calamity Jane, you can't know what it feels like, the long slow ache that never leaves, the ghost that encircles your heart."

But I did know, and I do. For by that time, I had already met Wild Bill.

THE FIRST TIME I saw him I was eighteen years old, or near enough as made no difference. It was 1874; the Great Depression had settled in the year before, and that's how I know the date still. The whole of the country was Depressed, but I was riding high on my happiness. I had left the hurdy-gurdy circuit and gone back to the camps, just for a change of scenery; I had followed the railroad camps for two years by then. I didn't confine myself to the railways; now and then I took up with a soldiering camp, the kind that ventured up into the Black Hills to look for Indians. I was a young woman, of the age when love is hard and real. I was already in love, already susceptible to the ache. But I hadn't yet fallen for any man—though I had my pick of the men, any night I pleased. Plenty prettier girls followed the camps, but I was the most popular, for I could drink alongside the men without losing my head, and most of them though it great fun to hear me cuss till my tongue turned blue. Besides, I was up for more adventure than any other girl I ever knew. I'd do more fancy tricks than anyone, except maybe for Backwards Kate, but she preferred the road houses in those days, and wasn't often to be found among the tents.

The boys back then was fair with their pay; even if there was a Great Depression somewhere Back East, we knew how to whoop it up along the train lines. Black iron rails might as well have been made from gold, for all we cared about money. Every foot of track the boys laid brought more coins showering down. Of course, we knew there was an edge to the world—a boundary beyond which the rail lines could never go. But we had yet to reach the end, so the money was still good and reliable. The Pacific was a long way off, and for us, the sun was far from setting.

It wasn't a man who'd captured my heart then, in the railway days. It was the land itself that enchanted me. I worked hard and earned plenty, enough to buy a real fine saddle for Silkie—that's what I came to call my big black mare. The saddle had only a few silver fripperies. Its real beauty lay in its tooling, intricate swirls carved into the leather, wild roses and asters and spikes of lupine like you see growing in the high wet meadows come spring. Every morning I would sling that pretty saddle up onto Silkie's back, and together we rode out from the camp—whichever camp we happened to call home that month—and took to the hills. Black Hills, dry hills, hills white with limestone or green after an April rain; hills streaked with red and ocher like spilled paint running down their sides. From the crest of a hill, I could see all the world, sweeping far away below me, a vastness of a land undiscovered, where in the shadowed clefts of mountains or in the sere golden earth itself, below its hot dry skin, there was gems waiting to be discovered, there was harmonies waiting to be found and laced together into song. There was nothing bigger than the plains and the mountains at my back. There was nothing greater than the sky, its blue solitude, its singularity, the very limit of what a mortal mind could know. There was nothing beyond, no God waiting to judge me for being who and what I was. There at the top of a hill—any hill would do—I could be myself. I could be free.

That was the great love I felt. The West had romanced me. I had fallen for its charms as any fool does, and gladly I threw myself into the sweet fury of love. By day I rode alone, with only Silkie for a friend, and come sunset I was back at the camp, ready to take to my work cheerfully, my spirit filled with the warmth of the high places, my heart overbrimming from the smell of dry grass and distant rain.

At sunset on a day in late spring, when the lupines still stood tall and blue in the cool, high meadows, I came back to camp just as another party arrived. This must have been in the Big Horns, on the Montana side, where the earth breaks up into deep red canyons striped like the muscle of a butchered ox. The memory of deep black clefts still lingered as I neared the tents and fire pits of our camp—the canyons seen from on high, a pattern of shadowed veins flowing along the landscape, the veins pulsing fast under my skin.

I pulled Silkie in beside my own small tent and watched the party of men arrive. There was a dozen fellas maybe, and a few pack mules. They came along briskly at a trot. Their horses was all sweat-darkened from a long ride, but looked to be in fine fettle, so I concluded that they must be men of experience and quality, for a quality man always keeps his horse fit and happy.

Molly b'Damn came out of her tent and stood beside me. We watched the new arrivals in silence. Molly had recently come from Ireland, determined to make her fortune on her back, and she was well on her way. She could cuss near as good as I could, and besides her forceful tongue, her golden hair and startling black brows made her a great favorite with the boys.

She said in her bright, funny accent, "Tis Gen'ral Sharr'dan. They've sent him up to find some way to fight the Indians."

The Sioux was a powerful nuisance in that locale (as every-where), though I can't say I judge them harshly for being a menace and a terror. Settlements sprouted off the rail lines like tendrils from a vine, and by then the Indians must have felt desperate and rather scared by the rapid rising of our tide.

I watched the troop ride past. The one in the lead was General Sheridan himself, I surmised—for though he wasn't decked out in military finery, he carried an air of command about him that even I (a young woman and a whore besides) recognized at once. Below the wide brim of his hat, the general's eyes seemed hard and far-seeing, and his mouth, though mostly obscured by a drooping dark mustache, still gave the impression of being pressed in long and careful thought.

Just behind him rode a personage who swept every thought of Sheridan clean away, the moment I laid eyes on him. Never before had I seen a man so perfectly beautiful. His was a carefully carved, masculine beauty made of strength, utility and an easy, self-assured competence—a special kind of loveliness only men may boast of. His mustache was alike to the General's, downturned and thick, but slicker and impeccably kept. His face was light, soft-looking, with the unchapped skin of a man who seldom removed his hat. The lines around his eyes spoke of many long years spent riding among wilderness; he was at least twice my age. And his hair…! It was marvelous, long and flowing as a woman's, a red as deep as canyon stone, tumbling with waves. He wore a fringed buckskin coat with a fleece collar, with Indian beads at the sleeves. The coat hung open, welcoming in the crisp mountain air.

He cast no glance to the side as he rode, took no notice of Molly or me. He was fixed on the Big Horn Mountains ahead, like a sailor attuned to his lodestar. And I believe it was that fixity, that firmness of place, that drew me so powerfully towards him. The mountains still sang in my blood; my body still ached from a long day's joyful ride. And that man, with his buckskin coat thrown open and his hair falling across his shoulder, was of the mountains—of the hills. He was a thing of the lonely, endless sky. My sky.

———

I DIDN'T WORK that night. I couldn't be convinced to; I was far too curious about Sheridan's presence in the camp, and the long-haired man who rode with him. I saw to Silkie, tethering her with the other horses in a meadow behind the camp. Then I took my tin cup and went walking through the rows of tents, searching for any sign of the newcomers.

I found them—or the red-haired one, at least—outside Boss's Place. Boss was a little Chinese fella who hardly stood as tall as my armpit, but he strode about the camp as if he owned the place, which was how he got his name. He had come out to work on the rails, laying ties with the other Chinese laborers, but soon figured he could make more money selling liquor to the camp workers. Selling liquor was far easier work than driving ties. Boss wore a long Manchu cue a-hanging down his back. He had a mustache wispy as a boy's, which framed a perpetual scowl. But though he glowered fiercely, I still got the impression that Boss was always happy to see me coming. And why wouldn't he be? I drank at least as much as the men did.

Boss's tent was spacious, with a makeshift bar inside made of planks pulled from the bed of a disused wagon. Fellas had already crowded around the bar, ordering up their drinks, and Boss's Place was as busy that evening as usual. The long-haired man from Sheridan's company had just settled into a game of faro in a circle of lantern light right outside the tent's entrance. I walked past him, hardly glancing his way like he wasn't anything a-tall. I headed straight for the bar, where a gaggle of my admirers set on stools and crates, talking over the day's business and enjoying their liquor as only men in a tent camp can do.

Behind the bar, Boss busied himself with a rag, doing his best to clean up his collection of cracked and mismatched glasses. He said, "You come for whiskey, Miss Jane?"

"When have I ever failed to come for whiskey? Fill my cup, good old Boss."

I put my coins down on the wagon planks, and Boss poured till the cup was brimful.

I said, "Who's that fella come in with General Sheridan? The one set outside right now, playing a hand of faro?"

Boss didn't know. "Nobody tell me nothing," he said, scowling as ever. "Nobody ever tell Chinese nothing. Think we are stupid, but I got all the liquor in this camp, so who's stupid now?"

The men at the bar laughed in appreciation of Boss's wit. One said to me, "That fella in the buckskin coat is Wild Bill Hickok. Ain't you never seen him before, Calam?"

I said I certainly had not, which was the truth.

Hickock was a Jayhawker in the war, the man told me, and a famed scout besides. He said, "That must be why Wild Bill has come over with Sheridan. Word has it he's been making his way as an Indian fighter since the war ended, and he ain't about to do soldiering no more. Not the kind of soldiering he saw Back East, anyways."

Another man along the bar, a few crates down from the first, piped up with his own opinion. "Bill Hickok ain't no Indian fighter. Bill Hickok is nothing but a yahoo."

"Don't let him hear you say that," advised another.

The sour man waved his hand like brushing away flies. "A gambler who's over-fond of getting in shoot-outs. That's all there is to Hickok. Like half the trash washes up in a railroad camp. Begging your pardon, Calam, for you are surely an exception."

The men all had a laugh at that, and I sipped my whiskey to hide my frown.

Another fella said, "Hickock is respectable enough. He's been a sheriff in Kansas."

"Sheriffs ain't respectable automatically," said the sour man. "If you think so, Jim, then I'd say you ain't met too many sheriffs."

Around that time, the talk at Boss's bar devolved into an argument over the merits of the badge, so I excused myself to the tent's exterior, where a small crowd had assembled to watch the faro game—or perhaps they had gathered merely to gaze on Wild Bill Hickok, whose reputation (whatever it may be) had surely preceded him. My curiosity was thoroughly piqued, as well as my pulse quickened. I edged into the crowd and found a place across from where Bill sat gazing calmly at his cards.

I had walked in on the heckling that is customary when men gather for a game. The boys paid me little heed, being focused on each other—on Hickok especially, whose unexpected appearance had ignited a sort of festival air. One of them, a rail laborer who I never spotted without a cigarette in his mouth, blew a stream of smoke and shifted the cards in his hand. Then he said, "Wild Bill, that long purty hair of yours is apt to incite the Indians."

"That is the idea," Bill answered, cool and unprovoked. His voice was smooth and low, like whiskey on the tongue.

"Ain't you concerned that your scalp might prove too tempting a target for a Red to resist?"

"Any Indian is welcome to try me." Bill never looked up from his hand.

One of the men watching the game reached towards Bill's hair as if he wanted to touch it but didn't dare. I couldn't blame him. Those marvelous auburn locks, spilling from beneath Wild Bill's hat like the cascades of a waterfall. The man said, addressing the crowd at large, "They call him Wild Bill, Devoid of Vanity."

"I am devoid of vanity." Bill tossed a few chips in to bid.

Most of the men hooted at his words, and I must confess I joined in their laughter. His coat may have been buckskin like any frontier rough, but everything about him—from the slickness of his mustache to the shine of the beads that trimmed his sleeves— spoke of a certain dandiness that could only come from vanity. I didn't blame him, though. I had always longed to be pretty, and if I'd been blessed with the fine good looks of Molly b'Damn or Backwards Kate or Wild Bill himself, I would have been vain as a peacock, and strutted and preened in a shameless display of pride. If the Lord gives you any gifts, you ought to take pleasure in them, and make the most of them, too. That's what I always say. Humility might get you into Heaven—I cannot rightly say—but humility makes for a dull, small life whilst you're stuck in the mortal realm.

I guess Wild Bill must have heard my laugh. I'm a big girl; always have been tall as a man, so many folks is surprised by my laugh, which is high and sweet. When I'm laughing (which is a rare thing nowadays) I sound like the giggliest little handful who ever bounced on a knee at the hurdy-gurdies. Bill looked up and caught me just as I raised the tin cup to my lips.

He caught me, and he held me with his eyes. Picked me out of all that crowd and saw me, as no one else saw me that night, as no one saw me ever. There was a quiet thoughtfulness in his gaze, which I appreciated as a permanent feature, not something he affected for me, not something I brought out in him. What could I bring out of any man, except the money from his pocket? But the *look* to him. The sadness in his gaze. And then, as I swallowed my whiskey and felt the smile die slowly on my unrefined face, Bill dipped a very gentle nod, lifting the brim of his hat with one long, graceful finger.

Somebody in the crowd said, by way of introduction, "That's Calamity Jane, the loudest and cussin'est wench in the Big Horns."

And I thought, but couldn't make myself say, *No sir, my name is Martha Canary, and I am pleased to make your acquaintance.* Instead of speaking, I downed the remainder of my whiskey in one long gulp and Bill returned to his cards. But that was the moment—just then, as his finger touched the edge of his hat—that his poisoned tooth found my heart.

WELL, I hardly think it suitable to recount the days that followed, for my behavior was undignified. I knew it then, and felt vaguely embarrassed by my hunger, my insatiable impulses—but I couldn't stop myself. I reasoned (and still half-believe now) that I was never a woman of propriety or grace in the first place, so putting on airs of dignity did me no service whatsoever. It was better to be myself, in all my miserable glory, than to put on a show I couldn't maintain for long.

I knew it was a shame, the way I followed Bill Hickok around that camp, hoping for some cast-off scrap of acknowledgment like a dog sniffing for crumbs below a table. It was a shame, but I didn't care. I got to know the men who circled Bill—his familiars —and they professed a certain bemused fondness for me, accepting my presence when they came to understand that I wouldn't leave them be. Bill remained maddeningly beyond my reach. A fancier lady might have called him aloof or untouchable. I had no such words, back then. I couldn't do a thing but stare. I followed his every step with my eyes, desperate, besotted, grinning like a fool—just the way a baby stares after its mother. I felt the least motion of his body—his hand plucking at the faro cards, his heel striking the ground in a smooth stride—snapping and humming down the fine lines of my own secret nerves. He was in me, deep under my skin. I couldn't get him out, and I didn't want to try.

Wild Bill might have kicked dirt at me—told me to get lost. He had no use for me, lurking as I did in the periphery of his days, haunting his every waking hour. But for reasons I still can't explain, he put up with me, showing the same kind and patient toleration that a much older brother gives a kid sister who can't be dissuaded from tagging along.

I made myself part of his retinue, and because I could walk like a man despite my long skirts and talk like a man and swear even better, I was accounted a natural part of Bill's inner circle. Never mind that he hadn't known me a-tall before he came to the Big Horns. Never mind that he hardly spoke more than two words to me at any given time. None of that mattered a lick, far as I was concerned. All that mattered was whether I could drift into Wild Bill's proximity a dozen times a day and bask for a moment in the sun of his beauty.

I couldn't have contained that longing for Bill, even if I'd been inclined to try. The dreadful, aching want was as powerful as the need that drove paying men to my bed. But it was made from something finer, something silvery and delicate—something holy. My adoration held no base desire—a simple itch in want of scratching. Mine was the yearning of like towards like. It was the same force that calls the rain down from the sky to soak the bare, thirsty ground—the same unseen magic that pulls one raindrop toward another as they race down a pane of glass. I loved Bill on first sight because he was the West, and the West was already deep inside my bones. And in those days, I was convinced—I am still convinced, when I'm quiet long enough to be honest with myself —that neither Bill nor I would ever be complete till we lay in each other's arms, till the broken parts of our spirits was at last made whole.

The trouble, of course, was that Wild Bill wanted nothing to do with me. I hung about, his useless shadow, while he conferred with General Sheridan in the big central tent—while they planned a series of scouting missions into the hills and the high green valleys, where the Sioux was rumored to hole up with their war bands. I contributed nothing to those meetings, as you may well surmise, and the general often paused in his plotting to cast a long, slow, narrow-eyed stare in my direction. In those moments, a thick sense of waiting fell inside the tent, as if Sheridan expected Bill to explain himself—explain me. But Bill never said a word about my presence at his side. Nor did he glance my way. I could have been a spaniel, curled on a cushion and gnawing on a bone, for all the notice Wild Bill took. I could have been a gnat whirling in desperate circles around his head.

All the days of Bill's presence in that rail camp, I never worked once. How could I have done it? In five years of giving men what they wanted, I had never balked at the task—it was only a job to be done. My work was no more onerous and no more escapable than the camp boys', who laid the railroad ties out across the land. But suddenly my bed had become the scene of something sacred, and all at once I found it wouldn't do for any man to join me there but Bill Hickock. I felt a deep, sharp loss just contemplating the possibility of inviting a paying customer to my small tent—for though I had entertained countless men, now I knew I had never laid down with love in my heart. I wanted to know how it was different—to take a man to bed for affinity, for love—not for money. And there was one man in all the world who might give me what I lacked—what I lacked, and what I wanted more desperately than the desert wants the flood.

On the fourth or fifth day, when I was dazed and aching from the mere sight of Bill (always walking away from me, tall and proud, the fringe on his buckskin coat swinging) I dragged myself back to my tent in an attempt to clear my head. I saw Silkie's fine tooled saddle there, and guilt struck me, for I hadn't taken her out riding in days. I knew she must feel restless and abandoned.

Molly b'Damn was setting outside her tent on a fold-up stool, having recently wakened after a long night of work. She sipped from a tin cup. I could smell her coffee, earthy and sharp. "You haven' been taking in callers, Jane," Molly said.

Wordless in my misery—pathetic with hope—I shook my head.

"Get your cup," she said, and raised a bottle of good whiskey from the grass at her feet. She had bought that bottle from Boss; it would be her prize possession till she drained it dry. I guessed she had added a splash or two to her morning coffee.

I got my cup and held it out to her. Molly didn't quite fill it halfway.

"Jane," said she, "ye must get back to work."

I made no answer. I couldn't find any reason to offer for my reluctance—no reason Molly wouldn't laugh over. I didn't want my friend to think me a fool—to know me for the fool I was.

She said, "Wild Bill Hickok is too fancy and fine a man for the likes of you. Jane, girl, you know gents of his sort don' fall in love with slammers."

I hung my head then. Molly had seen right through me, though as I stood beside her tent thinking it over, I supposed every damn person in the camp could see what was in my head and my heart. Even Bill. Knowing that Bill must think me pathetic—and a fool into the bargain—my heart felt crushed and shattered.

Molly b'Damn was sweet, though, for she didn't point out what was obvious to me and to everyone else: a man of Bill's caliber might indeed fall in love with a whore, if she was pretty and charming enough. Molly was the type of whore who could hope to land a decent man and step up from her low predicament into a world of hope and decency and love. Backwards Kate could have done it, too, or Em the Wrangler—even Smooth Bore. But not Calamity Jane. Calam, who looked like a busted hay bale on a good day. What did I have to offer any man that he couldn't find elsewhere—and in a much finer package, to boot? And a man as beautiful as Bill Hickok... well.

"I'm out of money," I said. "Can't even buy my own liquor."

"Nothing for it, then, but to get back to work. This bottle cost me dear; I won' give you another cupful. You know I like you plenty, Jane, but it's not as if you're sick or dying."

"If I don't work, that's more men for you."

"Aye, that's so," Molly said. "But if we ladies don' look out for each other, who will?"

She stood then, slowly and carefully, as if she was an old, old woman, though I think she was only stalling, so she wouldn't have to say the words she knew I needed to hear. But finally, she came to me and laid a hand upon my shoulder.

"Wild Bill will never love you," Molly said gently. "It's best to forget him now, while you still can, and move along with your life."

At that moment there was an awful whooping and hollering from up in the hills nearby. Molly and I both froze in fear, thinking—as all people thought in that place, at that time—that it must be party of Sioux preparing to fall upon us with their rifles and axes, their belts hung with white men's scalps. But then we detected words among the cries. We relaxed some; Molly even smiled at me. The words came as a welcome gift then. But now, I look back and wonder how my life would have been different— mine and Bill's—if neither of us had ever heard those words a-tall.

"Gold," someone shouted from up in the hills. His voice rang out over gully and meadow, rousing the whole camp. "By God, by jingo, by the Devil, it's gold! Do you hear?"

DESPITE MOLLY'S SOUND ADVICE, I still couldn't bring myself to go back to work. Not just yet. I did go riding on Silkie that day, the two of us alone under a wide indifferent sky, but riding had lost some of its savor. Silkie was cantankerous, bucking and crow-hopping as if to chastise me for my long absence. I took her rebuke without delivering any whacks in return. I figured it was my due, and a bad ride was the least of what I deserved for all my foolish ways.

Even the land I had so loved—the wide sweeping vistas in which I had reveled just days before—brought little comfort to my heart, and no relief from the thoughts that tormented me. I no longer felt myself a part of the land. For certain, my sins was no longer absolved by God's distance or the vastness of His creation. I was a small and wretched thing, and the farther I rode from the camp, the wors't my heart ached, for I sensed already the discovery of gold would bring irreversible changes to my life, and more darkness than I could bear. Hadn't that always been the way, ever since Pa made up his mind to set out from Missouri for Montana's empty promise? There I was, in that very same Montana. Gold hadn't entered my head in all the time I'd spent among the camps—yet now, I'd never be able to escape it. And the promise of gold would pull Wild Bill away from me—I was sure of it already—snatch him right out of my life forever, with no chance to learn whether he could love me (though the chance was ghostly-slim.)

I guess grim thoughts of my pa and the harrowing start to my life's adventure had riled me up some. I soon wearied of the open landscape and rode back to camp as fast as my horse could take the rocky trail. I made up my mind to find Wild Bill and speak to him face to face—force him to see me, as he had done that first day outside Boss's tent. Force him to confront the unbridled longing of my heart. When I regained the camp, I trotted straight through the place, perched high above the fracas on my big black mare. Men skittered around me, packing up their things, making ready to abandon the rail line and go charging up the untamed hills in pursuit of their fortunes. I kicked Silkie right through the ant's-nest of our camp till I found the tents Bill and his cronies called home. And there was Wild Bill, leaning on a tent pole while he chatted with one of his friends, lounging at his ease in the sunshine while the camp worked itself into a frenzy all around him.

He looked up as I damn near trampled his tent, but when he saw it was only Calam in the saddle, his expression of surprise faded, replaced by an air of cool toleration.

I swung down to earth and marched straight up to him. My heart pounded at being so near to Wild Bill. My heart always did so, when I found myself close enough to smell the soft, warm leather of his coat. I hoped the thrill didn't show on my face.

"You and I must have words," I said. I never knew how my voice remained so steady, so firm.

Bill's eyes met mine—locked with mine, and that look held me, so I couldn't break away. Then he shrugged. Not as if to put me off—just a casual acceptance of my demand. Without a word from Bill, his assortment of hangers-on vanished. I guess his friends all sensed there was something raw in me, and didn't want to watch me shame myself even further. Or perhaps—more likely—they didn't want to witness Bill's inevitable humiliation. There's a kind of code among men, a silent understanding that they will turn their backs when one of their own is ensnared by a female embarrassment like Calamity Jane. Bill's friends slunk off into the bustle of the camp, disappearing as completely as if they'd been blowed away by a cyclone.

When we stood alone, more or less (alone as a body can be in a busy railroad camp) I asked Bill the question I had come to pose. I let it thunder right out of me before I could think to hold it back, before I could be any wiser.

"Bill," I said, "why is it you never looked twice at me? I know I ain't much to look at, but I am good-hearted and at least I can ride. Don't that count for a thing with you?"

His body gave an involuntary jerk—just a small one, so subtle maybe no one but me would have noticed, for no one stared at Wild Bill like I did, no one had memorized his every movement and habit. His initial expression was one of shock so complete that for a moment I thought he'd been stung by a wasp or a pellet. I'd never seen his eyes open so wide—and oh, they were lovely eyes, a hazel-gray-green deep as river water. For a second, I saw humor flash across his long, refined features. I feared he might laugh at my notion. But then he returned to his typical calm, to the self-possessed, sad-eyed, slow contemplation that marked him. He stroked his mustache slowly, watching my face very carefully while he gathered his words.

Finally he said, "Calamity, I'll tell you why I never looked twice at you. It's because every time I saw you from the corner of my eye, you had that damn cup in your hand. You'll do yourself in with drink if you don't get your urges under control."

"I will not," I said in defiance. After all, I hadn't had a drink all day, since Molly had cut me off. I would have had more to drink by then, if I'd had a penny to pay Boss with, but that seemed neither here nor there.

Bill said, "You're young yet—and too young to look so damn rough. You ought to turn yourself around now, while there's still time."

"What a fine thing to say to a lady," I fired back.

"You ain't any kind of lady," said Bill, though not without a certain gentleness, "and there's no reason for either of us to pretend otherwise. Listen, Calam: whatever kind of woman I end up with, she won't be bedeviled by any vice. I could never love a woman of that sort. I just ain't that kind of man."

I looked at him squarely then, and set my jaw, and said, "You're surely bedeviled by vice yourself, Bill Hickok. Some vice or other —men always are bedeviled. And I've known far more men than you have, I bet, so I know what I'm talking about."

He stroked his mustache again and said, "Yes mam, reckon you have had the acquaintance of a powerful lot of men. And you so very young." He didn't say it with cruel amusement, to mock me. Nor did he sound disgusted. I couldn't decide whether his words held pity or a grim sort of respect. Bill said, "I don't deny what you say. Lord knows I do have my share of vices. But I do my level best to overcome them, Calam. You ought to do the same. Anyway," he added, straightening from the tent pole, abrupt and business-like, "I can't afford to fall in love with you. I'm leaving with Sheridan in two days."

I felt as if the world had fallen right out from under me. Dropped away into a terrible yawning blackness that had no bottom and no sides—that had nothing but the sick sensation of plunging downward forever. "Two days?" I nearly shrieked those words him.

"Yes mam. We was sent up here to this camp on rumor of gold, and, well… the rumors have been confirmed, as you surely heard this morning. Sheridan's company is going up into the hills to protect whichever men are brave enough to stake out a claim and begin mining."

"That's crazy," I said. "There's Sioux all over in the hills. They'll kill any whites who try it."

Bill pulled his gun from its holster. It gleamed like an autumn star. He said, "I'm to scout for Sheridan and keep an eye on the Sioux. There's no one better at fighting Indians than me. I'll clear out whatever Sioux still remain, and that'll be that. Reckon you and I won't see each other again."

I swallowed a hard, rasping dryness in my throat. Bill had sounded downright relieved at the prospect.

He strode off a few paces, then paused, turning back to look at me. He was kind enough then to give me a smile. It was small— half embarrassed—but it was the only thing Bill had ever given me, and I cherished it as much as I would have cherished a kiss.

"I wish you well, Calam," he said softly. "You're a sharp girl, for all your vices. You can go far in life, if you only will it. I do truly believe that, mam."

Then he touched his hat gently, just as he'd done the first time I seen him, with a graceful lift of his finger, with the barest and coolest of nods. And after that, he was walking away from me like he always did, all buckskin and swinging fringe, his auburn hair flowing. Walking away—taking every scrap of my new-found world with him.

A BREAST OF ALABASTER PURITY

WHAT CAN A WOMAN DO, ONCE SHE'S FALLEN IN LOVE? NOTHING but suffer with the pain of it. Nothing but give in.

I've met plenty of folks who would think the notion absurd: that a woman like me should ever lose her heart. Love is something reserved for pretty women—the fine ones, upright and respectable girls. Most folks find it a kind of blasphemy, I think, to picture a girl like me in the crystal palace of love. As if, like a bull in a china shop, a haystack of a woman might knock it all down, break all the prisms and shatter the rainbows and spoil love for everyone who comes along after. Plenty of times, I thought the same about myself, and tried to shut off the terrible deep longing I felt for Wild Bill. But I could as soon stop my poor heart from beating as stop myself from yearning for his touch.

We was parted, Bill and I, for more than a year. And while he passed through my every waking thought—every heavy, haunted dream—there was never a moment when I was fool enough to imagine he spared a thought for me. In moments when I was honest with myself—as honest as I could bear to be—I knew Bill was relieved to be rid of me, for what kind of man wants a sad, lost scrap of humanity dogging his every step? What good and worthwhile fella could ever find this type of girl worthy—or even respectable? I was not only a whore renowned for my cussing, but I was an ugly whore, too.

I worked hard, all that lonesome year—harder than I ever had before, moving from one camp to the next. I lived in rail camps and miners' camps, soldiers' squadrons, anywhere else I could light for a week or two. I wasn't choosy about location, as long as the camp was *out there*, away from towns and road ranches. *Out there* was the only place I felt I could survive—in the gray-green, wide-openness of the world—for if I couldn't be with Wild Bill, at least I could spend my days riding free beneath the sky. And there, with only the sun and the hot hills to judge me for a fool, I could give myself over to the giddiness of love and sing to myself, and let the stars come out in my eyes, and dream all my hopeless, wretched dreams. Sometimes I allowed my starry eyes to fill up with tears, in mute awe of the great force inside me—the unending, quiet torment of rapture. I worked all that long, dry, slow-burning year. I didn't want a single one of the men I took into my bed. But I needed their money, and now that I had a name—now that all the West knew me on sight as Calamity Jane—there wasn't no other sort of work I could find, however much I yearned to remake myself as a respectable and worthy lady, the kind of lady who might hope to win Wild Bill's heart.

Now that was an odd year in the West, one of the strangest I ever witnessed. Perhaps it was only the disordered state of my heart, reflected from within me and casting its broken shadow over the world, so that I saw things all askew, and noted misery and uncertainty everywhere I looked. But I think not. Even today, I believe it was simply the state of the world, for I also observed a great and optimistic restlessness, a gathering of hope. I think I saw the world honest and true that year—the year I turned nineteen. Every man and woman in the Hills—and on the prairie to the east, in the mountains to the west—seemed as jumbled-up and hopeless as I was.

You see, George Armstrong Custer was up in the Black Hills that strange, wild year, tangling with the Sioux. He had come to the area almost two years prior, and though I never saw him with my own eyes, I felt I would recognize Custer on sight if he came swaggering into a saloon while I was buying up a new ration of whiskey, or if chance took him through one of the railroad camps. Even if he lacked his fabled contingent of men, I felt certain I would know him, for his legend had so preceded him that he already seemed familiar, a force imbuing the whole West with his mighty presence.

Custer had first come to Dakota Territory back in '73, with a charge to stave off the Sioux so the men who plotted the railroads could take stock of the terrain and plan the course of the next long, reaching arm of track. He had done such a fine job of fighting the Sioux that the folks in charge became mighty impressed with him, and sent him up into the Hills to look for gold, just as they would later do with General Sheridan and my Bill. But Custer's expedition had struck a richer vein than Sheridan's in the Big Horns of Montana.

News of Custer's gold had spurred a right stampede into the Black Hills—packs of eager men, all raring for a chance to fill their pockets with gold nuggets and make themselves rich as devils forever. The sleepy little town of Deadwood boomed with a suddenness we could hear all across the West. The rattle of it shook our bones and echoed in our heads. Before the gold, Deadwood had been nothing but a faltering stage-stop, the last half-civilized place before the earth turned to white cliffs and painted slopes and Indians with ill intent hiding in the holes of shadows, out there in the treacherous Hills. Now Deadwood was as grand as a metropolis—or what passed for a metropolis in a sea of prairie grass, out where the rail lines tapered off to nothing.

I hadn't yet been to Deadwood. I saw no reason to go, for till the coming of Custer and the wild hope of his gold, Deadwood was a place better ignored, if not conscientiously avoided.

However, I did have occasion to ride back to Fort Laramie in May of '75. I had need of a few goods which I could only obtain from the trading post there, and besides, I'd grown tired of the dull routine of railroad camps—the long, lonely days when the air filled with the pounding of mauls against spikes, distant but oppressive in their repetition—a flat metallic clanging that went on and on. And each night in the rail camps, when darkness fell, my soul was overtaken by another rhythm, another pounding, just as wearying and fretful. So I was pleased to find an excuse to ride alone to Fort Laramie. I longed for the quiet of the trail, just me and my horse in the long grass, with the soothing quiet of stars at night and no one in my bed roll but me. I had no more fear of Red Nancy. If she still haunted Fort Laramie, she wasn't like to tangle with me now. Anyway, I had my pistol with the pearl star in its handle. If Nancy came for me, I'd only have to draw the gun to make her run screaming in fright.

On the day I rode into Fort Laramie, I wore my usual riding get-up: trousers in lieu of a dress, and a boiled shirt I had won off one of the other camp girls in a game of faro. (She had been given the shirt as a token of great affection from a railroad boy, a poor sod who thought himself sore in love with the girl. She, of course, had no use for the thing. Still, it was a fine prize for me, and fit me as if it had been made to order.) I had a dandy pair of buckskin chaps, too, which I found in an abandoned cabin somewhere out in Montana on one of my lonesome rides. I adorned my boots with two mismatched spurs—which I wore purely for looks. Silkie was a spirited horse, but not bad-tempered; I'd had no cause to give her anything worse than a hard word or a smack from my open palm. But what I liked best about my riding outfit wasn't the silver spurs, but a big, grand sombrero I'd bought at a trading post when I was eighteen. It put me in mind of the sombrero I had worn while driving Brad-dick's mules. Men and women alike thought it a great laugh to see me crown myself with that sombrero. And even with my boiled shirt and heavy chaps, the hat kept me cool on hot, sunny days.

As I neared the fort outside town, I noticed a great encampment stretching along the prairie to the west, a collection of tents aligned in neat rows. Such perfect order spoke of military precision. I was a young girl, but I'd seen enough of camps by then to identify the various sorts at a glance. This was most certainly an Army camp, evidenced by its fanatical tidiness and a conspicuous lack of whoop-up. I went about my business at the trading post, then asked the gentleman at the counter why the Army had come. I had some notion of attaching myself to a new camp, for the one I'd traveled with most recently was devoid of fun. Everything I valued was trussed up in my saddle bags, so I could strike out with a new band of boys as soon as a good opportunity came along.

"That camp," the man said, "is a mighty prestigious one, Miss Jane. It's led by Lieutenant Colonel Dodge and its mission is, as they say, scientific."

That caught my interest straight away. I had never been on a scientific expedition before. "Where they headed?"

"Up into the Black Hills," the gentleman said, "to see if they can confirm or deny once and for all Custer's reports of gold... before the fever for gold overtakes every man in these parts, and burns away what little is left of good sense."

"General Custer wouldn't make up stories," I said loyally. Everyone was loyal to Custer. In those days, he loomed as large as God Himself.

The gentleman held up his hands, a half-pleading gesture. "I never said Custer would do such a thing, Miss. Never said it. But Back East, the trains are filled near to bursting with men waiting to rush up into the Hills and stake a claim. It would be a disaster— a plum disaster—if there wasn't enough gold to go around. Fellows might turn to fighting. We might even have another war over it. So you see, a second opinion is required. Dodge will have a look for himself, then send word back to Washington, and if the

Hill streams are indeed running with gold, as everyone seems to believe, then the rush will be on, and we'll have nothing to fear. Though if the streams were running with gold, I do believe some of it would have washed down to Fort Laramie by now. Not that I've got a bad word to say against Custer, you understand."

A scientific expedition sounded like a leisurely change from the railroad camps. At least I wouldn't be forced to listen to the endless clanging of spikes into the earth. I said, "I got half a mind to take up with that expedition."

The man at the counter paled a little. His eyes shifted this way and that, as if he was reluctant to speak. "Miss Jane," he finally said, "from what I hear, Colonel Dodge is a mighty strict man. He doesn't mean to let any women follow this camp."

"Maybe he needs a guide." It was an absurd suggestion. I had no experience guiding. I could ride better than most men, to be sure, but I knew nothing of the Black Hills, and sure as you're born, I knew nothing about navigating through Indian territory. But the words came out of my mouth all the same. Something about Dodge's scientific expedition had got beneath my skin. It was calling to me. Maybe it was only the promise of a change of routine, but still to this day, I believe I was feeling fate's pull—though I didn't recognize the touch of its hand.

"Dodge has a guide already," the man said briskly. "Wild Bill Hickok has signed on to scout him through the Hills."

I don't know how long I stood and stared at that man, with one hand on the bundle of goods I'd paid for and my eyes stunned and glassy under the brim of my sombrero. If he said anything more to me, I never heard it. All I could hear was a roaring in my ears, as of water plunging over a fall, and all I could feel was that persistent ache in my heart, but it had yawned wider all-of-a-sudden, doubling with the force of my absurd, grasping, desperate hope.

I can't tell you how long I stood and gazed like a cow about to be slaughtered. However long it was, I surely disconcerted the man behind the counter terribly. But after a time, an idea sparked in my head. That spark lit a thin little flicker of a flame. I turned around and marched out of the trading post with my bundle under my arm—but without, I'm afraid, a thank-you-sir or a good-afternoon. I tied the bundle up on Silkie's saddle, then hurried across to the camp as fast as I could go, before my nerve could fail.

I strode right down the rows of tents as if I knew where I was going—and truth to tell, I did. One camp is mostly like all the others, though the soldiering kind has more order and routine. Even if his expedition was scientifical in nature, Colonel Dodge was a soldiering type, and besides, now I knew that the Colonel had no use for women trailing after his boys. I reasoned I had his personality pegged before I even reached the center of the camp. And as I neared its center, there I saw what could only have been the Colonel's tent—perfectly white, spotless, with its sides drawn taut as a drum between guy-lines that was all precisely of the same length.

My mind was made up. I would present myself to Dodge and talk my way into the camp—not as a follower, but as a junior scout of sorts, and one who would be more useful than most other scouts. I knew how to wash laundry like no one else God ever made—and when my back was against the wall, I could cook stew and bread that a body could choke down without too much suffering. I'd done it countless times on the lonesome trail.

I never got a chance to speak to the Colonel directly. The sight of a woman in chaps and sombrero raised a stir among the infantry tents; word traveled fast along the rows. Boys came out to stand in the mouths of their tents, wearing trousers and boots but nothing else, arms folded over their thin white chests as they watched me pass. They turned aside to laugh with their friends, or stood up from the shade where they lounged about playing cards, and shouted at me and whistled in an ironical manner. I didn't mind their humor, for I knew from long experience that if you laugh along with those who mock you, they soon enough become your friends.

Well, the hubbub I raised drew the alert of the camp's topmost men. I crossed an open patch—a parade ground of sorts, to judge by the trampled grass—and a thin little fella come out to meet me, scuttling from the door of the colonel's tent, tugging on his waistcoat in a great show of fluster. His hair was waxed into an elegant wave that wouldn't last long on the trail, I knew—and anyway, it had begun to go thin up top. But he did have the most glorious mustache I ever seen, so thick it hung right down over his mouth, so long on the ends it almost brushed the winking buttons of his coat. *God almighty*, I thought, sizing him up, *he must have been growing that mustache since the day he was born.*

He marched directly up to me and said, "Mam, I fear this camp is no place for a lady."

Some of the boys who stood closest to the edge of the parade ground heard his words, and hooted with laughter, for any fool could see I was no lady. The chaps and spurs should have been a give-away, even to a man who wasn't yet acquainted with the breadth of my infamy.

I said, "Sir, I ain't coming to you as a lady, but as a soldier of sorts. You see, I live here at Fort Laramie and I heard of Lieutenant Colonel Dodge's grand mission, and I thought to attach myself with my useful talents, since I am a great admirer of all things scientifical."

Even through the dense screen of his mustache, I could see his lips twitch, as if he was holding back an undignified laugh.

Before he could decline, I spoke up again. "I'm real handy at washing and mending clothes, sir, like you wouldn't believe. I can cook, too."

"We have a cook already," the man said calmly.

Thank merciful Heaven was all I could think. But I kept my relief to myself. I said, "But it's a hard ride up into the Hills, and your men will be better served if they don't have to patch up their own clothes or do their own washing. Besides mending and washing, I can nurse the sick real good."

He sort of raised up one eyebrow at that, as if to tell me he doubted the extent of my nursing skills. Or maybe he only doubted whether a creature like me had the necessary kindness and patience to care for the ailing. He was wrong on that count. Though I never worked in any official capacity as a nurse or healer, plenty of times I had helped care for sick and injured men along the rail lines. Nursing had never been any part of my usual occupation; I simply took to it when it needed doing, for any time I witnessed pain or suffering, I couldn't help but suffer right along.

The man said, "Young lady, my name is Dr. Valentine T. McGillycuddy."

I burst out laughing at that. I couldn't help it. The man had such a fine-and-fancy name—and it was sore out of place here on the fringes of Fort Laramie. "Sorry," I said, and controlled myself with some effort. "Don't think anything of me, Doctor. I'm rough around the edges 'cause my pa was a brave soldier killed by the Indians when I was but twelve years old, and my dear ma was consumptive, and never could stop me from running wild and seeking out adventure, though she was a very fine and respectable woman, well loved by everyone who knew her. I'm quite sure she turns over in her grave on the regular, to see her only child running about in britches and a sombrero, but if I don't make my way with some kind of soldiering, you know what kind of iniquity I'll be forced to turn to—me being a girl, and all. You wouldn't cast me down on iniquity, would you, Doc?"

Dr. McGillycuddy didn't respond to that. He combed his mustache with his fingers, narrowing his small eyes. His air was thoughtful. Finally he asked my name, and I gave it as Margaret Bird, not wanting to leave him any trail to follow back to Calamity Jane.

"Margaret," he said, "your type of woman is sure to follow

along after the camp whether you're welcome or not. But I must tell you frankly: we are about to embark on a difficult and hazardous mission. This is no jaunt through a park."

"My whole life has been no jaunt through a park," I said, and that was the truth, at least.

He said, "I suppose you do know how to ride—or else why would you be dressed in this strange attire?"

"I can ride better than any of your men. You needn't worry about my safety; I'll keep up."

"That's exactly what I fear," he said.

"Doctor, won't you speak to the colonel on my behalf? I'd like his blessing to ride along, and I know I'll be useful—and not at all sinful. I won't bring any shame or disgrace to a single one of his men. I'll do his name proud—you'll tell him that, won't you?"

"Lieutenant Colonel Dodge will certainly not permit you to follow this expedition," Dr. McGillycuddy said.

I just grinned at him then, wide and saucy and unconcerned.

He said, "If you make any trouble—any kind at all, young lady —you'll be sent back to Fort Laramie alone. We will not be able to spare any men to accompany you. If you have a scrap of wisdom within you, you'll take the road of safety and remain here, where you belong."

———

THEY CALLED those rows of tents the barracks. I strode among them happy and smiling, for I knew by Dr. McGillycuddy's tacit surrender that I would soon be riding into the Black Hills. The doctor knew, I believe, that whatever Dodge would have preferred, there was no way to keep men from women, nor women from men. Not in the West, anyhow. Perhaps in the fancy halls and mansions of the East, people was content to mind custom and propriety. But here beyond the crumbling edge of civilization, the world moved to a different rhythm. Our lives and actions was dictated by times and seasons no high-minded colonel could change, no matter what he believed. The rhythm that moved us was deep and powerful, essential and true.

I would soon make my way back to the hitching post to retrieve Silkie, and buy up the remaining supplies I needed for a lengthy expedition in the wilderness. But first I wanted to find him—first I needed to quell the quiver in my belly, or fire it up stronger than ever before, and lay eyes on Wild Bill after that long year of aimless, endless ache.

I found him far across the camp. Past the parade ground—beyond the rows of barracks tents, where the gathering fringed out into open field and the river ran by, swift and quiet—Bill sat on the sun-warmed ground, leaning against a pannier. A few stuffed saddlebags lay nearby. He had crossed one ankle up over his knee, and his hat was pulled down low, shading his eyes and his thoughts. He didn't face the barracks, nor the high wooden walls of the fort beyond. All his contemplation was turned toward the river and the distant line of blue mountains slung low across the prairie.

I stood still for a moment, staring at him—took in the sight of him, while the stillness of awe damped down everything else inside me. For a year I had heard nothing of Wild Bill's movements—though to be sure, I had gleaned from some source or other that General Sheridan had returned from his mission in one piece. But there had been no reliable news of Bill Hickock. Scouts and guides was often killed up in the mountains and foothills, for the country was confusing to the eye—I ought to know, from my many lonely rides. The Sioux was treacherous everywhere, but especially in the Black Hills, where they could shelter in the numberless gulches, unseen by the keenest white man's eye. But there Bill sat before me, whole and alive, exactly as I remembered him. He kept himself slightly apart from the rest, as if he knew how fine and grand he was with his dark red hair spilling down to his shoulders and his foot bouncing above his knee in a slow, idle rhythm.

The better part of the camp lay behind me now; I stood alone with Bill. I wanted to call out to him—some greeting or praise— but I didn't know what to say or how to say it, and anyway, I was half afraid that if I opened my mouth a lot of nonsense would come spilling out, or maybe something downright damning. So I stood there, away back where Bill couldn't see, and I trembled with the relief of knowing that he lived. I did my best to breathe.

At length, the desire to look upon his face overcame me—as did the need to hear his voice. I found I could speak after all. I said, "Hullo, Bill. Do you remember me?"

Bill started up at once, as if I'd rattled like a snake in the brush. I guess it was a shocking thing, to hear a woman's voice in that camp, among so many men. And though my looks have never been much to speak of, at least I sounded like what I was: a girl of nineteen, fresh as could be expected (given my circumstances) and bubbling over with life.

When Bill saw it was me, his eyes went blank for a moment. His face twisted in an odd sort of way, so quick I almost didn't see. For one painful heartbeat, I thought he would shout at me, tell me to get away and leave him be. Then he gave me a small, polite smile, just like the one he left me with—and though I knew it was only courtesy, nothing more, still that smile warmed me and thrilled me, all the way down to the soles of my feet. The feeling burned inside me, tingling, spreading through my stomach like a shot of powerful liquor.

He climbed to his feet, dusting off his britches with this hands. "Calamity Jane," he said, slow and drawn out, as if he savored a real pleasant and unexpected treat. "By damn."

"No sir, you got me mistaken." I winked, bringing him in on my deception. "My name is Margaret Bird and I have lived at Fort Laramie all my life. I'm a real plum of a girl, too, despite my scandalous attire. Never did nothing sinful in my life, nor drank a drop of whiskey in all my tender years. Nor have I ever cussed, I assure you."

Bill's smile was sober, meditative. "That's awful good to hear." He spoke those words with a certain emphasis, and my stomach turned over as I wondered how in Hell I'd ever live up to that image now.

But I was determined to make good on the promise. Bill seemed so genuinely pleased to hear that I was a reformed character, I felt a steely resolve to be exactly the woman he expected me to be. I was determined to prove to him that I could change— become as much a lady as any other girl in the world. The grim circumstances of my origins might have yoked a certain shame around my neck, but there was no reason why I had to drag that weight forever. I knew it was so, as I stood there smiling back at him, shivering with the desire to touch him, to feel his arms around me. Burning with the need for him, strong enough to catch myself ablaze.

"Well, Miss Bird," Bill said casually, "what brings you to this camp, all dressed to ride? If you're a woman unblemished by sin, then it seems to me you got no business following an expedition out into the wilderness."

I laughed as I answered him. "You pegged me wrong, sir. Colonel Dodge would never put up with scandalous behavior in his men, so I hear. Any woman of questionable morals would find it unfruitful to follow this camp. No, I ain't following, but working alongside. I'll be doing the wash, and caring for sick and injured fellows as the need arises, and maybe a bit of cooking if real misfortune strikes and I'm left as the last resort."

"Well," said he, "that sounds mighty respectable. I must admit I'm glad to see you've turned a new leaf. But you know, there's plenty of men here who've signed on from other camps, done other tours. I'm afraid your disguise won't last long. You'll be recognized, sooner or later."

I turned my eyes down to the trampled, dusty ground. "That

don't matter. By the time I'm known, we'll be far out into the wilderness. It'll be too late to send me back. Anyhow, I meant what I said; I'm reformed now." (How I prayed right then for God to make my words true!) "I'm coming along to do respectable work, Bill—to prove I'm a worthy woman after all."

He turned away from me, gazing across the river. "Just who you trying to prove that to, I wonder?"

He knew who. But I wouldn't disgrace him or me by admitting it. Instead I threw my arms wide, as if I meant to embrace the whole world. And indeed, in that moment I felt as if I had enough love and happiness to share with everybody. I said, "Everyone, Bill! Everyone. Soon enough the name of Calamity Jane will have a whole new ring to it. You'll see."

Bill deigned to look back at me then, and the spark in his eye felt downright encouraging. "I do hope it will."

THE SCIENTIFIC EXPEDITION set out from Fort Laramie five days later. Mounted on Silkie, and with a tiny new canvas tent tied to my cantle, I rode alongside Dodge's men and joined in when they sang their marching songs. We left the flat grasslands behind, climbing up through foothills scented with pine, dappled in light and shadow. Never in all my life had my heart felt so light, my soul so perfectly free. I truly felt as if I was riding away from the person I had been, leaving her far behind in her torn, degraded rags. Throughout the morning, as we progressed to the north and east, my spirit was light, my conscience easy.

It wasn't till mid-day that my head began to pound. My mouth went fearsomely dry. Then I knew for certain I was heading into trouble.

You see, Short Pants, I hadn't spent those last days lingering in Laramie as innocently as Bill thought. I knew a long trek lay ahead, and knew I'd be entirely without liquor all that while (unless I could negotiate some off of Dodge's men, which seemed unlikely.) So I made sure to get good and skunked every night at the fort, indulging in the best and most expensive whiskey I could find. It was my last hurrah—or so I thought—so I spent my last few coins on liquor and savored every drop. But I had lived so long with whiskey in my gut—almost every day since I was a girl of thirteen—that I wasn't prepared for the come-down. I didn't know how dreadful the bottle-sickness can be.

As the sun climbed higher and the mid-day sun beat down on the piney hills, I began to get some inkling of what the day would hold. Dodge called lunch; the men pulled hard sausage and cheese and raisins from their saddle bags, stuffing their mouths full while they rode, but by that time I had long since stopped my singing. The thought of eating revolted me. I sweated, swaying on Silkie's back with my dull, blurry eyes fixed on her withers, trying to ignore the sounds of eating all around me. When afternoon glazed the hills in a low, red light, I found myself hunched over the horn of my saddle, trying to prevent a string of drool dropping from my lip. By that time, my stomach couldn't bear the thought of swallowing. My head pounded as harshly as the railroad mauls—a steady, driving pain that shot down the length of my spine with a metallic clang, rattling my guts, slowing my blood till I felt trapped inside my own skin.

I lost track of the hours. I no longer heard the men who inquired after my health or called up to Dr. McGillycuddy to bring me a remedy. (McGillycuddy declined, it seemed.) As the day plodded on, I was aware of nothing but Silkie's mane bobbing slow beneath me—the only thing I could stand to look at—and a ceaseless, merciless thumping inside, fit to cleave my skull in two.

When Dodge called a halt for the night, I couldn't seem to make my hands or my legs do their work. The other horses stopped, but Silkie walked on a few steps till a hand stretched into my downcast field of vision and took the rein, pulling my mare to stillness.

"God damn, Calamity. You're a proper mess."

Though Wild Bill's voice was low and secretive, still it cut like a hot knife into my brain. I almost cried out from the pain of it.

Bill had ridden beside me—for how long, I couldn't say. He called out gruffly to a few men nearby. "California Joe—Sam, get over here and help the lady down from her saddle. She's taken on heat sickness."

I lifted my head with an effort that almost made me sob, for the bones and muscles in my neck had grown stiff and tender, and my jaunty black sombrero seemed to weigh a thousand pounds. I looked across a line of men strung out in the gathering dusk. Some was already putting up their tents in the clearing where we found ourselves—a flat, open space at the top of a hill. Deep-blue twilight closed in around us. In dim light and violet shadow, I saw the doctor standing beside his horse, watching me with a skeptical air.

"She hasn't taken on heat sickness," McGillycuddy said knowingly. "Better not let the Lieutenant Colonel see."

Wild Bill shot back at him. "Better not say a damn thing about it." His note of warning was plain to be heard. "Sam, Joe, pull her down."

Men's hands grappled with me, hauling the weight of my body over till gravity caught me and dropped me from the saddle. The boys didn't let me hit the ground. They got me more or less upright—and then Wild Bill was there beside me, pulling my arm around his neck, bracing his shoulder to support me.

"Get my tent up," he said to one of the men. "Then bring the big canteen from my saddle. It's got good water in it—still cool."

Bill half-dragged me to the edge of the clearing. He murmured close beside my ear all the while, as close as my sombrero and his hat would allow. "Margaret Bird, you remember how to walk, don't you? One foot in front of the other."

Stands of pine and brush stood like a palisade around our growing camp. Bill and I found ourselves some way apart from the rest, screened by a thicket of some dense, ferny plant and a few scrubby willows. He lowered me to the ground, propping me up against the bole of a skinny pine. I groaned and hunched over myself, a-throb with pain in my head and neck. I hated myself in that moment, for the agony of my bottle-sickness was so great that I had scarcely been aware of Bill's body pressed so close against mine. Such was the extent and totality of my misery: it even had the power to erase Wild Bill from my senses.

Bill sat down beside me, watching in silence while I dry-heaved and drooled into the dirt. When the fit had more or less passed, I threw off my sombrero and leaned my head back against the pine trunk, panting and suffering with my eyes shut tight against the lowering sun.

"God damn, Calamity," he said again.

I made no answer.

"You're coming down off liquor, ain't you?"

"Yes sir." My voice grated in my throat and in my ears. I felt powerful ashamed, like I was sinking into a dark pit of stifling cold slime, and knew it was exactly what I deserved.

I opened one eye a crack, looking sideways at Bill. I could barely make him out in the shadows of the thicket, but I saw that he was shaking his head, vigorously side to side, as if he couldn't believe any human being could be as much of a shameful wreck as Calamity Jane.

"You're just a girl," he burst out suddenly, with a passion of tender feeling I had only hoped one day to hear. "How old are you, anyway?"

"Nineteen."

"You ought to be at home baking pies with your ma."

"My ma's dead," I said coldly. "My pa, too."

I don't know why I felt so hostile toward Bill right then. Maybe it was only the pounding in my head that made me short and ill-tempered. Maybe I detected a kind of judgment in him, and resented it. His grand sense of right and wrong flicked on my last nerve. My ma and pa was both dead, and I was alone in the world since the age of thirteen, and what would Wild Bill have done if he'd been me—a child abandoned by cruel circumstance on the side of a wagon trail, with five little ones to care for? And I had been a female child, at that—bereft of prospects, except the few and shameful prospects I could manufacture for myself. The only assets I could trade on were those nature had given me, though nature had proved herself to be a stingy bitch where my form and features was concerned. What would Bill have done, in my shoes? I felt certain he wouldn't sit so comfortably in his lofty judgment if he'd-a had the least idea of what my life had been like since leaving Missouri.

And yet, even as my anger flared and I growled at him, I loved Bill more than ever before. For there he was, down in the dirt by my side, caring enough to tend me. There he was, lying to the doctor's face when he and McGillycuddy and every damn man in the camp could tell exactly what was ailing me. Through my pain, through my raw sense of unfairness—the whole damn-blasted world was unfair—I felt something weave in the air between us. I felt a queer reaching-out of my spirit and Bill's. Then I felt a silvery twining, as of hands clasping, or knots working themselves in an intricate, invisible lace. Something real existed between us now—something unseen, but binding. I couldn't give a name to our strange bond; language has no words to describe it. The bond was one of love on *my* side only. I knew that was true; the cruel, stark nature of my condition forced me to see clearly, and I understood that whatever Bill felt for me, it wasn't love. It wasn't the great, hollow, claw-fingered longing I felt for him. But it *was* an affection of sorts, and that was good enough for me. It had to be good enough, for it was the best I'd ever get from Wild Bill.

After a time, Sam Young appeared with the canteen. Bill unstoppered it and passed it over. I took a long swallow.

"Not too much," Bill said. "You'll sick it all up and be worse off than before. Take a little at a time."

The water was as cool and sweet as Bill had promised. I sipped it slowly till the fierce drumbeat in my skull diminished a little. I didn't feel much like myself, but I felt a little less like a dumb creature caught in the jaws of a trap. I handed the canteen back to Bill.

"So you got yourself drunk again," he said.

"I figured I ought to have one last hurrah."

"Hurrah," Bill cheered with irony. He swigged from his canteen.

I grinned at his joke. It made my whole face hurt, but I did it anyway.

"I do mean last, Bill," I said with sudden desperation. "I intend to get myself clean and be a proper lady—honest I do. And I mean to make a real life somewheres. A proper life. There won't be no liquor on the trail. Not for me."

"Plenty of the boys have brought along liquor. You'll light out after it the second you see it. Or smell it. Or hear the boys whooping it up at night."

"Dodge don't allow no whoop-up among his troops. The doc told me so. Anyway, I spent all my money at Fort Laramie, so even if I wanted to buy some whiskey, I can't."

"So this is to be a march of deprivation," Bill said—hint of a laugh in his voice, a low, affectionate chuckle.

"I hope I won't hurt quite so bad in the morning."

"No," he said, "I don't suppose you will. That's usually the way of a come-down. If you can ride out the first day, it's easier the next, and the next. But Calam—"

I winced at the name.

Bill amended himself with a tolerant nod. "Miss Bird, once a thing has got its hooks in you, like whiskey or women or any other vice, it calls to you again and again. A come-down is one thing, but leaving it behind forever..." He trailed off to dismal silence. I couldn't bear the weight of the words Bill left unspoken.

I said loud and strong, "I can kick it. I can kick anything. I'm ten times stronger than you think, Wild Bill. Just see if I ain't."

He reached out through the dusk, laid his hand gently on my shoulder. "Yes mam," he said. "I believe you are, at that."

———————

How I ever managed to fall asleep in my tiny canvas tent, I will never know. That night, I laid awake for hours, staring up at the black nothingness on the tent's inner peak, but rest evaded me despite my exhaustion. I believe it was the pain in my heart that kept me from sleeping. I felt a proper fool, for now Wild Bill could see me clearly: pathetic enough to attach myself to this expedition, just for the sake of being near him again—and still the wreck I'd been when he left me a year ago. I don't remember ever growing drowsy or drifting, the way you do when sleep overtakes you slowly. I was simply wakeful and suffering in the slim confines of my private Hell, and then I was awake again, and suffering still. Though I will confess that Wild Bill had been right: when I rose up next morning, dragging myself reluctantly from the privacy of my tent, my stomach clenched a little less fiercely, and the ache in my head wasn't quite as terrible as it had been the night before.

I hauled myself off into the brush to do what was needful. The men of the expedition pissed right against the trees, or even out in the open with their streams pattering down into the dew-wet meadow, but always with their backs turned to the colonel's tent, so as to be respectful. I envied them the convenience. It was clear I would have my work cut out for me, for under the colonel's eye— and McGillycuddy's—I must maintain a level of ladylike decorum to which I had never before aspired.

When I was finished, I returned to pack up my tent, wincing a little at the early yellow sunlight that still played sort of harsh on my eyes. I found two men not much older than me loitering in my small territory.

"Boys," I said in greeting.

One of them said excitedly, "You're Calamity Jane!" He was gangly and thin, sandy-haired. I thought he had more good looks than sense.

I held back a groan of despair and looked around the camp cautiously, but no one else seemed to have heard his words. I guessed another of Bill's predictions had come true: I would be known indeed, no matter how I tried to disguise myself.

I faced the men with as much dignity as I could muster and answered, "I don't use that name no more—not on this trek. I'm Margaret Bird, and that's all you can call me. And I don't do anything Calamity Jane does, so don't even ask. I didn't join up with this expedition to make money. I come along for adventure and experience—and I'll be earning my keep with honest work, not with anything Dodge disapproves of. Got it, boys?"

"I didn't mean nothing by it, Miss—" The sandy-haired one looked pained and embarrassed. He seemed about to call me Miss Jane or maybe Miss Calam, but he caught on quick enough and stopped himself. "Miss Margaret." He touched his hat, apologetic-like. "And," he said, "I didn't intend to ask you for… for anything of that sort. It's only that Sam and me, we heard all about your adventures. We thought you was sort of exciting, and maybe you had some good stories to tell. You know—to keep us from falling asleep in the saddle."

"It'll be a long and boring ride today," the other fellow said. He was shorter and more bullish, with brown hair that had already begun to thin. He held his hat in his hands and kept twirling it on one finger, absently, as if he wasn't conscious of the habit. In silence, I watched his hat make a few revolutions. In my dull, still-aching state, the spinning John Bull was enough to mesmerize me.

"Folks call me California Joe," said the tall and gangly one. He nodded to his friend. "This here is Sam Young."

Those names reached through my vague fog of misery and snapped me to attention. These fellas had helped me from my saddle the night before. I looked at them more closely now, with greater interest. They had pleasant, honest faces, the kind you didn't see much in the West.

I said, "What the blazing Hell made you think I'd have good stories?" Then I flinched, for my language was edging toward the blue. I had to keep my tongue in better check if I planned to stay on Dodge's good side. The truth was, I did have good stories, and more than enough to fill up a long day's ride. But all my stories was about my previous line of work. Those tales was thoroughly unsuitable to the new leaf I had so recently turned.

"Why, we read all about you in the newspapers," Sam Young said.

This surprised me quite soundly. Sure as I was born, I knew I'd never done a thing worth reporting in the newspapers. But I kept my startlement in cool check and gazed at those boys, waiting for them to tell me more.

California Joe didn't make me wait long. "You was with Custer at Big Hole, scouting against the Percey-Nezzy, wasn't you?"

Now, I never did hear a story as unlikely in all my days. It took all my effort to contain my laughter and keep a mask of perfect calm upon my face. I had no idea whether Custer had ever fought the Nez Perce Indians a-tall. If he did, I sure as hell wasn't there to see it. But Joe's question brought back a vague recollection of some six or seven months before, when (in a whiskey haze) I had attempted to distract an especially vicious faro opponent with tales of my supposed exploits, all made up on the spot, and wild as a summer squall. I didn't win that game of cards, but apparently the tales I spun in the attempt had grown legs and run off, all on their own.

"You read about my scouting in the papers?"

"Yes'm. Sam and me, we think it's awful neat to hear of a lady scout. And to meet you in person... well!"

"Has there been any other stories in the papers? Stories about Calamity Jane, I mean."

Had there been! As we rolled up our beds and tents together,

Sam Young and Cali Joe recounted every tale they'd heard of my great and glorious adventures.

—————

THE BATTLE OF GOOSE CREEK. I am outside the ring of the camp site, having left my place to attend to some duty or urge. A fifteen-year-old girl, black hair and gray eyes and a frame of five-foot-one, pretty as you please even in the garb of a soldier. Young and handsome Captain Egan is surprised. His camp is surrounded by Percy-Nezzy. The air rings with war whoops and the whistling of steel axes, which fly like bullets or birds. Because I am slender and light of foot, I slink among the Indians, who are so intent on wiping out Egan and his men that they take no notice of me. Fifteen and a girl, but my eye is experienced, my head steady, for I'm a true woman of the frontier, and expect no soft treatment from life on account of my sex. I fall on my knees beside Egan— wounded, and all his men demoralized, if they ain't already dead. There is but one good horse left in the camp. I get Egan into the saddle and swing up behind him, then ride away, knowing the country even better than the Indians do. I create a diversion (what kind? The papers don't say) and carry Egan to a place of safety. He gives me my name: Calamity Jane. And my fame like a wildfire spreads from the Dakotas to the western line of Montana.

A diversion. I picture it: a line of girls dancing the can-can along a dry red ridge, their white thighs flashing, skirts shivering in bunches of lace and silk. The Indians don't know what has hit them. They stare in confusion at the bouncing curls and the bright swish of velvet. The loud clack of ladies' prim boots against stone is like no music they have heard. They goggle at ample flesh squeezed into ripe round handfuls by tight laces and stoic stays. And the music plays out over hills and canyons, Streets of Laredo in double time, so jaunty and gay it sounds obscene.

THE NOTORIOUS LADY scout who has killed a score of Indians has staked a claim on a gold mine, the most productive Dakota has ever seen, and now she is prepared to hear the many men who come a-courting. She will consider their suits. Yes, boys: Calamity Jane is determined to settle down, and whoever can win her heart will get her gold, too. But what man is a match for the Belle of the Frontier, she who never goes without her rifle (or a pistol, at least) —she who can shoot as well as any gent? Her eye is as sharp as her face is pretty. Fellas must step lively and be on their guard if they hope to claim the prize of Calam's great renown and her rich vein of gold.

FACTS! FACTS! FACTS! INDISPUTABLE!

Just above the advertisement that reads in bold letters, We have the best and most complete line of men's, youths', boys and children's suits, overcoats, ulsters, ulsterettes, buffalo and blanket coats, snow excluders, German socks, rubber boots, boots and shoes, hats, caps, trunks, valises, blankets, quilts, etc.

One True Chapter, A Flash Light Section in the History of Calamity Jane.

(Not true at all, I'm afraid, but don't tell the Anaconda Standard.)

A driver shot by brigands out on the stage line, the one that runs out to Deadwood. Thirty miles away from the town, and I was riding in the sage—a scouting mission for Custer or some other luminary. I heard the crack of the shot and then the thunder of hooves, and the screams of women and children trapped inside as the coach careened up the trail. I galloped alongside, and with my spry slender girlish body I leaped from my saddle to the driver's seat, where I found a man shot dead, and the bag of gold that had been at his feet stolen clean away. (Why he had so carelessly transported gold in a sack at his feet is anyone's guess.) Possessed of an inborn skill with horses, I brought the team under control, thereby saving the lives of the innocents within, and with Indians and robbers hot on the stagecoach's tail, I drove it fast all the way to Deadwood and was acclaimed a true heroine, and a beauty besides, fit to steal any man's heart. My loyal horse followed me the whole way—being much enamored of my gentle spirit, and reluctant to leave my side. When I'd seen the ladies and their children to safety, I mounted my horse and said to all who had gathered, I'm the one they call Calamity Jane! And as the sun was conveniently setting, I rode off into it, disappearing in a fiery blaze.

SAM YOUNG and Cali Joe was so enamored of the newspaper tales that I hadn't the heart to tell them there wasn't a speck of truth in the lot. While they recounted the legends (breathless and thrilled), I sifted through the wild-eyed accounts and determined from where each one had sprung. A saucy remark misconstrued over cups of whiskey, or a joke told at a faro table, carried too far. Occasionally I had nothing a-tall to do with the stories; they was, as near as I could make out, wholly the invention of the newspaper men. I listened to the tales in silence, though now and again I couldn't resist nodding along or corroborating a glorious lie with a soft and mischievous chuckle.

And all the while, I wondered what this might mean for me— sudden, unlooked-for fame, the hard stamp of notoriety. Every one of those tales had made me out to be a real beauty, the kind of girl who can win a man's heart just by batting her lashes. *If this is what all the West believes me to be,* I thought rather miserably, *then I can't help but disappoint anyone who lays eyes upon me.* But Sam and Joe seemed to forgive my exterior. It was the stories themselves they loved, not the fantasy of the pretty young frontier hell-cat with a heart of gold. I might have no inkling of what my fame meant, but I'd be a damned fool and a liar besides if I tried to claim I didn't enjoy my few small trappings of glamour.

The longer we rode together, the more I came to like Joe and Sam. They was good, decent fellas, earnest and brave—and they had known Wild Bill for some time, having met up with him on his previous expedition into the Black Hills. We stuck close together, the three of us, and their conversation and general cheer distracted me from the pain in my head as my come-down resolved. I felt much better than I had the day before, yet the come-down still had me in its grips, and Lord knows I needed a distraction something awful.

Now and then, though, both Joe and Sam lapsed into silence, lulled by the heat of the day and the rhythm of their horses' walking, or drawn off by their own private musings to places I couldn't follow. And in those times, I fixed my eyes on Wild Bill, watching him surreptitious-like from beneath the black arc of my sombrero's brim.

I watched Bill emerge from a warped-glass ripple of heat, turning his mount to ride crosswise of the party's slow current. And halt, and pause, and as his head turned the heat would rise up from the earth and distort him till he merged—shoulders into stone, hands into dry earth—with the world around and behind him. The fringe of his buckskin sleeves was the waving of prairie grass; the smell of his body carried to me on the wind, sweat and horse and the oil of his well-shined gun, sun-roughened skin and the dark rasp of wood smoke. In the distance, the mountains hung blue—layers of blue laid one atop another, and when Bill ranged out beyond the snake-line of Dodge's party, the indigo and the violet-gray opened up to welcome him. He became a part of the hills, the embodiment of distance, and then he returned and rode close to me for a minute or two, and he was all shades of warm red, all shades of liveliness again. His auburn hair and his chapped hands. His knuckles hard and angular, skin split from weather but half-healed along their ridges. His horse was red, too, a glowing sorrel like a mountain sunset, like the evening's last light on the face of a high stone cliff.

Whenever he came near, I felt as if the mountains and the hills was bending down to touch me, brushing me with pale fingers of bear grass in bloom. And as he rode away again, with hardly a word spoken, the land swept out to reveal to me all the vast, painful beauty of creation.

THE NEXT DAY, I felt worlds better. I even started to perk up some. The party broke camp early so we could make tracks before the day got too hot and the deer flies (which was thick in the high elevations) wouldn't pester us more than we could stand. A grumble still lurked in my head, and a curious, heavy dampness seemed to weigh down my soul, but through the last of my come-down I did feel (for the first time in my life) that I could kick liquor for good and all, and become the kind of girl Wild Bill—or any other man, for that matter—might come to appreciate.

The camaraderie of Sam and California Joe reinforced that notion. We became proper chums by the third day, laughing at each other's jokes, lending a hand whenever a hand was needed. Sam and Joe saw in me real worth—I mean the true kind, that kind that went beyond the convenient proximity of my body and my always-bargain price. Anyway, they never got a bit of what I sold to other men on other expeditions. I meant what I said to Wild Bill: I was a reformed girl. The welcome friendship of Sam Young and California Joe—without any carnal expectation attached—assured me that I had a future as a proper lady.

By that time, Dr. McGillycuddy's hope that I would prove a poor rider was well and truly dashed. Silkie was a hardy thing, more than equal to keeping up with the soldiers' horses, and if I wasn't as feather-light as the newspapers made me out to be, I was still lighter than a man. Silkie found me a burden easily borne, even over the rough terrain of the Hills. My legs and behind was tough enough for the long ride; I never wearied, so if anyone tries to tell you that's how I came to be riding in a supply wagon, you'll know it's an outright lie.

Poor Silkie was tough, as I said, and well experienced with steep, rocky trails. She wasn't the only horse to slip as we descended a ridge near the strange, flat-topped, bare-rock spire the Indians called the Bear's Teepee. But Silkie was the only horse to suffer an injury. I can't lay the blame anywhere but at Bad Luck's door. Anyhow, when she was back on her feet, I kicked her away from the trail and slid out of my saddle to examine her legs. She had a nasty cut along one knee; it bled something awful. Joe and Sam helped me poultice it to stop the bleeding, but Sam said, "Oughtn't to ride her for at least a day, Margaret. Might go lame if you do."

Joe put up a request to the man in charge, but Dodge flatly refused to lend me a spare horse to ride. He said I could sit in the supply wagon till my mare was healed up. I think he hoped the humiliation of being hauled like a sack of potatoes would take me down a few pegs and put me back in a woman's proper place.

I didn't mind riding in the wagon, though I had forgotten how uncomfortable it can be. A wagon's movement is all chaos, without the fluid side-to-side and gentle bob of a single horse's motion. There was little hope I might accustom myself to the rattling—no looseness in any of my limbs could compensate for the wagon's ceaseless, weary rumble.

But I was far more concerned for Silkie than for myself. The black mare was my one good friend, if you didn't count Sam and Joe—who after all was only very recent acquaintances. I felt dreadful scared that Silkie might go lame for good, and all that day, I kept lifting my head and shoulders over the edge of the wagon to watch her gait, searching for any signs of permanent injury. She followed calmly behind California Joe, who had tied one of her reins to his horn; Silkie seemed content, untroubled by her knee. But still I crackled inside with worry.

To push my fears away, I made myself as useful as I could, for I was determined that neither Dodge nor McGillycuddy nor Bill—especially Bill—should find any cause to gripe over Margaret Bird. I took out my knife and peeled and cut potatoes while the wagon jolted up the trail. I made a private game of it, challenging myself to skin a whole potato in one long, curled strip. Then I flung the peels over the side of the wagon, so they lay like white snakes basking on the trail. It would have been better fun if Sam and Joe had been with me, for without their chatter all I could think of was Bill—or rather, Bill's absence as he rode out alone, this way and that, scouting for signs of Indians. I seldom caught sight of him from the wagon's bed, though I encountered him constantly in my thoughts, often enough that I nicked my fingers with the knife almost as frequently as I nicked potatoes.

Evening had almost settled in by the time we reached Lytle Crick. The ford was broad and gravelly, the water not especially deep but swiftly flowing. Wild Bill and Dodge set their horses and looked at the water for a long time, discussing the matter in quiet, earnest tones. The evening blued down around Wild Bill; new-hatched flies rose up from the brush to pester the horses, making them stamp and swing their tails, but Bill wasn't disturbed. He kept his eyes on the water and I watched him just as avidly, never caring who saw the hungry light in my face or the unwavering loyalty of my gaze.

After a time, Bill nodded. Dodge turned and barked an order to his men. A few at a time, they began crossing the stream. The horses held their heads up in a stiff show of dislike; they picked up their hooves with exaggerated care, and now and then a horse slipped on the slick rocks, with the current crashing around its feet, and almost went down. When half the party had crossed to the opposite bank, Dodge called for the wagon to ford the crick, too.

The horses pulling my wagon balked and snorted; they couldn't be made to enter the water. Eventually, someone tied a rope around one of their heads, and the men on the other side of the crick hauled at the rope till the wagon horses splashed in. They resented every step of the crossing. I was tense, gripping the side of the wagon with a fierce and desperate strength. I could feel the horses' fear in my own body, for I noted how the water shuddered against the wagon wheels, pounding and sucking and dragging with the force of a fast, cold current. Now and then a rock slid beneath a horse's hoof with a loud, hollow, watery scrape and the whole lot—team, wagon, potato sacks, and Calam—lurched and shivered with fear. But we made it past the crick's middle, and step by laborious step, the water receded from the wheels.

I had just begun to relax—scarcely allowing myself to believe I had survived—when the damn fool men on the opposite bank let go of their rope. The horses sensed freedom on the instant; they both danced sideways, and the wagon backed and shuddered with a sudden, sickening splash. A great chorus of fearful shouts went up from the men on both sides of the crick. I had time for one scream—embarrassing in its high, frantic pitch—before the wagon tipped up on its side. Then it turned over in a roar of water and a thunder of rolling potatoes.

The cold water hit me like a fist; I flailed with my eyes closed, though it was darker than pitch anyway. I clamped my mouth tight-shut, but water surged up my nose and into the back of my throat, bringing the taste of mud with it. Distant and muffled, as if behind a heavy barn door, I heard the men hollering and the team horses screaming. Water hissed; the rocks below me scraped and groaned and it was a sound I imagined one might hear down in the belly of Hell.

I'm about to die, I realized. The strangest calm fell over me—a peace of subdued acceptance. In that clear-headed quiet, I shut out the muffled sound of panic and realized that although I could hear the crick flowing hard around the wagon, the current didn't tug at my body. The water around me was absolutely still. Something was blocking its flow, and that something could only be the upturned wagon. The water was shallow enough where I lay— perhaps two or three feet deep. I felt the slimy stones beneath my hands and knees and pushed carefully upward, praying I'd find air above my head.

I did. My head broke the surface into a pocket of breathable air, trapped along with me under the wagon. I drew a shuddering breath. Then I pounded on the wood overhead with all my might.

"Calamity!" I could hear Joe crying out near one of the wheels. "Calamity Jane! Are you killed? Say something to tell us you ain't killed!"

Damn it all to Hell, I thought. *Now the cat's out of the bag for good.*

I yelled loud as I could, "I'm fine, curse you! Get this wagon flipped so's I can get out of here!"

A second later I heard hooves trotting boldly through the water and Wild Bill's voice shouting orders, all the cool detachment gone from him as he chivvied the men back into the water and set them to prying at the wagon.

"Margaret Bird," Bill called. "I'll get you out, girl. Don't you worry."

"I ain't worried, you bastard!" I shouted back. "I'm cold as your grandma's boot and more soaked than the sheets in a whore house. And it's black as Satan's balls in here!" Panic was rising fast in me, now that I knew I wasn't crushed to death nor drowned. I feared I might be holed up in that wagon till the end of time, though, like being buried alive—and I had to wrestle down the urge to scream in giddy fear. "Get this thing off me, you worthless shits! The fuck you waiting for? For it to grow a pair of goddamned wings and fly off me?"

At that moment the wagon heaved and tipped and crashed back over on its wheels. The violet dimness of dusk seemed bright as full noon; I sat on my ass in the shallows, hands bracing me up behind my back, and stared in wide-eyed wonder as coils of potato peels whisked away from me, traveling fast downstream. A pair of boots splashed down beside me. A moment later, Wild Bill hooked his arm through mine and hauled me up onto weak, shivery legs. Bill turned me around and marched me to the shore, though God alone knows how I managed to walk through the shallows. My legs was like water themselves.

With every step, I let fly another cuss. It was the only expression I could find of my terror, my disbelief—my sheer joy in finding myself alive. "Fuck, shit, damn, cock, fuck, damn, balls!" My boots squelched out cold water with every step.

"Margaret," Bill said softly beside me.

"Balls!" I yelled back. "Fucking big bouncing balls!"

"Margaret!"

I blinked and looked around me—really looked and saw what Wild Bill saw. Dodge and Doc McGillycuddy was right there in front of me, standing side by side like a palisade made of two sharp, stoic stakes. Neither of them looked the least bit glad to find me still among the living.

"Your language," Dodge said, "is unbecoming of a lady. And a woman has no business with this expedition."

"I knew you would prove a distraction," the doctor muttered, as if to punctuate Dodge's condemnation.

Bill still held me by one arm; I felt him draw up like a rattler ready to strike. "See here," he said. "She near about died under that wagon. You'd cuss just the same, if it'd been you trapped under there. And you sure wouldn't come down on me—or any of the other men—for cussing under such circumstances."

Dodge narrowed his eyes at Bill, an unmistakable warning.

Bill chose not to heed it. "Leave off," he said to the commander.

"A few unladylike words should be forgiven, all things considered."

Murmurs of agreement rose from the soldiers. Dodge's dark eyes slid sideways, as if he thought to glare around at his men, but his head never turned. He looked at me squarely then and said, "Young lady, you'd best keep yourself clean and respectable from here on out. If you don't, you'll be sent back to Fort Laramie just as soon as the supply wagon is empty."

Then he and the doctor turned as one and strode away.

Shivering with anger as much as cold, I stood with my arm hooked through Bill's and watched them go. When they was far enough away that they wouldn't hear, I whispered, "Balls!"

Beside me on the dark bank, Wild Bill laughed.

———

CALIFORNIA JOE LOANED me a change of clothing and soon enough I was dry. I was welcomed at my friends' fire, too, and set down with a big dish of potato stew and some newly made flat bread, still warm from Cookie's fire.

"Thought we just about lost you there," Sam said. He dealt out cards for a round of faro, including me in the game without my having to ask.

"Thought I'd lost me, too." I'd never been so frightened in all my life, though I smiled casually and propped my boots up heel-on-toe beside the fire pit, as if I hadn't a care in the world.

"Word's out about who you really are," Sam said with a note of contrition.

I waved his concerns away. "Wasn't nothing I could keep secret forever. And ain't nothing Dodge can do about it now."

A long, lean shadow moved toward us from the direction of the murmuring camp. An instinct in me—an automatic yearning —caused me to look up from my cards with a hunger that expected to be fed. Wild Bill appeared on the edge of the firelight's ruddy circle.

"Hullo," he said. "Mind if I join in your game?"

The boys made room for Bill. He sank down opposite my place. My vision seemed to slow, and time to stretch, so that every flicker of the flames was distinct, a slow spread of red fingers on a grasping hand. And every movement Bill made as he surveyed his cards left a trace of itself across my heart. His eyes sliding sideways, the corner of his mouth turning up in brief consideration, the curl and extension of one finger as he tapped and touched the upper edge of a single card, then moved on to another. All the while my feet remained propped, slowly wagging to a rhythmless, unheard song—as if I cared nothing for any of it, as if nothing in the world (least of all Bill Hickock) could break through the tight-shut doors and windows of my poor heart.

"How you feeling now, Miss Jane?" Bill asked at length.

So he had realized, too, that my secret was out. Word of Calamity Jane was already flying around the camp; no use trying to pretend I was anybody else. "Proper as can be expected," I said, "under the circumstances. And you know, Bill, I feel right good, in spite of being dunked and trapped like a half-drowned rat. That... that sickness that plagued me before. It's all gone now."

He looked up from his cards. His eyes met my own and he smiled, slow and warm, which sent a tremor right through me, a sweet burning down in my gut that felt better than the fire, better than any whiskey. "That's powerful good to hear," he said, and returned to studying his hand.

Bill said little else to me that night, but I felt a sort of good-natured comfort settle down between us, like a hen brooding warm and content upon a nest. The emotion that now bonded us together couldn't be called anything other than brotherly—for Bill's part, at least—but I was happy to have that much. I considered it rightly won, that gentle affection. After all, I had overcome the demon of liquor, and though I'd lost none of my proclivity for cussing, I did feel washed and made new, cleaner and more wholesome than I'd ever been before. I was well on my way toward winning Bill's heart. Till it was mine, I would remain content with the easy peace between us.

It wasn't only Bill who warmed me. Sam and Joe was fine companions, roping me right into their game and their confidences as if we'd grown up together and had always been a threesome. Long as it had been since I'd seen Cilus and Lije—or even heard word of their whereabouts—Sam and Joe felt like my true brothers that night. The only real brothers I ever had.

"Dodge a-comin'," Wild Bill said quietly, never looking up from his hand.

I tucked my cards under my thigh and affected a casual, patient air, making believe I was only watching the three men play their game of faro. Dodge stalked silently past our campfire with his hands clasped behind his back. The doctor trailed a scant step behind. As one, they both turned to look at me with sharp consideration, with a pinched uneasiness that spoke loud and clear of mistrust. I smiled like an innocent girl and waved a greeting, and they moved on, vanishing in the darkness between fires.

I CAN'T TELL you what pulled me from my bed that night—what soft, dark whispering called me out of sleep and tempted me from the confines of my tent with its black roof and its smell of close, slumbering breath. I crept out alone and tucked my blankets back inside, and stood up in the midst of a silent encampment.

A round, white moon gently touched the meadow where we had arrayed ourselves. Trampled grass smelled sweet and damp beneath the acrid memory of dung-fire smoke, and here and there an ember still glowed red-orange, smaller than a candle flame in the staggered fire pits. I felt instinctively—but didn't see—the slow tramp of night sentries moving in their cautious circuits. I felt, too, the comfortable, chummy weight of horses tethered in their lines. I imagined I could smell the dry-grass perfume of their hides, their soft and patient breath.

Somewhere in the darkness, Bill's tent stood. Somewhere he lay sleeping with his red hair fanned out across his roll, his eyes moving slowly beneath their lids, tracking a distant dream.

The stars was bold, forceful, spilled across the sky like nuggets of gold in a stream. I stood and stared straight up into that sky— for how long, I cannot say—till the sheer number of stars made me dizzy. Faintly, I could see the long black void that the Indians call the Spine of Night, and the pale powdery glow that surrounds it. I thought that glow must be made from many hundreds of thousands of stars, so far away that all that was left of them was a scattering of light. And then the thought of so great a number and such unimaginable distance made me dizzier still, but pleasantly so, and I swayed in awe on knees that trembled, swayed before the beauty and majesty of the sky.

Remade. Whole. Washed clean and new. The worst of what I was—what I had been—lay behind me now. I had ridden away from my past. Only good things waited on the trail ahead, and I would claim them all.

Now, remembering, I don't know why the crick called to me. Maybe I knew full well at the time, and have forgotten over inter-vening years. Perhaps I thought I had something to prove to the water that had tried to claim my life. Perhaps I felt some kinship with it now. It could well be that I was still rather fearful and wanted to put my terror to rest—the last black mark upon my soul. Maybe I just thought I needed a bath. But one way or another, I left the impossible, vast view of the sky alone. I returned to the bank where hours before I had thought myself drowned and dead.

The camp lay silent as a tomb, so I counted it safe enough to strip off my clothes and lay them aside on a flat rock that stuck halfway out from the bank. Boots, woolen stockings, britches and shirt, my short-legged drawers—I piled them up neatly, loosed my black hair from the bun I kept it in, and walked out into the water.

The crick was cold—so cold it made me gasp from the first step, and the water wasn't even up to my calves yet. I pressed on, biting my cheek, breathing harshly through my nose till I was used to the water's bitter chill. And then, when I made it halfway across the crick and the water reached up to my behind, the cold didn't matter no more. I sank down slowly, letting the current push against my chest, my back, even my face.

The crick had a respectable force, but with my toes curled around the smooth stones in its bed, I could stand up to the current all right. I faced the mad rush of dark water, leaned against it, felt my hair fan out behind me and tug at my scalp as it danced along the rippling surface. When I rose up, my skin was had raised in goose flesh all over, and my pale bareness was beaded by drops that sparkled like morning dew. I raised my arms and examined them. The light of the stars, hundreds of thousands, glinted on my skin. My small breasts, which had never been remarkable, was covered now in diamonds, and the black hair at the joining of my thighs was gemmed like a virgin's throat.

It was the first time in all my life—the only time, truth to tell—I ever thought myself beautiful.

When the water had run off me, I lowered myself again, and stood and held my arms wide like a queen before her subjects, though there was no one to see me except the trees and the little bats flitting overhead. The moon hung low against the horizon, a soft golden glow between the trunks of pines. The moon seemed to bow down before me. Again and again I dunked and arose, and each time I shimmered more than the time before. I felt nothing of the cold. All I cared for was the beauty of the night, and that beauty shone off of me—it *was* me, and I was, at last, as pure and pretty, as worthy as any other girl on the frontier.

I would have gone on like that forever, admiring my own firm and naked skin, but I heard a shout from the shore. A low, male voice—wordless but rough with outrage, even disgust. I dropped down into the water, crouching so only my eyes and nose remained above the surface. I hugged my arms tight around my body, shielding my breasts with my big, ungainly hands. A pair of sentries stared back at me from where my clothing waited. One turned and hurried off into the meadow, but he wasn't gone long. Moments later, Dodge appeared with Dr. McGillycuddy on his heels—his bristling lapdog.

Now the jig was up, and no mistake. I lifted myself so my mouth came clear of the stream and said, "Sirs, if you'll please turn your back so's I can get dressed proper, I'd be much obliged."

The men did not turn their backs. I could feel hot hatred burning out of Dodge's glare, though I was far enough away that I couldn't actually see the glint in his eyes. I didn't need to. His tense neck and shoulders spoke plain enough of his offense.

I waded toward them, hunkering low, trying to shield myself from their eyes as the water grew shallower around me. But they kept on staring, kept up their steely silence, till finally there was nothing for it but to stand up straight. I lowered my hands and made them look at my nakedness. It was nothing to me; I couldn't even count how many times I'd bared myself before men's eyes. I reasoned, if an eyeful was what they wanted then I'd sure as Hell give 'em one.

My flagrant display of nudity was too much for Colonel Dodge. He found his voice at last. "You are," he said in his stiff, formal manner, as if pronouncing a sentence on a prisoner, "Calamity Jane."

"The one and only," I spat back.

"I wanted no women on this expedition, but a woman of your ill repute least of all."

"Well, at least your potatoes got peeled."

Night air gnawed at me with fangs of cold; I shivered hard, but I made no move toward my clothing. Mad enough to spit nails at

Dodge, I resolved to make him face my nakedness—my female-
ness—whether he liked it or not.

A pack of men drew up around us, clamoring to see—not to
lay eyes my nudity, I think; just to learn what the midnight stir
was about. I caught sight of Sam Young and California Joe among
the crowd, and their expressions of pained confusion pained me
in my turn. They knew as well as I did that they couldn't stand up
to Dodge; they could say nothing to defend me. If they tried, it
would mean the end of the expedition for them, too, and they
needed the pay desperately.

"You will be sent back to Fort Laramie in the morning, along
with the wagon," Dodge said.

Finally I reached for my shirt, but I took my sweet time
shaking it out. "Sent back? All the way to Fort Laramie? Why
should I go there, when Deadwood's only a day or two ahead?"

"Do not question me, young lady," Dodge said. His words
carried more than a hint of danger.

A long, lean shadow slid through the crowd. "With respect, sir,"
Wild Bill drawled as if it made no difference to him whatsoever,
"it would be wiser to send the wagon on ahead to Deadwood.
Shorter trip. Easier on the horses."

I wanted Bill to look upon me naked, of course, and to do
more besides—but not like this. Not with me disgraced and
soaking wet, shivering in front of a crowd of soldiers. I hugged
my shirt against my skin and shrank back, trying to screen myself
behind some brush that clung to the river bank while I struggled
to pull my clothing onto my damp, resistant body. Bill didn't even
peek at me—not once. I couldn't say whether he understood my
need for privacy, or whether my bare hide held as little interest
for him as the cast-off core of an apple.

Dodge said, "Mister Hickok. When I have a use for your opinion, I will be sure to ask for it."

"Seems like a waste to me," Bill said, "to bring a man of my particular talents along on an expedition of this sort, and then disregard his opinion."

Dodge bristled. "That is enough, Hickok. The whore goes back to Laramie at sunrise."

I had my britches on now, and my shirt buttoned up enough that I could claim some small shred of decency. I rounded on Dodge, got right up in his face, for what did I have to fear by then? "You can go straight to Hell," I said, loud and wild so all the men in the camp could hear me.

McGillycuddy made a small choking sound. Colonel Dodge only watched me with emotionless calm.

I said, "I ain't going back to no god-damned Fort Laramie. Sam and Joe, pack up my things for me. Saddle up my mare. I'm leaving tonight, and going my own damn way!"

"Now, hold on." Bill stepped close to me, grasped me by the arm. His grip was strong, his hand large enough to encircle even my thick, tough limb. "Hold on, Calamity. You know it's too dangerous to travel alone. This is Sioux territory. I know better than anyone how deadly the Indians in these parts can be."

"No Indian has killed me yet," I said. Brave words, but my guts felt quivery inside at the thought of riding unaccompanied through Sioux territory.

Bill said, "I hate to think what they'll do to a woman alone if they catch you." He turned to Dodge and the doctor. "I'm going with her. I'll see her safe to Deadwood. Then I'll come back and find you along the trail. Won't take me more than four days at most."

"You will not go with her," Dodge insisted. "You're needed here, and you aren't being paid to escort road-house girls through the wilderness. She will ride in the wagon with an escort of men; her safety will be assured."

"I will not ride in no god-damned wagon," I hollered.

Bill cast me a pleading glance that seemed to say, *Shut your mouth if you know what's good for you, Calam.* But when have I ever known what's good for me?

I pulled my arm out of Bill's grip. My face burned so hot with shame and anger that I felt sure every man could see it, even in the darkness, with color all washed away by the stars. I said, "I can take care of myself, and I will, so Bill here can save his false concern for my welfare. Stay here with Dodge, Wild Bill; he's the one as pays your wages. For myself, I ain't gonna stick around to enjoy his civil company no more."

Joe and Sam was quick about packing up my things. They had Silkie there on the bank almost before I'd jammed my feet back into my boots. Joe handed me my black sombrero with his eyes downcast.

I swung up to Silkie's saddle, though my body was stiff from cold and from indignation. My mare pranced eagerly. Her injured knee seemed as good as it ever was. I shivered hard, still more wet than dry, but I was ready to be off, just like my mare was. I crossed back over the crick with a great, loud splashing of Silkie's hooves and soon enough found the trail the expedition had left, a gouge of dark wheel ruts and hoofprints through the silver-and-black forest.

"Damn it, Calam!" Bill called to me from across the crick. But he said no more.

I recalled that some ways back, there had been a fork in the trail, a split that ran off past the Bear's Teepee. And not far from the Bear's Teepee stood the Cuny and Coffey Road Ranch, where I had worked for a week or two in the past. I could make it safe to Cuny and Coffey's, if God was willing. To distract myself from the considerable shame I felt, I thought about that road ranch with anticipation—the loud music, boisterous dancing, the burn of whiskey in my throat.

But before I'd made it far from Dodge's expedition, I heard a distant splash in the crick. Then the pounding of hooves along the trail. I pulled Silkie back to a slow walk and allowed the rider to catch me.

I wasn't surprised to find Wild Bill, tall and straight on his big sorrel gelding. He fell in beside me but held his tongue.

"Dodge won't pay you if you come with me," I told him.

"To Hell with Dodge," said Bill. "You need a guide; that much is clear. For one thing, you're headed the wrong way if you mean to get to Deadwood."

"Ain't going to Deadwood."

"Back to Fort Laramie?"

I shook my head, but I didn't reveal my destination. I didn't think Bill would like to hear that I was planning to take up my old trade again. And there was little to do at a road ranch except drink. I guessed I had to admit to myself that I was planning to take up that old pastime, too. Why not? All the beauty had been stripped from me, trampled into the mud by Dodge and his god-damn ideals. I was what I always had been: a worthless whore. There was no point in pretending otherwise.

"You ain't going to accompany me," I said to Bill. "If you think so, then you can go to Hell right alongside Colonel Dodge."

"Is that any way to talk to your friend, Calam?"

"Are you my friend?" I looked at Bill squarely then. I held his eye, daring him to speak—to say, *No I ain't, not really, for you can't never be anything to me.* Or to say, *I'm more than your friend because I find myself powerful in love with you and want you for my wife.* Both possibilities were absurd, I knew. And yet I couldn't have said which I longed to hear more: the truth, or the lie.

Bill didn't respond—not with words. To this day, I think he was wise to keep quiet. I was riled up then, boiling with vinegar, and I don't know how I might have reacted had he said anything a-tall, even if he'd merely coughed or clicked his tongue at his horse.

Instead he reached down to his holster and drew his gun.

For a second, I thought maybe he'd shoot me, though I'd given him no cause. Maybe in that moment, I just wanted it to end—the shame, the ache of my dreams shattered, the ridiculous nature of my love for him. But he reached across the space between us and handed his gun to me.

I took the pistol, looking down at it for a moment. It was well polished and perfectly clean, shining like the moon on the horizon. It smelled of oil, bitter and sharp—just like Bill did.

"I already have a gun," I said.

"You might need another, if you come across any Sioux."

That decided me. I pushed his gun through my belt.

"Stay safe, Calamity, wherever you're going."

I thought, *You coward. If you was a real man, you'd ride along with me, no matter what Dodge thinks.* And even as that thought tumbled through my head, I scolded myself for thinking it, because wasn't I the equal of any man on the frontier? Didn't I have to be a man's equal, since I never would be pretty enough or worthy enough to land a man of my own?

"I'll be safe," I said shortly. "Ain't no sense in worrying about me."

Bill reined his gelding to a halt. When I was good and sure his horse had stopped on the trail, I kicked Silkie into a jog-trot. We made our way back through the wilderness alone.

THE MOST RECKLESS BUCHARIO IN
THE HILLS

RIDING OFF ALONE THAT NIGHT RANKS AMONG THE MOST DAMNABLY foolish stunts I ever pulled in a life defined by damn-foolish things. My horse made slow progress, for the terrain was steep and hard, much rougher than any of the previous trails I followed on my own. And of course it was night, ill-lit by a low-slung moon, which only added to my fears and to Silkie's hesitation. With every step Silkie took into treacherous darkness, I recalled with dreadful lucidity the scenery I took in from the safety of the supply wagon: limestone cliffs falling sheer and straight a hundred feet or more, the sudden ravines revealing themselves among the hills, all black shadow with hard edges, opening like rips in fabric. I had thought the landscape pretty, when I'd ridden secure among sacks of potatoes and flour. Now my heart pounded every time Silkie's hooves skidded down a bare stretch of slope, for I felt sure we was about to plunge over the lip of a canyon or a cliff and fall to the great, cracked boulders below.

Wild Bill couldn't have done a thing to save me from such a fate, but he might have been some use against Indians. The Sioux was up there in the Hills, without a doubt. I couldn't soothe myself with comforting lies that the Indians had all packed up and left when they'd seen the expedition coming, for I spotted an encampment that night when I gained the crest of a hill. As I rode up the steep trail, nothing showed ahead but white stars spattered across an ink-black sky. But the moment Silkie reached the summit, I reined up short in fear—for directly ahead, level with our vantage, I could see the banked embers of at least two dozen fires glowing red against the night. I sat perfectly still in my saddle, silently pleading with my horse not to call out to the Indian ponies, not even to snort nor swish her tail, for the night had disoriented me, and for some long while I couldn't judge how far off that encampment lay. I knew my only saving grace was Silkie's dark color, which would obscure me from the eyes of sentries for a few minutes at least. I sat staring at the campfires, my mind gone blank and useless with shock, heart pounding so loud in my ears that I nearly took the sound for Sioux war drums. Only very gradually did my eyes adjust to the new source of light, and then I could see that the camp occupied a different hilltop entirely—one that stood at least half a mile from my fearfully exposed perch, perhaps even farther.

When I realized I wasn't about to ride directly into the middle of a Sioux encampment, I relaxed some, settling back in my saddle with a quivery sigh. Silkie, sensing my relief, let out a soft whicker, as if to ask, "What now?" I didn't know what to tell her— didn't know what I ought to do, where I should go. *To think*, I scolded myself bitterly, *you once thought to fool Lieutenant Colonel Dodge into taking you for a scout. Why, you wouldn't even know which side to fall off your horse if you was shot with an Indian arrow.*

The relief of knowing I hadn't blundered upon my death all unawares—not yet, anyway—made me feel terrible tired. All urgency to get away from the expedition evaporated. Now there I was, well and truly away from Dodge, and my body realized all at once that it was night-time and I was sore tuckered out from a long, harrowing day. Exhaustion struck me so hard I began to tremble. Silkie sensed that change in me, too, and tossed her head in confusion. I knew I had to make some decision before she began to fuss. I was no scout—that was damn sure—but I had enough common sense to know that the Sioux wouldn't all have taken to their beds. Watchers had their eyes wide open, searching the Black Hills for any sign of the white men who'd come sniffing after gold. Wild Bill's words came snaking back to me through the night. *I hate to think what they'll do to a woman alone if they catch you.*

If I stayed at the crest of that hill, the Sioux would spot me sooner or later—either that night, when an Indian sentry turned his eyes to the west and picked out the silhouette of a rider against the stars, or in the morning, when the sun fell upon my dark horse exposed on a pale, bare hilltop. I knew I must get down low, preferably into one of the canyons, if I hoped to evade the Sioux. I dismounted to make my whole assemblage as short as possible and led Silkie step by sliding step down the other side of our hill, one eye fixed to the distant glow of Indian fires, holding my breath each time my mare's hooves or my clumsy boots sent a stone rattling and bouncing down the black trail ahead.

By and by, I lost sight of the fires altogether, and I reasoned I'd descended into a protective gulch. I found a flat patch of earth just big enough to accommodate Silkie and me, stamped around carefully to shoo off any rattlers, and rolled out my bed. There I caught a couple hours of much-needed rest. I slept with both guns laid out to either side of my head—the pearl-handled pistol and Bill's gun, the dull gleam of which I stared at till weariness finally dragged my eyelids shut. Then, an hour before true sunrise, I was up and riding again, picking my cautious way down a steep path in the whispery blue half-light before dawn.

As the next day wore on, I did my level best to behave like the scout I knew I was not. A grim truth revealed itself to me as I floundered alone through the Black Hills: I didn't really know what the Hell a scout even did—what knowledge they held that made them so valuable, what skills they'd honed out on the lonesome trail. I reasoned that they must have sharp eyes, so I kept mine open and trained on the ridges and ochre-banded hillsides that towered above, frantic for any hint of the Sioux. I hadn't the least idea what to do if I spotted an Indian, and I tried not to dwell on what would happen if an Indian spotted me first. I concentrated on riding among the willows and shrubs that clung to the lowest places, the sandy bellies of ravines and dry washes, hoping the rustling leaves and the shadows they cast afforded me some protection from eyes much keener than my own.

But all the while as I rode, I kept the Bear's Teepee within my sight—in sight, and always at my right hand, for I knew the Cuny and Coffey Road Ranch stood not far to the west of the mountain. Afternoon blazed across a merciless blue sky, and the heat raised clouds of lazy deer flies from the brush to torment Silkie and me with their searing bites. Anyplace that wasn't covered by clothing was soon covered in bleeding welts. Silkie's countless bites dripped red along our path, and her hide never ceased to twitch amid that hellish onslaught. The flies was such a plague of misery that I considered riding up out of the gullies to higher ground, where the wind would chase the flies away, Indians be damned.

Just before sunset—when I despaired of ever finding my way out of those damnable hills with my skin intact—the ravine I'd been following for hours opened out onto a wide sage plain. The Black Hills lay behind me at last, and there in the distance, across a flat gray meadow of summer-dried grass and gnarled brush, I spotted the welcome palisade that surrounded Cuny and Coffey. I had found the road ranch at last; I had hauled myself through the terrors of the wilderness alone, and had survived the trek more or less in one piece.

I would have let out a whoop of glee and lit out for the ranch at a gallop, but my shoulders still tensed and twitched at thought of Sioux in the hills behind me. I didn't much care for the possibility of drawing their attention, no matter how near or distant they might be. So I kept quiet and urged Silkie to a cautious trot, and by the time the sun had disappeared behind the far horizon, I was pounding on the road ranch gate, hollering for them to open up and take me in.

Accordingly, I was ushered into the protected grounds of Cuny and Coffey, and never in my life was I so glad to be shut up behind a fence. The moment the heavy timber gate closed, I slumped in my saddle, almost weeping with relief. The familiar grounds seemed to swim in my vision, the stock pens and boarding cabins and the big cheerful saloon rippling and blurring as if I looked at them through moving water, or through the squares of a cheaply made window. I scrubbed the tears from my eyes with a blood-spattered sleeve before anybody could see that I'd been on the verge of crying.

"Calamity Jane. I'll be damned." Jem Coffey, one of the owners of the road ranch, came limping out of his cabin to greet me. He had always limped, since I first met him—was shot through the leg by an Indian arrow, or so he told anybody who'd sit still long enough to listen.

I swung down from my saddle, but I had to lean against Silkie to compose myself, for my legs was shaking with the residue of fear. I reached out to shake Coffey's hand. He turned my hand over so's he could see the fly bites welted all across my skin, the blood dried hard and brown along my knuckles, cracked and flaking. Then he peered closer at my face, wincing at sight of me. "What in Hell happened to you, girl?"

"Ran into a swarm of deer flies. Ain't nothing to worry over." I tried to make myself sound cheerful, full of pluck as I'd been the last time Coffey had seen me. "Listen, Jem—I come all this way up from Fort Laramie to work for you again."

"Last I seen you, you said you'd had enough of the road ranch life and you meant to light out after some other pursuit."

"I know—but I need the money. A girl has to support herself one way or another, after all."

I was conscious of my filthy trousers, my trail-stained shirt. I had nothing suitable to wear among my personal effects, for I'd sold off all my nice dresses long ago. But I hoped the reputation I'd built while touring for McDaniels might be enough to save me. If word of the girl trick-shooter had spread far enough since my McDaniels days, I might not need to rely on fancy dresses to make my way. Trousers and buckskin might prove sufficient to get me by.

Jem Coffey sized me up, sweeping a long, considering look from my black sombrero down to my weathered old boots, pale with the dust of my journey. For a moment I feared he'd tell me he had no use for me—that unless I looked like a proper girl, he couldn't let me work the saloon. Then his sharp eye returned to the two guns resting on my hips. His craggy face broke into a slow grin, and I could see that I had him where I wanted him.

"Could be nice to have some new entertainment here," he said. "Word gets out, you might even draw some folks over from the nearest towns, on purpose to see you shoot."

"I'll start tomorrow, if you like," I promised. "I only need a little time to clean myself up and rest. I've had a long, weary trek to get back to you."

"That smallest cabin is empty, down at the end of the row. But see here, Jane—you take any boys inside, you owe me a quarter of whatever they pay. Consider that your boarding fee."

I slapped my palm against his, fly bites and all. "You got yourself a deal."

"Now go get cleaned up. There's a well and a pump out back of the saloon. You can put your horse in with the rest. I'll make sure no one sells her. I got some salve that might do for those fly bites, too."

By the time we finished our negotiations, dusk was well on its way. The long shadow of the palisade faded, giving way to gathering night. But I could still feel that sturdy timber wall at my back, and I was grateful for its presence. While I went about the business of settling into my new domain, I resolved to build a wall around my heart every bit as high and impenetrable as the palisade. For after that mad and reckless jaunt through the border of the Black Hills—all for the hope of one kind word, one loving look from Wild Bill—I knew Molly b'Damn had been right. I was better off forgetting Bill Hickock. Gents of his sort didn't fall for slammers like me, and a slammer was the best I could ever hope to be.

A YEAR PASSED SWIFTLY at Cuny and Coffey's Road Ranch, and before I knew what had hit me, my twentieth summer dawned. I think that's why I made up my mind to leave the shelter of the palisade and strike out for new prospects, new adventures— because I was twenty years old, and feeling my oats, as do all wild-and-free types in that most adventuresome of decades. I had put by a fair sum of cash—not as much as I'd made in the hurdy-gurdy days, for Cuny and Coffey was a remote place, there at the edge of the Hills, and was never like to attract big spenders. But I had enough scratch to see me comfortably to anyplace I wished to go.

In early June I bid farewell to Jem Coffey, who pleaded with me to stay till the fall at least. His prediction had proven right: my shooting demonstrations, scheduled special once a week and staged in the open space between the saloon and the palisade wall, quickly drew crowds from the nearest towns—none of which was really all that near. The fellas who came looking for a little enter-tainment often found themselves trapped by encroaching dark-ness, and having no wish to venture out into the borders of Sioux territory after nightfall, they usually stayed at the road ranch till dawn. Of course, that meant extra income for Jem Coffey and his partner, Mr. Cuny—as well as for the eight girls who had become regular fixtures of the place. I was sorry to leave the lot of them. I'd become something of a star attraction, and my utility in bringing men to the palisade made me popular among the whores. That year was the first time—and just about the only time —I enjoyed real friendship with any other woman.

I had a special fondness for Lilah Dean, a half-Negro beauty with a round face and a rounder bosom, whose talkative nature and fondness for jokes made us fast friends from the moment we first met. Lilah and me got up to new mischief just about every day, playing good-natured tricks on the other girls that most often set them to laughing right along with us. When she heard I was leaving the road ranch, Lilah clung to me weeping and wouldn't let go.

"You can't leave me now, Jane," she wailed with her arms around my neck. "It'll be too dull without you. Nobody else will get into trouble with me; I'll just die of boredom!"

I was sore tempted to stay on forever, purely for the affection I felt for Lilah and the other girls, who lacked all the hard-scrabble meanness of the pack I'd met at Madam Robair's pool hall. I thought it likely I would never find such pleasant girl-friends again in all my life, but a firmness of mind and spirit had recently come over me, and I knew it was time for me to move along.

I disentangled myself from Lilah's embrace and kissed her on both cheeks. "I ain't much good at writing," I told her, "but I can write some, so I'll send you letters often as I can. I promise. And when I got my course set clear ahead of me, I'll come back this way for a visit."

"What is your course, anyhow?" Lilah dabbed away her tears with a lace kerchief I had given her. It had been a present from one of my gentleman admirers. Whatever he'd thought a buck-skin-wearing she-buffalo like me would do with a dainty lace kerchief was beyond my reckoning.

I didn't answer Lilah's question, for I had no answer yet. I just kissed her one more time on that round, rosy cheek and swung up

onto Silkie's back, and waved a last good-bye to the Cuny and
Coffey crowd. There was nothing I could have told my friend,
anyhow, that would have made her understand. She would have
counted me a fool, and I would have had no defense against such
an accusation, for I most certainly was a fool, but powerless to
change my heart.

You see, all that year I told myself I must forget Wild Bill and
move on with my life. Day in and day out, even while I squinted at
my targets before a rapturous crowd, I tried imagine a future and
a life without Bill Hickock, for no matter how I longed for that
man, he assuredly wanted nothing to do with me. But more often
than not, the gun I fired was Bill's gun. And sometimes late at
night, when I took a traveler to my bed, his arms reminded me of
Bill's, wrapped tight around me as I swayed with whiskey-sick-
ness in the brief and sacred privacy of that small pine grove. To
forget Bill was a plain impossibility—a feat far beyond my
strength. I might as well have told myself to fly up to the moon.
To picture a life without Bill in it was to envision nothing but gray
—a featureless, colorless expanse, a dull and empty nothingness
that stretched on forever. I was twenty years old and feeling my
oats. I knew for a certainty that a life without Wild Bill was no life
for me.

So you can see, Short Pants, I was right back to the state of
mind in which I'd found myself the previous summer, at the start
Dodge's great expedition: determined to reform my character, to
polish the rough stone of my spirit into a gem of a woman, fine
and upstanding—or failing fine and upstanding, then at least
respectable enough that I might hope to win Bill Hickock's heart.

That's why I went to Cheyenne. This time, I had no intention
of hitting the hurdy-gurdy circuit. I'd heard tell that Cheyenne
had grown considerably since I last seen the place. I thought I
might reprise my ancient role as a maid in a boarding house, for
surely the quantity of boarding houses had grown along with the
general population. Now that I was a woman of twenty, possessed

of a righteous aim to become respectable, I even daydreamed about opening a boarding house of my own. If I was diligent and saved every penny I earned—and kept myself away from the whiskey—I might reasonably expect to buy my own house in two or three years. (At least, that's what I told myself. The truth is, I had no idea how much a big house might cost in a growing city of Cheyenne's caliber.) I pictured it all as I rode south toward my destination: the grand place I'd own someday soon, smack in the middle of town, with a peaked roof and dormer windows and every room rented out, every room earning me a fat, respectable profit. Wouldn't Bill's head just about spin when he rode to Cheyenne someday and inquired after the finest temporary housing available—only to find his old friend Calam, dressed in the ruffled frock of a proper respectable lady, holding open her door to welcome him in!

I reached Cheyenne a few days later. Reports of its growth didn't go halfway far enough. Dozens of new buildings lined the main street—not only houses, but several general stores, a dress-maker's shop, a handful of restaurants, and two new hotels. I recognized the saloons from my prior tenure, but they seemed grander now, their façades brighter and more cheerful than I had recalled, and they bustled with activity. The entire town was lively as an ant hill, in fact, with wagons so thick along the hard, bare road that at times I was obliged to weave Silkie in and out of their lumbering paths. Two stage coaches passed by, one headed east and the other west, with their window covers rolled up to take in the sight of an expanding city—Cheyenne perched on the edge of its former humbleness, fledging into an honest-to-God metropolis.

There was even a brand-new sheriff's building, complete with jail, the whole thing constructed from smooth red sandstone blocks. I stopped to admire the clean, square novelty of that build-ing, smiling to myself over the ingenuity of fancy scrolls carved into the uppermost corners near the roof. On that fine day, I had no idea that me and the jailhouse would soon make a more intimate acquaintance.

McDaniels' hurdy-gurdy house was gone—replaced by three or four others—but its disappearance didn't trouble me. I hadn't come to Cheyenne in order to fall back into my old profession. My aim was noble, free from sin. My first order of business was to seek out a place to lay my head, and I found that in the rather crowded halls of Skipton's Boarding House, a big mismatched lurch of a building out on the northern edge of town. Skipton's looked as if somebody had rounded up all the tumble-down shacks for miles around, herded them onto one barren patch of hot, red earth, and stitched them together willy-nilly without much regard for whether the finished result looked welcoming— or even stable enough to stand up to a stiff breeze. But the rates was cheap, so I paid up for a week in advance, hoping I would find respectable employment by then, and could justify a less dodgy accommodation.

Mrs. Skipton, a stout and blustery dame somewheres around fifty years of age, showed me to the narrow closet that was to be my room. Then she wagged her finger in my face. "No gentleman visitors of any kind—you hear me? Not even ones as are already boarding here. I don't run a cat house, miss!" I guess she could feel my history emanating from my person, the way you can sense a ripple of body heat before a gentleman visitor touches your bare skin in the dark.

I tucked my few belongings into an undersized chest—the only bit of furnishing, aside from my bed, that would fit in the rented room. Then I inquired after the best livery stable in Cheyenne, and duly boarded Silkie with all the comforts she deserved. I set out on foot to explore the booming town, grateful for a chance to stroll and stretch my legs after days in the saddle.

I spent an awkward hour with a dressmaker, standing with my arms held wide while the woman measured every part and portion of my big, ungainly body. I needed to be cautious with my money, I knew, but I had also perceived that no high-class boarding house was like to hire me if I wore shirt and trousers. Hell, no middling-class establishment would hire me, neither, and probably not even a dive like Skipton's. If I wanted a proper lady's work, I must do my best to look the part. A dress would act as a disguise of sorts, too, shielding me from my reputation as the girl shootist of Cheyenne—for it had been only a few short years since my previous habitation of the town, and I had no doubt that some men could still recognize me at first sight. A frilly get-up would help me blend in with the women of Cheyenne till I secured a place as a maid. Or at least, that's what I hoped.

The dressmaker scratched a few figures in her little notebook. She tutted and squinted at the difficulty posed by my broad shoulders, my startling height, my disappointing bust. She disappeared into a back room partitioned by a fine curtain of olive-green velvet, and I listened in on an extensive course of rustling and bumping and the occasional curse, whispered in a small, genteel voice, so faint I almost couldn't hear. At last, she re-emerged with two dresses slung over her arms: a cream calico dotted with blue flowers, and a pink-and-white check.

"The waist will be too big," she said. "I made these for a much stouter lady who never paid me for the work. But you can wrap a woven scarf around your middle and draw them in tight. That will be stylish enough, I think."

Style was the least of my concerns. I needed to go about decently while I hunted up a new living; that was all I cared for now. I bought both dresses and a blue sash for the sake of my unremarkable waist, then hastened back to the Skipton house where I bathed and clothed myself as quick as I could.

I spent the next five days tramping up and down the streets of Cheyenne, inquiring at every boarding house, restaurant, and laundry I could find, but no one seemed inclined to hire me, even decked out in my new dresses. The end of the week was fast approaching; my prospects had begun to feel distinctly

small. An odd malaise had settled over me from the first day of
my search, too. At first, I thought the strange weight of discomfort, the dragging reluctance of my every step, came only from
the dresses. I hadn't worn a dress since the start of my hurdy-
gurdy days, after all, so I reasoned that the sensation had
become unfamiliar, and convinced myself I'd feel right as rain
once I fell back into the habit of comporting myself more or less
like a lady. But as the week plodded on, that distant, haunting
melancholy took on a note more ominous and troubling.
Perhaps I was only feeling the effect of so many shaking heads,
so many doors closed firmly in my face. But looking back now, I
can't quite make myself believe it. A curious tension ran through
the streets of Cheyenne. Something was bubbling all through
the population, a strange disquiet that grew day by day. As I
walked one street, then another, I noted men tumbling out from
saloons and restaurants to shake their fists in one another's
faces. I saw women scold their children, and their voices grew
harsher every day. Even the sun seemed to beat down with
concentrated fury, so the heat of the day felt impatient—or
vengeful.

On my sixth day in Cheyenne, I came to understand why.

That morning, my route took me up the main street and past
the jail, which happened to stand right beside a freshly installed
news printer's shop. The newspaper had landed in town only a
couple months before I had, and was still such a novelty that
ladies and gentlemen alike found it good fun to stand outside the
shop waiting for the paper, each one hoping to be the first soul in
Cheyenne to clap eyes on whatever news of the world had just
traveled across the telegraph wires from every far-flung location
they could imagine. I had seen the morning crowd on my first day
searching for work. The gathering was significantly larger now—
more than double its previous size, and that same curious tension
I'd sensed in the town at large fairly boiled outside the news
printer.

I worked myself into the edge of the crowd, listening to the conversation around me.

"There ain't nothing to worry about," one man said to his friends. "You think the greatest hero of the Civil War can't handle a mess of Reds?"

"The last news we heard was of 'the biggest village ever seen.' That's a mite more than a 'mess of Reds,' I wager."

"Don't matter how many Indians there is. Custer can lick 'em all."

"So we all must pray," said a gray-haired woman. She was dressed in widow's black, high-collared and severe, and she had the look of a humorless schoolmarm or an overworked mother. "For if Custer can't put this village to flight, there will be no one left to stop the Sioux."

Somebody deep within the crowd chuckled at her words. "Stop the Sioux from what? All the Indians is running now. They know what's good for them."

"Stop them from raiding one town after another." The gray-haired woman's voice rose with every word. She seemed barely capable of holding herself from the edge of hysteria—and she wasn't alone. As she spoke, men turned their hats nervously in their hands or kicked their feet in the dust, and women whispered in one another's ears. "Certainly, the threat seems far away now. Montana is a long way off. But you know as well as I do that Indians travel fast. If God doesn't grant Custer this victory, the Indians will take it as a sign from their heathen spirits. The raids will begin again, but worse than before—worse! We'll all be in terrible danger, even here in Cheyenne. Don't think the modernization of this town will keep the Godless menace at bay!"

"Have a little faith, Grandma," a man called. "Or if you got no faith, then have some respect, at least. It's George Armstrong *Custer* you're talking about. If God ever made a man better fitted for war, then I never heard of him."

I stepped closer to the woman in black. "Please, mam," I said, "I been on the road for an awful long time and ain't heard news of the world for many days. What has happened out there?"

She looked me over carefully before she answered. Her mouth twisted in judgment when she saw my ill-fitting pink-check dress and the blue sash that contained it. But she answered politely enough. "We would all like to know what has happened out there, young lady. We've had no news of Custer for several days, and I'm afraid it has put us all on edge."

"What news should we expect to hear? I been traveling long enough that I ain't heard a peep about Custer for months."

She raised one doubtful brow at that and looked me over more sharply—no doubt wondering just where I'd sprung from, and what suspect purpose had brought me to Cheyenne. At length, she said, "My goodness. You must have traveled some lonesome roads indeed, not to have heard what has transpired with General Custer. But surely you know that the Seventh Cavalry has been engaged on the Montana frontier, in the unceded territory, all spring and summer."

"Certainly," I said, though in truth I hadn't heard much about it, saving a few moments of idle chatter gleaned from visitors to Cuny and Coffey's.

"Well," said the woman in black, "we've heard nothing here in Cheyenne since our last news of the Seventh Cavalry. That was more than a week ago. It was a tale daunting enough to rob us all of sleep; I can tell you that much. The Seventh fell into a battle at a place called Rosebud Creek. They were routed by the Indians. Our troops retreated—and that's all we've known from that day to this."

"I can understand why everyone's hopping about," I said. "That's a powerful long time to wait, when you're fretting over news."

"The printing is almost an hour late by now. I suspect some important telegraph came in and has delayed publication. I'm a wreck of nerves, to tell you the truth. The unceded territory isn't so very far away, and if the Seventh has lost ground, I shudder to think…"

The woman didn't finish her thought, but she hardly needed to. I shuddered to think, myself.

At that moment the door to the newspaper office creaked open, a small and hesitant motion. A young man in a felt cap poked his head outside and looked around, wide-eyed. When he saw the size of the waiting crowd, he turned rather pale and sickly.

"What news?" someone cried. Then the whole street burst into one great clamor, men and women alike shouting at the tops of their voices for word of Custer and the Seventh Cavalry.

The newsman cringed at the sound. He shrank back into the building, then suddenly threw the door wide, heaved a stack of papers out onto the boardwalk, and slammed the door shut again as the crowd surged forward.

I knew the news was grim long before I saw a paper myself, for a great moan of despair went up from the crowd, spreading up and down the street in waves. Then the men began to shout again—a ruckus of outrage, of disbelief, of violence itching to be unleashed. I pushed through the pack of bodies, trying to get close enough to a paper to read the news on my own, for I thought the odds slim that I could convince anyone to pause and speak to me now. The crowd was too riled, each person stunned and reeling within the confines of their individual shock. Papers flitted hand to hand all around me; I craned my neck or turned on my heels, trying to track each flapping, rustling bird before it flew away. I could scarce be called literate—truth was, I struggled even to read my own name—but the urgency and commotion seemed to sharpen my wits, and whenever I caught sight of the hard black headline, the words burned themselves into my eyes, echoing like rifle shots inside my head.

MASSACRE!

3 DAYS DESPERATE FIGHTING
GEN. CUSTER AND 261 MEN LOST

THAT NIGHT, I stayed out late on the streets of Cheyenne. Dread
had gripped the whole town, and the streets was full to busting
with an air of wild abandon. A desperate certainty had fallen over
Cheyenne: certainty that doom would soon come—indeed, that
some dark and foreboding fate would shortly envelop the whole
West. That sickening air of impending disaster made men rowdy.
They was all unpredictable, reckless and loud. Every sensible
woman had shut herself away at home, there to weep frightened
tears into her kerchief. But I had never been especially sensible—
and anyway, a private melancholy all my own settled over me,
making me near as desperate and wild as the men. I had no reason
to believe Wild Bill had attached himself to Custer's Seventh, but
Bill had been a soldier in the war, and the last time I'd seen him it
had been in Indian territory. The two facts seemed most
ominously connected. I couldn't shake a terrible certainty that
Wild Bill Hickock, my true and abiding love, was laying dead
somewheres along the banks of Rosebud Creek, bloated like a
dropped deer, his pretty hazel eyes picked out by vultures, leaving
nothing but black pits and a void where his spirit used to be.

I spent a few fruitless hours drifting about the streets,
searching for some way to drive the image of Wild Bill's corpse
from my head. The alleys and lanes of Cheyenne was all filled
with angry shouts, with the tight, coiled tension of violence
waiting to be unleashed. Big and strong I may have been, but I
didn't wish to encounter any men that night. Their fear and grief
made them unpredictable. I wasn't keen to be any man's victim, so
I stuck to the patches of light that spilled out of taverns and
saloons; I hung about the hitching posts and patted horses' necks,
listening to cries of disbelief that seemed never to end—listening

to the pianos in the bars, playing too loud and forceful to sound happy. An ill omen had descended upon Cheyenne, all right— maybe on the whole damn West.

Finally, I knew my lonesome state would drive me mad, even there in the midst of the crowded Cheyenne streets. I resolved to find a card game and join in, just for the sake of having someone to talk to, though I knew already that no one would talk of anything but Custer's disastrous battle. And joining a card game meant stepping foot inside a saloon. I had kept myself well away from whiskey since leaving the road ranch; the persistent headaches had only vanished a couple days before.

You ought to go back to the boarding house and take to your bed, I told myself even as I made for the nearest bar. *No good will come from putting yourself within reach of a glass.*

But I couldn't bear the thought of laying in my hard, narrow bed, staring up at the dark ceiling. There, I would read no answers to the questions that chased themselves around and around inside my head. Shut up at home like a proper lady, the not-knowing would eat away at my soul. Long before morning came, I would surely go mad with fear on Wild Bill's account, and then I'd be of no use to anybody, least of all to myself. I needed answers—or at least some conversation to distract me from my thoughts. That's how I found myself in a saloon called the Swinging Bucket, bellied up to a game of faro with three subdued and pale-faced young men.

One of them looked up from his misery long enough to study my face. "Ain't you Calamity Jane?" he said. "I swear I saw you shoot in a fancy dance hall some two years ago."

"No sir," I said, lowering my eyes to study my cards. "My name is Margaret Bird. But I heard a time or two before that I resemble the famous Calamity."

That was enough to throw the boys off my trail—or so I devoutly prayed. Talk turned at once to the news of the day.

"Damn shame about the Seventh."

"Damn shock, is what it is."

"I call it treason," said the third fellow. "There's no way a pack of Reds could have pulled one over on Custer. Some white man turned his coat and slipped the Reds some secret or other—the General's plans. I guarantee it."

"Martin Wells, that is the stupidest fucking thing I ever heard you say, and by God, I've heard you say more than your fair share of stupid things." That fellow tossed a few chips into the kitty, then seemed to recall that I was there. He nodded in my direction. "Begging your pardon, Miss Margaret."

"I promise you, some traitorous white man was involved," Martin said. "The truth will come out, sooner or later."

The man who had begged my pardon sighed, long and deep. "You've always underestimated the Indians. That's your trouble. You can't conceive of the Sioux defeating Custer because you think they're all as dumb as you are. If you ever dealt with them yourself—if you seen what I seen out there with Dodge—you wouldn't make such a foolish mistake."

I studied my cards even harder while my cheeks burned. So that man had been on Dodge's expedition. He wasn't the fellow who had seen me shoot, and I had counted it unlucky enough to encounter one man who might recognized me. *What about this other fellow?*—I couldn't help but wonder. Dodge's rider hadn't so much as blinked when I'd given my name as Margaret Bird. Maybe he never came close enough to see me, on that trek from Fort Laramie to the fateful crossing of the crick. Or maybe recognition just hadn't caught up with him yet. *I should have gone back to the boarding house, after all. Martha, you damn fool!*

Warily, speaking with the most casual tone I could muster, I said, "Oh, was you on Dodge's expedition in the Black Hills? What was that—more than a year ago? I recall I heard some tell of that expedition, months gone by."

"Yes'm, I was on the very same detail."

"He was only there for half of it," Martin said peevishly.

"Makes out like he's some great Indian fighter, but he spent a couple weeks riding with Dodge—that's all."

Dodge's rider cut his friend a long, dark stare. Then he said to me, "True enough, that I was only along for a few weeks. I didn't join up till the end of the summer. Had to make my way out from Kansas first, and by the time I got to Fort Laramie I missed the departure and had to wait around till a shipment of supplies went out. I joined up then. But," he added, "a few weeks of action was plenty of time to become acquainted with the Sioux. And plenty of time to know that you, Martin, are full of shit."

I slumped in my chair while the game went on, for the relief of knowing I wouldn't be recognized had turned my backbone to water. I played my hand rather half-heartedly and listened while my table mates ribbed one another without the least mercy, and predicted in dire tones what Custer's defeat would mean for Cheyenne. They was all unanimous in their belief that the tragedies at Rosebud Creek and Little Bighorn brooked nothing good for any white man. Or woman. I ought to have fretted more over the promised disaster, and I knew it—but till I'd heard some definite word of Wild Bill's fate, I could attend to nothing else.

After a spell, a lull fell over the conversation. I took advantage straight away. "Say, that trek you made with Dodge. Wasn't there a fella attached, by the name of Bill Hickock?"

The rider perked up at once. "Wild Bill?" He tossed another handful of coins into the kitty and grinned at me. "Sure was. He was a damn fine scout, I must say."

"A dandy is what Bill Hickock is," said Martin sourly. "I never heard of no fancy-man being much good for anything."

"Then I reckon you haven't met an awful lot of fancy men," said the third player. He leaned over the table, looming toward Martin Wells. "You better tread carefully, son. Never know who's hiding his fanciness under his clothes."

I broke in before they could inflame themselves enough for a fight. I didn't much care whether they took it out into the street or not, but I wasn't about to let the talk die out before I'd learned what I could about Bill. "No reason to come to blows, friends," I said. "I was only curious. I must have read about Wild Bill in a newspaper back in Fort Laramie. I heard he's the best scout who ever lived, and a great Indian fighter, too." I swallowed hard, toying with my cards to stall for time. I longed to know, yet I was frightened of the truth, too. "I guess Wild Bill must have joined up with Custer, seeing as how Custer went to fight the Sioux. Nothing much else makes sense."

"If he joined up with Custer," Martin said, "then he's nothing but a pile of bones on the banks of the Little Bighorn now. Fat lot of good Wild Bill's vanity did him, in the end."

My heart stopped beating. I felt it freeze in place, felt the surge of panic and pain, the rush of blood to my head. My ears roared loud as a waterfall, loud enough to drown out the wails of despair and drunkenness from the dark streets of Cheyenne.

Then Dodge's rider spoke, nice and short and dismissive. "Very likely Wild Bill would be dead, if he'd been with Custer. But he wasn't."

"He wasn't?" Cards fell from my trembling fingers; I scrambled to retrieve them before the men saw what I'd held. "How do you know?"

"'Cause I seen him." The rider laid down his cards—a devastating hand—and scooped the kitty towards himself. "After Dodge's expedition, all manner of patrols went out around Wyoming to search for more gold. I ran into them plenty, while I worked here and there. I caught sight of Bill Hickock at least half a dozen times over the past year, and never was he in proximity to General Custer."

"He's a coward; that's why," Martin said.

I rounded on him at once. "Bill Hickock ain't no coward. I never heard such horse shit in all my days."

The men laughed in appreciative shock—even Martin. Then

he said, "How would you know whether he's a coward or not, Miss?"

"Just what I read in the papers," I muttered, and tossed my useless cards down on the table.

"You all right?" asked Dodge's rider. "You come over flushed all-a-sudden."

"I'm fine. Guess the news about Custer is finally catching up with me." I pressed my hands against my burning cheeks. My heart was a drumroll inside my ribcage, loud and rattling. Never in my life had I known such relief; the sheer giddiness of certainty made my head spin, even though I was sitting down.

"You look just about sick, Miss Margaret."

"I feel all right. Don't you boys worry none about me."

"You do seem awful peaky," said the third man, the one who had threatened Martin. "You ought to have a tonic to bring you back around. Let me buy you one. Least I can do, since you was kind enough to call Martin out on his horse shit."

Wild Bill was alive. He hadn't been slaughtered with the Seventh Cavalry. He had been roaming free throughout Wyoming Territory—free and easy, blending into the vast beauty of the land that was his and mine. My joy in that moment was boundless—so great and fierce and shivering, it made me reckless.

"If you're buying," I said, "I'll have a whiskey."

"By God," Dodge's rider chuckled. "She swears and she drinks. No wonder you've oft been mistaken for the infamous Calamity Jane."

Moments later, the glass bumped down in front of me. I could smell the warm welcome of liquor, the biting promise of revelry and comfort, and above all else, forgetfulness. Whiskey was the only door I could close between myself and the assortment of dreads and terrors and black, looming shames that haunted me in my lonesome moments. What did fear and shame matter that night? What did Custer matter that night, or the Sioux, or the

inevitable downfall of the West? Wild Bill was alive, and I alone—
of all the residents of Cheyenne—was in the mood to celebrate.

———

YOU WON'T BELIEVE ME, Short Pants, but I don't recall much else
of that night. Next I knew, my three friends from the faro table
was gone. So was the Swinging Bucket Saloon, and God knows
how many empty glasses—which I had drained, I suppose, while
my new friends cheered me on. First I became aware of a terrible
chill—a biting cold—and the faint dampness of dew in the air, the
smell of dew-covered sage. Then the pale gray half-light that
looms up from the eastern horizon just before the sun rises. I
heard crickets in long grass, and the first twitter of a lark, away
off across the prairie.

And then I heard a man shout, "Miss, I said to put it down and
come toward me. Keep your hands where I can see them. Miss!
This is the sheriff talking!"

There was something bunched up in my hand. Cloth. A great
quantity of cloth, and it was slightly damp from the dew, just like
all the rest of the world. I let the bunch of fabric unfurl from my
hand. It was a woman's dress, fine and beautifully made, with
pintucks and ruffles all down the chest and silk ribbons at the
collar. I stared at the thing astonished, never knowing how it
came to be in my possession, nor why I was standing in the
middle of Cheyenne's main street just before dawn, far on the
south side of town.

———

I'LL SPARE you a recollection of my trial. It's a long and sordid tale;
even now I blush with shame to remember. All you need to know
is this: I was spotted nicking dresses off of clotheslines in the
yards of all the best homes of Cheyenne. It seems that day a great

many women forgot to bring in their wash, which is understandable, considering they had all convinced themselves that an army of Sioux was likely to descend upon the place any minute and scalp them all to death—now that the protective talisman of General Custer had been so thoroughly destroyed. I was over-bolstered on whiskey, and took it into my head to improve my wardrobe—or so I presume. I can't imagine what else would have inspired me to go raiding from clothesline to clothesline in the dark of night.

I spent three weeks in that beautiful new red-sandstone jail for theft, as well as for a general raising of Hell. The jail wasn't near as pretty on the inside, and those three weeks of confinement rank among the worst days of my life. I had nothing to do but dwell on my foolishness, endlessly berating myself for the whiskey and my gluttonous tendencies. The whiskey had proved itself an abominable way to celebrate Wild Bill's continued survival, for hadn't I sworn I would come clean and never touch the stuff again, all for his sake? Worse, I had ruined my fresh start in Cheyenne, and no mistake. If I'd thought it tough to find honest work before, I knew I'd be in for a devil of a time now that I'd become a known quantity in that city.

The only saving grace of my tenure was that the sheriff had been kind enough to retrieve my goods from the Skipton House. He carried my boarding fee to Silkie's livery stable, too, so my horse was safe and seen to while I did my time. The sheriff stowed my personal effects in an apple crate at the far end of the jail, well beyond my reach, but I scarce took my eyes off that box while I stewed in remorse. Wild Bill's gun was among my goods. I never would have forgiven myself if I had lost my true love's pistol.

By and by, my three weeks of imprisonment concluded, and I was escorted from my cell to a small, stuffy room furnished only by a table and two chairs. Through a narrow window, I could see the prairie stark and yellow, dried and oppressed by the violent summer sun. The flat plain rippled in the heat, all the way out to a pale-blue horizon, to the line of the Medicine Bow range crouching low in the distance.

The sheriff entered the room carrying my box full of goods. He had found my black sombrero, too; it sat atop the whole lot like the finial lid of some improbable tureen. He set the box on the table. "You gave your name to the court as Margaret Bird," he said. "You were under oath, so I must assume you told the truth, even if I can't quite make myself believe you."

I swallowed and said nothing.

"Let me tell you how it'll be, *Miss Bird*. This town has enough troubles just now. The night I picked you up, the whole place was on the verge of a riot on account of Custer's downfall. It took my deputies considerable effort to restore order to Cheyenne, and I am not eager to see that order dashed again. There's no place in this town for a woman who drinks herself into wildness and then flits around in the dark of night, outraging her neighbors with larceny. Such behavior won't be tolerated again. If you don't behave like a proper lady—" Here he paused and lifted my sombrero gingerly, as if he feared he might find a rattler sleeping underneath. Instead he found my trousers and my guns, which he seemed to consider equally upsetting. "—you will be sent out of Cheyenne for good. We are upstanding citizens, here. We aim to make this a fine city—fine as any Back East. If you can't keep yourself under control, you'll find yourself on the road to Fort Laramie or some other place. Do I make myself clear?"

"Yes sir," I said at once, "perfectly clear. And I'm real sorry for my bad behavior."

He pushed the crate toward me. I was free to go. But of course, after three weeks ruminating in a small, dark cell, I was convinced —and rightly so, I believe—that no one in Cheyenne would give me a chance now. My only hope was to leave the town altogether and light out for a new destination.

Now, seeing as how I'd been gifted free room and board for three weeks, courtesy of the town of Cheyenne, I had more money in my purse than I had expected. And I liked the look of my worldly possessions packed neatly in that crate; it made a nice change from my usual state of affairs, which was to cram everything I owned willy-nilly into saddle bags. I determined to give myself a little treat, and leave Cheyenne in higher style than I'd entered, so I proceeded at once to the livery, where I sprang Silkie from her own confinement, retrieved my tooled-and-silvered saddle, and rented a cracking sharp buggy with a team of four.

The livery man squinted at me in doubt when I put forward my request. Ladies didn't drive themselves unless it couldn't be helped, but I had learned the secrets of driving a team many years prior, and I was itching to relive the experience. Besides, I didn't look much like a lady by that time, for I had changed out of my calico dress and back into trousers and chaps—a more agreeable costume by anyone's standards. It took a fair heap of cajoling and the addition of some extra pay, but by and by, I wore that livery man down and drove out of Cheyenne alone, perched proudly in the driver's seat with my team of four stepping out smartly to my command and Silkie tied to the back. I ain't too proud to admit that as I left Cheyenne behind me, I saluted the whole place with one vigorously extended finger, a gesture I learned from an Italian railroad man who had called on me more than once during my hurdy-gurdy days.

Many a story has followed me over the years; many legends have attached themselves like burrs to my name. Some are untrue —dreamed up by scribblers like you, Short Pants, all in the name of earning a buck. I bear you no ill will, nor any of your kind: the dime novelists and sensationalist writers who have come west seeking my legend, seeking the ghosts I left along my countless lonesome trails. We all must earn our pay; no one knows that better than old Calamity Jane. Most of those stories can only be called fabrications, but some ain't—or at least, some contain more truth than fiction.

The famous tale of how I drove ninety miles from Cheyenne

to Fort Laramie blind drunk, though—that is a scurrilous lie, and
I will insist it's a lie till I finally turn to dust and blow away on a
prairie breeze.

I am so vociferous in my denial because once I was let out of
jail, I was dead set on coming clean. I knew Wild Bill still lived,
and so my motivation to transform myself redoubled. God and
the Sioux may have taken Custer from all of us, but my love had
been spared. I was apt to believe in miracles that summer—even
the most unlikely miracle of breaking whiskey's hold on me for
good. New wings of gratitude had me flying high; I faced the
lonesome trail and my future with pluck and vigor. No thirst
plagued me on that journey, save what I could slake at any ordinary crick or spring. I had no clear idea of where I ought to go, for
every town in Wyoming Territory seemed as unlikely to afford
me comfort as Cheyenne had been. The budding city fell away
behind me—its haphazard boarding houses, its beautiful new jail,
its bubbling Custer-induced fear. But I didn't mind. I had set my
heart not on fear but on love, and I chanted under my breath as
the team of four swung out onto the open prairie. *Take me wherever Wild Bill may be. Take me to my love.*

———

BY AND BY, I found a broad, flat road running north, and despite
the glaring sun and the thirsty dust hanging over the prairie, that
road looked smooth and inviting. Fort Laramie lay to the north—
the last town where I had seen Bill Hickock. Fort Laramie seemed
as good a destination as any other; maybe lucky into the bargain,
so I turned my team northward and settled back to enjoy the
drive.

The day was hot, but I kept an easy pace, wending my steady
way through sage and grass, always following the promise of my
chosen road. A herd of buffalo moved lazy in the distance, and
once a great flock of black birds scattered up from the road ahead,

twisting in the air above me like some wind-tossed storm cloud. In time, the heat eased and evening set in, followed by a fleeting sunset. The stars blossomed in a cooling sky, paving my road with gentle silver light. Starlight seemed such a blessing that I knew I couldn't be far from my goal—my endless, aching need. My love, Wild Bill.

I arrived at Fort Laramie just after dark and surrendered my rented buggy and the team of four to the livery. "They're from Cheyenne," I told the fella who ran the place. "Wire down and tell them Calamity Jane has turned in their buggy and team in fine fettle. And tell the whole damn town to go stuff their heads while you're at it, just as a favor to me."

I mounted Silkie and rode through the dark, narrow lanes of Fort Laramie, with my worldly goods stuffed once more into my saddle bags and one eye keenly open for a likely place to rest my head. I passed plenty of saloons—the Fort had grown up considerable since I seen it last—but I felt no temptation to venture inside. I reasoned I would spend one night at Fort Laramie, then strike out for the next destination (whatever it may be.) I intended to keep moving from town to town and fort to fort till I'd criss-crossed the whole West, ever on the lookout for Wild Bill. And once I found him, I wouldn't leave his side again, not even if he tried to drive me away with a club. Fate had spared him, preserving him from Custer's grisly end. Foolish girl that I was, I couldn't help but believe—with the dead-certain conviction of an idiot in love—that fate had kept him safe specifically for me.

Seeing as I was thoroughly determined to keep myself on the trail till I found Wild Bill at last, you can imagine my surprise at almost riding him down in the black streets of Fort Laramie. I had just made a circuit of the town, but had found no vacant boarding rooms—so I decided to cut back to a grassy, unbuilt square and make a rough camp there, just as I'd done with my brothers and sisters in Salt Lake City. I wheeled Silkie around in the middle of a narrow street and kicked her into a brisk trot, but at that very moment a man came striding out of an alley, bursting into reality sudden as a snap of lightning. Silkie reared and very nearly threw me; I cussed and fought the reins till my horse was back on all four feet, snorting and wringing her tail.

"You damn fool," I shouted, "why don't you look where you're going? Or at least don't wander around drunk in the dark of night. Somebody'll take you for a thief!" Didn't I know all about that.

The man planted himself in front of my horse, stalk-still, and stared up at me in disbelief. Even in the darkness I recognized him—the long tumble of hair, the proud carriage, the buckskin coat with its swinging fringe and Indian beads along the edges of his sleeves. And his eyes—sharp, intense, as piercing and considering as ever. I recognized him, and yet I didn't. I couldn't really believe I'd found him, easy as that, just by wishing and dreaming I would. And so I set like a bag of rocks in my saddle, mouth hanging open, unable to do much more than stare.

"I'll be damned," Bill said at last. "Calamity Jane."

The sound of his voice. Like nothing I'd heard in all my life, better than any music, sweeter and more compelling than the wind in the mountains. I wanted to close my eyes to listen— wanted to distill him to an essence of himself, pure sound, concentrated and singing all through my blood—but I was afraid the sheer force of my longing had conjured up a vision, and if I took my eyes off him, even for a second, he would disappear.

He said, "What are you doing in Fort Laramie? And riding like a breakneck fool in the middle of the night?"

"It ain't the middle of the night," I managed to say. "Not yet." I swung down from the saddle, took a few halting steps toward him. "I just come up tonight from Cheyenne. What are you doing here, Bill?" His name on my tongue tasted better than molasses taffy.

"Arranging another expedition, I'm afraid." He swept off his hat, held it against his chest in a sheepish display—a false display, for Bill had never been meek nor humble in all his life. It was one of the things I loved best about him. "I'm bound for the Hills again soon. I aim to stake out a claim among the gold fields."

"An expedition," I said, perking up some. "That's good luck for me. I'm coming with you, Bill, come Hell or high water. I won't take no for an answer. You'll find me real useful and pleasant, I swear. I haven't had a drop to drink in a proper long while."

I omitted the fact that I had been penned up in jail for a proper long while, too, and that accounted for my dryness. What Bill didn't know wouldn't hurt him.

Bill chuffed a little laugh and sort of settled on his feet, leaned his weight in a comfortable fashion. "Now why in God's name would you want to join up with another expedition? I would have thought your last adventure was enough to put you off the idea for a lifetime, at least."

"I want to be a gold miner," I said, without taking the time to consider whether it might be true. I would make it true, if Bill agreed—I'd become the best damn gold miner who ever dipped a pan in a crick. "I been real respectable since we parted ways, but it's getting harder all the time to find good work. I tried, down in Cheyenne—tried real hard. I thought I might keep a boarding house, but there was no house that'd have me. And there ain't no boarding houses here at the Fort, far as I can tell. I don't want the kind of work that'll just keep me barely fed, though; I aim to get rich someday and live like a queen."

Bill chuckled at that. He turned his hat in his elegant hands.

"Why not?" I said, defiant. "Ain't I got as much right to live like a queen as any other woman? And I'm willing to work hard to get there—harder than most ladies will consent to work, I wager."

"I guess you got as much a right as anyone else," Bill said. I liked the warmth in his voice, the note of chummy gladness. "And I guess gold mining ain't less respectable an occupation than the one you held in the past."

I sensed my advantage and pressed it most shamelessly. "I'd say gold mining is a damn sight more respectable—at least if you was to ask a preacher for his opinion. Come on, Bill—let me join up. You know I'm strong and hardy, and I can ride as well as any man."

"I dare say you can, at that."

"I'll be just as handy in the gold fields. I can do the same work a man can do."

Bill's mouth twisted in a slow, considering fashion, and a veil of doubt seemed to slide across his eyes.

Before he could tell me no, I said, "It's a long way from here to the Hills. And expeditions require a powerful lot of money." I didn't know that to be true, but I figured they must be costly affairs. Otherwise, a body would run into ten new expeditions for every mile of trail they rode. "I can earn quick money along the way. I'll give it all to the expedition. You know I'm good as my word."

"Earn money? Calam—"

"Not through any sinful means. I developed a reputation as a trick shooter. Look, Bill, I still got your gun, and I can shoot real good, too. People come from miles around to see Calamity Jane trick-shoot. All the money is yours, Bill—whatever I can earn. Just take me with you up into the Hills. Let me have a chance as a gold miner. Let me take my one shot at living like a queen."

Bill turned away, but not to reject me. He stared out into the lightless calm of Fort Laramie, silent and still while he weighed my offer. Crickets called everywhere in the night, one clamoring chorus of joy. My heart seemed to beat as fast as the rapid pulse of their song.

Finally Bill looked at me again and nodded. Just that—but it was all I needed.

"Bully!" It was all I could do to keep myself from hollering that word. "We're going to get rich, Bill—you and me."

"Come along to where I left the rest of my crew. You might as well start bedding down with all of us tonight. They're a good bunch; they won't give you no trouble, long as you return the favor."

I led my horse through the night, and Bill fell into step beside me. When we reached the expedition's encampment, out on the edge of Fort Laramie, I realized Bill had carried his hat the whole way. Just as a gentleman would do in the company of a real, proper lady.

A ROMANCE OF THE SILENT TONGUES

I'VE TALKED A STREAK ALREADY, SHORT PANTS, AND DRAWN THE picture of my life, as far as my poor skills will allow—drawn out every beautiful and ugly facet, laid my whole world bare. But how can I describe the bliss of riding again with Wild Bill? I look back on those weeks, when we made our way from Fort Laramie to Deadwood, and I find words fail me utterly. Perhaps there's no language sufficient to describe the beautiful pain of love. The torment of proximity, the longing in your bones—in the fiber of your flesh—a need to touch so compelling, your hands will catch fire unless you reach out to take what you can never have. It's a hunger so deep, no food will satisfy; a weariness so consuming, no sleep can ease it—and anyway, in sleep you find only dreams of the love you cannot speak, the rip you cannot mend.

Even if Bill had loved me—if he had deigned to hold me close, as lovers do—my longing would have gone on forever. My love for him was too powerful by then. Mere touch would never quiet that force. A kiss, a lingering embrace—nothing could have cured the sweet, the endless ache. Even the stark act wouldn't have been enough; I yearned to know Bill's mind and heart so desperately, nothing could have contented me except to merge with him—

body, mind, heart—till his every private thought became my own, till I felt his breath in my own lungs and heard his voice spilling from my throat.

An impossibility—that's what my love was.

I knew it was impossible, knew I could never be happy again, even if God granted a miracle and Bill decided he could love me after all. I was miserable with the knowing, even while my heart soared to heights of bliss I hadn't imagined might exist.

I thrilled to every moment of that journey, each passing heartbeat—for I had grown closer to Bill than I had dared to dream. (I mean closer in the physical sense—riding by his side—as well as in our friendship.) I was willing to tolerate the precious agony of an unfulfillable longing, so long as I rode next to Bill, and shared a laugh with him now and again. So long as I could watch Bill ride out onto the trail ahead, scouting the way, while the edges of him blended into the land and the land melted into his beauty.

On Dodge's expedition, I had come to appreciate that Wild Bill was a part of the West. But it wasn't till our trek to Deadwood that I came to understand Bill's perfection of place and spirit. I felt his belonging in that vast, open world the way you feel a line of poetry, or the strain of a poignant song. The sight of Bill on his red horse, perched atop a red bluff—or traversing a ridge at evening time, singular in the cooling night—reverberated in my blood, so that even when Bill returned to his place on the trail beside me, I could still see him there—away out there, a ghost drifting apart from the ordinary world, a memory patterned against the sky in skewed and vivid colors, as when the vision of a candle flame remains imprinted on your eyes, dancing violet and blue against all mundanity of ordinary sight. I savored those visions of Bill in the wilderness more than I ever savored whiskey. And Bill among the world—his true and rightful world—brought a thrill far deeper and richer than whiskey, too. I came to understand that Wild Bill was a habit I could never shake. With enough motivation, I could hold myself clear of liquor—I knew that by now. But my hunger for Bill—the sweet, trembling pain of my insatiability—would haunt me all the rest of my days.

We didn't travel alone, Bill and me—more's the pity. Don't take me wrong; the fellas he chose for his expedition was all good men to a one, and whenever Bill went off scouting, I enjoyed their company immensely. Three gents accompanied Bill and me, each hopeful of enough gold to make him rich as a lord. There was Joe McAllister, whose pappy came from Scotland, and who played a dandy fiddle by the campfire every night. Timothy Crutch was a Negro boy about my same age who didn't talk much but enjoyed my stories plenty. The more fanciful and improbable my stories became, the more Timothy laughed and prodded me on. And Jasper, of no particular last name, was the oldest of our lot—old enough to be a grandpa, I think, but strong and vigorous with a respect for Wild Bill almost as great as my own. I enjoyed the company of those boys whenever Bill rode off on his own, but the moment he returned, I cleaved to his side like a loyal spaniel pressed against its master's heel. Truth was, Bill paid me no more heed than he paid Joe or Jasper or Timothy. But he paid me no less heed than he paid the boys, either. I counted that a wealth and a blessing.

I made good on my promise to perform at every road ranch and town along the way. The name Calamity Jane drew modest but predictable crowds, and my fancy shooting oft' inspired enough whooping-up from my admirers that I sometimes brought in extra funds to put toward our gold claim. Long before we reached Deadwood, Bill began to look at me with greater respect. By and by, the pity he had once felt for me eroded, replaced by the warmth of genuine esteem. He never said a word about his shifting opinion of old Calamity Jane, but I read the change in his eyes, in the way he squared his shoulders in my presence and asked me for my thoughts on the towns and road ranches we passed—whether I accounted them worth a stop-over, or whether we ought to press on toward Deadwood. I drank down Bill's tacit praise, thirsty as a man at a desert well.

What I liked best about that trek wasn't my shooting shows at the road ranches, nor even the way Bill smiled when I handed over my earnings. What I liked best was the nights. Our little expedition bedded down beside some trickle of a stream, or away out in the sage with nothing around to mark our camp—any flat place would do, chosen because sunset had come, and we was all dropping. By night, I stoked up a fire of buffalo chips, and the five of us cozied up around the blaze, swapping lies and eating heartily even though the food was terrible. We cussed and laughed and basked as much in the warmth of our friendship—all us comrades together—as we did the heat of the fire. The light from our flames set Bill's face apart from the darkness, and bounced from the golden ring he wore, shaped like a snake with two garnet eyes. And when the flames had dithered down to a few glowing embers, we all took to our bedrolls. Then I lay with my back turned to Bill, whose back was turned to me. But my every sense was attuned to his smallest movement—the sound of his breath, the way it slowed and deepened as he sank towards sleep. I lay awake, shivering from the nearness of the man I loved, aching to touch him—knowing I never could. And all the while, high above, the stars wheeled drunk on their own light, brighter and more numerous than they had ever seemed before.

We took our time traveling to Deadwood, for that summer was especially hot, and the season carried something wild and frenzied in its long, yellow days. Outrage over Custer hadn't abated. In fact, it seemed to grow with every settlement and ranch we encountered. Long before we reached Deadwood, the summer felt like a tinder box—close and confined, yet packed to bursting, liable to blaze out of control at the first and smallest spark. The people was all frightened, and fear makes most men angry, aggressive, boastful. All across't the West—or at least across't Wyoming and Dakota—men seemed harder, less trustful, less worthy of trust. We made up our minds to tread with care and watch what we said, for the most harmless of interactions was apt to end in a fist fight, or worse.

But even at our leisurely pace, we did find Deadwood at last. Bill stopped our party beyond the edge of town, at the crest of a rise, all hard-white earth, dry and exposed, baking under a merciless sun. Deadwood lay before us, just far enough to look like a toy village scattered by a child at play. All its buildings was small and fragile, clustered self-consciously around the feet of the Black Hills. The town seemed half-forgotten in the vastness of the landscape.

"I don't fancy staying in the town itself," Bill said, staring long and sober at Deadwood. "You seen how het-up everybody was, all along the trail. But we've come up against the hottest weeks of summer, too. There ain't no sense going up into the Hills just now. It'll only go harder on us than it needs to."

"We should wait out the last of the summer here," Jasper said. "Head up into the Hills once we see the rain clouds gather in the high country. Then the cricks will be flowing again for sure, and the going will be easier."

Bill nodded, but he still kept his eyes fixed on Deadwood. "Exactly my thoughts, Jasper. Let the rest of the summer pass. We'll benefit from the extra preparation, anyhow—more time to get our supplies together, time to be sure we've got the best equipment available. Two weeks, then—and we'll see how the weather goes. But I don't like the thought of boarding in town. It'll cost too much money, for one thing. Jane has worked hard to keep us in cash; I ain't keen to squander her earnings. We'll use our money to buy more goods for our mining operation."

For one thing. Bill harbored other grim considerations, which made him shy of boarding inside Deadwood. He never spoke his worries aloud, but I could guess well enough. Even at a distance, I could feel Deadwood vibrating with the same queasy tension we found in every settlement along the trail. Bill was no coward, you understand—I won't hear a word against him, even to this day. He was sensible; he thought it better to keep us all out of danger in the first place, rather than fighting our way out of the pickling brine.

We set up camp a good half mile beyond Deadwood in a shallow wash. A muddy trickle of water still ran among parched and sun-baked boulders, but plenty of willows grew among the boulders, too, and the shade was nice. Many a pleasant hour I spent lying on my bedroll at midday, soothed by the cool, water-scented air below the willow boughs, watching their thin, gray leaves paint pictures against the sky. In those happy hours, I idly picked out among the ever-shifting shapes the profile of Wild Bill, or a brief image of him on horseback silhouetted against the hot blue sky.

We made a short trek into Deadwood at least once a day, where the fellas took any odd job they could scare up, and I danced the liveliest of reels with sharp, intense men at every saloon and pool hall the town had to offer. Folks was willing to pay a few coins for the novelty of dancing with the notorious Calamity Jane, famed swaggerer and swearer of Dakota Territory —but I did nothing else to earn my pay. For one thing, Bill wouldn't have approved. I had no great wish to spoil his image of me, now that I had gained his respect. For another thing, I had no desire to poach in the rightful territory of the fine ladies who occupied those pool halls and taverns. I had renounced my former profession, but I still felt something of a sisterhood with the kind-lier whores—and feared the mean ones enough to give them no grief. Besides, if I had stopped dancing even for a minute, I would have been too tempted to wet my throat. The livelier I danced, the more the boys paid me, and the less chance I had to smell whiskey on the air.

While me and the boys brought in cash, Wild Bill set about taking meticulous stock of our goods. By the end of our first week in Deadwood, he had worked out a list of all the tools and supplies we lacked. Then he hunted up and down the streets, seeking to fill the holes in his inventory. Every evening at sunset, we converged on our camp site among the willows, each of us weary to the bone. We pooled our money in Bill's hands. Then we settled around our fire to listen to Joe's fiddle, slapping mosquitoes and dreaming of the vast riches yet to come—the certainty of our success, the brilliant future we could all sense waiting some-wheres just head.

One night, Bill was late returning to camp—so late that I began to fret, for the fire had almost burned itself out and the night felt close and pressing, still uncomfortably warm with the day's remembered heat. The longer Bill stayed away, the more worried I became, till I dropped out of the talk altogether and sat huddled with my knees drawn up to my chest, staring into the guttering flames.

Timothy watched me a minute. Then he said, "You all right, Calam?"

"Fine," I answered. "Just tired. Long day at the pool hall."

The boys looked at one another, then at the empty space where Bill ought to be. I could feel them all staring at me, weighing my silence. They must have puzzled out my secret by then, but they was gentle enough not to mock me for my hopeless love.

Eventually, the boys took to their beds—but I remained awake, wondering if I ought to head into town and scare up Bill Hickock, and picturing all the ways I might find him if I was fool enough to try. Knocked out cold in an alley, the victim of some damn, drunken idiot still smarting over Custer. Or worse, knifed in the chest by the same sort of damn, drunken fool. I might find Bill too drunk to walk, despite his admonitions against liquor—and then what would I do with him?

What really held me back, though, was a growing, howling suspicion Bill that had occupied himself with a girl. For though Bill claimed to disapprove of whoring, he was only a man—and I ain't never met a man who will hold out terribly long. He might berate himself the next morning, but once the urge takes him, he'll forget all about his lofty morals and dive right into the first bed he finds. What pained me most about the possibility wasn't the thought of Bill as a hypocrite. I could forgive him that. What hurt me was the images that kept running through my head—me busting down a crib door to find the man I loved taking pleasure in another girl's embrace. I couldn't bear such a scene, when Bill hadn't yet touched me—and seemed likely never to touch me a-tall.

But despite my fears about pretty whores, I soon reached such a state of despair that I was willing to brave the town, even if I did half expect to find Bill in another girl's arms. It just wasn't in Bill's nature to stay away so long, without a word... And when I did find him, I intended to scald him for making me worry so, even if he was slumped over in an alley with a knife sticking out of his guts. I rose abruptly from my place beside the fire and stalked off through the willows, gritting my teeth against my fear. Then I spotted Bill making his way toward me, a dark figure slinking through the night, picking his way between boulders and patches of scrub.

I went to him eagerly, my whole body prickling with relief, though I moving with great care so as not to wake the other boys. My feet had begun to tingle and my knees to quake; I didn't quite trust my legs to hold me upright. Bill stopped at the sound of my approach, waiting for me in the dark. I found him behind a dense patch of willows. The scraggly growth screened us from the camp, in case any of the boys awoke.

"Where in Hell have you been?" I whispered. "I been sick with worry. I thought you got yourself killed."

I had expected Bill to chuckle, then to rib me some. That was our way, after the long trek to Deadwood and the bond it had forged between us. Instead, he looked at me steadily in the faint starlight. I drew myself up rather defensively, for I could see that pity had returned to his eyes.

"You know, Calam." He spoke in a slow, reluctant way. "You know… last year, I went and got myself a wife."

I stood there. For longer than I care to admit. Staring at him. His revelation had stolen the breath plum out of my body; I couldn't do nothing more than gape at him, and wonder why I was still on my feet—why I hadn't fallen over dead from grief and loss.

After a spate of my silence, he said, "Right after I came back from Dodge's expedition. I figured it was time."

"Oh." That was the best I could manage, just then.

"I guess she's about to have a baby. Any day now, if it ain't come already."

I nodded.

"Thought it best to tell you," Bill said. "Thought you should know."

I progressed rapidly through shock, disbelief, rejection of the whole damn idea. Then I settled into calm acceptance. I didn't want to know the woman's name; I didn't care. Or that's what I told myself. There had never been any real hope that Bill would come to love me, and I knew it—had known it all along, from first sight of him riding behind Sheridan. So what if he had gone and married his fool self off to some woman? Some woman who couldn't possibly love him as much as I loved him. Nothing had really changed between Bill and me. I would still love him just as powerfully, just as doggedly, even if he had a dozen wives.

"Where you keep her?" I was pleased that my voice sounded so causal, unhurt.

"Just outside Fort Laramie."

"Does she mind an awful lot, you going off to prospect in the Black Hills?"

"Not a terrible lot. She told me she was looking forward to getting rich and building a big, fancy house inside Laramie proper. Said to bring back plenty of gold and she'd forgive me any long absence. She's a good enough girl, but she's the type who can look after herself. I don't think she'll miss me much till I come home."

"I'm the type of girl who can look after herself."

"I know you are, Calam," Bill said gently.

"Well," I said, trying to make as if the news had already blown right past my heart, "what were you up to so late in town? Now that I know you gone and married yourself off like a fucking blind idiot, I guess it's even less likely you was dallying with a whore."

Bill laughed, low and quiet. "Never that. Ain't never been my way."

Of course it hadn't been his way. Beautiful as he was, Bill had no need to pay for affection. I could see it now—could see what a shameful fool I'd been all that past year, riding around the prairie and yearning for Wild Bill Hickock as if he would ever have any cause to love me—as if he would look twice at me when the most respectable and upstanding of ladies would gladly tumble right into his lap, without his needing to trip them first. I thought, but didn't dare say, *Your wife must be surpassingly beautiful.* Why would such a fine-looking man bother to marry unless the bride was as delicate and rare as a china doll? Standing there before him, with my heart falling down into the pit of my stomach, I thanked God for the dark of night. In the dark, Bill couldn't see me so clearly— couldn't see my bigness, my ugliness, the dirt ground into my skin. The last thing I wanted just then was to know for a certainty that Bill was comparing me to the astonishing beauty he had left back in Wyoming Territory. His wife.

A pause hung between us. At the time, I was too distracted by my turmoil to notice the awkward air, the tension lingering around Bill while he weighed his next words with care. I didn't notice then—but all the countless times I have relived that moment, I have taken note, and wondered at the feeling.

Finally, Bill said, "I ain't been seeing any girls in town, Calam.

Truth is, I've taken up playing faro to earn a little extra money for the expedition."

I recalled the first time I'd seen him, sitting cool and unmoved outside Boss's tent, among boys who had ribbed him for his good looks. Faro game, cards held easy in one hand, all the confidence of long experience. The way he held his cards put me in mind of my pa. A bone-deep certainty. Knowing he would win—or believing he would win, at least, even when luck wasn't on his side. Always that same belief, the endless knowledge that fortune would favor him. Next time, if not this time.

A queasy suspicion rose inside me. My chest felt so tight, I could hardly draw a breath. I said, "You play cards a lot?"

Bill shifted on his feet, turned his face so he didn't have to look at me. "Some."

"It's more than 'some,' Bill. I can tell."

"You can't tell a thing, Calam."

"Hell I can't. You think I ain't seen shit like this before?" He scowled at me over my coarse speech, but I was beyond caring for his high ideals. What was the point now in trying to make myself into a woman Wild Bill could love? "I should have known it when I first met you," I said. "Known it just by the way you held your cards. And this seals the deal: you slinking back to camp so late, any reasonable person would have thought you dead. You're hooked on games, ain't you?"

"No." The way he said it most certainly meant *yes*.

"Damn it, Bill! I worked in pool halls and hurdy-gurdies long enough to know what's setting right before my eyes. And if that long experience wasn't enough to convince me, I can compare you easy enough to my pa. It's all over you—the gambler's look. I can see it now. God help me, it's a wonder I never saw it before. You got some real nerve—riding me over my whiskey, telling me I ought to give up drinking when you're hooked just as strong."

Bill took offense. He didn't like being compared to a drunk—not one bit—but I knew full well how apt the comparison had been. He rounded on me, stepping up like maybe he might consider throwing a punch—though I knew he would never do such a thing. Bill wouldn't have struck any woman, not even a big, mannish creature like me.

He said, "Faro never hurt any man, except to lose him money. Nobody loses his dignity playing cards, the way you—yes, you, Calam—lose your dignity when you're down in a bottle."

"Faro never hurt a man, like Hell," said I. "My pa died for a game of faro. Faro's the reason I ended up an orphan, all alone on the trail with no one but me to look after my little brothers and sisters. Faro's the cause of all my woes, far as I'm concerned—and all my disagreeable characteristics, too, for I never would have taken up this life if my pa hadn't been killed over a damn fool card game. Whatever faults you find in me—whatever you lay at my feet, Bill Hickock—you best take those complaints to faro's door, not mine."

"All right," he said, gesturing with his hand as if to coax me to silence. "Careful now, or you'll wake the boys."

"I don't care if I do. Off gambling into the night—imagine! Betting away all the money we raised for our claim, too, I wager."

Even in starlight, I could see how Bill's face darkened. "I can get it back. All of it."

I groaned. "So you have lost our money. How many nights you been out gambling, Bill?"

"Not many."

"Which means all of 'em."

"Not all, and you'll make me real angry if you keep up this harangue, Jane."

"Bully. You won't get half as mad as I am right now. I thought I never could feel anything but good towards you, Bill. Now I see I was wrong. Terrible wrong. You put our expedition in danger and you blew money we all worked damn hard to earn. And you ain't concerned yourself a-tall with the dangers—the men who might come after you."

"I don't cheat." Bill was icy.

"You don't need to cheat to find yourself on the wrong side of a fight. All you need to do is set across the table from the wrong sort of man. You know how many fights I seen over cards? Seen men killed, too—more than just my pa. And to top it all, you had the nerve to make me swear off drink when you was hooked on something yourself! Where'd you find balls big enough for such a thing, I wonder? It's damn sure you wasn't born with 'em."

Bill sighed. His shoulders slumped a little; there came over him an air of relief, as if he was glad to have found himself entangled in this fight, and glad to have lost it. "You're right, Calam. You are. I ain't too proud to admit you're right. It's a nasty habit, and I ought to let it go—particularly now, with a family to think of. It's long past time. Got one more game coming up, tomorrow afternoon. It should be an easy one. I'll be able to win back what I've lost, and—"

"No," I said at once. "Back out. You can't ease out of these things, Bill. Once something has its hooks in you, it don't let go as easy as you think. You got to tear yourself away in one quick motion, and never go back for any reason."

"But the money for our claim—"

"Find another way to earn back the money. Take up bull-whacking, like Timothy and Joe has done. You got to listen to me, Bill; I know what I'm saying. It's been almost six weeks now since I touched a drop of liquor. I know what it takes to get free. Please just listen to me, or before you know it, you'll have lost more than money. You'll gamble away all your treasures in life—everything that's really precious to you, all the things you can never get back. I saw my pa do it. Everything he cared about was gone before he could blink. Then his life was gone, too. I don't want that to happen to you, Bill. Not to you."

He sighed and nodded. "I'll heed what you say." Then he took a gold watch from his trouser pocket, unclipping the chain from his belt. He passed the watch to me. I stared at it, the golden disc swinging in the space between us. "Go on; take it."

I did, slowly and with no small amount of trepidation. The watch was cool in my hands.

"You can keep hold of my irreplaceable treasures," Bill said, "and that way I can't be tempted to gamble them away. Give them back when I've kicked the habit for good—which I expect will happen up there in the Hills, for we won't have much opportunity for real gambling when it's just us—the boys and you and me."

"Don't put this on me," I said. "I can't be your conscience. I ain't fit to be anyone's conscience."

"You don't need to be my conscience, Calam. Just my safebox."

He slipped the gold ring from his finger, the snake with garnet eyes. I wondered whether it was his wedding band. Did his beautiful wife choose it for him? Did she have it made special? If so, she knew him well. The snake was a perfect symbol for Bill: smooth and enduring, ever-present in the dry, hot world, confident and unafraid.

Bill tried to pass his ring to me, but I stepped back. "I don't want it. I won't touch it."

"Don't be a fool, Calam."

He reached out and took my hand. Bill's touch spread fire all through me on the instant; I thought of the man I'd met with the snake-bit ankle, the red and black lines running out from the place where the poison had sunk in. Bill lifted my hand, so he could see what he was doing. He slipped the golden snake over my thumb, and it fit there perfectly, as if the ring had been mine all along. My chest quivered. I scolded myself for a damn, unforgivable fool, but I couldn't help feeling as if Bill had betrothed himself to me with that garnet-eyed ring. I knew full well that to entertain such thoughts would only bring me pain, in the end. But I couldn't drive the thought away. When Bill released my hand, I turned the ring around and around on my thumb, feeling the shape of the snake and the small glittering eyes, feeling the metal warm against my skin.

Bill leaned in suddenly. His kiss landed on my cheek so swiftly, I didn't have a chance to savor it. He was there—then he was gone, stepping back into his private sphere, the separate world that was Bill's alone, his atmosphere of cool confidence, his untouchable realm.

"You're a real good friend," he said. Then, "We ought to get to our bed rolls and catch a little sleep. Tomorrow is another day."

YOU CAN GUESS how much sleep I caught that night. I lay awake almost till dawn, toying with the snake ring on my thumb, picturing the woman Bill had married, wondering what she'd say if she knew Bill had given me the ring to hold.

By and by, I managed to achieve a restless, unsatisfactory slumber. I woke late in the morning feeling groggy and sick. Most of the boys had cleared off—Bill included—and only Timothy remained, for it was his turn to watch camp while the rest of us ventured off to Deadwood.

I found a spot to piss, off among the willows, then wandered back, one hand newly adorned by the red-eyed snake. Sunlight kept flashing and winking up from my left thumb as I crossed the gully, making me blink—making tears spring to my eyes. The other hand I kept in my trouser pocket, where no one could see my fist locked tight around Bill's golden watch. A sick feeling of dread followed me as I went about my business. I told myself my heavy fear would soon enough abate, lifting like a winter fog. I told myself we would leave Deadwood any day now, for I was certain the summer heat was letting up. Soon we would be up in the Hills, where no one could tempt Bill into a disastrous game. He would overcome his addiction to faro, just as I had overcome the whiskey. All would be well.

I wandered back to camp and struck up a conversation with Timothy, trying to make the day fly by faster—trying to carry my heart beyond Bill's last game of faro.

"Late morning," I said.

"I thought it best to let you sleep in."

"Been dancing too much, I guess. I needed a good, long rest."

"How rested you feeling?" Timothy asked. "Up for a trek to Deadwood? I could use a few things from the general store, and I'd be much obliged if you would pick them up for me."

I agreed, and in the end, Timothy sent me with all his most recently earned bullwhacking money—a few loose coins for the hard-goods store, with the rest of his cash tied up in a little leather bag. I was to locate Bill and give him Timothy's money that very afternoon. I considered telling Timothy to keep his money and deliver it to Bill that night, for there would be no more venturing into town on Bill's part. But Timothy spoke up before I could, and said he hoped Bill could make use of the funds while he was still in town, gathering more pick axes and shovels and gravel pans for our expedition.

What was I to say then? I set off just before noon with everything Timothy had given me. My feet dragged as I paced out the half-mile to Deadwood, for I was caught somewheres between excitement and dread at seeing Bill face to face in the light of day. After the strange intimacy of our conversation the night before—and his fleeting kiss, which I could still feel hot and vivid on my cheek—I wasn't sure how Bill would react to my presence. By day, I felt sure he would see only my blunt face, my broad shoulders, my lumbering buffalo stride—and he'd recall what a disagreeable woman I was, and thank his lucky star that he had married a proper, pretty young thing, rather than saddling himself with a catch like me. He would take back his ring and his watch, fearful I would tarnish those beautiful things with my ugliness. All that worry over what Bill might do or say—unprotected now by the mercy of starlight—had me so twisted up that by the time I entered Deadwood, I made up my mind to deliver Timothy's money to Bill first thing. I would not linger more than a minute, and that way, Bill would have no time to think ill of me.

I set about searching for Bill, peering through the swinging doors of every saloon and pool hall, listening for the sound of his voice. He never spoke loudly, but I was so attuned to him that I could have picked out his murmur or his whisper among a thunder of men. I hunted up and down the main street, but I found no trace. All I discovered was outrage—more of that same boiling anger over Custer's defeat, more fear of what the Indians would do now that the magic talisman, the undefeated general, had fallen.

The heat of high noon beat down on the streets, so I leaned against the wall of the general store, cooling myself in the shade of its awning. A narrow alley stood to my right; I could hear two men somewhere in its depths, talking over the Custer misfortune while they pissed out their whiskey in relative privacy.

"I tell you, Clive; them Sioux will be feeling their victory. They ain't stupid, like some folks says. They know Custer was our best fighter. They know what it means, to have killed him outright and slaughtered the Seventh Cavalry good and proper. They got the upper hand know. They'll act on it, soon as they feel the time is right."

"But they ain't organized. Everybody says so."

"They *can* organize, and right quick. Shit, son; ain't you ever learned a speck of history?"

"Not an awful lot of specks, no."

"Folks Back East used to say, 'the Indians won't never organize', too. And I guess it was true enough, till it weren't true no more. Along came Tecumseh, and that brother of his who said he could see the future. Raised a whole army of Reds, so vast and wild, they near-about wiped out every settlement in the East."

There was a pause. Then the other man said quietly, "You think such a thing could happen here?"

"I know it. There's a chief up in the Hills, name of Red Cloud. I already heard he has sworn to carry Indian vengeance beyond the Little Bighorn and Rosebud Crick. And sure as you're born, the closest white town to Red Cloud is this one. Deadwood. We'll be dead for sure if we stay here any longer."

I didn't want to listen to their talk anymore. I shoved off up the street again, never mind the heat—and I shivered despite the sun, for I recalled with fierce and sudden clarity my fear that night in the Black Hills, when I had ridden alone up a rise and found the patient red embers of an Indian camp there before me in the darkness. The sooner I located Bill and gave him Timothy's money, the better off we all would be. Deadwood was a place best put behind us, all right, before danger closed like the spiked jaws of a bear trap.

At last I reached the only remaining saloon, one I hadn't searched yet. The sun had crossed its pale meridian; afternoon had arrived. I told myself Bill might be caught up even now in his faro game—the one he had sworn would be his last. There was no-place else Bill might possibly be, except inside that saloon. Eagerly, I stepped inside.

Though the day was young and hot, still the tavern was crowded, close with a smell of liquor and sweat, the stench of men's rage. The names Custer and Red Cloud seemed to roll off every tongue. I edged through the crowd, doing my best not to brush against any man, for I didn't like the crackling in the air, the lightning spark ready to ignite Deadwood's tinder.

As I neared the back of the room, I spotted Wild Bill. His back was turned to me where he sat at the card table, just cashing into his first round. There was no mistaking him, even though I couldn't see his face. He had slung his buckskin jacket over the back of his chair, and his hair was so red, it looked like a flame in the dark. I let out a quick, short breath, a sigh of relief. This business would soon be over, and by nightfall we would all be off, putting Deadwood and Red Cloud and the whole damn combustible world far behind us.

I gripped Timothy's money and started toward the faro table, intending to drop the bag on Bill's lap and depart once more. But before I could reach Wild Bill, somebody else reached him first.

The man separated himself from the crowd, and I could tell by the way he moved—the purposeful step, the eager tightness of his face—that he intended no goodwill. I froze, halted by the hate that rolled off that man in a black, oily wave, a billow of coal smoke. My eyes fixed to the green scarf knotted at his neck. That was how I knew he spelled ruination—for Bill and for me. I saw the scarf, the gun in his hand, the hateful steel of his eyes, the curl of his lip. I saw it all, and I knew.

"No!" I shouted, and surged forward, reaching for the man—as if I could do a thing to stop him. But even as I leaped toward Bill, the killer pulled his gun from his holster and fired a single shot.

I saw...

What did I see?

Memory comes back to me—memory has never left, but it's fractured, broken. Fragments passing through my mind like shards of glass busted from a window, pointed and shining, tumbling in the light of knowing. Vanishing again in a great black suffocating pain.

Bill lurching forward, tipping.

Chairs knocked back as the other players sprang to their feet.

The cards falling, and blood—hot, red, red as the bluffs. A fan of red across the table, spreading out from Bill's slumped body, his face flat against the wood.

A drop of red on the face of a card. And the smell of sulfur hanging in the air. Fuck off outta here, girl, before I shoot you too.

The tavern erupted in shouts and screams. I could hear it all through the terrible muffled ringing in my ears, the impact of the shot. And I could hear myself howling—a wordless, agonized cry that went on and on, even after I ran out of breath. I kept on screaming as I reached for Bill, kept screaming till there was nothing left in me—but still my body shook with the force of my hollering. I was out of breath, but my cry went on. I believe I howled the very spirit from my body.

IF YOU THINK ALL I did was stand there above my slain true love, screaming like some useless woman, then you haven't learned much about my nature by now. The man in the green scarf shoved his way through the thrashing, disoriented crowd, thrusting toward the door. I stared after him, wild-eyed, and I saw that the men of the tavern scrambled to get out of his way, fearful he might pop off again with his gun. No one made a move to apprehend him; they was all too frightened, the pack of sorry dogs. So with a great force of will, I sucked in one long, deep breath, and my body stopped shaking. I lit out after the killer, every nerve afire, burning with the need to catch him—hurt him, beat him, make him weep. Take his life for what he did to my Bill.

I didn't have either of the pistols with me that day—my pearl-handled gun or Bill's bright and shining piece. But I wasn't about to let my unarmed state prevent me from doling out justice. I surged through the crowd, silent as a hunting wolf, and followed the killer out into the streets of Deadwood.

The sun struck me with all its brutal force; I squinted, blinking tears from my eyes. I kept my purpose fixed to that man's dark, sweat-blackened shirt. By that time, the commotion inside the tavern had spilled out into the street. Anyone pacing the boardwalks or riding past was obliged to scramble and flee as scores of hollering men poured out the tavern door. I ignored the lot of them. Dogged, desperate, I pursued Bill's killer. I shoved aside both ladies and men, anyone who had the misfortune to step into my path. I wanted to shout for the sheriff, but my voice was gone. I had no breath for words—only for running, only for revenge.

The killer and me both broke free of the confusion, onto an open stretch of road. He was only a few paces ahead; I don't know whether he knew I was on his heels, but he ran as if Hell itself pursued him. Hindered no more by the crowd, he lit off down an alley. I stuck to him tighter than a burr. Now and then, I came almost close enough to tackle him, but by sheer luck he evaded my hands. I could hear men shouting along Deadwood's main street—"He went down that alley, Sheriff!" "He's still armed!"— and the pounding of hooves. The law was coming for him. He must have known it, surely as I did. I ought to have yielded the chase, let the sheriff do his work. But that man had stolen the one good thing in my life—ripped Bill away in a clap of thunder. I had a right to vengeance, and I intended to take it.

By that time, the killer seemed to know the sheriff was after him. I could see his rotten head twisting this way and that on his coward's neck as he ran. He was searching for a hole to dive into —must have realized he wouldn't get out of Deadwood alive, at least not till nightfall, when he might hope to evade the law under cover of darkness. The killer and I spotted an empty butcher shop in the same moment (no doubt the butcher and his customers had taken off running when they heard the riot from the tavern, curious to see what grim and inevitable fate had befallen the town.) The killer dodged inside the butcher shop, and I followed hard on his heels.

The interior of the shop was cool and dim; as I sucked desperately for breath, the thick, coppery taste of blood filled my mouth and damn near closed my throat.

The killer swung around to face me over the great, flat bench of the butcher's block. The wood of the block was pitted and lined with chop-marks. Flies rose from blood that had pooled here and there along its surface. A cleaver, shining like fury, was stuck point-down in the wood.

The murderer gasped for his breath, staring at me in disbelief.

"You fucking pig!" My voice came roaring back. It filled the shop, shook its walls, silenced the buzzing of the flies. "You rotten heap of shit! Why did you do it? Why?"

The man just stared at me, dumbstruck by my size or my rage or by the hellfire emanating from my eyes, from my raw, burning throat.

"Why?" I demanded again. "Tell me, you cockless shit-stain. Tell me why."

He found his words. They snaked out of him with a greasy little laugh. "Got sick of his bragging. And his cheating at cards. The great Indian fighter won't swindle nobody no more. Pretty boy Hickock is dead, just like he deserves."

I surged toward him; my hips hit the edge of the butcher's block and its legs screeched against the brick floor. My hands was like claws, bent at a desperate angle, sharp with the need to catch him—to savage him, make him bleed. He dodged around the block, keeping it between him and me.

Because I couldn't catch him—not yet—I screamed at him. I screamed. "I loved him. I loved him, you scum, you worthless bucket of piss! I loved him!"

The man laughed again. "Guess old Wild Bill's luck ran out in more ways than one. Who'd want to be loved by an ugly bitch like you?"

He raised his gun, pointed it at my chest. I went silent and still in a heartbeat. I stared into the dark hole of the pistol's muzzle. That gun had ended my true love's life minutes before. It was fitting that it should take me, too—take me out of this world of misery. Let me go wherever Bill was then—let me ride beside him in the ineffable bliss I had found with him on the trail. Let me never take my eyes off him, the West cloaked in the flesh of a man, all beauty and brilliance made whole. I accepted my death in that moment. I even welcomed it. The killer's thumb pulled back the hammer with a soft click. I waited placidly for my end.

But when he pulled the trigger, only a small, pathetic snap issued from the gun. I raised my eyes to his, and found him staring in confusion at his piece, turning it slightly in his hand as if to ascertain what went wrong. Either he had fired his last bullet into Wild Bill's head, or the piece had jammed. Whichever the case, I wasn't about to die—not that day.

The realization that I must go on alone, without my Bill, resurrected every scrap of my considerable fury. I wrenched the butcher's cleaver from the block and darted around the bench before the killer could train his gun on me again. Then I kicked the piece right out of his hand, so hard that the force of my blow spun that bastard halfway around. He cried out in pain while his gun went skittering across't the floor. Then clutched his hand against his chest. I think I broke a few of his fingers. My only regret is that I didn't kick his hand clean off his wrist.

Before the cry had even died on his lips, I shoved him hard against a wall, pressing the bloody cleaver to his throat. He strained up on his toes, trying to edge away from me—from my weapon, from my unchecked hatred.

"You pathetic fuck," I hissed in his face. "You low-down, yellow, whipped-ass dog. You sorry excuse for a man."

He twisted, but I leaned my whole weight against him, pinning him hard, holding him at my mercy.

"You'll do exactly what I say, you son of a bitch. You're gonna come with me outside, and I'm gonna hand you over to the sheriff. And as God is my witness, I'll see to it that the sheriff hangs you by your worthless neck. I hope it's a slow and miserable death. And when you get to Hell, be sure to tell the Devil it was Calamity Jane who sent you."

WITH BILL GONE, there seemed no point in avoiding liquor. There seemed no point in living, I confess—and since the killer's gun had failed to do its job, I suppose I resolved to do the job myself. Once I handed that stinking murderer over to justice, I hauled my numb, stupefied self to the nearest saloon and ordered up a whiskey. Then another. The barkeep kept them coming till my senses and my sorrow both dulled down—till I had no more awareness of anything but the taste of the liquor and the way it never stopped burning a path down my throat, into my splintered soul.

Some time later—I knew not when—I found myself lying in an alley. I could tell it was morning 'cause birds sang from the rooftops of Deadwood, even though the alley was dark with shadows. I laid on my stomach, pinning both my arms to the ground, and the first thing I did was feel for Bill's snake ring. It was still on my thumb, just where he had placed it.

Through a thick haze of confusion, a terrible pounding in my head, I puzzled out that the barkeep must have rolled me outside and left me there to tackle the night however I would. I guess no one had noticed me in the alley. If they had, they surely would have robbed my half-dead corpse. Carefully, I shifted onto my side and reached into my trouser pocket. The watch was still there, too.

And then knowledge of all that had transpired came back with cruel, inexorable force. I cried, though I was so dried-up from liquor that no tears fell. I laid on the cold earth with the stench of alley piss all around me. I sobbed out my grief till the sobs turned to heaves. I spewed out a thin stream of bile, then I wept all over again, for I knew if Bill could see me, he would never approve.

But Bill would never see me again.

By and by, a murmur of familiar voices edged into the boundless reach of my misery.

"There she is."

"Is she alive?"

"Yes, thank God."

"Shit—look at her. What a state."

Someone crouched beside me, tapping my cheek as if trying to rouse me. "Calam. Can you hear me? Calam!"

I groaned, tried to roll away.

"Made a mess of herself," said the man who had settled near me. Timothy—his name came back to me, and I thought of the camp under the willows, and Bill in the starlight, sliding his ring onto my finger. "Joe, go back and get her a change of clothes. Bring a few canteens of water, too, and whatever cloth you can find. We need to clean her up. Poor girl."

I fell flat on my back. High above, the sky was a pale blue band, a strip of searing light between the sides of two buildings. My head throbbed with the agony of sunlight, but I squinted up at it, defying the pain. I had a vague idea that pain was no more than what I deserved for being such a useless thing, a waste who had let that bastard pull his gun from his holster.

"We heard about Bill," Jasper said, low and regretful. "Guess you heard about him, too."

I seen him killed, I wanted to say—and did not want to say. I just shook my head side to side, wordless in my grief, and waited. Waited for what, I cannot say—for my friends to tidy me up, for the sky to open like a mouth and swallow me, for my heart to give out and spare me any more suffering. But time and life went on and on, and I was scarce aware of Jasper and Timothy by my side. I was cognizant of nothing but the agony in my head and my heart, and certain of nothing, save this: Wild Bill Hickock was dead.

In time, Joe returned, and the boys wrangled me to my feet. They stripped my soiled clothes from my body, right there in the alleyway, and cleaned me up as tenderly as a pack of new fathers washing a helpless baby. Then they wrestled my calico dress over my head and forced my swollen feet back into my boots.

"You need water," Jasper said, "and a bite to eat."

"Don't want to eat."

"I know you don't, but you're going to anyway."

"Let me starve. I don't care."

"You're going to eat, Jane. And then we'll all go together to Bill's grave and pay our last respects."

Bill's grave. "He's already buried? How long have I been—"

"Two days," Joe said, in a gentle, consoling tone. "Now come along, Calam. Lean on me if you need to. We can't do a thing to change what's passed. All we can do is keep moving forward."

I did eat and drink, though nothing had any savor. I did whatever the boys asked of me, automatic and unthinking like some trained animal, grateful to surrender all thought to my friends. By and by, I felt steady enough to walk on my own, and Timothy took me out to the crick that ran behind Deadwood—the same crick that wended through our campsite, though we was far from our camp by then. We stood together in silence for a long time, listening to the gentle bubbling of what remained of the crick—what the summer had left us.

"Where is he buried?" My voice sounded dull and small, even inside my own head.

"Out back of the church. 'Bout a quarter mile from here."

I nodded, though moving hurt my neck and my eyes. Around the roots of the willows, in the perpetual mercy of their shade, sprays of blue forget-me-nots still bloomed. The flowers were as small and ragged as my hopes had ever been. I picked them all—every flower I could find—and when I had gathered two great fistfuls of blue, I turned to Timothy and said, "I'm ready now. Take me to his grave."

WILD BILL WAS LAID to rest in a dirt hole like any other. There wasn't any stone to mark his final resting place—not yet—but the freshness of the new-dug earth was as clear a marker as anyone would need. I laid my flowers at the head of his grave, then sat in the dirt beside the low mound. Sat all day, while the boys came and went, patting the earth that covered their friend, coaxing me into a sip of water here, a bite of bread there. They drifted to the grave and away again as the hours passed and sunset came on. I remained, watching the forget-me-nots fading and withering, wishing I could be down there with him, knowing I must go on alone.

During my long and silent vigil, the realization came that I never had learned the name of Bill's wife. I felt powerful guilty at that, for I thought it was only fitting that news of his death should come from me. I, the woman who had loved Bill more completely, more perfectly, than anyone had done. I imagined our shared grief —mine and the widow's—and thought perhaps in the unity of mourning, we might come to understand one another. But I didn't know her name. I had no hope of reaching her. In time, she would learn of her husband's death, but the news wouldn't come from my lips.

Timothy returned to the grave as twilight set in. He found me there, right where I wanted to be.

"We got to get back to camp," he said.

"I don't care about that damn camp. I don't care about the expedition, nor gold, nor anything else. Now that Bill is dead, there's nothing for me in this life. Nothing. Go away and leave me be."

Timothy hung his head, then admitted quietly, "I know, Calam. I know how you felt about Bill. I saw it all. I—"

A sudden turmoil of sound startled Timothy to silence and shook me from my stupor. These wasn't the ordinary sounds of anger that had plagued Deadwood since our little expedition had arrived, some week and a half before. Shouts and screams rang through the night, high and frantic. Now and then a loud bang— gunshots?—boiled up from the town.

"Good God, what now?" Timothy said.

The screams grew louder, more desperate. A sickly glow bloomed and spread among the gathering dark—a fire, I realized. Somebody had set a building on fire.

"It sounds like a riot," I said.

"All the more reason to get out of here."

I let Timothy pull me to my feet. I don't know why. I should have stayed and allowed death to claim me. But we made our way back through town, clinging to alleys, skirting the backs of shops and houses. Deadwood had indeed fallen to riot. Men shouted and barreled through the streets, waving their guns, clutching at screaming women who clawed their faces and fought to break free. Away on the northern edge of town, I could see flames leaping above a rooftop. I thought it might have been the tavern where Bill was killed.

"For fuck's sake," I said, more annoyed than frightened, for the riot had intruded on my private sphere of grief. "What's the cause of all this?"

Timothy and me didn't stagger more than a dozen more steps before we saw the cause. The crowd broke and scattered, yielding the street to a tall gray horse and its rider—a man who whooped and cried like a wolf in a hunting pack. The gray horse ran at full tilt, throwing up its head, mouth white with foam. We shrank back into an alley as the horse and rider thundered past. And just as he flashed by our hiding place, the rider raised his arm. Something round and dark dangled from his hand, bouncing with his horse's stride. A flash of passing torchlight illuminated the thing he held. I gasped, lurching away from the scene, and Timothy caught my arm to keep me from running, blinded by my fear and disgust.

The man on the gray horse carried aloft an Indian's head.

Deadwood, I realized that night, was far worse than a tinder box. It was a keg of black powder, and the fuse was already lit.

"The sooner we're gone, the better," Timothy said.

I didn't try to argue no more. We kept our heads down and hustled out of Deadwood, retreating into the kinder arms of night.

THE BEAUTIFUL WHITE DEVIL OF
THE YELLOWSTONE

THE BOYS AND I RODE AWAY FROM DEADWOOD THAT NIGHT. WE
reined in at the crest of a hill—the same one we'd paused atop less
than two weeks before—and I turned in my saddle to take one last
look at the town, Wild Bill's resting place. Shouts and screams,
and the occasional crack of a pistol, carried through the night to
our vantage. The fire had spread, too; most of Deadwood's
northern edge smoldered in the dark, a smear of orange-red
spilled across the barely-seen foot of the Hills. None of us spoke a
word; we just set despondent in our saddles, watching Deadwood
burn, listening to the chaos erupting all down the length of its
streets. In time, Joe McAllister turned his horse and descended the
opposite side of the hill, vanishing into the waiting night. One by
one, the rest of us followed.

Our journey was largely silent, for we was all heavy with the
weight of contemplation—the weight of my inconsolable grief.
We rode without aim for the better part of a month, each of us
wilting and fading under the relentless heat of the sun, each of us
sagging in our saddles under the burden of sorrow. Bill had been
the force holding our small band together; it was he who had
provided us with purpose. Without him, all our dreams of

prospecting dissolved—turned to trail dust, blowed away on an errant wind. I can't tell you now whether we simply wandered without a destination, or whether Jasper (who had taken up the task of leading, rather half-heartedly) lost his direction. However it came to pass, we four battered souls meandered from one settlement to the next, finding small comfort where we could, speaking only when one of us had need.

I recall very little of those dark days, save for a constant, thick sorrow that sickened me by day and left me sleepless every night. I do remember laying in my cold bed roll, staring into the camp-fire flames while the other fellas retreated into sleep. In the dance of flames—in their twisting, fleeting shapes—the image of my love came back to me, Wild Bill's face and form repeating cruelly before my swollen eyes. I saw the color of his hair, the planes of his face, his tall proud silhouette against the darkness. I could even hear his voice in the soft murmur of burning wood—that low, slow way he had of speaking, the easy confidence that was his by nature. When the wood shattered and sent a stream of sparks flying high in a column of red, the crackle sounded like Bill's laugh, sudden and bright.

The only sense that penetrated my sorrow—the only reality I knew, beyond my private misery—was the danger pervading every town, a fearful alertness. In Custer's wake, the West had been left on edge, waiting to plunge over the cliff of civility. By then, a fall seemed inevitable. Somewhere beyond the gray haze of my misery, I was braced—certain that the world as I knew it would shatter like a dropped china plate. That restless tension of rage and disbelief had caused Wild Bill's death—at least in part. If the West hadn't given itself over to hopeless terror and readiness for violence, then the man in the green scarf never would have raised his gun in the Deadwood tavern. I convinced myself that was the truth, during our long and terrible wandering—though today, I ain't so certain.

More than a week after leaving Deadwood, we learned what

became of the town we fled. Jasper led us to a small village, situated where the Whitewood and Yellow Cricks join—I can't remember the name of the town, and it has surely vanished by now. Jasper intended to sell our mining equipment at the hardgoods store and divide the money evenly, and while he was negotiating with the shopkeep, he inquired anent Deadwood's fate. I hung back among the bins of sugar and corn seed, listening to the talk—keen for the first time since Bill's death, for I expected the shopkeep to wail and wring his hands and recount a most dreadful tale of woe. If the man had done so, I would have reveled in the story, I'm sorry to say. I would have taken a sharp, bitter joy in knowing Deadwood had been destroyed. Nothing else seemed fitting to me, except that the town where Bill had met his untimely fate should fall as he had fallen.

But the shopkeep perked right up when Jasper asked about Deadwood. "Had a spot of trouble, I know," he said, "but all's well now. The Army sent George Crook right up from Fort Laramie."

"Who?" said Joe McAllister.

"George Crook. Captain of the Army. Distinguished himself in the war Back East and has been dealing with the Indians ever since. By God, son—ain't you never heard of George Crook? The Reds call him 'Chief Wolf.' That's how fearsome they account him. Anyway, he'd been waiting down at Laramie, readying his men for a foray against the Sioux. Intended to put down that damnable savage Red Cloud, or so I hear. But it seems some feller from Deadwood did the job for him."

"I'd just about say he did," Timothy said. "Jane and me—we saw Red Cloud's head when his killer rode back into town."

"Must have been a real sight," said the shopkeep.

"One I'd sooner forget." Timothy shared a glance with me, and I nodded in agreement.

"Anyway," the man went on, "Crook came riding into Deadwood with a unit of his men—must have been a rapid march, to make it up from Laramie so fast—and he put out every fire in

Deadwood. I mean every fire—the real ones and the ones that only burned inside men's heads. Seems Crook settled the whole place down right smart, and just in time, too, for folks was all set to form a mob and light out after the Indians. I don't know how many Indians they expected to find up in the Hills, with their chief dead and all. I reckon they must have all took off like a lot of scalded cats. But I suppose no good would come of giving pursuit. Not many men in Deadwood can call themselves proper scouts. The whole mob would have been lost up there in the Hills—lost and dead within a few short days."

I had known one man in Deadwood who could call himself a scout. I turned away so the shopkeep couldn't see the pain rising to my face.

He said, "Old Crook settled the whole place down and told them what-all is happening with the Indian war—I guess, a town remote as Deadwood, they don't get a powerful lot of news. Whatever he told the townsfolk must have cheered them up considerable, for I heard they had a dandy of a ball at Crook's insistence—sort of a way to cool the whole place down, you see. Like kissing and making up. And from what I heard, Deadwood has been peaceful as you please from that day to this."

"A ball," Jasper said, dubious.

"Sounds like a fine state of affairs," said the shopkeep. "Wish we'd have a dance in these parts once't in a while. Good excuse to watch all the girls get dolled up and go about in their fanciest dresses."

Crook's ball sounded like a fucking stupid idea to me—like tying a bandage over a festering wound. The fear that had turned Deadwood into a powder keg still infected the West. My friends and me, we felt it all along our aimless journey. I was certain no mere bandage or ball could tamp down the hysteria for long. Custer was dead—Wild Bill, too. What might become of us next? Seemed anyone's guess, by my reckoning.

By and by, our flagging expedition parted ways. It happened

naturally, quiet as dispersing mist, without any hoopla. Joe was the first to break away, deciding to settle himself in Scooptown, where he aimed to take up steady work as a bullwhacker. We sent him off with a round of whiskey at Scooptown's fanciest saloon, then rode on our way one man poorer. Jasper peeled off at Rocky Pile back in Wyoming Territory, and then it was just Timothy and me.

I figured it was a matter of time before Timothy found himself a new gig and a brighter future, and then he'd be obliged to set me down and shoot straight. *Listen, Miss Jane,* he'd tell me, *I got my life all figured out now, and you haven't. I'm sorry for your plight, but it's time to go on to whatever's next for you.* It would be a hard speech to give, for Timothy was tender-hearted and sweet as you please; he had cared for me loving as a brother when he'd found me in that Deadwood alley, dirtied by shame and grief—and ever since that day, too. I made up my mind to spare him the difficulty of breaking my heart all over again, turning me loose in a cold, uncaring world. So I waited till he fell asleep one night beside a small, smoky fire of chips and slivers of juniper wood. Then I bundled my bed roll as quiet as I could, saddled my horse, and scratched in the dirt where I had lain my head:

GON BAK TO RAIL CAMP. SO LONG, FREND.

My WORD to Timothy was good: I did go back to the rail camps for a spell. How long? I can't quite recall. Might have been six months, or the better part of a year. I find the months after Bill's death run together into one great stream of featureless gray, like a bank of smoke or a wall of storm clouds. But I was a camp follower once more, and I made good money at the work, for by that time, Calamity Jane had garnered enough reputation to draw the curious—if not true admirers—into her unpredictable orbit.

Following the rail camps again, but I can't recall a single night I spent with any of those boys. None of them meant a thing to me. None of them ever could, after I'd tasted the purity of joy—the sweetness of riding at Bill Hickock's side.

If I'm honest with you, Short Pants, it may also be the case that I stayed too drunk that year to remember much of anything. I guess I don't need to tell you that I ran straight back into the arms of vice—my own particular vice, that hankering for strong drink that never quite left me, not even while Bill had lived. Without my love to restrain me—without the hope that he might someday come to love me in return—I saw no point in keeping clean. I threw myself back into whiskey with headlong abandon, consuming the stuff so thirstily, I believe I might have been trying to drink myself to death. Anything to ease the agony of my loss—anything to still the ghost that haunted me.

I remember this all now, and I can't tell you why I didn't take the easy way out. Why I didn't put Bill's pistol to my head, or to my heart, and end it just as fast as his own radiant life was ended. I guess something deep down inside me wanted to live. Or maybe there was a part of me that didn't believe Bill had truly died. Sometimes I still felt his presence there beside me, when I looked out over a canyon in evening light, or when I felt the endless green prairie wrap me in its sweeping embrace—oh, those long and lonesome rides. And in those moments, when I was alone with the land, I felt Bill so close I thought I would find him there if I only turned in my saddle to look.

I never did turn, though. Part of me knew that presence, that longing, was only the desperate need of my battered heart. I had no desire to undo the comfort Bill's ghost imparted. I preferred the fantasy, the slimness of the not-quite-possible—the thought that Bill might be there, not far back, following me up the trail.

I did keep his gun wrapped in an oil cloth, stowed in my saddle bag. I kept his gold watch in my pocket and the snake ring with the garnet eyes on my thumb, exactly where Bill had placed it.

And each night, when my latest caller left my tent and the railroad camp filled with its accustomed night sounds—the distant music of fiddle and mouth harp, gusts of laughter rising and falling abrupt as autumn storms—I looked at Bill's things by the light of a lone candle, and pressed those artifacts to my heart, and kissed their cold metal with trembling lips. But none of that ever brought his memory any closer. It sure as Hell never brought him back to life.

I CAN TELL ALREADY how this little chat will end. You'll soon grow weary of my talk, for my memories don't get any clearer from here on out, and they sure as shit don't get prettier. After Bill, all the color drained right out of the world. What memories return to me now come back in shades of gray—gray and blurred, like those old photographs you sometimes see, where the figures in the foreground are indistinct, and their eyes and mouths almost don't seem to exist a-tall. Where the only clear and recognizable feature is a line of distant hills against a blank white sky. Gray and blurred, or sepia. Take your pick. It's all the same to me.

AT SOME POINT—I know not when, neither the date nor the season—I abandoned the rail camps in a fit of restless pique and I became a town girl again. By that time, I seldom needed to work on my back, for folks was ready to part with a few coins just for the pleasure of watching me shoot. My reputation had grown steadily. The legend of the untamed girl shootist of the West had taken on proportions that far exceeded even my impressive frame. A demonstration or two outside a decent-sized village could set me up with money for board, livery, and whiskey for a week at least—and then I moved on to the next town, just as my reputation began to sour and more lawmen than curious spectators came sniffing after Calamity Jane.

I certainly did raise Hell in the towns I blowed through—more towns than I can number, in every trembling Territory, Montana to Utah to Colorado, Dakota and Wyoming, the jagged green- and black-basalt beauty of Idaho. I even ventured into some of the States (Nebraska and Kansas was often kind to me) for a while, anyhow, till the whiskey settled deep in my stomach and I began to whoop it up again. I never intended to raise any Hell whatsoever—even to this day, I swear to that truth, solemn as you please. But somehow Hell came rearin' up out of me, regardless of my wishes or my good intentions.

The Hell-raising nights always began innocent enough: a game of cards shared among some new friends (I always set with my back to a wall, for I had learned Bill's lesson, even if he hadn't.) Those nights ended in fist fights and wrasslin' matches, or with property smashed or stolen. And once a saloon was set ablaze, though I still insist that particular mischief belonged to someone else, not me. But whether I was truly responsible or not, Calamity Jane often took the heat for any ill luck that befell the towns she visited. I can't say as I blame anyone for blaming me. I made a tempting target: a woman big as an ox, dressed in a bullwhacker's gear, drinking and shouting and carrying on like some damn fool of a man. I stood out, and so I paid the price, even when the price wasn't rightly mine to pay.

A very thin margin of my thoughts did remain clear of whiskey, and in that margin, I was keenly aware that my notoriety as a Hell-raiser was beginning to eclipse my reputation as a skilled shootist. If I was to hold onto my livelihood, I knew I must set that situation to rights. So I made up my mind to perform a good deed—no matter how my heart would break from the doing. In the early summer after Bill's death, I found myself orbiting slowly around Fort Laramie, creeping from one town to the next, always with the Fort and its surrounding settlements at the center of my reluctant spiral. For I had determined to seek out Bill Hickock's widow and bring her the news of her husband's demise—or if she had learned of his death already, then I could at least reassure her that Bill's killer had been delivered to justice.

I reasoned the best place to find the widow's whereabouts was in the town of Fort Laramie itself, so I entered just as bold as you please. But all too soon, my skimpy nerves failed. I knew I couldn't look upon the woman Bill had chosen over me. I couldn't face her beauty without comparing myself to her perfection—without knowing how hopeless my love had always been. The widow was sure to be delicate and lovely, soft-spoken, with manners befitting a lady and a face blushing like a rose. If I was to look upon her—if I was to hear her melodious voice—she would only remind me of all the ways I had failed as a woman. Besides, she'd been fixing to have a baby, which would certainly have arrived by that summer. I would have given Bill a dozen children —and gladly so, if he had only wanted me. I couldn't set eyes on the child he had made, and not hold that child to my breast, as my own.

So I backed away from the whole idea, and cringed within the alleys of Fort Laramie knowing myself to be a coward—with no good deed done, to boot. That's how I found myself dangling at a loose end inside Fort Laramie. I made my pay in the usual manner —two days of demonstrations at the edge of town, riding Silkie fast around a circuit of old barrels and tent poles, standing in my stirrups to ping tin cans and whiskey bottles off fence posts as I galloped by. I had added a bullwhip to my routine, too, flicking its long lash at my targets, wrapping the whip around the tent poles, then wrenching the poles from the ground. Everyone found the bullwhip a jolly distraction.

After two days of work, I bedded down at the finest boarding house available and lived for a spell like a queen. I reveled in the softness of a feather bed; I whiled away pleasant hours listening to the faint, jolly clamor of the piano downstairs in the house's parlor. I liked the boarding house so well that I paid for another week in Fort Laramie, even though I had already done my demonstrations and the time was fast approaching when I ought to move on.

This boarding house came with two square meals a day. The mistress was a dandy cook in addition to playing a fine piano. She was a real educated lady, too—the sort of woman I had aspired to be when I last visited Cheyenne, elegant and independent, well respected by all and sundry. She always spread the town paper on her breakfast table, so her boarders could keep themselves informed of the Indian War. I was not much good at reading, but I could make out enough of the written word to glean something here and there from the headlines.

One morning, the headline I read near-about caused me to choke on my porridge and eggs.

CALAMITY JANE WREAKS HAVOC IN FORT CASPAR
  Wild Woman Wanted for Grave Misdeeds

I swallowed hard and read on, laboring over most of the words.

The notorious female outlaw Calamity Jane has been identified as the party responsible for breaking two windows and destroying several bottles of valuable spirits at the White Horse Saloon. Witnesses to the crime insist that the vagrant woman appeared at Fort Caspar around the tenth of June, already in a shameful condition due to the whiskey she had elsewhere consumed. The White Horse barkeeper asked her to vacate the premises due to her unruly behavior, upon which she drew her pistol and shot out both the saloon's windows, then attacked the bar with a bull-whip, which she wore slung across her person as more dainty and proper women wear gay-colored sashes. Damages total $75. The Sheriff has sworn to arrest the notorious no-good woman if she ever shows her face in Fort Caspar again.

At least half of what that columnist had written was damn lies. I had been in Caspar around the tenth of June, and though I cannot swear it, I doubt I was already skunked when I arrived. However, the barkeep at the White Horse never asked me to leave, and I never shot out no damn windows, nor took my whip to the bottles. A fight broke out over a game of faro—a game I hadn't even played—and I skittered out of that saloon right quick, along with every other person who had half a brain in their skull. Yet all the blame was laid at my feet, merely because I was notorious.

That a fella could get away with spreading so much hogwash was already enough to make me see red. I glanced toward the kitchen, where the boarding-house mistress hummed softly, going about her work. I wondered whether she had read the news yet—and if so, whether she had come to see me as more liability than welcome guest.

The more I set and stared at that filthy, lying paper, the angrier I grew. What was my odds of drawing a good crowd to my next demonstration if the whole town of Fort Laramie regarded me as a menace instead of pleasant entertainment?

Such fury overtook me then as I had never felt—not since I chased Wild Bill's killer through the streets of Deadwood. I pushed myself up from the breakfast table abruptly, retrieved my bullwhip from my room, and stormed out of the house. With my whip coiled around one shoulder—slung like the gay sash of a dainty, proper lady—I took myself straight to the office of the Fort Laramie Examiner and barged in.

As I threw the door open, all the printers and wire operators shouted, leaping up from their chairs, milling about in a panic. A couple of men tried to stop me—tried to point me back toward the open door—but I wouldn't be dissuaded.

"Where's your boss?" I roared. "Which low-down snake-in-the-grass is in charge of this lying, two-cent operation?"

A thin, balding fella with wire-rimmed specs came scuttling out of a back office. He raised his hands before him, as if he sought to placate me or fend off my considerable rage. But I wasn't in the mood to be mollified.

"Please, Miss," the fella cried, "only tell me what the matter is, and I'll make it good!"

"You in charge here?"

"I am the chief editor," the balding man said. He swallowed hard; I could see how a-scared he was, but he talked smooth enough. "Tell me how I may assist you."

"You," I hollered, pointing one finger right at his nose. "I'll tell you how you can assist me. I'm Calamity Jane—herself, the very one, in the flesh—and you gone and fired me right up with the lies you printed about me."

The editor paled; I could see him trembling. His staff had gone quiet around me. The only sound was the clicking of a telegraph wire.

I dropped the loop of my bullwhip off my shoulder. "If you ever print another unfavorable story about me again, it won't go well for you! I can tell you that!"

"Very well," the editor said, backing away. "You have my word, Miss Jane. Now please, put down that—"

I lashed out with my whip, but not at the editor. I never intended to hurt him—that wasn't my way, not even in anger. Instead, I licked a lamp clean off somebody's desk and sent it crashing to the floor. The thick scent of oil filled the room. Then I cracked my whip at a fancy vase set upon a cabinet; it broke with a satisfying pop.

"Please, Miss!" The editor squealed, dancing back to keep himself far beyond the range of my lash.

I went on lighting into the office, breaking up whatever could be broken, setting into disarray what I couldn't break. I swept papers and notebooks from desks, kicked the sturdy oak cabinets, pulled the telegraph wires from the walls. I knew what I did was miserable, and would only serve to hurt me worst in the end. But I couldn't stop myself, once I begun. All the terrible feelings I had

stewed way down deep in my heart since the occasion of Wild
Bill's death came bursting out of me at once, and even while I
pleaded with myself to rein it in, I also reveled in my fury. It felt
proper good to finally let loose—to give my pain a voice. Even if I
could have stopped my reckless outburst, I ain't sure even to this
day that I would-a done it.

Finally I barged into the editor's private office, intending to
cause more mayhem with the whip. But I spotted a fancy oil
portrait of that very same editor hung up above his desk. My plan
shifted in that moment. I leaped across the room and snatched
that portrait from the wall so fast, the editor could only let out a
feeble squawk of protest. Then I bolted from the building with my
whip trailing behind me, slithering like a black snake in the
Laramie dust.

I was quick on my feet, and neither the editor nor his staff
could apprehend me, though I know they tried. I could hear them
skittering after me, shouting for someone to call the sheriff, for
Calamity Jane had gone plum crazy in the office of the Examiner,
and now she was on a rampage through Laramie's streets. I knew
the law would come for me—I figured I'd do more time behind
bars. But before the sheriff caught me, I intended to have my
vengeance on the Examiner and its prig of an editor.

The Gem Saloon stood just ahead; I made as if to run right
past its doors, but at the last moment I turned and darted inside. I
knew I hadn't much time before the sheriff came, so I jumped
right up on the first table I saw, scattering a perfectly good game
of faro in the process.

"Listen up," I hollered, "My name's Calamity Jane, the one and
only, the famous girl quick-draw of the West!"

A few men hooted in appreciation.

"It has come to my attention, boys, that the editor of your local
paper is a low-down, no-good bastard."

More cheers. Either I wasn't alone in my opinion, or the fellas
liked my show. Either way was fine with me.

"He has printed the vilest slander against me. But do you think Miss Calamity is like to take such outrage sitting down?"

The men raised a ragged chorus. "No! Show him what for, Calamity!"

"See what I got here!" I held the portrait high above my head, so everyone in the saloon got a proper eyeful. "You know this man, don't you?"

They hissed.

"You think I can plug him at twenty paces?"

The men about went wild with enthusiasm. A path cleared through the heart of the saloon; I realized they was setting up a little shooting gallery, all for me. I hadn't intended to blow holes in the portrait right there inside the building—such a thing could be dangerous. But more men came pouring in from the street, drawn by the commotion, and the barkeep gave a helpless shrug, as if to say, *I can stand a few bullet holes in my wall if all these fellas buy a drink.*

I set the portrait against a wall I knew didn't adjoin any other shop—I had no intention of firing through the planks and injuring some innocent dressmaker or cobbler on the other side. The men began to chant "Calamity! Calamity!" as I propped that fancy painting up on a table and paced out the length of the saloon.

I could hear the editor outside the swinging doors, speaking frantically, imparting to someone—the sheriff, I assumed—everything that had transpired. I didn't have much time left.

Quick as a striking rattler, I spun on my heel, drew my gun, and fired. The pearl-handled pistol bucked in my hand. I managed to let fly three rounds before the law made its appearance. One bullet through each of the editor's eyes, one through his flat and sallow cheek.

"Drop the gun, Miss," the sheriff bellowed from the door.

I eased my pistol back into its holster, raised my hands above my head, and turned to face the law. As I did, the rowdies in that saloon raised up such a cheer as nearly blew the roof clean off the place. By the time I met the sheriff's eye, I was smiling.

WELL, of course I did a little time at the Fort Laramie jail in exchange for my mischief. But still to this day, I account it a fair trade. Not only did I have my revenge against that damned fool of an editor, but news of the exploit spread faster than a wildfire. My notoriety was set, double what it had been before. In fact, the small fame I cobbled together before the incident at the Examiner wasn't a patch on what came after.

When my sentence was up, the sheriff ushered me out of Fort Laramie. But by the time I reached Cheyenne a few days after, two eager reporters was waiting there to meet me, and a dime novelist, too. Neither the reporters nor the book-writer had known I would visit Cheyenne next; they had merely hoped, or perhaps had thought to use Cheyenne as a jumping-off point to search for me, scouring every sagebrush plain and slot canyon till they'd rustled the infamous Calamity out of hiding. The fact that I had brought myself to them fairly sent the lot of them over the moon.

Each night, a different writer plied me with whiskey and opened their notebook, and I obliged them merrily, giving interviews and accounts of my life that grew wilder with each retelling. A few more writers came racing in along the Overland Line, shouting questions at me just as fast as they could hop down from their stage coaches. Seldom a day passed but I found myself surrounded by eager young men—and even a few women—scribbling down my lies as fast as I unspooled them from my tongue.

I didn't see any harm in those wild tales. It was all a game to me. I figured I was putting on another kind of show, less physically taxing than my shooting and bullwhipping demonstrations. And I will confess that I liked the attention, too—the company of a new writer every night cheered me considerable, kept me from dwelling too long on my sorrows. I always found writers to be agreeable types—much more so than editors. That's why I picked you out of this crowd, Short Pants. I could tell you was a writer before you even said boo, and I wasn't wrong, was I? You been good company, too, all these many hours. I've set like this with many a writer in my time, spinning the most fanciful of yarns, but never have I told a writer the truth. And you know, it feels damn good to spill out my real history after all these years.

Well, I supposed I never thought a one of my tall tales would actually get printed. Because it was only play to me, I assumed it was all good fun for the dime novelists, too. But it was deadly serious to them—the kind of story that could make a career, securing both fortune and fame. I believe those atrocious fibs did make one or two of those writers well and truly famous. I hope they never learned the truth—never came to know how badly I duped them all. I think if they knew I fed them lies, they would have recalled our nights of whiskey and tale-swapping with grim disappointment, and I couldn't bear such a thing—for those memories (all those nights of chummy good fun with my new writer-friends) are a great comfort to me, even still.

Like I told you, I never expected to see my stories in print. But one day I did, sure enough. I had just paid to board at a house in Fort Collins. The town had growed up considerable since my last visit a few years before, and the house I chose was a fine new one, pretty as any Back East mansion. I sighed as I settled into my room, laying back on a glorious feather bed, soft and warm as a summer cloud. But something on the bottom shelf of the bed-stand caught my eye. It was small, papery, with a yellow cover—a little book forgotten or abandoned by the last resident, and over-looked by the mistress of the house, or by the poor orphan girl of thirteen who turned the rooms.

I picked up the book in idle curiosity, having no intent to read it, for reading was always such a toil. But I liked the soft ruffle of its well-thumbed pages, and the smell of paper pulp and dry ink was soothing and compelling. I examined the cover: an intricate engraving of a woman riding a horse at a mad gallop down a narrow trail. Long black hair streamed out behind her, flying on the wind. Above the woman, in a fancy script that took me some time to puzzle out, the title read: *The Beautiful White Devil of the Yellowstone*.

What have we here, I thought, and opened the book, expecting some inconsequential tale of adventure with perhaps a lurid passage or two. I read the first page in my halting, strenuous fashion, and straight away I realized the book was about me.

Well, Short Pants, I stayed in my room all the rest of that day, agonizing over every page, piecing together the tale that yellow book told. Wouldn't you know, the story wasn't just about me. It was about me and Wild Bill Hickock. Oh, Bill wore a guise, to be sure: the novel called him Deadwood Dick, and his hair was yellow instead of red. But nothing could hide my true love's nature from my eyes, my ravenous heart.

As I turned one slow page after another, consuming the story with desperate greed, I had a recollection of a tavern somewheres up north—maybe as far north as Montana—where I had invented this very tale for a young writer from Pennsylvaney who had come west especially to find Calamity Jane. Of course, the writer fancied up my tale with pretty words, many of which I couldn't make out for the life of me, but the core of my wild imagining remained the same. The tale was just as I had spun it for that writer-fella more than a year before—and I had spun it from the depths of my need, from the raw fiber of unfulfilled longing.

This is how the story went.

AWAY ACROSS THE PRAIRIE, at the foot of the Rockies, the Indians came to fear only one person, the only soul brave enough to chase them into the heart of their hardest and most treacherous territory, where the ground steams like a kettle, where the earth will break beneath you if you set one foot wrong, and you'll fall into the underground pits of boiling water. This brave soul was no man, but a lovely, black-haired woman, young and slender, wild and free. The Indians called her the Beautiful White Devil, and feared her because of her courage and her wily nature. The men of the West all longed for her legend, for none but she would make a worthy wife—yet no man dared to find her, for she dwelt in the wildest places and could vanish like a mountain lion if she didn't wish to be found.

Only one man was brave enough seek her out. His name was Deadwood Dick, the hero of countless adventures. Heartsick already, though he hadn't yet laid eyes on the Beautiful White Devil, he rode both day and night to seek her and win her heart. But as Dick neared the White Devil's territory, the Indians fell upon him and harried him and almost took his life.

It was the black-haired girl who saved him from his fate, appearing like a hawk diving from the sky, descending upon the attacking Reds in a sudden fury worse than any hailstorm. She rode with the reins gripped in her teeth and fired her twin pistols from either hand, and in short order she drove all the Indians away. Then she held Deadwood Dick tenderly in her arms and treated his grievous wounds, and by and by she nursed him back to health and strength. Private and protected in the mountain stronghold of the White Devil, she let all her wild ways go, and she was tender and kind as any proper woman, and she was the most beautiful creature Deadwood Dick had ever seen, besides— so he fell in love with her straight away, and declared that he would marry her, for no other woman would do. No other woman was as beautiful or as brave, and Dick would have no wife but the bravest and the prettiest, for he was the great hero of the Plains and deserved nothing less.

The White Devil held him tenderly in her arms and swore that she would become his wife, for he was the best and bravest man she had ever known. But before she would consent to marry him, she must confess her real name. And that was Calamity Jane.

Deadwood Dick laid his noble head on Calamity Jane's alabaster breast. In the solitude, in the quiet of their perfect love, he whispered that he would be hers forever, and she would always be his. And they lived a long and happy life together, with never a tear to fall between them.

OF COURSE, I invented that story wholecloth; it was one damn lie from cover to cover. But reading it on the page made it real to me. Real and true, maybe realer than the world around me. I turned those creased and softened pages, and smelled the mercy of ink and paper, and I convinced myself that maybe there was another world existing somewhere alongside my own, or behind my own, cast like a shadow. And in that shadow world, this precious story was no lie. In that shadow world, Wild Bill still lived. And he loved me, and I was the beautiful untamed girl with raven-black hair, free and lovely as the West itself.

Except for that editor's portrait and a few crusts of bread to feed my brothers and sisters, I never stole a thing in my life. I should have turned the book over to the boarding-house mistress, for it wasn't mine to keep. Instead, I slipped it in my saddle bag straight away, and from that day on, wherever I rode I carried the book with me. I carried the possibility of another world, glimpsed like an image in a mirror—like a scene through a window as reflected in the dim gray surface of a mirror. Present and yet not present. Gone when you blink, gone the moment you look too directly.

QUEEN OF THE SADDLE AND LASSO

WHATEVER WAS LEFT OF THAT BLEAK AUTUMN FADED TO A DIM GRAY winter, and by the time the snows hit, I found myself in Rapid City. I figured it was as good a place as any other to settle down—to surrender myself to fate. I still had the trinkets Bill had given me to hold, and I had the book with its comforting fiction of our great love. Nor did I have the gumption—nor even any intent—to keep myself clear of the whiskey. Drinking was the only act that could separate me from my misery—for a short time at least. Whiskey was the only power I had over the ghosts of pain that haunted me, waking and sleeping.

But though I no longer pretended I would keep myself clean, I did still hold some notion that I ought to be the kind of woman Bill could have favored, if he had lived. Bill had trusted me with his most treasured personal effects; an honest stab at decency seemed the least I could offer in repayment of that trust, the smallest gesture to honor my true love's memory. That's why I decided to marry in Rapid City: give up my wild ways and lonesome ramblings, take up the venerable mantle of Wife. Just who I ought to marry made no difference. One man was exactly the same as any other, in my estimation—for none of them was Wild Bill, and thus all fell miles short of my ideal.

I took up with a whole string of husbands, one after another, starting that very winter. It may surprise you to learn that Calamity Jane was any man's wife—the infamous heartbreaker, the untamed beauty of the West, restless as a prairie wind. But God's honest truth, I was. Least-a-ways, I was some sort of wife to each of those men, even though I never stood before a justice nor a minister with a single one of 'em. I never spoke no vows. There's some sort of fancy law that governs the spousal situation into which I blundered, time after time. A trick of those barristers and judges that makes two people husband and wife in all but name, provided you live together under the same roof. I never understood the ins and outs and all the particulars. They didn't matter a whit to me then, and matter even less to me now.

George Cosgrove was the first of my several husbands. I met him in a saloon, as you might expect—and he professed a great interest in my skills at faro and my prodigious thirst for whiskey. I figured that sort of admiration was reason enough to take up as his wife, and so I did, not long after.

I can't tell you what I expected from marriage, but I know for a certainty I didn't expect what Cosgrove gave me. He was a mean fucker, with a hard eye and a harder fist. Don't I know it; George Cosgrove gave me a taste of his fist all too many times. Straight away, before the first month of our unorthodox marriage had come to a close, I came to understand all the woes of wifehood, and I saw clearly why a wedded life had never set well with my dear dead mother or with Emma Alton.

"Listen," I said to my husband one day, when his temper had cooled, and he settled into his favorite chair to smoke his pipe at ease. "You got to stop beating on me. I had enough."

George laughed, but he didn't have that mean spark in his eye, so I knew he wouldn't lash out at me—not that evening. "You damn fool," he sneered. "If you don't like it, go off and find yourself another husband. See if anyone else will have you, big ugly buffalo that you are."

"All right," I said, "I'll just do that."

George laughed again and refused to look at me or speak to me all the rest of the night. He only set staring into the fire, sucking on his pipe, self-satisfied and wholly assured. I could tell he was certain he had the final word, and I would come to my senses soon enough, and meekly allow him to go on walloping me like a proper wife should. But I spent that night quietly packing up my things—I didn't own much, even as an established wife—and well before dawn, I saddled my loyal horse and left Rapid City and George Cosgrove both, for good and all.

If I had any sense, I would have called that experiment in marital bliss a predictable failure and gone back to my wild ways —which, to be sure, suited me a damn sight better than cooking and cleaning and simpering for some dirt-crusted, pipe-smoking, womanizing old piece of leather like George Cosgrove. But I was young, and still far too foolish for my own good. And of course, the ache of my love for Wild Bill had settled way down deep in my spirit, and wouldn't allow me any peace. So when I found myself in Coulson, Montana, I took up again with another man, a fella all of Coulson knew as Darling Jim.

Jim was a real treat to look at, I must admit: six foot two with a square jaw and sparkling blue eyes, and hair so deep a shade of gold it looked like birch-sap candy. Darling Jim took a shine to my name and my reputation much more than he did to my actual person, but that was all right with me. We spent most nights beside the fire downing whiskey and rehearsing Jim's schemes to make hay out of my identity—for he was a clever man, and hadn't failed to notice how many dime novels bore my name. He knew there could be real good money in notoriety, if we only worked our angles just right, and if I stuck diligently to the business of being Calamity Jane.

But Coulson in those days was far off the beaten track. No

matter how Darling Jim schemed—no matter how I persevered at my cussing and whooping-up along the streets of the town—his plans never got too far off the ground. There simply wasn't enough visitors from the East. We had a shortage of tenderfeet—those credulous gawkers in their dapper Back-East duds, always willing to spend a few coins if they thought they could get their picture made with a real, honest-to-God legend of the West. Still to this day, I think Darling Jim and I could have made a fortune if we had lived in Cheyenne or Salt Lake City, where tenderfeet was never in short supply. But stuck as we was in Montana, we never made more than a handful of cash, and all too soon our marriage soured. Darling Jim and I parted ways with no hard feelings between us, and I moved on to the new state of Colorado, lighting like a weary bird in the city of Boulder.

There I found another husband in short order—a fella by the name of Frank Lacy. Frank was nothing to me, just like George Cosgrove and Darling Jim—for as you know, Short Pants, my heart had been Wild Bill's from the day he rode into camp on Sheridan's heels. There was no room for any other man within my soul—and even if there had been, I wouldn't have let Frank Lacy in.

Frank was as mean a cuss as Cosgrove had been, and he had a liking for theft besides. Worse crimes, too, I suspect. I never pried too far into Frank's habits, for some small and frightened instinct told me I didn't really want to know what my quiet, flat-eyed husband got up to. Some nights he stayed out till all hours, then came home wild, all a-quiver with some foul excitement that made me feel defenseless, big and strong though I was. But on the nights when Frank went out roaming, he would leave me alone, and wouldn't raise a fist for a good week after—so I made myself content with leaving Frank to his questionable devices. Whatever he got up to on his midnight ramblings, I think he needed me as cover—a dutiful wife kept in a passably proper home; the sort of existence one would never think to question. That's why he took me in, I guess, and made me his spouse.

Aside from his temper and his mysterious late-night forays, Frank Lacy was a good enough provider. He worked as a delivery man by day, just like old Mr. Braddick, though Frank ran a team of oxen rather than a team of mules. Often I would stand on the sagging front porch of our tumble-down house, watching Frank drive his wagon down the lane and out to the open road. In those moments, my heart yearned for the carefree days of my youth, when I had only the route and my mules for company, yet I was more perfectly content than any girl on her own ought to be. And all the days Frank stayed away with his wagon and his team, I dreamed that I was the one driving those oxen. I imagined the sights Frank took in on the open trail and hungered for the freedom he surely felt in the great spaces between towns and encampments. And when he came home, I risked his impatient slaps and his ugly words so's I could linger close beside him, breathing in the smell of sage, the smell of his ox-team's sweat rising from his body.

I stayed married to Frank Lacy for more than six months, right up till he divorced me by finally landing on the wrong side of the law. I kept myself mostly ignorant of his charges; I could only feel a wash of relief when the sheriff came a-knocking at my door to inform me that Frank Lacy would remain in prison for ten years at least due to the severity of his crimes. I think I did an acceptable job of feigning wifely shock at the length of his sentence, but when the sheriff imparted his next piece of news, not even God himself could have kept the grin from my face.

"Seeing as how you are his wife, mam," the sheriff said, "all of Mr. Lacy's assets now belong to you."

"Do they?" said I. "We never married in front of a justice."

"That doesn't matter, mam—not here in Colorado. The common law regards you as Frank Lacy's wife, so everything belongs to you. This house, his business, and his team. You'll want to keep the house, I suppose, but if you need assistance selling the business and the ox team to a more suitable party, you need only ask. I'd be happy to help you find a buyer. The profits should keep you till Mr. Lacy is set free—if you live frugally, as befits a woman in your predicament. You know where to find me, Mrs. Lacy."

The sheriff tipped his hat, then went on his way. But I had as much intention of selling the ox team as I had of wiping the damn-fool grin off my face. For all the trouble he'd put me through, Frank turned out to be good for something, after all. When he landed in jail, I landed in legal possession of a thriving delivery business and a healthy, experienced team.

That's how I became a bullwhacker, just as quick and easy as you please.

I TELL YOU WHAT, Short Pants: I was a damn sight better at bull-whacking than Frank Lacy ever was. The lessons I learned with Braddick's mules returned quick and easy, and I found oxen almost as agreeable in temperament. They ain't as quick or agile as mules, but every ox can pull at least three times the weight of a single mule. As a team, my reliable old beasts could haul astounding burdens out across the prairie, or over the foothills, with no more trouble than a dog hauls its fleas. Most often, I transported great pieces of machinery from the rail lines out to the distant camps where young men built the offshoot branches of the Transcontinental. The bed of my wagon was reinforced with iron bands, and my oxen was all steady and strong from long work along their routes. Weather permitting, I could coax faster delivery times from my team than Frank ever could, for I ruled those beasts with sympathy and understanding, not with Frank's hard will and harder fist. I soon built a reputation as the best bullwhacker anywhere along the Transcontinental, and the business flourished till I had enough scratch to buy three more wagons and teams, and to hire men to work along with me.

How I loved those long, leisurely drives—the solitude of my routes—the company of memory. Wild Bill's poison still burned in my heart, but out there on a remote hill, with nothing around me but the endless waves of grass and a sky pale with racing clouds, the burning didn't hurt quite so bad. Bill's agony took on a poignant significance, a weight suspended somewhere between blissful memory and searing loss. And even the loss felt beautiful, though it pained me something terrible—for alone among the sage with only the slow, steady tread of my oxen and the creak of my wagon's axles, I came to feel a kind of holy perfection in my love for Bill. Because that longing could never be fulfilled, it could never be sullied by the countless disappointments and fears that had shadowed my marriages. My love for Bill would remain pure and whole all the days of my life, and though I would have given my own life gladly if it would have brought Bill back from his grave, at least I knew he would remain unchanged within my heart. That was the next best thing to having him back again.

Wouldn't you know, I found it easier to stay away from whiskey on the trail. Not only would I soon drink up any supply I brought along (leaving myself bereft of liquor for the rest of my slow-plodding route) but the work was taxing enough that I usually found myself bone-tired at the end of every day, with little inclination toward whooping up when I reached my destination.

Now, that ain't to say I never ventured a drink. One of the rail camps I visited most often lay very near Fort Pierre, in Dakota Territory. After a good rest, and just before turning my team south for Colorado, I often found myself riding my horse along the streets of Fort Pierre in search of one night of distraction.

I seen plenty of rowdy settlements in my day, but few compared to that town. Tenderfeet rode the rails from the grand

cities Back East in droves, dispersing among Cheyenne and
Laramie and Boulder. And all those fancy Back East folks
earnestly believed they'd come for a taste of the real, wild West.
But I tell you what: if those tenderfeet had the misfortune to find
themselves in Fort Pierre, they would have walked all the long
way back to Boston or New York rather than wait for the next
train to whisk them off to safety. There never was a wilder
example of the West than Fort Pierre. Folks of that town never
bothered with the law; if two fellas had a dispute, they shot it out
in the streets, and a body was as like to be felled by a stray bullet
as bit by a flea. A few small gangs of cattle rustlers banded
together into one great mob of bullies, and extracted pay from the
citizens of the town in exchange for not burning down their
houses or shooting all the menfolk dead. No one liked to live in
Fort Pierre, but everybody who was there was stuck good and
tight, like a boot bogged down in thick mud. Lord have mercy on
the poor souls who couldn't pull themselves free.

Despite its infamy, I found the town pleasant enough, as long
as I kept my wits about me and paid heed to the prevailing mood
—though I'm sure I only found Fort Pierre passing decent 'cause I
didn't have to live there. Whenever a gun fight seemed likely to
erupt, I returned to the livery and hunkered down under my
wagon till the immediate danger passed. Then I hitched up my
cattle and drove away, fast as I could persuade those lumbering
beasts to go. But by the time I made another delivery, Fort Pierre
always settled back into its wheel-rut, and more often than not, I
had a perfectly enjoyable time among its taverns and saloons.

I grew especially fond of the Triple Star, a tavern right at the
heart of town. I loved the Triple Star not for its whiskey (though I
sampled enough of it to know it was top notch) but for the
company of Angus, the barkeep. Angus came to know me well,
too, for I often stopped for a single drink before I returned to the
road, and the old fella always enjoyed the stories of my past
adventures. He was right amiable—put me in mind both of Mr.

Braddick and Timothy Crutch at the same time, with just a touch of California Joe and Sam Young, those fellas who'd been so keen to hear my tales in the glory days when Wild Bill had ridden at my side.

Angus, gesturing with one of the cigars he never ceased to smoke, always drew a crowd over to the bar the moment I stepped into the Triple Star. Those fellas bellied up and listened while I held forth, spinning the most fanciful yarns about my past, sparing not a single cuss. The Triple Star rattled with laughter whenever I hit the high note of a story, and Angus poured me a second drink—not whiskey, but a bracing tonic or a good, spicy sarsaparilla—without my saying boo. He seemed to understand that I struggled to keep myself clean, and declined to make that task any harder for me. A less honorable man would have kept the whiskey flowing, and pocketed every coin that fell from my inebriated hands. But there wasn't a dishonorable drop in Angus's blood. He liked me as I was, and aimed to keep me that way—not falling-down drunk, just for the sake of his own profits. I was grateful for his friendly discretion.

Angus didn't mind if I took up my old trade, neither—the very oldest. He kept a comfortable room upstairs for just that sort of occasion, and only took a small cut of my earnings. The gents of Fort Pierre paid well for a night with the famous Calamity Jane, and Angus's upstairs room made for pleasanter accommodation than my wagon in the livery shed—that's for damn sure.

Since I found success as a bullwhacker, I felt no more need to take up as any man's wife. I felt no more compunction over plying a trade on my back, neither. Those men didn't mean a thing to me, but their money sure did. With two regular sources of income, I began to make out the shape and color of a steady future somewheres just ahead. Before long, I thought, I would have enough money to sell that tumble-down house in Boulder and move my operation elsewhere—wherever the growth of the railroads dictated. And once the bullwhacking trade fell all to pieces (which was inevitable, I knew, having learned Braddick's lesson well), I would have saved enough money to open the fancy boarding house of which I had so often dreamed.

Yes, a pleasant turn to the road of my fortune was waiting just ahead—so close I could already see it. After the long, harrowing slog of my life, a suitable reward for my patience and fortitude was practically at hand.

That was when calamity found me again, and dashed all my dreams to pieces.

You see, I fell pregnant in Fort Pierre. Of course, I had employed all the usual tricks a girl of my trade learns early on. A copper coin stashed right up in your nook-and-cranny was the most effective measure, but when the coin trick failed—as it often did—I took regular doses of tansy and pennyroyal tea to keep my belly in a pleasantly unoccupied state. But this time around, none of the usual tricks worked. I was stuck with a child, and I plum despaired, for I knew would make a piss-poor example of a mother.

I brooded over the coming disaster for months while my waist thickened (it had never been especially slender to begin with) and my belly began to protrude over the top of my trousers. In time, the boys I hired for the bullwhacking business discerned my condition, and insisted I remain at the house in Boulder, over-seeing the deliveries and keeping the books, as far as I was able. They took all the joy of the open road for themselves, and how I did resent my confinement.

I resented that little mite growing inside me, too, for I never wanted him to begin with. Even less did I welcome him now, pulled as I was from my beloved trail, mired in boredom and misery.

But a funny thing happened as my condition progressed. The bigger the baby grew, the more real he became in my mind. I began to imagine what he might look like—quite against my will, at first—and I saw again the faces of my little brothers and sisters, remembered them as the babes I had cared for so tenderly while my ma and pa had occupied themselves with their own interests. A grudging affection developed for the child to come, and little by little, a sweet anticipation displaced my resentment. I began to talk to the baby, for it was the only company I had most days. I stroked my belly almost constantly, certain he could feel my touch; I made grand plans for the two of us, and all too soon I was looking forward to becoming a mother, though I still labored under no illusion that I would make an especially fine specimen of maternity.

For the sake of the baby, I resolved to build a decent future. I counted my growing cache of money—not a fortune by any means, but enough to set myself up with a proper home, enough to meet a little one's most pressing needs. I had never tried to sew before, and I knew I would be terrible if I tried, so I went about town buying little dresses and bonnets from ladies whose children had grown too big for their old clothes. How I did fuss and fawn over all those pretty little things, despite their stains and patches. Every night I set beside my fire, rubbing my tight belly with one hand, smoothing with the other an embroidered crib dress or a stack of diaper cloths. To my surprise, I found myself downright excited to have that baby—to finally meet the little thing, to look into his wrinkled red face at last. The expected date in early November couldn't come soon enough.

What is there to tell you? The date came, all right, and my boys sent for the midwife, just as anxious as if they was all the father. But my child never drew a breath.

It was a little boy. Somehow I had known all along that it would be a boy. He was perfectly formed, with my black hair. He would have been beautiful—far more beautiful than his mother—if not for the bluish cast to his skin.

I held his lifeless body for a few cold hours. Then, too stunned and weary to cry, I surrendered him to my boys without a word. They buried my son in a tiny pit out back of the house, under an apple tree, at the edge of the ox-team's pasture.

The boys never asked what name they ought to paint on the little wooden cross they stuck into the earth to mark my son's grave. But I would have called him Bill, if he had lived.

SHE HAS GROWN RECKLESS IN ACT AND ROUGH IN LANGUAGE

THE THREE YEARS AFTER MY BABY'S DEATH DON'T HOLD MUCH remembrance for me. They appear to me now like a canyon filled with mist—the dense, heavy fog of autumn settling into low places, obscuring everything from my sight. I kept up my bull-whacking—I hadn't any idea what else I ought to do—and though my business didn't exactly thrive, it did hold steady enough to keep me going from day to day. I suppose I must credit the boys I'd hired for the continuation of my deliveries, for I don't believe I was of any real use to anybody during those years. I went about my life, responding automatically to the push and pull of season and fortune, unthinking as a gear or a shaft within the great black engine of a train.

One bright spot of color do I recall amid that long and feature-less stretch of gray: the day I learned the whereabouts of my brother Lije. While delivering a load of mechanical goods to a rail camp outside Fort Washakie, I listened in on the men who checked over and unloaded my wagon.

"That's a right fancy vest you got there, Paul," one fella said with a hint of a sneer.

The one called Paul sported some outrageous attire, including a vest all done up in Indian beads, far too bright and dashing for a rail camp worker. He said, "I'm right proud of this vest, I'll have you know."

"Proud as a peacock."

All the fellas laughed.

Then Paul said rather slyly, "I won this dandy garment off Lije Canary down in Lander."

Before anyone could respond, I turned to Paul desperately—so fast I had no time to ask myself whether there was a lick of wisdom in what I did. So frantic was my approach that Paul shrank into his beaded vest, as if he feared I might take a swing at him. I seized him by his shoulder, bunching my fist in his shirt. "Did you say Lije Canary?"

"Yes mam, the one and only." He laughed and looked around at his friends, silently pleading for their help. "You see? This gal knows who I'm talking about: the famed faro player of Lander. No man can beat him, or so his legend goes. No man except me!" He tugged at his vest, pulling it straight, for my excited grip had knocked it askew. "Won this right off his back in a hand we played at—"

"Is he still there? In Lander?"

Now the fella could see the hunger in my eyes—and, I suppose, the desperation. He flushed, uncertain what my keenness meant. "I don't know, mam. He was there this winter past. Played almost every day down at the Horse Trough Tavern."

I realized then what I must look like to him—to all the men. A woman keen for a man—and one man in particular. If they had spoken of Wild Bill, still living and sitting in for a round of faro, I wouldn't have minded their assumption. But it was my own brother they spoke of! I let go of Paul's shirt and laughed as easy as I could, and set their minds at peace with some off-handed comment that I'd like to try my luck against that famous card player. Soon enough, they returned to their work, and I drove away the moment my wagon was empty, at once troubled and intrigued. Lander wasn't terrible far away from my base of operations in Boulder. Only a few days' drive with my team. I had only to convince myself to make the trip—and I wasn't a-tall sure I could do it.

For more than a year and a half, I wrestled with thoughts of my brother. Assuming he had remained in Lander all that time, I could only guess whether Lije wished to see me again. So many years had passed. Perhaps all my ponderings was futile, I told myself; perhaps Lije had moved on, or cultivated a deep hatred for me. By day I would make up my mind to ride to Lander and call on him, if the was there a-tall. But by the time I crawled into bed at night—or wrapped myself in my bed roll if I was out along the trail—I convinced myself Lije wanted nothing to do with me, and thought me a terrible stain on his past for having given him up to the Richardson ranch.

Finally, though, I grew weary of the endless conflict within my heart. I knew I would never rest easy till I saw Lije face to face. If he hated me, then let him profess his hate and have done with it. At least then I would know what esteem my brothers and sisters still held for me—if any. The time had come to seek Lije out, and learn what I could of his life, and the lives of the other children I had sacrificed so much to protect. Whether they loved me or hated me, or even regarded me with indifference, at least that part of my past would haunt me no more. I put the sharpest fella on my crew in charge of the business and saddled up Pie, my youngest and sturdiest horse. Then I set out alone for Lander. It was 1885. I was twenty-nine years old.

I reached Lander late in the month of May, and promptly set about inquiring after Lije Canary. The man I'd met in the rail camp claimed Lije was a card player of some renown, so I thought to check the taverns and saloons. I hadn't seen Lije since he'd been a small boy, of course, but even so, I suspected I could spot the Canary features—tall, broadly built, and black of hair—at a hundred paces or more. But searching from tavern to saloon, I located no man who might pass for my brother, and so I began to inquire about the famed faro player.

"Lije Canary," said a grizzled old fella at one bar. "Yes mam, he does still live here in town, but you won't find him playing cards these days. He has turned a new leaf, I'm afraid. Just recently got himself sprung from jail."

"Jail, you say?"

The old man chuckled. "Landed himself in a spot of trouble. Had something to do with rustling cattle, I understand—a sordid business. But you'd have to ask Lije himself for the details; I don't know any more than that."

"Where can I find him, if not playing cards?"

"Don't rightly know, mam, for I've only seen him now and then at the general store. But you might ask his sister."

At those words, all the blood rushed to my face in one surging beat of my heart. "His sister, you say?"

"Yes mam, Missuz Lena Bourner. Her husband John runs that big farm right at the mouth of the valley on the other end of town. Lena operates a laundry in a shed out back of the house, and it's the finest laundry in Lander. If anybody knows where Lije has got himself off to, I reckon it's bound to be Lena Bourner."

I hadn't counted on finding Lena, too. I wasn't prepared to face my sister. Lena had always been a prim and proper girl, which was a real accomplishment, considering she'd been born a Canary. She certainly wouldn't approve of me as I was—dressed in a bullwhacker's trousers and chaps, with a grim history and no small amount of infamy dragging along behind. I had never forgotten what Lena looked like the last time I seen her in Piedmont—walking away, hand in hand with her brand-new ma, hardly sparing a backward glance for me. She had seemed relieved to renounce her family, and I can't say I ever blamed her. I knew straight away that Lena wouldn't weep tears of joy to find me, come knocking on her kitchen door.

But hadn't I come to Lander for that very purpose—to see my

kin again? Though I trembled over the prospect of confronting Lena face to face, I swung up onto Pie's back and headed for the valley at the edge of town. All too soon, I located the very farm that must belong to my sister and her husband. It was a pretty place, neat and tidy with a small but beautiful farmhouse all painted up in white with snappy green trim. I reined in my horse at the end of the lane and stared at the place for a good long while. A tidy garden surrounded the farmhouse. I could see a flock of hens pecking and scratching near the porch steps. A pasture, gold-struck with afternoon sunshine, stretched from the house to the banks of a crick lined in willows and cottonwoods. A field of green hay rippled in a soft springtime breeze, giving up its scent of lush grass with an undertone of damp, dark earth. The place was like something out of a dream or a storybook. It was the kind of home I had never even dared to hope might one day be mine, peaceful and picturesque. Lena had done well for herself. Whatever would come from this day's work—whatever tears might wait for me on the road just ahead—at least I could feel grateful that Lena (perhaps she alone, of all the Canarys) had landed on her feet.

By and by, I became aware of a dog barking, and then a man calling out to silence it. I looked around, past the hay field, and spotted a sizable patch of potatoes. The man came strolling up the furrows towards me at an unhurried pace. A hoe was slung over his shoulder. His leisurely stride told me he assumed I was a rider with a message or a delivery. I should have turned and ridden away before he ever got to me, but I sat transfixed, staring—for indeed I recognized my brother Lije, even at a great distance. I should more rightly say, I recognized my mother. Everything about Lije reflected my dead ma: his upright frame, his slow but confident stride, that black hair tousled by the wind. I couldn't move, couldn't speak, and so I sat and waited for my past to catch up with me.

Lije came to the edge of the field and lifted a hand in greeting.

"Hullo," he called out. His voice was so low, so manly. That startled me. I realized with a foolish tremor that I had expected him to still speak the way he had when I had seen him last, in the high, sweet tones of a little boy.

He paused, taking in my face. His jaw fell first. Then the hoe toppled from his shoulder. "Martha? I'll be damned. Martha—can that really be you?"

I swung down from my saddle and ran to him, and he came a-running towards me. We threw our arms around each other, laughing, pounding one another's backs. Of course I got all mistied-up with tears. After a moment, we pulled away from one another, and Lije took me by my shoulders—my ungainly Canary shoulders. He grinned at me. I could see my pa in that smile, for certain. Maybe my mother hadn't carried on with other fellas as often as I assumed.

"Thought I'd never see you again," Lije said.

"I thought the same. I tried to get back to you, when you was at that ranch outside Piedmont—you and Cilus. I tried." But my face went hot with shame, for I knew I hadn't tried hard enough.

Lije's eyes took on a glaze of distance at mention of the ranch. His smile slipped. But he recovered himself quickly, almost before I had a chance to notice. "That's all right," he said. "All's well now."

I chuckled. "*Now*. Heard you just got yourself freed from jail."

Lije whooped with laughter. "You heard that, huh? My legend precedes me."

"I also heard you was accounted a great faro player. Is that the legend that saw you locked up in a cage? Or was it something to do with cattle rustling, as the rumor goes? You can tell me without shame. I'm no stranger to the inside of a jail cell, myself."

"'Course you aint," Lije said with no small amount of admiration. "You're a Canary. No, I must admit it was a damn sight worse than cheating at cards. Even simple cattle rustling would be a preferable charge. I'm afraid it was fraud put me behind bars. I am ashamed to admit it, but it's true."

"Fraud?" Even I had never done anything to terrible.

"I ain't proud of it," Lije said again, "and I done my time. I'm a better man now—or I aim to be. Two other fellas and me, we cooked up a scheme among us. We'd buy up a herd of cattle and take out an insurance policy, claiming we was fixing to set ourselves up as ranchers. Then we'd drive the cattle down to the railroad tracks in the dead of night and leave 'em there. When the trains come along, the cattle would either be hit and perish, or would run off in a stampede. Either way, we cashed out our insurance, then ran the whole game over again. Guess I should have foreseen that it wouldn't work more than two or three times before the law caught on."

"That's a dirty trick."

"I know it, and as I said, I ain't proud. But I'm settled into a new life now. Guess you heard this is Lena's place."

I nodded.

"She and her husband John have been real charitable. They took me in when I was released. I promised to work for John here on the farm for three years at least, and then I'll set out on my own with some money honestly come by, and make of myself a respectable man." Lije interrupted himself. "Damn, but it's good to see you, Martha. I wondered about you so many times since we parted ways, and hoped you was all right."

"I wondered about you all, too." *Feared for you*, I thought. "And Martha—no one has called me that in a terrible long time. These days, everybody calls me Jane."

Lije looked at me more closely—squinted at my trousers and my shirt, his mouth pressing hard and thin with suspicion. "You ain't, by any chance, Calamity Jane?"

"The one and only."

Lije hooted again. "Wish I could say I was surprised to learn it! What adventures you've had. Why, I heard—"

"None of what you heard is true. All lies, I'm afraid, cooked up by those crazy novelists and dirty newspaper writers. My life ain't been half as pretty as they made it seem."

He was sober now. "Guess nobody's life has been a bed of roses."

I hesitated, fearing to ask the question I knew I must. "That ranch you and Cilus went off to…"

Lije nodded. "It wasn't the best of homes, but I can't say it was the worst. The Richardsons worked us hard—damn hard. After a few years, they did make good on their promise and teach Cilus and me reading and sums, but mostly we was unpaid hands to them—and just about the only hands on the place. I guess neither Cilus nor me had much of a childhood, but we survived. That's the important part."

"Where is Cilus now?"

"Can't say. The both of us took off from the Richardson place when I was eighteen and Cilus was about to turn twenty. We traveled together for a spell, went up to Montana and played with the idea of becoming prospectors. But the longer we cooled our heels in Montana, the less certain we became about what we ought to do next. Cilus had all kinds of ideas. Becoming a minister—though I can't think of a wors't preacher than Cilus Canary. I believe he took a shine to the idea just so's he could lay his head in a nice house for free. Then he cooked up some crazy scheme to go Back East and get into a college somewheres, become an educated man. I told him it was a damn fool idea, that he couldn't read well enough to get into no fancy schools. He took it bad; we quarreled. We parted ways that night, and he told me he'd come back by and by, when his temper cooled. But he stayed away for months on end, and so I left Montana, too."

"Do you suppose he could be—"

"Dead? No, I don't think so. Somebody would have contacted Lena or me if Cilus had met his end. No, he's off East, I wager, still trying to weasel his way into a fancy gentleman's college."

"What about Isabelle?"

"Still living in Piedmont, and about to marry. She wrote Lena and told her all about it. Lena and John are welcome to come to the wedding, she said—but not me, and nobody else from the family if they should chance to turn up. Isabelle is sure Lena is proper company, since she has a husband and a farm and all. But she don't look too favorable on any other Canarys."

The news pained me. I remembered how Isabelle had cried when her new mother had taken her away. She had wanted to remain with the boys and me—wanted to keep the family together. I suppose over time she came to view the hardship of the trail in a different light, and was glad to put the past behind her.

"Guess I deserve that," I said.

"Guess you don't. None of us deserves it. We're all family, Martha, no matter what misfortunes have come our way. Isabelle might kid herself that she can keep some distance, but family never can stay apart for long. Or at least, not for good. Before you ask, no one has heard tell of Sara, and not for lack of trying. Cilus and I tried to find her several times. Lena and John have tried, too. I expect that Mormon woman who took her in changed her name, and never told her nothing of her real origins."

For one wild moment, I thought to ask Lije whether he or Lena had ever tried to find me. Then I thought better of the impulse. It was a fair bet I'd rather not know the answer to that question.

Lije glanced toward the prim white farmhouse and perked up. "Kitchen fire's on. Lena must be done with her laundry, and started cooking supper. Let's go in and see her."

"I shouldn't." If Isabelle wanted nothing to do with me, then Lena would want me even less.

"Don't be a fool, Martha. Come on; let's bed your horse down and get to it. Lena will be surprised, but she won't be hostile. I know her well. You must trust me where Lena is concerned."

A sickening weight of anticipation fair-about numbed all my senses as I followed Lije from the barn (where Pie was rewarded for his service with ration of grain.) I moved toward the house in a state of discomfort; my clothes all felt much too tight. The world around me seemed to have shifted, retreating from reality into the vague, half-solid realms of a dream—or more likely, a nightmare. The afternoon bore me along on its current. I could not slow time's rapid flood, nor alter the course of my drifting. Lije led me up the back steps, into a small but tidy kitchen with a clean-swept, spotlessly scrubbed red-brick floor. The smell of wood smoke and fresh-baked bread wrapped all around me. I kept my eyes fixed on the bricks below my feet.

"Supper will be ready in about an hour." It was a young woman's voice, smooth and high, pretty as a song. And it plucked a nerve inside me, sent a jolt of recognition traveling up my back till my scalp tingled and my heart went sick all at once with love and longing. I knew it was my sister's voice, yet it sounded so much like my mother's. I had scarcely thought of Ma, all those many years since we left Missouri. She leaped back into my awareness, vivid in memory—and once again I saw her knees showing below her pushed-up skirt; I saw pale dust flying as her horse sprinted away, bearing my ma beyond my reach.

"Turn around and have a look, Lena," my brother said. "Look what the cat dragged in."

I couldn't raise my eyes from the clean-swept floor, but I did see the hem of Lena's skirt, pink flowers on white, rotating slowly as she turned from her stove. I could see the toes of her boots now, pointed and brown, as clean as the bricks. Lena held perfectly still and faced me. Silence flattened itself between us and lay there, cringing and thick.

"Don't you know who this is?" Lije asked.

"Of course I do." Lena sounded half-choked. "I... I never thought to see her again, that's all."

I could read no emotion in her voice. Only dull, cautious shock.

After a spell, Lena said, "Hello, Martha."

I'll never know how I convinced myself to speak. "Hello, Lena. You sure have a pretty place here." I was still staring at the toes of her boots.

"All thanks to John—my husband. He's a hard-working man." She cleared her throat and moved out of my sheepish, downcast vision. I heard the scrape of a chair across't the floor. "Well," Lena said briskly, "I suppose you ought to sit down. I'll put the percolator on."

Lije gave me a gentle push towards the table. He joined me there, grinning eagerly, looking from me to Lena and back again. Timid, I risked a glance toward the stove and found Lena in profile, busying herself with a copper coffee pot. She was very pale; her brows had drawn together in a stern frown, or perhaps that was just the way she looked whenever she worked. Her hair was like mine, dark and gently curled, but glossy where mine was always dull from trail dust. She had swept her hair up into a fashionable roll, too, with a little puff standing up at her forehead and the whole arrangement held in place with a tortoiseshell comb. She had our mother's eyes—keen and dark, with a spark of hardness to them, but so prettily shaped you couldn't help but stare. As I took in the sight of my sister, I realized Lena was only a few years older than my ma was in my favorite memories. She must have been twenty-five in 1885. Lena was much smaller in stature than I was, and finer in the face and hands. But still she bore the unmistakable stamp of our family—a firm presence, a carriage far prouder than a Canary ought to be. Once in my hurdy-gurdy days, I had heard a woman called "statuesque," and that word came back to me as I gazed at my beautiful sister. She looked just like a marble carving, valuable and set high upon its plinth.

When she had put the percolator on the stove to boil, Lena approached the table with the grim resolve of someone determined to see to an unpleasant task. Her belly pushed out a little, filling her skirt. She was pregnant—six or seven months along, from what I could tell. The pain of losing my son had eased a little by then, so I could be more pleased for her than envious.

"You're gonna have a baby," I said.

"Yes—my first. I guess he'll come by the end of summer."

"It's a dreadful thing, to be pregnant in the summertime." I feared she would ask me whether I had any children, so I added quickly, "Or so I hear tell."

Lena smiled rather tightly. "I will manage." She flicked a cautious look at Lije, and I blushed at my own stupidity. It wasn't fit, to talk of bearing babies where a man could hear.

Lena said, "What brings you to Lander, Martha? And in… such a state?"

"Oh." I brushed my big, clumsy hands down the front of my shirt, fidgeting in my trousers. "You must excuse me for all this. I been running a delivery service out of Boulder, Colorado. The work is so terrible dirty, I find it more suitable to dress like a man than a lady." Lena couldn't quite disguise her scowl, though I saw her try. I added, "But of course, I always wear a dress to church on Sundays."

"Of course. You made a delivery to Lander, then?"

I swallowed hard before I spoke again. "As for what brought me here—to tell you the truth, I heard tell that Lije was in Lander. I thought to find him. I didn't know you was here, too, till I arrived this afternoon. But I'm right glad to see you." Suddenly all the reservation broke within me like a breached dam. Words—desperate explanations—poured from my mouth. I couldn't have stopped talking if I'd tried. "Lena, I thought about you every day since we parted. You and everyone else. I fretted over you so often, I could never count all the times. You can't imagine how it soothes my soul, to see you set up so well in such a pretty house, and married to a man you like, with a baby on the way. Oh, all the times I wondered what became of you! I feel as if I'm witnessing a proper miracle, right here and now. I could jump up and sing a hymn."

Lena smiled, but it was a small and tentative thing. A good deal of confusion tensed the corners of her eyes. She made herself laugh. It sounded forced. "There's no need to sing. And yes, I am well; thank you for your concern. I work hard—John works hard, too, selling meat and vegetables to the Army and to other expeditions that pass through the valley. But one small farm alone can't provide the sort of future John and I have planned for. So I have taken up the laundry business." She sighed; there was no mistaking her weariness. Then she shook her head and asked, "What of you, Martha? Where did life take you after... after we parted ways?"

I didn't know how to answer such a question. I had no doubt Lena wouldn't care for the truth. If she knew even half of my sorry history, she was like to toss me out the kitchen door on my backside. So I said, "I met with hardship, here and there."

All the pains I'd felt over those sixteen years—and the loves I had lost—rose up and struck me all at once, a concerted blow harder and meaner than any man's fist. I longed for my family with a hunger I had never felt before, never since leaving Piedmont. I had only the two of them now, Lena and Lije, but I knew I couldn't part with either one, even if Lena scorned me. My heart would break at the separation. I had found my family again—what scraps of family remained—and I knew this time, I mustn't let us fall apart.

"You're tired," I said. "You work hard, as you say. Let me work for you, Lena. You need to rest, with that baby on the way. I done laundering before—plenty of it. You'll find me a real good worker. And you don't need to pay me one cent; I got money enough to live on, thanks to my bullwhacking. You don't need to put me up here, neither; I can board in town and ride to work, or walk, if you prefer."

Lena looked perplexed, at first—then almost angry. She turned her face away, staring at the wall, and her frown returned, the fine black brows drawn together.

Lije said, "You talked about hiring a girl to help you with the washing, Lena."

She shot our brother a withering stare. Lije only shrugged and leaned back in his chair, grinning, satisfied. He seemed confident already that Lena would accept my offer, but I wasn't so sure.

"Martha ain't half wrong," Lije went on. "You need help more'n ever, with a baby on the way. Who better to lend a hand than your own sister?"

Lena shifted uncomfortably on her chair. She didn't seem much inclined to meet my eye. Then the percolator began to chatter, and she jumped to her feet, grateful for the distraction.

"How about it," Lije said.

Lena sighed, turning away from us both. "Yes, all right," she said. "Very well."

I HASTENED into town that very evening and sent a telegram to my boys back in Boulder. The bullwhacking business is yours, I told them—all yours. Sell it if you please, and divide the profits among you, or keep running it—it's all one to me. I've found my missing family, and I don't aim to leave any time soon. Or words to that effect; I don't recall their precise nature now. All I remember with any certainty is the hope I felt blossoming in my breast, unfurling like some bright and miraculous flower. Now, of course, I know what a fool I was. At the time, I thought my travails had come to an end, and only happiness lay before me. I should have known better. My life has only ever been fit for calamity.

I worked for Lena all the remaining months of her pregnancy, driving a cart into town to fetch her customers' garments, sorting them all into stamped bags, and returning their goods after me and Lena washed and pressed them. It was hot and tiring work, made all the more miserable by the fact that I was obliged to work in a dress. Lena's sense of propriety demanded nothing less. But I toiled for her gladly, taking on the brunt of her labors—especially as the summer waxed and the heat took its toll on her health.

Lena was never especially warm with me. I can't say as I blame her, for by that time, we was little better than strangers. But she was tolerant and patient with my early mistakes, and seemed honestly determined to make the best of our strange situation. In time, as I grew used to the rhythms of her laundry shed, Lena even came to appreciate my work. She thanked me often. She seemed to admire my strength, my refusal to wear down. But she never grew especially friendly towards me.

At the end of a long day of labor, I often joined Lije at the edge of the potato field, reclining in the shade of the cottonwoods. Or we wandered down to the crick together, wading up to our knees in the bitingly cold water, splashing and joking exactly like we did as children, when we had played in muddy ditches between the Missouri fields.

One hot evening, while Lije and I stood in the lazy current of the stream, I worked up the gumption to ask him why Lena still treated me so distant and cold.

Lije stared down at his bare knees showing below his rolled-up trouser legs. I could read his hesitation in his silence. But at last, he heaved a sigh and said, "Sometimes I think Lena blames you for the way things went. You know—when we was small."

I felt hot tears pricking at my eyelids. "I done my best."

"I know you did, Martha. I know." Lije waded closer and put one arm around my shoulders. "But Lena was such a tiny thing back then—just a mite. She don't recall those days the same as we do."

As twilight settled over the valley, I walked to my boarding house in Lander properly dejected. That night I lay awake for hours, fretting over the past. Sixteen years of silence between my sister and me—all those years when Lena despised me. I couldn't do a thing now to change what had befallen the Canarys. I couldn't have done a thing back then, neither, when I was a desperate orphan girl of thirteen. I was a child in those days, as much as Lena was. But she had carved her version of the Canary history deep into her heart. I saw no way to change Lena's mind now.

As her belly expanded, Lena's temper grew shorter than a bug's leg. She was often cross with me while I toiled over my kettle of steaming lye. I took her temper in the best stead I could manage. But the colder and angrier Lena became, the less ready I was bear her scorn. Lije had been right; I could see that plain. Lena had nursed her anger at me for sixteen years; she couldn't keep it in check. But I knew the truth of what had transpired long ago, when we found ourselves orphans on the trail. I thought it a great injustice, that I should be made to suffer when I had done everything in my power to love Lena and treat her as kindly as fate would allow.

One day, when Lena had treated me especially bitter, I pulled a chair out from its place beside the wall and bade her sit.

"I won't," she said. "There's too much work to be done." But she was already drifting toward the chair, even as she spoke— moving toward the mercy of a rest. She sank down with a long groan, rubbing the small of her back with both hands. Her eyes was screwed tightly shut against the pain.

I sat, too, on the empty crate where we folded shirts. I faced my sister and braced myself up. The time had come to thrash out all the sourness remaining between us. "Listen, Lena. We can't go on arguing day after day. It ain't good for your health, with the baby about to make his appearance. Let's have it all out right here and now, or we'll never work together peaceably."

She stared at me for a long moment. I could almost hear all the words she wanted to say, but dared not speak. The accusations she longed to sling in my direction: her life had been harder than she had deserved, and it was my fault, for I had been the leader, back then. Every poor decision had been mine to make; every sorrow she suffered was one of my invention.

To her credit, Lena controlled herself with that same icy resolve. She said only, "Very well, Martha. What do you wish to say to me?"

"I know you blame me for the way things turned out," I answered quietly. "I guess you can't help but blame me, for you was such a small girl at the time, but—"

"Of course I blame you, Martha! How should I not?" In the months since making her reacquaintance, I had never known Lena to burst out so passionately. It fair took me aback. "For mercy's sake, *you gave me up*! You sent me away!"

I stared at her so long, I swear I felt the Earth slow in its course around the sun. Finally I said, "Lena, you asked me to send you away. You told me to find you a good family to care for you, like I did for Baby Sara. You didn't want to stay with us any longer—me and Lije and Cilus."

"That's not true!"

The memory returned to me, so cruel and stark I could smell the dung of the oxen, taste trail dust upon my tongue. I could feel my sister, small and frail, curled in my lap while I sang close beside her ear. I remembered the firelight dancing fitfully on her black curls, the softness of her cheek against mine. I remembered how my hands ached from washing, and my back ached from walking, and my heart ached from all the ways I had failed.

"It is true," I said, and for once I was cold and hard to my sister. "I swear it's true. And even if you hadn't asked me to do it, I still would have given you away, if I had to make the decision again. For you had a good life, Lena—a kind and loving mother to raise you, a father to provide for you. A happy home, a comfortable future. It's more than the rest of us got. It's damn sure more than I got. I wouldn't have changed a thing, for your sake. And you're too damn foolish to see the truth."

Heartsick, hating myself for giving her up in the first place and hating myself even more for cracking down on her now, I stood and left the laundry shed. I kept on walking through the fields, to the pretty little lane, away from the story-book valley altogether. I never went back. Nothing good could ever grow between Lena and me. I seen that truth in my sister's eyes. All too soon, after just three months with my family, the time had come for me to strike out on my own—to make my life anew, just as I had done so many times before.

BY THE TIME AUTUMN CAME, I found myself in Crawford, Nebraska, and if I never set eyes on Nebraska again, then by God it will be much too soon. An uglier and deader place you cannot imagine. And if I had any power over you, Short Pants, I'd forbid you from ever going. I wouldn't have tarried in Crawford a-tall, but by then my small supply of money had plum run dry—for I had left what remained of my bullwhacking profits in a little cloth bag atop Lije's bunk, along with a note directing him to hire a girl to help Lena with her laundry till the baby was one year old. That was my final act of kindness toward my sister. I halfway convinced myself she'd appreciate it.

In Crawford, I set myself up once more as a trick shootist and scraped together enough money to live in a rat-hole of a boarding house. It was a dreadful place—and so damn expensive, I lived on bread and water, without even a few coins left over for a rare sip of whiskey. I'm afraid my circumstances was direr than ever. The legend of Calamity Jane was scarcely profitable in Nebraska, yet my legend was the only asset on which I could hope to trade, for Crawford was full of pretty girls and I couldn't compete in the brothels. Besides which, I was thirty years old, and had lived a difficult life. What paltry-few looks I had once possessed was rapidly fading. I knew I must earn my keep some other way, for the days when I could squeak by on a whore's earnings was behind me. By and by, I even grew desperate enough to sell the gun with the pearl star in its handle, for I had sore need of the money. But I couldn't part with Wild Bill's gun, nor his watch nor his ring. They was far too precious; I could as soon sell the artifacts of my heart as I could saw off my own leg.

If I hadn't been so hard up, I never would have fallen in with Bill Steers. And save for the one precious gift that man gave me, I would have called my life blessed (despite its many harrowing stretches of darkness) if I had never met Bill a-tall, let alone taken up with him. No hardship I'd endured could ever compare to the terror of Bill Steers.

Steers began showing interest in me after one of my shooting demonstrations, and I suppose in some strange way I found it intoxicating, to be stared at so intently by a man. Even in my whoring days, no fella had ever looked on me so keenly. Fool that I was, I took the intensity of his gaze for romance—and though I found is cold, craggy face remarkably unappealing, I was flattered by the interest. That's the way of a lonely heart, I suppose. To this day, I believe Steers read the lonesome heartbreak on my face the way learned men read a book. In my sorrow, Steers found his opportunity. He knew exactly how to draw me in: with kind words and sweet gestures. But he never meant a word he said to me. I learned the truth of Bill Steers, all too soon.

I don't know whether Bill intended to profit from my name, the way Jim Darling had hoped—or whether he merely enjoyed shoving and hitting and hurting women. His motives don't matter to me now. They didn't matter then. All that mattered was that I get away from his fists with all haste—a matter made fearfully difficult when I fell pregnant. Unlike with my first (the poor baby boy I left buried in a cattle pasture outside Boulder) this time there could be no doubt about who had fathered my child.

I couldn't stomach the thought of raising an innocent, fragile baby under Steers' shadow. Escape was easily dreamed of, but much harder done. For in addition to his cruel words that often made me weep with shame and despair—and in addition to his kicks, his hard slaps, the crack of his fist against my jaw—Steers

hid all the money from me, even the money I earned, so I would
have no means of caring for myself till I found a new home. It's a
damn blind miracle he never found the watch and ring, my
precious mementos of Wild Bill—nor Wild Bill's gun, neither. I
cut a slit in the bottom of our mattress and pushed those treasures
up inside, and every day I fretted and prayed that Steers would
never discover them.

As my pregnancy progressed, I grew more desperate to escape.
I came to understand that if I wished to be truly free of Bill Steers,
I must leave Crawford altogether, for he was too well known in
the town; I could never hope to evade him for long. Either that, or
I must get that man locked up for a good, long while. I went to the
sheriff and showed him my bruises; I begged him to take Steers to
jail. He did, but only for a few days. And when Steers was let out
of the pen, his rage was ten times worse than it had ever been
before. He beat me so bad, I couldn't get up off the floor for a day
and a half. It's a wonder and a miracle I didn't lose the baby.

After that terrible beating, Steers got slyer about his methods.
He found ways of hurting me that left no mark, so I couldn't run
to the sheriff again. As his outrages against my person became
more frequent and more inventive in their cruelty, I felt my body
gathering its strength. My labor would come soon; I was frantic to
get away. On the night when the first faint pains began, I knew
the time had come. I must make my escape without any money—I
must throw myself on God's mercy, or the mercy of whatever
force exists in lieu of God. I could only pray I would land somewhere safe before the baby came.

That night, I took special pains to be meek and sweet to Steers.
I gave him not the least speck of trouble, but poured his whiskey
and encouraged him to drink—which was always dangerous, for
it sparked his darkest moods, but I knew if he drank enough, he
would sleep deeply, too—as deep as death. All the while, I turned
my back whenever a pain took me, for I didn't want him to notice
the strain—or my grim resolve. I was determined to make him

believe nothing was amiss, determined to lull him into compla-cency and guide him gently to a few hours of black unawareness.

When he finally descended into sleep (snoring so hard I could smell the whiskey fumes hanging around his head) I threw a few changes of clothing and some blankets for the baby into a small trunk, barely two feet wide. I buried Wild Bill's pistol under the blankets and slipped his watch and ring into a tiny cloth bag, which I tied to the strings that held up my knickers, so my greatest treasures was disguised beneath my skirt. Then I hefted the trunk that contained all my worldly goods and crept out of the house, taking care to shut the door soft as a whisper behind me.

It was a cold night; winter was just around the corner and I was frightened, shivering, uncertain where I ought to go. I knew only that I must keep moving away from Steers—as far as I could get before my labor became too intense and I could force myself to go no farther. There was no hope of riding in my big and desperate state; I had been obliged to leave my horse Pie in Steers' corral, though I hated to part with that fine animal. I left my beau-tiful saddle, too—the one I'd had since the expedition days, when I had ridden my black mare Silkie alone among canyons and buttes. It stung to leave that saddle behind, for I knew Bill would sell it the first chance he got. But I also knew Bill would kill me, sooner or later, if I stayed. He would kill my child, too, and that I would never allow.

The baby moved restlessly inside me. I felt a terrible pressure, inside and outside, as if all the cold world was telling me my time was damn near up. I near-about went crazy at the sensation; I was desperate enough to try anything, to go anywhere if I could hope for a little shelter and aid. I walked through the dark streets of Crawford lugging that box against my fat hip, sweating and curs-ing, aching all over. My stomach roiled with a dreadful certainty that the birth was upon me.

Then I spotted a stage coach paused outside a livery. Two women perched inside, their delicate profiles white against the

dark of night. They was fine and fancy ladies, indeed, and traveling alone, as far as I could see. I didn't hesitate; I set my box
among their bags at the back of the coach and heaved myself into
the vehicle.

"My goodness," one of the ladies said as I clambered grace-
lessly into their carriage.

"Good evening, mam," I said to each of them in turn. "You
mustn't mind me. I was supposed to take a different coach, but I
just got word that it has been delayed. As you can see, I'm in a
particular state; I must make my trip tonight, so your driver was
kind enough to agree to carry me." I settled on the leather seat and
sighed, smiling like it was the most natural and expected thing in
the world, for a nine-months-pregnant woman to climb aboard a
coach in the dead of night. "Don't you worry about a thing,
Misses. I won't give you a speck of trouble."

"You, er—" The elder of the two women paused, eyeing my
vast belly where it rested on my lap. "You must be close to your
time."

"Yes mam," I said, "fairly close now, but it's nothing to trouble
yourself over." Even as I spoke, all cavalier, my belly cramped with
another early pain. I believe my brows pinched together, but I
would allow my distress to reveal itself no further.

I settled back in the seat, pressing my big body as far into the
shadows as I could manage, and held my breath while the driver
returned from inside the livery. My heart beat so wildly, I
expected the two women to hear. Would they call out to the
driver, ask about my unexpected presence—demand my dirty self
be evicted from their dandy carriage to wait for a more suitable
rig? But the two ladies held their tongues, thank God, and only
blinked at me in mild confusion. Then the stage coach rocked as
the driver climbed up to his seat, and when it lurched into
motion, I let out my breath in a long, shuddering sigh of relief.
Crawford, Nebraska and Bill Steers fell away behind me, swallowed by the night.

BY THE TIME a peaky dawn edged the cold horizon with pink light, I could no longer hide the extent of my pains. I huddled over my taut round belly, gritting my teeth and groaning as each labor pain took me. The younger of my fellow passengers had taken my hand sometime in the night, murmuring comforts and casting desperate glances at her companion, who counted the miles to the next stop—a town called Douglas—where she swore I would find help.

"We've reached Douglas now," the older woman said, pressing her cheek against the glass window, watching the town take shape in the frigid morning light. "Hold on but a while longer, my girl. Help is at hand."

We rolled into Douglas; the stage coach stopped outside a livery.

"We must go to the town midwife at once," said the elder lady.

But the next moment, the driver opened the doors to let in the morning light. All three of us blinked in the unexpected glare. The fine ladies cast timid glances between me and the driver.

"What in all Hell is this?" the driver exclaimed.

"Please, Mister," I began. I didn't get no farther than that. The strongest pain yet gripped me; I could no longer keep my voice in check. I bellowed and hunched, for my body felt ready to rip itself in two. The baby would make its appearance all too soon, and there was nothing I could do but center myself in a world of pain.

Dimly, I was aware of the other travelers pleading on my behalf. "You can see her state. There's nothing to be done."

"Like Hell there ain't," the driver said. "She never paid me a cent."

"She's a poor woman, and she must be fleeing desperate circumstances."

"I don't give free rides. Not to anybody."

"Have a heart, sir!"

The driver had mislaid his heart, and seemed in no hurry to find it again. He shook me by the shoulder. "Out, you. Out! This is the end of the line for you. You won't go a mile more—not in my coach."

"Please, sir," I began.

That devil wouldn't let me speak another word. "You heard me; out! Be glad I don't turn you in to the sheriff. It's only because of your... your *state* that I don't. Thank your lucky star, or you'd be dropping that whelp in a jail cell."

The younger of the two women jumped down from the carriage and offered her hand. I leaned on her heavily as I stumbled out. I managed to gasp, "My trunk..."

But before I could make my way to the foot of the stage coach to retrieve my belongings, the driver beat me to it. He slapped his palm down on my humble box. "I don't expect you've got a damn thing of any value in here, but I'll take it, just the same. Consider it your fare."

"Mister, please!"

The women exclaimed at his cruelty, but they made no move to pay my fare in coin, neither. (Maybe I'm unkind to think them stingy. Could be they had no more money left between them.)

"Go on; get out of here," the driver said. He kicked dust in my direction, as if I was a feral dog. "Don't let me see you hanging about. I'd rather call for the sheriff than look at you for one more second!"

I would have fallen to my knees and begged for his mercy, or wept out of pure desperation right there in the street. But my condition didn't allow me. Instead, I stumbled to the nearest hitching post and braced myself against it, supporting the impossible weight of my agonized body. There I cried as I never had before—choking on my ragged breath, pummeled by a grief I hadn't felt in years. It wasn't only fear of the strange town that had upset me so. I had lost Wild Bill's pistol, and all the memories it held. I would never touch that gun again, never recall the way it had fit so easily in my true love's hand. It was gone forever, just like Bill himself. But I remained, lonesome and in pain, to carry on in a cold, heartless world.

All too soon, another contraction shook me. Then I stopped sobbing and choking, and wiped the snot from my pinched-up face, for I had pressing business and it certainly would not wait. I told myself I could give over to grief once the baby was born. Till I had delivered that child safe and sound, I could spare neither thoughts nor tears for the cruel world.

I lurched away from the hitching post and set about finding a bed. I truly had nothing now—no money, not even the pistol to trade—but I thought I might scare up a little charity, if I could find a church. I squinted at Douglas, searching through my swimming vision for a white-sided church with a beckoning steeple, like the one I'd found in Piedmont. In the blush-dawn light, the buildings and streets blurred around me. I swallowed down my fear, praying I could find my sanctuary before another pain struck.

Then I saw it, across the street and three doors away. Something far better than any church: a dance hall. I staggered up to the door, pressed myself against it while another contraction seized me. Panting, groaning, I waited out the pain. The sweat of my brow burned in the morning chill. When the pain ebbed a little, I pushed open the door and called out, "Help me! Please, Madam, take pity! I'm in an awful way."

I almost fell to the ground, for I was quaking with weariness. I caught myself on the edge of a pool table and hung over it, palms braced against smooth green felt. Beyond the realm of my fear and agony, I was aware of women—their voices, their hands—gathering all around me. And then a sharp clap, and the dancing-girls skittering away. The madam stood before me, her aging face too brightly painted, looking me up and down with a glint of skeptical disappointment.

"Madam, you must take me in," I said.

"In your state? You must be mad, girl."

"I can earn you money, once this baby's born."

She laughed rather grimly. "I doubt that."

"I don't mean by dancing," I said. "I'm too big and ugly for that. I'm about to bust open, besides. But I'm Calamity Jane—the one and only. I know I don't look like much right now, but you must believe me, Madam; I swear I'm the famed wild girl of the West. My trick-shooting shows bring in real good money. All of it's yours—all of it, for the whole next year—as long you'll give me a room to stay in, so's I can birth this baby someplace warm. I'll need a pistol, too, for I lost my last remaining gun."

A murmur spread among the girls the moment I confessed my name. The madam silenced them with another sharp clap. "Why should I believe you?" she said to me. "Ten girls have come to me in the past year, all claiming to be Calamity Jane. The West is full of Calamity Janes; they're worse than a plague of locusts."

Even in my desperate state, I perked up at her words, for it was news to me. "You haven't any reason to believe me, I guess. Except this: would a false Calamity appear to you in such a state? No! Only the real thing would come crawling in like this, claiming such an infamous name when she's in terrible dire straits. You got no reason to believe me, Madam—yet still I say it's the truth. And I'll make you a rich woman, if you only take pity on me and trust me. Please, Madam. I can't have this baby out there in the street. It's too cold; the little thing will die."

That was so miserably true that I burst into fresh tears. I don't think that madam trusted me one bit—not yet. But my tears moved her to pity. She rolled her eyes and turned away, but she did give me lodging—and not a minute too soon, for by the time the dancing-girls helped me up the stairs to a cramped, musty room, the birth-water gushed down my legs and my labor began in earnest.

The madam sent two of her girls running for the town's midwife, and a few hard hours later, my baby girl drew her first

breath in the confines of a whorehouse. She cried first thing, the
moment she slid out into the midwife's hands, and that strong,
defiant wail drowned out all my fears that she would be born cold
and blue like her brother.

When the midwife wrapped her in a blanket and pressed that
precious bundle into my arms, I set up in bed and turned toward
the dusty window pane. I watched the October sun shining on my
angel's features. She was beautiful—perfect—with wet black curls
and porcelain skin, dark lashes and a nose like a rosy little button.
I named her Jessie.

The longer I stared transfixed at my daughter's round, red
face, the stronger grew my resolve to do right by that child. I had
a dreadful premonition, a sick fear way down deep in my aching
guts, that I would fail to be a proper mother, the kind of mother
my little angel deserved.

I would fail, but by God, I would try.

HER PROSPECTS HAVE SUFFERED SADLY FROM HER NEGLECT OF APPEARANCES

SHE WAS A RIDER FROM A RIGHT EARLY AGE, MY JESSIE. SET UP ON the saddle before me, she learned the sway and rhythm of a horse's gait before she learned her own. We left Douglas as soon as we was able—just a few weeks after my year-long promise to the madam was fulfilled. Then Jessie and I and drifted from town to town (whatever town would have us) with Jessie carried in a cloth sling against my heart till she was big enough to set upright. Everywhere we lit, I took up work as a laundress or a maid till I lost my place again. Then we found ourselves mounted on our horse once more, plodding across an expanse of hot grass, following the slim black line of the train tracks from west to east and back west again.

Those first years of Jessie's life was a trial, I suppose—or at least I know it ought to have felt like a trial. One woman alone in the wilderness, with a tiny child to care for. But now, when I cast my thoughts back to those days, all I can feel is the sacred joy of my sweet little girl held tight in my arms. All I can see is the straightness her tiny back, how proud and confident she always looked in the saddle. I remember the way her fine, black curls bounced when I kicked our horse's flanks, and clucked with my tongue, and we started off at a trot down another long and lone-some road. Jessie never minded our untethered state, our restless circuit of the towns and forts spread out across't the prairie. All she cared for was the ride—and oh, how she laughed to feel that horse go.

The weeks we spent riding are the greatest treasures of my remembrance. I cherished our time alone, traveling from one town to the next, for it was just me and Jessie—no searching eye to seek out my sins and my failings, no one to judge me. Freed from all constraint, with no one to heed but the little girl wrapped tightly in my arms, I painted pictures for my Jessie with a thousand beautiful lies. They shone in the brightest colors.

I told myself Jessie was never Bill Steers' daughter, but Wild Bill's. Steers never could have made something so pretty and good. Come to that, I never could have made a child as beautiful as Jessie, either. Wild Bill's spirit had found its way into my daughter's soul—into her very making, somehow—through some process of angels and miracles, the nature of which I had no power to understand. Don't look at me that way, Short Pants. I knew it was all a fantasy; I know it still. But I wanted it to be true. I longed for that truth so hungrily, to this day I suspect some part of me really did believe.

The tales I wove for Jessie was wilder still, but I justified the lies because the stories I told my girl was sweeter than honey—to me and to her.

"Your mother's name was Charlotte Burch," I told her. "She was pretty as a blackbird flying. Charlotte was my daughter; that makes me your grandmam."

Had anyone ridden along beside us—had anyone but Jessie heard the story—I doubt they would have questioned my claim. I couldn't have been older than thirty-three, but hard living had taken a brutal toll. I'm afraid the hollow, broken state of my heart was visible from the outside; I looked at least twenty years beyond my real age. But while we journeyed across the prairie with the tall grass brushing my feet in the stirrups, there was no one else to hear, no one to shatter the delicate filigree of my lies. And Jessie resembled my mother so very much, I found it easy to believe the tale, myself. So I recited the familiar story as many times as Jessie liked to hear it—which was plenty.

"Your ma Charlotte Burch was a real beauty, and a fine upstanding lady, adored by all who met her. She loved you more than the moon loves the stars, and always treated you gentle.

"Your pa was Wild Bill Hickok, a brave and fine hero of the war, a renowned scout who treated everyone he encountered with wisdom and justice. His hair was red as the sunset, and his eyes was sad and kind, and he was the beautifullest man anyone ever seen.

"Wild Bill loved your ma with a purity and passion even the angels envied. He intended to marry her and make an honest woman of her, but General Sheridan wouldn't let him, for he needed Wild Bill for his grand missions. And your pa was so righteous and upstanding that he did his duty by the General, even though his heart cried out for your ma. On the last day he rode out with Sheridan, Wild Bill said to his men, 'When I get home to Deadwood, I will make Charlotte Burch my wife, for there never was a finer woman in all God's creation, and her child is mine, and I intend to raise Jessie up proper, for she is the most beautiful and sweetest-tempered baby in the whole of the West, and when she's big enough I intend to give her a pony of her own and teach her how to ride.'

"But Wild Bill never came back from that ride. He was killed saving General Sheridan and ten other men from an Indian ambush. He sacrificed himself, so the rest of the men might get away. He was a hero and a gentleman, and he never had no vices. And he loved you, Jessie girl. He loved you with all his heart.

"The only bit of Wild Bill Hickok that made it back to Deadwood was a lock of his long red hair. When Charlotte saw that lock of hair, she knew it meant Wild Bill was dead. She fell down in a faint from heartbreak, straight away, and I'm afraid she never did recover. She expired of a broken heart; her love for Wild Bill was the very blood in her veins. I set by her bedside, holding her hand the whole time she ailed—and she looked so fine and delicate and pretty, though I could see how sorrow made her cheeks go pale and made her eyes flame with the last passion of her heart.

"She came around just long enough to clutch my hand and say, 'Mother, my dearest mother who was always good and loyal to me —you must take my baby Jessie and raise her up proper, for I shan't be able to. And tell her all about her ma, Charlotte Burch, who treasured her more than any mother has ever loved a daughter before. And tell her about her pa, Wild Bill Hickok, the finest and handsomest and most respectable man who ever rode the Hills.'"

By the time Jessie reached her second year, I could have recited the legend of her origins in my sleep—and did a time or two, for I recall jerking awake in the stillness of night, murmuring those familiar words into the darkness of a boarding-house room or beside the embers of our lone camp fire. When she was two, I dressed Jessie in a little frock of scarlet, which I paid a girl in Douglas to sew. That dress was dandy with pintucks and frills, and it put me in mind of the bit of red cloth my mother had flung at the neighbor-lady back in Missouri. "Take that cloth and make a dress for that bastard of yours," she'd said, and then she thundered away, leaving me in the dust with only my awe of her and the taste of molasses candy lingering on my tongue.

Those warm days in the saddle. Jessie talking happily in my lap, the horse moving steady through the knee-high grass. I used to sing to my girl—songs I picked up from the boys in the saloons, or learned long ago at the rail camps. Although my voice had never been accounted very fine (or even acceptable, truth be told) Jessie laughed and clapped and looked up at me with shining black eyes whenever I broke out a tune.

I sang Oh Johnny, Oh Jonny, Oh and funny songs I gleaned

from the Englishmen and the Scots who'd come searching for
gold.

> I'm a broken-hearted keelsman and I'm or-head
> 　　in love
> with a young lass down in Gateshead and I call her
> 　　my dove.
> Her name is Cushie Butterfield and she sells yeller
> 　　clay,
> and her cousin is a muckman and they call him Tom
> 　　Gray.
> She's a big lass and a bonny lass, oh and she likes her
> 　　beer,
> and her name is Cushie Butterfield and I wish she
> 　　was here,
> she's a big lass and a bonny lass, oh and I'm sore in
> 　　love,
> and her name is Cushie Butterfield and I call her my
> 　　dove.

That year—the year Jessie was two and dressed in her little red
frock—when I was twenty years beyond my real age, wrapped in
the comfort of my beautiful lies—I passed through more towns
than I could count. Everywhere I went, I put on a different name,
fearing my reputation had preceded me and wrecked up all my
prospects before I'd even arrived. Sometimes I was Mary King,
and sometimes Margaret Bird. I was known to call myself Charlotte or Isabelle or Lena, and I pulled out the surnames of my
various husbands whenever the need arose. Now and then I was
even Martha Canary, when I felt haunted by the past and ready to
atone for my sins. A patchwork of identities, but never did I admit
to being Calamity Jane. Jessie deserved better than that. She was a
sunny child with a real sharp mind; I couldn't stand to cover her
in the shadow of my infamy.

I suppose we never can escape our nature, though, no matter how we try. As I told you, I would begin working in a laundry just as soon as we arrived at a new destination. I fell quickly into the routine of my new job, but once life began to get easy for me again—once I felt, as it were, my feet on solid ground—then the whiskey called. It always called, sooner or later, and no matter how I insisted that this time would be different, this town would be different—in the end, I succumbed to my vice.

No—in truth it wasn't whiskey that called to me. I can see that now. Rather it was memory a-calling. It was sin and hurt and a vastness of loss, endless as the sky. It was the lightness of Baby Sara in my arms, and Lena in my lap, asking me to find a place for her. It was the man in the sugarloaf hat tucking my pa's money into his saddle bag and saying, *Fuck off out of here, girl.* It was a stick cracking down on a burned palm, a rattle of wagon wheels rolling away, and most of all—most of all, it was Wild Bill saying, *You know, Calam, I went and got myself a wife.*

All that came first. The whiskey came after.

But the whiskey always did come.

I MIGHT HOPE to last two months, maybe three at best, before calamity caught up to me and sullied the good reputation I built in town after town. Rather than allow my past to overtake me and swallow up my Jessie—my Cushie Butterfield—I moved on before any sheriff could toss me in jail, or any sharp wit could connect my habits and style with the reports that circulated the Plains and Hills—the legend of Calamity Jane.

It helped some that by that time—late in 1893—the West was overfull with Calamities, full to the point of busting. Anyplace where a girl got herself into trouble and whooped it up a little too hard, she claimed her initials was C. J. I heard tales of girls robbing one another blind in the cat houses, and laying the blame at Calamity's feet. There was even one intrepid lady who tied a black scarf around her face to hide her identity, then held a stage coach at gunpoint till she collected every last bit of gold off its driver and its occupants. As she rode away, the thief hollered, "You just been robbed by Calamity Jane, the fastest gun this side of the Mississippi!" It surely was not me, for I have never approved of thieving. But the law never caught up to the stage coach robber, and I must admit I find something admirable about her ploy. It was clever, even if it was a damn dirty trick. Calamities wrecked up rented carriages and set saloons afire. They beat their husbands and rustled cattle; they took out stakes in the Black Hills and built companies of all-lady miners. In the streets of damn near every town, some Jane or other drank to excess and made a scene, or stole bottles of whiskey right off the shelves, or fought bare-knuckled in the alleys, spitting cusses along with the blood that dripped from their broken noses.

That state of affairs suited me just fine. By then, I was content to pass the mantel of notoriety to girls who actually wanted to wear those accursed rags. I surely had no more desire for infamy, or the keen attention it brought. I was content to be Martha Burch, loving grandmother and half-assed guardian of Jessie— daughter of the Blackbird of the Plains and Hero Wild Bill. I kept one eye on the newspapers and took in each fresh tale of a new Calamity, and every time some wild girl incited outrage, I breathed a sigh of relief. For if the law sought Calamity Jane in some piss-pot of a settlement a hundred miles away, then no one was likely to spot me where I actually was, right under their noses.

And when I gave in to the call of memory and whiskey—when the true Jane revealed herself at last—I moved along the very next day, for moving on was easier than getting the Devil out of me for good. Moving troubled me not one bit—not those first years, anyway. As long as I still had Jessie, I reasoned, I could make it through any turn of fortune.

But after a time, my predicaments became somewhat harder to flee. Jessie's third birthday was fast approaching; I had lighted in scores of towns by then and fled them all when the whiskey had taken too strong a hold. We was running short of destinations; after three years of sin, Martha Burch had accumulated almost as dire a reputation as Calamity Jane. Me and Jessie found ourselves in northern Wyoming, having fled a succession of towns and forts at the heart of the new-made state. A string of ill-advised behaviors dragged along behind me (maybe a few warrants for my arrest, too.) It was autumn already, and the season was getting late. To the south, foul weather had already set in, burying the plains under bushels of snow. I knew I would never make it down to Utah or Arizona with Jessie, young as she was. Fate obliged us to hole up for the winter, and there was only one town in our vicinity where I could safely go to ground—where I hadn't already made a nuisance of myself.

Long before we reached Suggs, Wyoming, I was fearful of the place, for men I met along the road cautioned me that Suggs was about boiling with danger. "Go to Deadwood," travelers advised time and again, "for the Negro-haters are wild just now in Suggs, and they are a damn sight more dangerous than the Indians."

(There was a certain faction in Suggs, I guess, who objected to the camps of Buffalo Soldiers who had worked in the hills nearby for damn near twenty years. I never understood the misliking some whites have for black folks. Up to that point in my life, the only men who ever showed me any genuine kindness—except for Wild Bill—was Reverend Wilkes and Timothy Crutch. But many a time had I seen the hate burning in white men's eyes when they talked about the freed Negroes—who they expected would set about the business of raping every white woman from Carolina to California, any day now, any day. The freed slaves certainly had not set a precedent for such behavior. Thirty years after the Emancipation, it didn't seem likely to me that they was about to begin their rumored campaign of vengeance against every white person they could lay hands on. But hatred never thinks; it only feels. Seems to me, the most dangerous man is one who won't use the head on his shoulders, regardless of the color of his skin.)

I didn't like to bring my daughter to any place that was boiling over with hate. Men lose all control when they're ruled by hate— all control, and any claim on good sense they might once have had. Whenever men lose control, it's always women and children who suffer worst. But I couldn't go to Deadwood—not ever again. I'd be recognized there for certain, before I even swung down from my saddle. And winter was coming on fast and hard; I could smell snow on the air, blowing up from the south, smoky and biting—and the winds that came down from the Rockies was cold enough to raise tears.

Suggs was my only choice, so to Suggs we went, with me singing to hide my worries and my arms wrapped tight around Jessie to keep the cold at bay.

SUGGS, Wyoming was one of those small, scrappy towns, half pale wood (new-cut) and half gray boards, old and weathered by sun and prairie wind. Suggs wasn't much more than a few houses, all built after the same simple style, ringed around the usual saloons and cat-houses you could find in any village that grew up along the rails. The whole lot of Suggs was perched on a bank of the Powder River. The town boasted a new ferry, of which its citizens was inordinately proud, for they was all certain the stage line that ran between Buffalo and Sundance would make ample use of their crossing—and thereby turn the gray huddle of Suggs into a bustling metropolis, the likes of which the world hadn't seen since New York City come along. I very soon learned not to cast aspersions on the ferry. There was no surer way to turn a citizen of Suggs against you than to make light of their big-city hopes.

I very soon learned, as well, that there was little work to be had in town. I inquired after laundries, but it seemed a certain Miz Sugarmarsh had the laundry game in lock-up. No one worked for her unless they was born into her family; she didn't even deem her daughters-in-law fit to bruise their knuckles on her washboards. There wasn't a hotel in town, for Suggs hadn't yet reached its lofty expansionary goals, and the few boarding houses was never full enough to warrant hiring help.

I thought to inquire whether any of the local bawdy houses needed a madam. I reasoned Suggs might be the kind of town where my lack of experience on the madaming side of the business could be overlooked. But when it came to the bawdy life, the only claim I could make was as Calamity Jane. As for working on my back again—well, even if I'd been willing to expose my daughter to the ridicule, I was long past the point of trading on any meager looks I had once possessed, infamous identity or no. Nor could I hire on with the stage coaches, nor even whack bulls again without admitting my real identity. Suggs had me in a trap, all right. I didn't know how I'd ever find my way out.

I did still have a small reserve of money—not much, but enough to board for a week or two while I plotted my next move. I took Jessie down from the saddle and took my coins from the saddle bag and led her into a saloon. There I ordered up a whiskey for me and a sarsaparilla for her with a dash of real vanilla and a pickled cherry, and the bartender was so charmed by my darling sunshiney child that he put two extra cherries in the cup and winked at Jessie as he handed our drinks over. How vanilla ever found itself in Suggs, Wyoming is a mystery I cannot puzzle out, even to this day.

I took Jessie outside, just in case a fight should erupt at the faro tables. We set down on the wooden boardwalk to savor our drinks in the brisk autumn chill. I liked to keep her out of saloons as much as I could, for well did I remember their wicked draw from my whoop-up days. No matter how predictably we fell on hard times, I didn't mean for my daughter to ever whoop it up if whooping could be avoided. I was damn determined that Jessie would live up to the legend I had crafted for her: beloved daughter of an elegant, upstanding woman and a heroic man. I figured it'd be pretty justice if one of us, at least, managed to do our legend proud.

I set and sipped my whiskey nice and slow, reasoning that if I paced myself, maybe I'd feel satisfied and wouldn't go back for another. I had to measure out my money with care till I found a job to see us through the winter. Jessie was a regular catbird, gloating over every sip of her drink and giggling when the bubbles tickled her nose. I did my best to laugh along with her, but inside I was on the verge of crying. We could go back to Deadwood, I thought—we could just about make it to Deadwood before the snows got real bad. Then it would be all over, of course: the pretty canvasses I'd painted for Jessie would tear themselves asunder; the haggard portrait of Calamity Jane would be exposed underneath, there for my girl to see, undeniable as sin. But at least I might find some work in Deadwood. At least we wouldn't starve.

As we set on the boardwalk outside that saloon, a few folks did pass us by, progressing on foot or horseback to and from the ferry. I had to admit by then that Suggs' ferry was doing a reasonable trade. I lamented my lack of ferrying skills, for with my big strong frame I might have convinced the owner to hire me on as a hauler. But without experience to bolster me, he would likely laugh a woman right out of town. Except to muse dismally on the ferry, I didn't take any note of the passers-by who came up from the river—not till one of them stopped right in front of us.

At first, I didn't see any part of that man but his boots: old, worn-out, scuffed things with tired, slouching leather tops. The kind of boots that had seen many a long day of good, honest work. I set with my eyes fixed to his worn-down boots while he said in a bright voice—to Jessie, of course— "My, honey, you sure are having a good time, ain't you? And pretty as a picture, you little bee."

He sounded so sweet, so genuine and happy, I couldn't help but look up at his face. He as a spot younger than me—that is to say, younger than my real age—with a soft, round face and a long mustache, which he waxed into two jaunty curls like a Back-East man. But his big black hat was all West, and his hair was yellow as straw, which only made him seem all the younger. He bent over at the waist to grin at Jessie, just as if he was her favorite uncle. I liked the kindness in his eyes and felt drawn to him most powerfully—for neither Jessie nor I had seen such pleasantry in another human spirit for an awful long time.

I looked up at him, and that was it. My ruse was all over. He glanced at me once in polite acknowledgment, then turned back to coo at Jessie some more. But he stopped and looked at me again, sharper this time, and the smile slid from his face, replaced by the slow awe of recognition.

He said, "Why you're—"

"Don't, Mister. Don't say it." I gave a little jerk of my head, the smallest nod toward my daughter. "She don't know nothing about it, and I aim to keep it that way."

He straightened with a thoughtful air. "Yes mam. Reckon I can see the sense in that."

I said, "I'm trying to leave that all behind—the way I was. For her sake, you see. But it's harder than I thought it would be."

He gazed down at me, speculative, but not with the sharpness that means a man is fixing to do you wrong. He just stood and looked at me, as if he felt called to do something but couldn't make up his mind what that something was.

I said, "I only need work; that's all I'm after here in Suggs. Good, honest work. Do you know where a lady might take a proper job to see her through the winter?"

"No mam, I do not," he said, and twisted the curl of his mustache around his finger for a minute—thinking, weighing the consequences. Then, when I was about to shout and throw what was left of my whiskey in abject despair, he said, "But you won't be out for the winter. You'll have a place to stay with me—you and the girl both."

———

THAT WAS how I came to take up with Clinton Burke, and by God, if I ever learn what good deed I did to deserve that kindness and mercy, then everything I have suffered in my shadowed life will be accounted fair. Clinton was the gentlest soul the Lord ever made. He didn't have much, save for a two-room cabin on the bank of the Powder, with a potbelly stove and a fiddle hung up beside the door (and he played that fiddle every night.) But everything Clinton had, he shared with me. He didn't do it because he expected a damn thing in return. It was in his nature to share, to offer kindness to every broken thing he found—to mend whatever could be mended.

Clinton lived to make little Jessie smile, and oh the nights when we would sit around that stove, stoked up to a red-hot glow, choking down the inadequate soups I cooked from ham hocks or cow's tail, while Clinton played the fiddle and Jessie danced, twirling in her red dress till she fell down breathless with laughter.

That's why I did what I did—because Clinton wanted nothing in return for such tender mercy. Never before had I felt myself so heavily indebted, and yet I knew Clinton never expected me to pay him a cent for the Christian grace he offered. Because he was good-hearted enough to demand nothing, I gave that man everything I had.

"Clinton," I said one night when the snow was piled thick outside. We had just tucked Jessie into her little bed beside the stove; she was fast asleep already. "I have an idea, and I don't know how good it is, but you'll tell me if it's even worth thinking."

"All right," he said softly, so as not to wake the child. "Tell me, then."

"I gone to a lot of trouble to hide Calamity Jane from the world, ever since Jess was born. But what if we brought her back?"

He didn't know what to make of my nattering, so he hung up his fiddle on its peg beside the door and waited for me to clarify my thoughts.

Cautious and trembling, I said, "I think there's some money to be made in Calamity's name. There must be—else, why would so many girls claim to be me? They must feel they can turn a profit if they can convince somebody—anybody—that they're Calamity Jane. If there's any money to be made from Calamity, I'll let you in on it. I'll give you half of whatever we earn, whatever my old notoriety will pay. If you'll agree to just one condition."

Still Clinton waited, patient as ever.

I swallowed down my fear. "Tell everyone you're Jessie's father." The words came out in a rush, for the dam of shame that had held them in for so long finally burst. My grief and hope and love couldn't be stopped; they scoured me, and fair swept Clinton away on the current. "Let's you and me pretend we was always married, and that Jess is your girl, and nothing was ever bad or sour. I don't ask it for my sake, for I know I'm not the kind of woman any man would be eager to take up with. But Jessie... she deserves better than I can give her on my own."

Clinton smiled then, warm and serene. He crossed the tiny room and bent over my chair, and kissed me on the cheek—a brotherly kiss that made me feel as if I had always been his, as if I'd never been in any danger, and all the world was warm as springtime.

"Why, Miss Jane," he said then, using the forbidden name for the first time since our acquaintance, "I think it's the very worthiest thought you ever had."

WHEN THE THAW CAME, and the Powder River swelled to the edge
of its banks, we picked up and moved to Billings, Montana—the
town I had once known as Coulson—right in the heart of the
fabled fields of gold. We found no golden fields, of course (my pa
would have been sore disappointed) but we found plenty of
prospectors eager to scratch out a fortune.

Clinton opened up a modest hotel on Billings' main street. He
had a big sign painted in fanciful, scrolling words outlined in
golden leaf. He hung that sign above the hotel's front steps:

HOME OF THE ONE TRUE,
THE LEGENDARY
CALAMITY JANE

From the very day Clinton opened his doors, business was
cracking and brisk. I didn't even have to play the role of maid; so
many people came to Billings in search of their fortunes that we
hired proper workers right from the get-go, including a damn fine
cook who about made Clinton and me fat as swine. My only duty
was a light one: to dress in buckskin and a big black sombrero,
just like the one I'd worn as a much younger girl, and make our
visitors say Ooh and Aah with my feats of riding and shooting.

Clinton cleared a broad yard out back of the hotel, ringed by a
pretty birch forest, and there I impressed a nightly audience with
a half hour of shooting and trick riding. My audiences paid a
quarter a head to see the One True Calamity Jane—and just as I
galloped the final circuit, pinging the last cans from their posts
with my two dazzling pistols, Clinton's cook would throw open
the kitchen doors, so the smell of roasting chickens or apple pies
wafted out into the yard. My audience about went mad with
hunger. A quarter a head to watch me shoot, and a dollar for the
finest supper in Billings. Clinton and me, we prospered more than
we'd ever imagined possible.

We passed two beautiful years that way, living in ease and

happiness, content with one another's company. Clinton was good as his word: he proudly claimed he was Jessie's father, and Jessie herself came to think of him that way—though I'm certain she still retained, in some sweet corner of her precious thoughts, the tales I had long-ago spun about Wild Bill. Jessie loved Clinton as much as he loved her. She thrived upon his knee. And every day, I over-brimmed with gratitude that my darling child should grow up safe and happy.

Clinton bore a great affection for me, too, which I returned in kind. He was the best-tempered man I ever did know, patient and fair, so sensible he could have been a doctor or a preacher. Not a day passed but I thanked God for this welcome turn—the crossing of Clinton's path and mine. Attached to such a quality man, no one dared question my morals, even if I was the True and Legendary Calamity Jane.

Would that we could have gone on that way forever, living in simple harmony, happy with plain companionship. But that state of affairs wasn't destined to last over-long. For two years, Clinton seemed glad to exist in an amiable partnership. But around the time Jessie turned four, I caught Clinton making calf eyes at me now and then, when he thought I wasn't looking. I would tuck Jessie into bed—she had her own room now, in the pretty little suite the three of us shared at the back of the hotel—and I would straighten up to find Clinton leaning against the door frame, watching the whole proceeding with a misty fondness. He would catch my eye and smile, but his smile would linger just a moment too long. Or at the supper table, he would pause with his fork halfway to his mouth and stare at me, wide-eyed as if something had struck him an unexpected blow—as if some fearful realization had come upon him all at once, and startled the very breath from his body.

I knew what that change in Clinton signified, though I couldn't quite believe it was true. He was falling in love. It seemed damn impossible—too ridiculous. No man had ever fallen for me;

not even when I was young enough that my youth held some
small measure of desirability, if not my specific features. I couldn't
claim a shred of youth now. Yet Clinton Burke had found something in me—something worthy of his love. I didn't understand;
the situation tangled me up inside, and made me tense and short-
tempered in his presence.

My life would have been a damn sight easier if I could have
loved Clinton back. God knows, he deserved all the love any
woman ever heaped upon a man. But the more I noticed his
yearning stares—the longer his glances lingered on my unremarkable face—the more I fretted and ached. I would have gladly given
my heart to Clinton, but it wasn't mine to give. My heart had been
buried in Deadwood. It lay beneath the cracked, dry earth and a
handful of faded blue flowers, in eternal darkness, among Bill
Hickock's bones.

LIGHTING A CIGAR AT FULL MOTION

CLINTON KNEW, OF COURSE, THAT I DIDN'T RETURN HIS AFFECTIONS. How could he help but know? We never spoke of it—the unfinished task that hung between us, that hopeless longing he bore for me. I was so astonished by the fact of his love that I couldn't puzzle out the right way to raise the subject. Nor did any time seem right to turn our frank attention to the business of our hearts. I believe Clinton would have breached the subject himself, sooner or later—some evening when Jessie was dreaming in her fine, soft bed, when Clinton sat pensively chewing the stem of his pipe and I worked my way (word by faltering word) through yet another novel about Calamity Jane. He would have raised the issue if I gave him half a chance. Many a time I felt Clinton go tense and quiet beside me, burdened by his need to speak. But I already knew what he wanted to say, and I think Clinton knew what my answer would be. *I don't love you and I can't, Clinton Burke, because I have always loved another.* He couldn't bear to hear those words any more than I could bear to say them, so silence remained in its place, a wall between us, a palisade defending the comfortable routines of our shared life.

When summer came on, Clinton had grown so restless under that burden that he couldn't stomach the idea of staying put. The hotel was well established, he said—its care and operations now resided in the capable hands of our hired staff, who after all showed more proficiency than Clinton ever had in the duties and specifics of hotelling. Clinton took the owner's cut, but little work remained to keep him occupied. The only thing that kept him tethered him to Billings was me.

That's why it came as no surprise when Clinton announced his intention to pass the summer out at Ekalaka, a settlement of cattle ranchers and sheep herders scarce bigger than a postage stamp. Clinton had been a cattle driver in his younger years. He missed the life, he said, and wanted a taste again. He meant to revel in the freedom of wide-open places while he was still young enough for revelry. Seeing as how I was intimately acquainted with wide-open places, I could find no cause to criticize his plan, even though I suspected his sudden yen for the range had more to do with the fact that I wouldn't be there. I didn't like to embarrass him by pointing out that fact, so I only said it was a bully idea, and wished him a glorious summer.

You know, I believe that summer would have been a glory for me, too—for my life had elevated itself to a pinnacle I never dreamed possible. That's not to say I was rich, by any stretch of human imagining. But I was comfortable and secure, and after a lifetime of hardship, what small comfort and security I now possessed seemed better than mountains of gold.

Bitterly do I wish that state of affairs would have carried on indefinitely. But the unrest that fell over the West after Custer's demise had never entirely abated. Indian raids wasn't near as frequent as they once had been, yet the papers still clamored with grim news of attacks, with graphic descriptions of entire families cut down somewheres out on the prairie, or tales of white children abducted by Indians, never seen by their weeping mothers again. Such wild rumors kept white men scared enough that they was always quick to violence, and getting quicker by the day. Resentment of the Buffalo Soldiers down in Wyoming was spreading, too, like a summer fever—so was mistrust of the Chinese who worked along the rails. Fear and hate seemed to rise up on all sides, growing thick as the prairie grass. I suppose it was inevitable, that the twin demons of fear and hate would soon find their way to Billings. After all, gold was supposed to be hiding somewheres in the vicinity, and gold is the one force on God's green Earth that can motivate a man stronger than fear or hate.

Now, I must admit that Billings had been roughening around its edges since Clinton and I first arrived. But the summer Clinton took off for Ekalaka was especially bad. Tempers ran short as a matter of course. Fights often made the papers, for there was precious little else to report on, save fist fights and gun fights, and the jail sentences of the hot-headed men who perpetrated them.

Oh yes, we had our share of gun fights in Billings. But it wasn't till the Mulkey gang came to town that I really began to fear. The Mulkeys was a family of rowdies—brothers and cousins, from what I understand—infamous throughout Montana for their cattle rustling and card-cheating. Strength In Numbers seemed to be their clan motto; the Mulkeys ran in such a sizable herd that no sheriff's posse could suppress a shudder at thought of squaring up to the gang. Bad as their cheating and rustling was, what really made the Mulkeys frightening was their quickness to do violence. Everywhere that pack of feral dogs roamed, breathless accounts followed, filling the papers and telegraph wires with news of their dreadful exploits from Cheyenne to Pocatello.

I had taken note of the Mulkey gang in Billings' newspaper, reading each account of their numerous outrages with growing disbelief. When the Billings paper fell silent on the topic of the Mulkeys, I sensed trouble coming. For Billings didn't yet have a big enough posse, nor a sheriff powerful enough, to handle the menace of that gang. I perceived that the editor of the newspaper thought it more prudent to drop the subject of Mulkey outrages altogether, rather than risk the family's ire. And that could only mean the Mulkeys was headed straight for Billings. Me and Jessie set right in the path of the storm. There was nothing a fretful mother could do, except hunker down and pray the danger would soon pass.

The atmosphere of Billings darkened considerably as soon as the Mulkey gang appeared. A few of them took up residence at the hotel, for it was the best accommodation in Billings. The hotel staff went about its duties quick and quiet, heads down, praying every moment that no Mulkey would take exception to an offhanded comment or an unthinking gesture. Day and night, the air seemed to crackle with a dreadful energy, the tension of fearful waiting. A lump rose to my throat and stayed there; my back ached from constant worry, for the town had become a powder keg, and above all else, I feared the first lethal spark would fly within my own hotel, blowing my good life apart in the blink of an eye, landing innocent bystanders—and maybe my daughter, too—in an early grave.

Well, the powder keg certainly did ignite just a few weeks after Clinton left for the ranch. I'll never know what set off that gun fight. I suppose the cause is of no real consequence now. All I know for certain is that I was putting Jessie to bed one evening, while a long summer sunset lingered peaceful and red among the pines. Just as I bent to kiss Jessie's brow, the crack of gunfire split the night.

The odd shot from rile or pistol was a common enough occurrence, rarely worth marking. But wound up as I was over the gang's unwelcome presence, I crouched beside my daughter's bed and waited, wide-eyed, for more. More fire was certainly coming; I knew it, way down deep in my bones. Sure enough, that first report was answered by an over-eager blast from somewheres close by—so close, I near-about jumped out of my skin and barely stifled a shriek of surprise. I tore Jessie from her bed and laid her flat on the floor, then covered her with my half-crouched body. Another shot rang out, then another, and all at once Billings was swallowed in a constant roar of gunfire.

I couldn't do a damn thing, except press my daughter to the floor, praying all the while no stray bullet would splinter the wall and find its way to Jessie's heart. Neither of us made a sound—not that we could have heard one another over a thunder of endless violence. Now and again, when chance brought half a second's respite from the fire, I could hear men screaming in rage or in desperate agony. The panicked groans of horses came to me, as well. Sure enough, all-out war had broken out between the Mulkey gang and the town's insufficient posse.

Me and Jessie huddled on the floor of her bedroom for damn near half an hour. By the time the last gunshot finally sounded, evening light had faded, replaced by the deep-blue chill of night. When I heard no more shots for a proper long while—only the hollering of men and the pounding of hooves on the road outside —I sat up slowly, staring down at Jessie. She never cried out, but tears streamed from her eyes. She trembled where she lay, frightened as a hunted fawn, and clung to my hand with all her small might.

I watched my daughter's pale face among dusky shadows, and I considered my options. The sheriff's posse wasn't likely to have won that battle—I knew it was true. The Mulkeys far outnumbered the law; they was wily and hardscrabble, to boot. But even if (through some unaccountable miracle) the law had come out on top, I made up my mind right then and there to spirit Jessie out of Billings till all danger was past.

"You get some sleep," I told her, lifting her back to her rumpled bed. "In the morning, we will take to the trail again, just like we did in olden days. We'll go to find your daddy at that ranch out in

Ekalaka. We'll pass a lovely summer out there, among the horses and cattle, and come back to run our hotel again in the fall."

To myself, *I promised, We won't be back again till the Mulkey gang has left Billings for good. And if they never leave, then so be it. I won't keep my daughter in a town where she's as like to get shot as trip over* her own feet.

WE SET out for Ekalaka at daybreak, just as I promised. The streets of Billings lay silent—not with the righteous peace of rest, but with the hunkered-down, cringing silence of a whipped creature waiting for its cruel master to return. Shutters had been drawn across't every window. Wherever morning duties forced a body out of doors—tending to stock or assessing damage done in last night's storm of gunfire—work proceeded at a tentative pace, with the small rustlings and scrapings of mice creeping between walls. Now and then, a fella turned his wary eye at the sound of my horse's hooves, peering from the marginal safety of a livery corral or peeking around the corner of a building. When my watchers saw that I was just one woman—and riding with a small child, at that—they shook their heads with scorn at my foolhardiness. No one but a plain idiot would ride out where the Mulkey gang might see; not after last night.

Once we put Billings at our backs, the fog of danger lifted. All the bliss I had known some years before, when I had ridden in blessed solitude with my sweet Jessie, returned with fulsome strength. The Montana terrain was a welcome departure from the prairies and long, dry valleys I had known in Wyoming. Great, flat-topped buttes surrounded the town, pale sandstone cliffs all slanting at the same angle up toward an astonishing sky, broad and blue, still colored at its eastern border by the rosy flush of sunrise. Canyons split the earth between those layers of mesa, and the canyons was damp and fragrant with gathered dew, or with trickles of water that still came down from higher ground, even in the heat of summer. Wherever water collected, forests of birch and slender evergreens crowded in. The breezes smelled of pine sap and flowing water; the morning was lively with the music of foraging birds.

Jessie would see her fifth birthday that autumn. She was a big girl, far more talkative than she had been on our last trail ride. She asked me to sing the old songs, of course, but she soon took over, changing the words in ways that made me chuckle and hug her closer to my heart. She invented stories, too, spinning her own legends about Bill Hickock and Charlotte Burch, the fabled beauty of far-off Deadwood. In Jessie's stories, Bill never died. He came home and married Charlotte, and they lived in happiness all their days, with never a sorrow to trouble them. It gave me a pang, to hear my daughter weave such pretty fancies. I wished her stories was true.

We journeyed more than a week, leaving the forested canyons behind as the land returned to the flat, bland monotony of the prairie. By and by, we found ourselves among the Medicine Rocks, strange outcrops of pale stone standing upright in a sea of sage. The Medicine Rocks towered above us; smooth-sided holes pocked every face of those strange monuments, and evening shadows settled into the holes, giving the impression of countless eyes that turned to watch us as we passed. The effect was nothing short of eerie. I didn't like being among the Medicine Rocks, for the sight of them made my skin creep. But I knew they was a sign-post; Ekalaka lay just ahead. So we made our night's camp at the foot of one of those odd, upright stones, and in the morning I woke Jessie early so we could press on.

One final stretch of trail lay ahead before we reached Clinton's ranch. The trail led through a gully cut by a bubbling crick. The water smelled spicy and welcoming, and the air in the gully was cool, so I slowed my horse to a lazy walk and took my time traversing its length. Jessie was deep in one of her stories about

Wild Bill; I listened only halfway, for I couldn't shake the lingering anxiety that had tightened my chest and clouded my thoughts since we'd made camp among those rocks the night before. The day was bright, the sky cheerful with little sheep-flocks of bustling white clouds. Yet still I felt as if I rode under a heavy shadow, and not even the summer sun could drive away my chill.

Just before we reached the end of that gully, we came across't a forlorn huddle of shacks clinging to the banks of the crick. I reined in quick; my immediate fear was that I had stumbled onto a Sioux encampment. But of course, the Sioux lived in teepees— not these haphazard lean-tos made from pine branches and scraps of tin. Naught but white men could have built those shacks. Yet the sun was well up, and the camp was silent—unnervingly still. The only sign of life was a peaky stream of smoke rising from a rusted chimney pipe. I set rigid in my saddle, clutching my daughter hard against my body, and stared at that smoke as it drifted up into the whispering pines.

After a spell, Jessie said quietly, "What is it, Grandmam?"

"A camp," I answered. "A miners' camp, I guess."

"Ain't nobody there?"

"I don't know, Cushie Butterfield. Guess we ought to find out before we go any farther."

I sucked in a deep breath, more to steady my nerves than to power my voice. Then I shouted, "Hullo!"

No one answered. I couldn't even hear a stirring from inside those shacks, nor from the strip of woodland around us. The birds went on scolding in the pines, and the crick tumbled and pattered over the rocks, but the camp was quiet as a grave.

I should have ridden on with my daughter and thought nothing more of that blasted encampment. But the persistent still-ness struck me as too odd to ignore—maybe dangerous, as well. I had to learn the cause of the silence, for if the Sioux had recently struck, they might still linger in the vicinity. They might even carry their violence on to Clinton's ranch, unless I warned the ranchers first.

"You stay here," I said to Jessie. I put the reins in her small hands. "If any trouble should befall me, you kick that horse and go straight ahead—same direction we been riding. You follow this crick right up to your pa's camp and don't stop for nothing. Understand?"

Jessie nodded, but she was mute now with fear. I could sense her reluctance, her sudden consciousness of her own small and fragile self. All I could do was pat her little arm and tell her everything would be all right. Then I slid from the saddle and approached the shack with a rusted chimney pipe. My hand never left my pistol the whole while.

"Hullo," I said again as I edged closer to the lean-to. "Anybody home?"

No answer came. A bit of canvas hung across the lean-to's opening, a door of sorts. Cautiously, I pushed the canvas aside, bracing my guts for what I would find within.

What I found inside that shack was ten times wors't than the remains of an Indian massacre.

Two cots dominated the shack's interior; a small potbelly stove crouched between, running its chimney up through the pine-bough roof. Two men lay abed among a scattering of filthy blankets; their limbs hung limp and feeble from the edges of their cots. The stench of sickness walloped me so hard I reeled on my feet, covering my mouth with one hand, fighting not to gag and puke up my breakfast right there in the doorway of the lean-to.

But the smell wasn't the worst of it—no. Worst of all was those men's faces. And their hands. Every bit of skin that showed had blistered and raised into hideous, pale boils. They looked more like lizards than men—or like demons sent up from Hell. The boils crowded around their eyes and mouths; I could scarce make out their features through *those painful, weeping distortions.*

So this is where my dark *mood has come from, I told myself. This* is what haunted me all morning long.

I had never encountered the smallpox in my life, yet st*ill I knew t*hat devil at firs*t sight.*

They're dead, I told myself. They must be. Surely no man can survive such affliction.

But even as I comforted myself with those words, one of the men groaned in helpless suffering and the other shifted a little—just the barest motion of his hand, yet I saw the movement. I couldn't deny the truth. Those poor men still lived, lingering in agony at death's welcome door.

I stepped back from the lean-to, let the canvas curtain fall. With my hands braced on my hips I breathed, slowly and deeply, desperate for some useful thought, warring with my instinct to bolt in fear and loathing—to get my child away from that place, quick as I could go. My eyes rolled frantically, searching the other three shacks for signs of life. How many prospectors? More than the two I had seen, of a certainty. I had to know the extent of the illness—had to know what to tell the ranchers at Ekalaka. They needed to know the smallpox was coming; that disease was every bit as deadly as the Sioux, and every bit as feared, too.

Resolute, I marched to the next shack, then the next, and peered inside every one. Seven men lay in misery, some on cots, some felled upon hard bed rolls. And all of them suffered terribly —that was plain enough to see. Even when I backed away from the last shack, I could still hear those poor boys' rattling breath, still smell the tainted air, though a fresh wind was blowing down the gully, sharp with the scent of juniper and sage.

I scrambled back to my horse and swung up into the saddle. What else was I to do? I could only pray I hadn't carried the infection with me—straight to my daughter. But I couldn't leave Jessie alone. Despite my command to ride on to the ranch, I knew the odds was small that a girl of her tender age could find the place on

her own. There was nothing for it but to mount up and ride on—
and beg God to spare my girl from that dreadful affliction.

"What did you find, Grandmam?" Jessie asked.

"Nothing, darling girl—nothing a-tall. The shacks was empty.
Guess all the prospectors went out looking for gold."

We pressed on towards Clinton's ranch, and after a spell Jessie
took up with her stories again. I had half-listened before, but now
I couldn't seem to hear my daughter's voice. That hellish rattle,
the rasp in dying men's throats, filled my ears; a vision of their
distorted faces hung before my eyes, imposed like a veil over
everything I saw. The suffering I had witnessed ate at my heart.
Before we reached the ranch camp, I had already made up my
mind what to do.

By afternoon, Jessie and me could see a distant cluster of tall,
white-canvas tents ringed around a stand of pines. Temporary
corrals dotted the prairie, and great herds of cattle moved across't
the grass, rivers of flesh warm and flowing beneath the summer
sun. I could make out riders working their stock on quick cow-
ponies, and the sight of so much industry cheered me considerable, for it meant the smallpox had not yet come.

As we drew nearer to the camp, a lone rider broke away from
the corrals and loped toward us. Long before he reached us, I
recognized Clinton's appy-loosy horse, white with red dots like
the pelt of a leopard.

Clinton's grin was about a mile wide when he circled us, then
fell in beside. "I'll be damned. I never expected to see you here." I
couldn't quite tell whether he was glad or regretful; that grin
might have been purely for Jessie's sake, not mine.

"Billings got real bad, and fast," I said. "The Mulkey gang came
in—shot the place up. I had to get Jessie away. It ain't safe to stay
in Billings just now. Didn't know where else I should take her."

Clinton said nothing. His lips pressed into a thin line beneath
his curled mustache—a grim sort of acceptance.

I said, "Guess we ought to stay here till the summer's out. I can be of some use with the stock, but I got to keep Jessie safe."

"I suppose it's best if you do stay. There's a good camp set up for all the ranching folk and their families. Nice, airy canvas tents —a mess tent for eating, too, and the cook's real good." He reached across't the space between us, patted Jessie's knee. "There's even some other children for you to play with, little bee. You can pass the summer here happy enough." To me, Clinton said, "With any luck, Billings will have settled by the fall. You can go back then."

You can go back. Not we.

"That sounds fine, Clinton, but you got to take Jessie to the camp yourself. Get her all settled in." Jessie looked up at me, confused and maybe a little frightened. To her, I said, "There's nothing to fret over, Jess. I got some business to tend; that's all."

"Business?" Clinton reined to a stop and I did the same. He squinted at me below his broad-brimmed hat. "What's this talk?"

I picked up Jessie and passed her across to Clinton, who settled her on his pommel. Then I untied her roll from the back of my saddle and handed that to Clinton, too. Only then did I speak. "I passed a prospectors' camp back some ways, down in that gully past Medicine Rocks. The men was all down with the smallpox."

Clinton flinched. His arm tightened around Jessie's middle, locking her in a protective grip. "You didn't touch anyone, did you?"

"No. Didn't get close enough to touch. But I saw them, Clinton. God help me, I'll never forget the sight."

Clinton stared out over the cattle herds for a spell, frowning, considering the news. Finally he said, "That's bad, Martha, but nothing to be done about it."

"The Hell there ain't. I'm going back to tend those men."

"God sakes, Martha. Don't talk crazy."

"I ain't talking crazy, Clinton Burke. I thought about nothing except those miners since this morning. I can't leave them to suffer."

He shook his head in denial, but he was helpless to stop me, and he knew it. "You can't do it! You'll take the sickness yourself, Martha. You'll die."

Clinton sounded so pained by the prospect of my death, I was almost convinced to heed his warning. But I couldn't release myself from the memory of those men, trapped in a web of suffering without anyone to fetch a sip of water or hold their blistered hands and ease them toward their end. "It ain't right, to leave sick men with no help. If I die, then at least I'll have done some good in this world. And there's no one else to give them aid, Clinton. No one else to bury them when they die."

"Let some of the men from the ranch go down and bury the dead."

"No. They all got families here, from what you said. They shouldn't risk taking the pox themselves."

"You got family here, too." Clinton spoke those words so quietly, so reluctantly, they caught at my heart and filled me with caution. But then he sighed, surrendering to my mule-stubborn will. He reached towards me; I took his hand and held it, squeezing his fingers tight. "Why do I feel I'm saying good-bye to you forever?"

I thought it more than likely this would be our final parting. I said, "You take good care of Jessie, if I never come back."

"You know I will. I'll be praying for you, Martha."

I blew a kiss to my daughter, then another. I would have given much to wrap my arms around her. But I had already risked Jessie too far. I knew I mustn't touch her again till I could be sure the smallpox had passed me by—if it passed me by a-tall. I turned my horse around and rode back toward the gully, blinded by tears. As much as I treasured my daughter, I couldn't leave suffering men to face their torment alone. My tender heart wouldn't allow it.

NIGHTFALL FOUND me back on the banks of that crick, riding slow among the darkly shadowed lean-tos. The mining camp was as silent as it had been before, and the steep walls of the gully seemed to tip toward me, hemming me in, threatening to close overhead like the mouth of a bag pulled shut by its drawstrings. My heart hammered sharp and heavy inside my chest; my stomach churned with fear. But I dismounted and took my time pulling the saddle from my horse's back. I meant to stay a good long while—maybe for what remained of my life. There was nothing for it but to settle in.

Starlight glinted off something smooth and round near one of the lean-tos. I crept closer, squinting through the darkness. Someone had left a kerosene lantern setting on a birch stump; when I picked it up, the oil sloshed inside the chamber and the wick looked like it would serve. I lit the thing straight away; a ring of light wrapped itself around me, driving back a small portion of my fear. That lantern gave me the courage to set about my work.

The nearest I'd ever come to smallpox was at Cuny and Coffey's, that year after I first made Wild Bill's acquaintance. I had taken a fellow with a pox-scarred face to my cabin and entertained him there, and after our transaction he told me harrowing tales of his illness, and stories of the nurses who had cared for him back in Nebraska. I hadn't liked his stories—I never took kindly to tales of suffering, for I have always had a tender heart, and can't help but feel the pangs and sorrows of those around me as if I was afflicted myself. But I did recall that boy's description of the nurses with their faces tied up in clean white cloths, with their hands always pink and raw from endless washing. It was any man's guess whether those Nebraska nurses took the smallpox in spite of their precautions. The boy at Cuny and Coffey's never mentioned their fate, and I guess he wasn't like to know. But his word was the best guide I had on that dark night. Before I laid a hand on the suffering miners, I set about armoring myself as best I could.

I rummaged in my saddle bag till I found the cleanest shirt I possessed. It wasn't especially spotless, to be sure, but it was the best I could do at short notice, a day's ride from anything resembling civilization. I tore the shirt into wide strips and tied a double layer around my face, covering my nose and mouth. Then I took the lantern and looked in on the ailing miners, leaning my cautious, cloth-bound head into the dark recesses of their inadequate shacks.

The situation was much as it had been at the start of the day: men flat out on their backs, skin bubbled and weeping with putrefaction. Six still clung to life, though their grip was rapidly failing. One of the men had succumbed to his disease. I found him in the door of his lean-to, one hand stretched out before him as if he had reached for the wide-open world in his last agonized moment. He must have crawled from his bed roll when he knew death had arrived. As if you can run from death. As if you can escape its slow-blinking eye.

I stood over the dead man for a while, lantern light flaring and receding over his lifeless, pox-ravaged form. My breath was close and rapid in the confines of my mask. I hadn't stood in the presence of death since Wild Bill. The loss of my true love shook me, as it always did when I allowed myself to remember. The slump of Bill's body over the faro table, the spray of red across't old wood. For a minute I knew myself a coward; I told myself to get back on my horse and ride away, run and never come back to this dreadful place. Then I shrugged and hung my lantern from the edge of the lean-to, on a splintered piece of pine wood. I grabbed the dead man by his sleeve and dragged him well away from the camp, out among the rocks and willows. Then I set to work digging his grave.

Being a prospectors' camp, at least there was no shortage of picks and spades. I fetched my lantern and took up a spade from where it leaned against a shack. Then I made the deepest pit I could manage in the hard, rocky soil near the gully wall—which to be sure was not especially deep. When my spade hit stubborn rock no matter how I plunged and pried, I rolled the dead man into his grave and stood over him, looking down. Shadows deep in the pit already covered the body, so I could make out little save for the toes of his boots, poking up to where the lantern light could touch them.

"Afraid this is the end of the line, fella," I said. Then, more solemnly, "God rest your soul, whoever you may be."

When the dead prospector was properly buried (resting place marked with a flat stone from the crick) I found canteens and empty whiskey bottles, and filled every one with cool water. Then I made my rounds of the lean-tos, trickling water into each man's mouth by turns, doing my best not to see the horrific yellow nodules that distorted their faces. At least my double thickness of a mask cut down some of the stench. I wanted to tear down the flimsy walls of the shacks and let fresh air blow through, but I feared the night's chill would only heap misery on misery.

I believe I made the rounds of those shacks for two hours or more, doling out water in sparing sips till at last I noted results from my ministrations. When my light filled a shack, its wretched inhabitants turned their blistered heads toward me. The nightmare slits of their mouths moved in entreaty, yearning for a drink. I watered them all one last time. Then, weak with exhaustion and shivering from the cold, I stumbled out to the stream.

Sometime that night, I located a bottle of whiskey among the prospectors' goods. I thought to take a pull at it, merely for comfort's sake—but I had seen spirits used now and then to clean doctors' knives and bone saws. I reasoned the whiskey might do just as well on my hands, so I tipped some into my palm and scrubbed myself up to the elbows, holding my arms out to dry in the cold night air. I removed the rags from my face, dunked them in the crick, and draped them over a willow branch to dry. Then I hauled my bed roll as far from the camp as I dar*ed go and toppled, bone-weary, into bed.*

*My last thought before sleep took me was, You'll wake up wit*h blisters for sure. Jee-zus, you are a dumb little bitch sometimes, Martha Canary.

I DIDN'T TAKE the smallpox next day. Nor the day after that, nor the week after. Truth to tell, I cannot say whether the cloth I kept tied around my face saved me, or whether I simply had some miraculous immunity lodged within my blood, alongside my propensity for cussing and my native stubbornness. Whatever the reason, I was spared—and so I went on caring for the sick prospectors, day after day. I gave them water every hour, and fixed up a thin gruel from the rations of oats I found among their supplies. It took some doing to make them all eat, but I cajoled or bullied each one into two small meals a day. I stripped off their clothes (moving with tenderest care, for the blisters had spared no part of their wretched bodies) and washed away the foul suppurations with cool water from the crick. I held pots for them to piss in, once they started pissing again, and talked to them all the while, telling them what good boys they was, how brave, how strong, and how their mothers loved them.

And every hour, every minute, whenever I looked down at my laboring hands, I expected to find the pustules bursting from my own skin, rising like mushrooms from a stump. I would take the illness soon enough, I knew, and perish. There would be no kindly nurse to look after me. The end was coming; I couldn't avoid it. I could only work to save these men as long as my strength held out, and pray my labors would spare at least one life.

Yes, I was resigned to my fate, and I tell you what, Short Pants: I even felt a curious peace in the face of certain death—for at least I had seen my daughter to safety. At least I knew Jessie would live, safe and sound in Clinton's care. And each night, when I dropped into my hard, cold bed, my thoughts turned to Wild Bill, pensive and calm. When death finally came for me, would I find my love in the world beyond? I imagined the scene: Bill standing among the clouds, just this side of the Pearly Gate, his arms wide open to embrace me, the fringe of his coat swinging on a Heavenly breeze. In the Great Beyond, Bill would be eager for my company, as he never had been in life. I was certain it would be so—and with that sweet promise hanging before me like the morning sun, I was almost cheerful in my grim and weary duty.

Two more men perished of the disease despite my constant efforts. I buried them beside their fallen comrade. But four recovered, little by little, marshaling more strength every day till they could even sit up in their cots and speak.

Nine days into the ordeal, I stepped inside a shack with a whiskey bottle, newly filled with crick water. My patient had raised himself, trembling, on one elbow. Some of the blisters had subsided on his face; I could see his eyes more clearly than I ever had before, and he stared at me with an intensity that stopped me in my tracks.

"Who are you?" His voice, a dry and painful rasp, sounded like a grinding stone.

I didn't know what to tell him, save for the truth. I shook my head helplessly, then admitted, "Calamity Jane."

I sank to my knees beside his bed and held the bottle to his lips. He drank with more vigor than he ever had before. When he'd taken his fill, he nodded, paused, and swallowed. Then he said, "You're an angel, ain't you? I died. I died and now I'm in Heaven, and you're an angel."

I laughed at that. I couldn't help it. Through my cloth mask, I said, "Mister, I am the farthest thing from an angel you're ever like to meet, believe me. Just look at me. You ever heard of an angel who looks like the wrong end of a mule? I'm afraid you ain't dead

—not yet. I can't swear you'll get into Heaven when you do die, someday—but today ain't that day."

He laid back in his cot, but those bright, adoring eyes never left mine. "If you say I ain't dead, I guess I must believe you. But God's honest truth, you are the most beautiful woman I ever seen. A pure angel. Thank God for you."

After three weeks of ministrations, the prospectors grew strong enough to see to their own needs. The worst of the disease had passed. They was all still weak and shaky, but I knew they would survive; they grew stronger by the day, and the blisters had vanished, leaving raw red scabs behind. I waited till the dark of night, when they slept around their potbelly stoves. Then I packed up my bed roll, saddled my horse, and followed the crick upstream, away from that camp forever. I had no wish to make a grand farewell, no wish to hear those boys plead with me to stay. I done what I set out to do—and I saved more lives than I thought possible. There wasn't no point in hanging around any longer.

I headed out into the wilderness, riding under a gentle sweep of moonlight. But I didn't go to Clinton's ranch, as you may have thought—for I still feared the smallpox, and fretted that I might bring death to my daughter, and to the rest of the innocents camped outside Ekalaka. Instead, I aimed to spend the remainder of that summer on my own, away up in the sandstone buttes, waiting for the smallpox to take me. If by some miracle the autumn found me still kicking, I would return to Ekalaka and claim my Jessie.

I would claim Clinton, too, if he still had a hankering for my heart. For that summer, I had drawn near enough to death that I treasured the small joys my humble life contained—Clinton foremost among them.

THERE'S little I can tell you about the tail end of that summer. I camped at the top of a butte directly across the valley from Ekalaka. From my vantage I could just make out the distant ranch: specks of white canvas tents encircling the low, blue shadow of the pine grove; swaths of darkness, slow-moving and ever-shifting in form, the vast herds of cattle tended by Clinton and his friends. I had taken enough rations from the mining camp to see me through the rest of the summer—with three men down, the surviving fellas had a surplus—and I lived humbly, dwelling in the private halls of my thoughts while autumn crept ever nearer. I watched the valley below surrender its green to the coming season, watched the earth deepen into gold, drying and fading a little more with each passing day.

I had dwelt among death for the better part of a month—and a harrowing month it had been. Alone on my butte, with only my horse and the pine jays for company, I found I could think of little else but the world to come. But for all the time I spent considering death's relentless progress, now I can recall very little of my revelations—if indeed I had any revelations to speak of, up there in my lonesome camp among white birches, with my daughter's distant safety my only view. Now, of course, I understand death's nature —its enduring truth. Now I can see more clearly what lies beyond. Death in its shifting colors, the shades of green and gold.

There's a funny thing that happens, once you've gone. Time ceases to matter, or it maybe it matters in a different way; its shape and utility change. It folds back upon itself. In thick and dusty layers it lies, and the nap of time's velvet settles and crushes against your skin. Time pulls itself this way and that; each indi-vidual thread that makes up the weave shifts and bends. Now it is dark, now light. Now it lies down smooth, and the next moment something stirs—a memory or a moment relived—and time is alive beneath your hand, and your fingertips trace patterns through it, and the patterns remain.

If you know the way to do it, time will allow you to pick up its very substance and shake it out. And then you fold it again, so this part touches that, and it lies in a different way, with its grain running across't itself in new directions. But there's the pattern you drew before—the track of you, a dark line sunk in the shining substance, all down the length of the velvet.

There is something that connects us, like the underground rivers that bear sweet water or water laced with sulfur to widely separated springs. Not all of us are connected. I mean to say, we aren't all made from the same stuff, but each of us has our river, our network of commonalities. That summer, set among my silver birches, I would have said the Almighty made us this way, all of a purpose—I would have told you that He cut some folks from this cloth, and others from that, and stitched us together in subtle ways after His own design.

I know better now.

There was no grand purpose to our making; there was only ever chance. But the lack of purpose makes our affinities no less powerful. Every one of us goes through life looking—always searching, with a weather eye peeled for that sense of sameness in others, the proof that we are made from the same substance, cut from the same cloth. And when we find those who are like ourselves—whose springs taste of the same water—we never lose our way back to them, even when death divides us.

Bill and me never touched in love. He never embraced me—not the way I wanted him to. But still I carried him inside me. He is with me even now. His faro game is smooth and cool in my hand—the tip of one finger rests on the rounded corner of a card, its edge pressing into the callus. I feel his hat on my head, the familiar cling of its band; his hair brushing my shoulders, the place on his shoulder where a mosquito bit and the welt and the itch remain. At night in the scouting camp, my body lies in his bed roll, tired and relaxed, and my hands are folded behind his head while he listens through the darkness, through the smoky air beyond his tent, to the sound—far on the other side of camp—of Calamity Jane singing.

You tell me these are memories, and broken ones at that—fractured by time, put back together in the haste of my miserable longing, so the pieces are skewed and misaligned. But I know better by now. I have folded time's velvet. I have laid Wild Bill and me nap upon nap. I have sunk into him, or he has sunk into me, water into parched earth, drunk down to fill an empty hollow. And the common stuff that makes us has mingled, so that everything I was and everything I am becomes Wild Bill—and he, poor soul, becomes me.

WHEN THE FIRST leaves fell from my birches, I saddled up my horse and rode for Ekalaka. I passed through the gully above Medicine Rocks; the old miners' camp was gone, the shacks disassembled and scattered into the brush. Nothing remained to mark the camp, save a couple of charred black fire rings and tramped ground—and the three stones I had laid to mark the graves, the three souls lost. I scarcely paused to take in the sight of the camp where I had labored for a terrible, treacherous month. I rode on, and reached Clinton's ranch by nightfall.

The ranch was a merry place, it must be said, full of music and laughter. The rising notes of a fiddle far off in the twilight brought to mind the first rail camp I had visited in my mulewhacking days. As I rode along the rows of canvas tents, searching for my family, smoke from a dozen campfires pricked my eyes and brought on the hot flush of tears. But they was tears of happiness—of gratitude, for I had survived my ordeal, and the future that lay before me seemed fresh and new as a budding rose. A stir of campfire talk mingled with the distant lowing of the herds. Away across't the valley, I could hear wolves crying, and the sound gave me a comfortable thrill. My solitude had ended; I was back where I belonged, with a pack full of rowdies eager to whoop it up proper, embraced by warm fire light.

Now that I was certain I wouldn't die of smallpox, I longed for Jessie more forcefully than any hunger that had ever afflicted me. I stopped at a campfire to inquire where I might find Clinton Burke, and the fellas directed me to a tent on the edge of the encampment, then lifted their cups in cheerful salute as I rode away.

Long before I reached Clinton's tent, I could hear Jessie's high, sweet voice cutting above the sounds of the camp. I couldn't make out her words just yet, but I could tell by the cadence of her speech that she was telling one of her stories. I sniffed back a few more tears and rode around the corner of the last tent—it had to be Clinton's—and there at last I saw my girl, seated on a little stool beside a jolly, crackling fire. Even though she was seated, swinging her legs and bouncing on her bottom, I could tell Jessie had grown. The sight of her—happy and whole, thriving like a flower in the sun—wracked me with a shiver of love and relief so powerful, I damn near fell right out of my saddle.

Clinton set beside the fire, too, grinning at Jessie, enthralled by her words, chuckling now and then as she spoke. And there was a stranger at Clinton's fire—a woman whose back was turned to me. But even so, I could tell the woman was young and slender. Straight, black hair fell across't one shoulder and down her back. At the sound of my horse's approach, the woman shifted on her stool, turned to glance into the darkness. Her beauty struck me, even in silhouette against the fire's ruddy glow. Her bold nose and high cheeks proclaimed her half-Indian, if not more than half. She smiled in welcome when she saw me—and that smile struck me cold. There was nothing unfriendly in the woman's demeanor, but even so, I knew my road to happiness ended at her smile.

Jessie saw me next. She stopped speaking; her little legs ceased to swing. The girl stared at me for a long moment. Then she shouted, "Grandmam!" and sprang up from her seat.

I vacated my saddle so quick, maybe I did fall to earth, after all. Jessie was running to me, and I strode out to meet her. I scooped her into my arms, covering her with kisses, laughing like a damn fool from the sheer bliss of holding my baby again.

"Cushie Butterfield," I said when I could speak through my tears. "I missed you, girl."

Jessie giggled, wrapping her arms so tight around my neck she could have choked me. I didn't mind. "I missed you," she said. "You was gone a awful long time."

"I sure was, but I had very important work to do. Otherwise I never would have left you. But all my work is finished now, and I don't aim to leave your side ever again."

"Promise?"

"Cross my heart and hope to die, and if I'm lying, stick a needle in my eye."

"Martha."

Reluctant, I pulled myself away from Jessie's soft curls. Clinton stood there before me, kicking his feet at the edge of the firelight. He was hesitant, shame-faced. His old warmth had cooled a little. Not in anger—his eyes shone with gratitude for my return—but there was no more light of longing in those eyes, neither. Not when he looked upon me.

"I convinced myself I'd never see you again," Clinton said. It sounded like an excuse.

"Well—here I am." I didn't know what else to say.

"God, but I'm glad to see you. I was terrible feared you would..." He glanced at Jessie in my arms, then cleared his throat. "Feared you might not find your way back."

"Nothing in the world could keep me from Jessie."

"Of course not. No."

The dark-haired woman had crept up beside Clinton, casting a timid glance between him and me.

"Martha," Clinton said, "I'd like you to meet Sally. Sally, this is my... my friend Martha."

I nodded at the woman. "How do you do." There was no need

for Clinton to explain what Sally meant to him. I could see the truth already.

Jessie yawned in my arms, then rubbed her eyes.

"Come along, Jessie," Sally said, stretching out one hand. She had a kindly voice, a gentle manner. "It's late. Let me put you to bed."

Jessie kissed my cheek one last time. I allowed her to slide to the ground. She went meekly into Sally's care; a moment later they disappeared into the tent.

"So," I said to Clinton.

He nodded, then sighed. He couldn't quite make himself meet my eye. "Only natural, I guess."

It was the naturalest thing in the world. I wasn't inclined to argue. "I got no right to be jealous. I turned you down, after all. Not in so many words, but I guess you knew I wasn't inclined toward you—not in that way. Not back then." I sighed, too, heavy and hollow. "You're fair game for another woman. And she is a real pretty woman, at that. Can't say as I blame you."

"She's good with Jessie."

"She better be, or I'll relieve her of her head."

Clinton laughed a little, grateful for my humor. He folded his arms tight across't his chest, still shuffling his feet in the dust.

"I was a fool," I said, "not to take your love when you was willing to give it." Clinton perked up, on the verge of making some reply, but I held up a hand to stop him. "I was a fool, and I regret it. You're a damn good man, Clinton Burke. I was lucky to share my life with you while I did. I'm grateful for all you've done for me."

"Come on, now, Martha. Don't sound like you're about to go off and leave. Not when you only just come back."

An ironical smile pulled up one corner of my mouth. "I can't go on living with you—not now."

"Why not? I've grown so fond of you, and Jessie—"

"Don't talk like a fucking idiot, Clinton," I said gently. "You got to make your own life now—not tend to mine. And truth is, I don't want to go on living with you as we have done. Not if it means I'll be forced to watch you loving on some other woman. Not now, when I come to understand how good you really are… and what you *mean to me*. *I was a god-dam*ned idiot; *that's all there is to say. It's my loss to bear. I expect it'll* eat at my heart all the days of my life." But I've borne wors't pains, I though. Even wors't has gnawed at me, leaving me bare as a dug-up bone.

Clinton said nothing. He only squeezed his arms more tightly around his body and nodded, eyes on the ground.

I said, "I wish you better luck in love than I ever had." I meant it, too.

Silence fell between us again. I could feel Clinton straining against that silence; I also longed to break it. But neither one of us understood how to break it proper. Neither of us knew what was right and good to say in a moment such as this.

I heard Jessie's voice again, gentle and sweet, muffled by the tent walls. The girl was happy there—thriving under Clinton's care. And she had gone right to that pretty lady with the long black hair, just as happy with Sally as she'd ever been with me.

"I think I ought to leave Jessie with you," I said before I could think better.

"You know I'll look after her—gladly. I come to think of her as my true daughter."

I smiled at Clinton then, though I could scarce see him through the hot blur of my tears. But I knew I couldn't give Jessie up. The moment those words crossed my lips, my soul reeled back from the precipice, and my head pounded with a sudden rush of blood. Jessie was all I had in the world, now that Clinton wanted no more of me. To leave my daughter with anyone else—even a man so beloved as Clinton Burke—would have shattered my heart. Parting with my girl would have destroyed me, broken me under an agony worse than giving up my brothers and sisters.

"I can't do it," I said. "I just can't, Clinton. I'm sorry. Maybe I'll damn myself someday for being too cowardly, but I can't give away my only child."

Clinton drew a deep breath. "I understand," he said softly. "I understand."

"In the morning, you must tell Jessie good-bye."

"I must tell you good-bye, too."

Then at last he came to me, crossing the emptiness between us. He wrapped his arms around my trembling shoulders and pulled me to his chest—embraced me, like a brother holds his sister. He held me that way for a long time. He never minded when my tears soaked through his shirt and ran down his shoulder.

BY THE TIME Jessie was eight years old, I knew I must settle down and build a proper life. And so I set my sights on the one town I had always avoided—for I knew Jessie would never find happiness till I made good on my own legend, and woke Calamity Jane from her long slumber. For the sake of my daughter's future—whatever future I could provide—I was determined to make hay while my feeble sun was still shining.

Deadwood, 1895. The town had grown up considerable since I seen it last. A proper school now stood out on the edge of town, and I resolved to get Jessie into that school, though the cost was daunting. But a photographer had set up shop in Deadwood, too, aiming to make his fortune off the flocks of pop-eyed tenderfeet who rode the train into town, searching for the untamed West.

I found my opportunity in that photographer's shop. I had several pictures made of myself (all dressed up in the dandiest gear, a fringed coat of buckskin and good trousers, holding *a rifle as if I knew what to do with it.) The photographer printed a stack of copies, complete with a few lines of text designed to spur my infamy back to life.*

The legendary CALAMITY JANE, wild woman of the West,

heroine of novels, renown scout and Indian hunter who can ride standing up in the saddle and light a cigar at full motion.

I lingered on the train platform or at the stagecoach depots, selling my image each time a new gaggle of tenderfeet came flapping and squawking into Deadwood. I didn't make enough money to buy a proper house. I was obliged to take up residence at a boarding house—and a middling one, at that. But I did scratch together enough cash to send Jessie to that bright new school.

She was glad as Christmas day the first week or so, and how I delighted in sending her off to her lessons. I dressed her in a pretty, blue-check frock with a smart pinafore embroidered with forget-me-nots. She proved a brighter student than I expected her to be. But though she loved her lessons and doted on her beautiful young teacher, Jessie often came home from school wrought out, her face red from crying.

The first few days, she refused to tell me what had upset her. She only sulked in a corner of our boarding room, knees drawn up to her chest, arms folded atop her knees, her dear little face hidden from my sight.

But one day, I coaxed the truth from her.

"The other children at the school poke fun at me," she muttered. "They say I'm Calamity's daughter."

My heart froze in my chest; I actually felt it stop beating, felt my throat swell with sudden panic.

"Is it true?" Jessie demanded, raising her indignant eyes to mine.

I couldn't look away from my daughter's pain. Nor could I lie to her any longer. At least, I couldn't lie much. "I am Calamity Jane." I dragged those words out, slow and heavy as a sledge pulled through mud. "That much is true. But I'm your grandmam, Jessie—not your ma."

"But is it really so?" the poor child insisted. She must have seen truth in my eyes—must have read my shame and reluctance as easy as she read those school-house primers. "Are you my grandmam for true?"

"For true," I said. "I swear it. Your mother was beautiful Charlotte. Your father was the hero of the West, Wild Bill. Why, he's buried right here in Deadwood. Someday I'll take you to see his grave."

Jessie buried her face in her arms again. "I don't want to see his grave."

She no longer believed the story—the pretty fantasy I had made for her, an escape from the hard, heavy weight of reality. But how I wanted the old tales to hold together! Not for my sake, but for hers. I cursed myself for not leaving her with Clinton, where at least she would have been happy—and free from the burden of my notorious past. If I was to maintain any slim hope for my daughter's joy, I had to put some distance between Jessie and me. I had to spirit my girl right out of Deadwood.

A solution presented itself the very next morning; seldom had fate proved so kindly or expedient. I was on my way to the photographer's shop, due to pick up a new stack of souvenirs. I breezed past the dry-goods store, but a paper tacked *up beside the door fluttered and caught my eye. I paused and leaned close, studying the print, puzzling out the words while a growing sensation of luck flowered in my heart.*

To open in *STURGIS*, Dakota,
May 1:
Saint Francis Convent School for Girls
Room, board, and
SOUND RELIGIOUS INSTRUCTION
Along with
ESSENTIALS of EDUCATION
For girls age 8 to 15
Monthly cost: $80.00

Room and board. Sturgis was a good two days away from Deadwood, if you rode overland. A long day's journey by stage coach. Far enough, I hoped, that my legend would leave Jessie in peace. And a convent school—surely the sour old nuns in charge of the place would brook no mention of a sinner like Calamity Jane, even if the legend preceded me.

But how could I hope to afford eighty dollars a month? We hardly scraped by on the few dollars a week I earned selling my photographs at the depot.

I could feel the watch in my pocket, just where I always kept it. It seemed to heat against my thigh, burning me, urging me to do the unthinkable. I might hope to get a year's worth of schooling for Jessie, provided I could find a buyer who believed my story that the watch had once belonged to Wild Bill Hickock.

Even as I summed up the value of Bill's old watch, my gut tied itself in knots at the thought of selling. The loss of Bill's gun still pained me; that had been eight years before. I couldn't part with his watch or his ring—not even for Jessie's sake. I must find some other way to send her off to that dandy new school in Sturgis.

I turned away from the notice and pressed on toward the photographer's shop, frowning over my sad dilemma. A shout halted me again. "Miss Jane! A moment, please."

I turned, bracing myself to face a gawking tenderfoot—but I found the postmaster bustling out of his little office, waving something above his head.

"Letter for you, Miss Jane. I've been hoping to catch you; you never step into the office anymore."

"I never expect any mail."

"Well, this has come for you. It has been waiting for some days now."

I took the letter and opened it, then nodded my thanks to the postmaster. He retreated to his office; I sank down on the edge of the boardwalk and began again the laborious process of reading.

My dearest Jane:

You must forgive my rude manners in addressing you by your Christian name. I have been unable to locate your surname, so "Jane" will have to do.

Madam, surely you have heard tell of Bill Cody, promoter of the greatest Wild West Show from New York to California. I am that same Bill Cody, otherwise known as "Buffalo Bill," and I write you now seeking your talents as the most singular performer of the West, legendary star of novels and all manner of exciting tales.

I offer you a chance to perform with the greatest display of Western entertainers yet seen on this Continent. The pay is VERY GOOD and the work rewarding.

I have heard you may be reached in Deadwood. Write me back with your interest, dear Jane, and let us further discuss this opportunity (not to be missed) for fame and fortune.

Yours,

"Buffalo" Bill Cody

Well, Short Pants—I don't mind confessing that my first reaction was one of outright revulsion. I earned my living from the tenderfeet who crowded Deadwood's streets—cooing over the quaint town, fancying themselves a part of the West, for one day at least—but I didn't like those bastards, not one lick. The damn fools had recently found the graveyard, and had so cluttered up the place that the groundskeeper had built an iron fence around Bill Hickock's grave to keep the careless herds of tenderfeet in check. I had never seen a Wild West Show before, but I knew just by the sound of its name that it would only draw the sort of folk who flocked to Deadwood for a gander at the place, then left again in a puff of dust. They had no proper respect for the West— the world I knew, the world I loved. All the bright and fleeting beauties of my land—my heart—was nothing but caricatures to the tenderfeet. Like the funny drawings you find sometimes in newspapers: exaggerated and false, printed for amusement, easily forgotten the moment you turn the page.

No, I had no great liking for this Buffalo Bill, or his vaunted Show. In fact, I plum hated the idea of accepting his offer.

But I was damn sure I could earn more from Buffalo Bill than I would ever make hawking my photographs at the stage coach depot. Cody had offered more than a job: he had given me the best shot I had to make Jessie happy.

I resolved to respond that very afternoon, and accept Bill Cody's offer.

THE BUCKSKIN-CLAD BELLE OF THE PLAINS

BUFFALO BILL NEVER INSPIRED MUCH PRAISE FROM THOSE OF US who knew the real West, for his vaunted show was nothing but trickery and tales—wors't damnable lies than anything my many writer friends scribbled in their novels, and more egregiously told. But I will say this in Cody's favor: he dispatched a generous advance against my future earnings upon receipt of my letter (I paid the mistress of the boarding house fifty cents to write that letter for me, since my own writing fell somewhere south of chicken scratch, in terms of readability.)

Cody's money arrived just a few weeks later in the hands of a tight-laced, stodgy young woman by the name of Josephine Brake. I knew I was destined to butt heads with Josephine the moment she stepped off her train and onto the Deadwood platform. She wore a meticulous dress of cream and wine-red, with a big flounced bustle over her behind and a jacket with a ruffled collar. Even the most fashionable girls in Deadwood never donned such a get-up; Josephine Brake fairly dripped with city living. As I watched her brush the dust from her skirt, I thought I could just about smell the Back East life rolling off her person like a thunderhead blown by an ill wind. Even from across't the platform, she stank of coal smoke, fancy perfume, and down feathers—all the odors of easy living. Her chestnut hair was swept up in a tidy roll, crowned by a cream velvet hat with a huge red flower canted off to one side. I could already see the Black Hills dust clinging to pale velvet, discoloring her finery with the dry grit of the hard West. She had eyes that could skewer you with a single glance, and a turned-down mouth that let you know she brooked no nonsense without her needing to speak a word. Josephine was a tenderfoot, all right—but she carried herself with a steady determination no tenderfoot ever showed. She had come to Deadwood on business, and that business was me.

I threaded my way across the platform, conscious of my buckskin jacket and my patched trousers as I never had been before. Stood up next to that woman's finery, I was sure to disappoint. I was powerful annoyed with myself, too, for I had never cared a whit what any tenderfoot thought of me. But this lady wasn't just any Back East visitor; I reminded myself of that fact while I brushed through the milling crowd. Josephine held my daughter's future in her hands. Even if I disliked her showy style and her hard, suspicious eyes, I had to make a favorable impression for Jessie's sake.

"Good afternoon mam," I said when I reached her side. "I guess by the description you sent me in your last letter, you must be Miss Josephine Brake."

"Indeed I am. And you are Miss Jane." She pulled off an ivory glove and offered her hand. When I took it in my awkward grip, one corner of her mouth twitched. Guess she didn't much care for my calluses. "I mentioned in our correspondence that I am an agent of Mr. Bill Cody. Do you understand what that means?"

I was older than that chit by a good ten years—and I looked at least thirty years her senior. Her habit of speaking to me as if I was a small and especially stupid child didn't exactly thrill me to my toes. But I swallowed my irritation and shook my head in what I hoped was a mild, friendly sort of way.

"It means Mr. Cody has authorized me to speak and act on his behalf, Miss Jane."

Josephine bent over the handled case waiting at her feet, slipped her ungloved hand into a side pocket, and withdrew a piece of paper. She flashed the paper with a kind of stately flourish. I could see that it was scrawled all over with fancy writing, and a very special scrawl crossed the bottom of the page, which I guessed might be Bill Cody's personal signature. To read the page would have taken me a good five minutes at least, and I had no desire to keep the agent or myself waiting out in the hot Dakota sun. So I nodded, and Josephine tucked the paper away.

"We are terribly pleased by your agreement to perform with the Wild West Show, Miss Jane. We feel certain your act will bring an element of adventure and delight our many avid viewers."

Inwardly, I cringed, for I didn't like the idea of any passer-by hearing that Calamity Jane (the One and Only, the Authentic Wild Girl of the West) had sold her soul to Buffalo Bill and his three-ring circus of lies. But I reasoned the tale would get out sooner or later.

"Can I carry your case?" I picked up Josephine's bag before she could answer. "Guess you'll be wanting to stay the night at the best hotel in Deadwood. That would be the Shelby. I'll walk you there." The last thing I wanted was for Josephine to choose her accommodations on her own. She might pick a boarding house where Calamity Jane was a well-known commodity, and hear one too many tales of my exploits. I couldn't have this agent go scampering back to Cody without me, still burdened with my advance.

I had no cause for fear on account of my money. The moment Josephine checked into her room, she paid me forthwith. Three hundred and fifty dollars—more than I had ever held in my hands; more than I had earned for years at a time. I made as if the astonishing sum was all in a day's work to the great Calamity Jane, and stuffed the wad of notes in my trouser pocket with a word of thanks.

"I imagine you will need some time to arrange your affairs here in Deadwood," Josephine said. "Can you be ready to travel in three days?"

I certainly could be ready. Cody had already written to inform me that an advance was forthcoming; the moment I'd been sure of his money, I arranged for Jessie's enrollment in that fancy convent school and made all necessary plans to transport my girl safely to Sturgis. I took my newfound fortune back to my boarding house and enlisted the aid of the housekeeper, a firm and reliable widow whose age had been no detriment to her energy or her sharp good sense. The housekeeper agreed to accompany Jessie on the train to Sturgis, and to escort her safely to the convent school, as well. I paid her an extra dollar on top of her transport fee. That was so she could write to me, in care of the Buffalo Bill Wild West Show, and tell me when Jessie had lighted safely among the nuns—for I would be inconsolable with worry till I knew my girl had reached her comfortable new future in one piece.

All that remained was to tell Jessie. I set her down on the edge of the bed we shared and brushed her dark curls away from her forehead. They sprang back into place the moment I moved my hand.

"Jessie," I said, "I know you ain't been too happy in this school, on account of the children being so cruel. I don't like to do it, for I'll miss you something awful, but I found another school for you —a better one, with smarter teachers and kinder children."

"Why will you miss me, Grandmam?"

"Because..." I faltered, and found I couldn't speak a-tall for a spell. I stared at my hands in my lap, and there I found the gumption to go on. "Because I must send you away from Deadwood. The school is out in Sturgis. But it's a right dandy place, all brand-new, and you'll live behind its walls just as if you was a princess in a castle, safe and sound. And the ladies who run the place won't take kindly to any mention of Calamity Jane. Nor any other notorious persons, I bet. No child at this new school will know a thing about me—and if they do, they won't be quick to speak of it. I hear nuns can be awful generous with their switches when children break the rules."

I looked up at my daughter's face, expecting to find Jessie wrestling back her tears. Instead she beamed at me and threw her arms around my neck, and kissed me again and again on my cheek. And with a heavy heart I understood that I would miss Jessie far wors't than she would ever miss me.

WHEN THE FATEFUL DAY DAWNED, I took Jessie to the town bakery and bought her a pretty little cake with lemon frosting. I watched her devour that sweet, rosy-cheeked and eager-eyed. Then I walked with her to the train depot, where the staid old widow stood waiting. I kissed my girl one last time, and watched through misted eyes while she boarded the train. Then I meekly followed Josephine Brake to our own train: a sleek, new one shining like a jewel, even if it was one of those oddly compressed narrow-gauge conveyances.

Me and Josephine, we slung our bags into the hold and took our seats, pressed shoulder-to-shoulder. Josephine took a little book from her handbag and settled in at once to read—travel by rail was nothing startling to such a worldly, sophisticated type. But though I had eye-witnessed the exterior parts of more trains than I could ever remember, I had never actually been inside a train car before. Cramped against the window, I turned my head this way and that, taking in the gleaming wood panels and the short curtains of green velvet, drawn back and tied beside every window. The car smelled of new leather, ladies' sweet perfume, and the lingering odor of cigar smoke. I had smoked cigars more than once in my life—most usually during my trick rides—and I craved one powerfully then. What a distraction it would have been from my tangled-up nerves and the raw pain in my heart, my sadness over parting with Jessie. I longed for that compelling tingle on my lips, the soothing effect of a cigar's thick blue smoke —better than any nerve tonic I knew. I might have approached one of the gentlemen in our car and offered him fifty cents for a smoke, but a glance at Josephine's prim, austere face (in profile, turned down over the marbled cover of her book) put me right off the idea. I might have been hired to play the part of the Buckskin-Clad Belle of the Plains, but I sensed instinctively that Bill Cody's hard-eyed agent expected me to confine my performances to the stage, and to comport myself like a lady at all other junctures. Or as much like a lady as I could manage, anyhow.

The train whistled and gave a jolt as its engine came to life. The narrow car shuddered, then crept forward; a high wine emanated from its wheels. The train found its speed, holding me subtly against the padded leather bench with a force and pressure I had never felt before. I pressed my cheek against the window, watching Deadwood vanish in a hot white haze behind.

The land became a blur outside my window as we traveled east, but for hours, the world around me didn't change. Morning aged into afternoon; the Black Hills followed our route, keeping their distance, a raised plane of ochre and limestone-white strung along the horizon. Not only the unchanging world, but also the motion of the train became monotonous, and a thick, oppressive discomfort settled in. My head ached as much as my heart. It gave me a dreadful sense of doom, to be shut up in that cramped car when I had been accustomed to roaming free whenever the mood took me. I longed for my horse and saddle with a passion so sudden and fierce, I was obliged to blink away my tears lest Josephine catch me weeping. I fretted that I had made the wrong decision, after all—but now it was much too late to halt all the changes I had set in motion.

Josephine noticed my anxious fidgeting and offered me a book to read. But I didn't like the thought of that pinch-faced agent watching me from the corner of her eye, measuring how long it took me to turn every page. I politely declined and resolved to keep my attention fixed to the world outside, giving every impression I was absorbed in the unchanging landscape. I did my best not to fidget anymore.

As evening came on, small, ragged settlements appeared, crouching out along the prairie, flashing by and disappearing before I'd had a chance to observe them proper. Then the widely scattered settlements became real towns clustered around the tracks, with well-built houses and church steeples, stores and liveries and stage coaches rolling along their broad, dusty streets. I caught sight of people working on small farms or in fenced gardens, glimpsed so rapidly through a blur of motion that they seemed stilled forever, captured in time, like photographs in full color. Homes and shops became more numerous, crowded under a purple, dusky sky. And then there was no more space to speak of between one town and the next. The train leaned slightly as it took a long bend, curving around the foot of a hill. When the track straightened and the hill receded from view, I caught sight of Minneapolis in the distance: a thousand orange lamps glowing against the oncoming night, lights so numerous they might as well have been the stars overhead. My mouth fell open at the sight. I made no attempt to hide my awe. Not even Salt Lake City had been so large, so vastly populated. My heart beat high and rapid in my chest, till the pulse roared in my ears.

Less than an hour after my first sight of Minneapolis, we pulled into the station and stepped off our train. I knew I was out of my depth that very moment. The noise of the city pressed in all around me—a constant hum of voices, of carriage wheels rattling over brick pavers, the clamor of music coming from every direction at once. Gas lights burned in square cages atop towering lamp posts; the whole world was cast in the ruddy monotone of the flames, and a current of smoke from trains and towers of industry flowed down every street. Josephine invoked the name of Bill Cody at once. Our bags was fetched and loaded onto a waiting buggy, a far finer conveyance than any I had seen in the West. I stepped up uncertainly into the gleaming carriage, settling on a padded bench. The rocking of the carriage on its springs and the hostile night outside the window reminded me of the night Jessie was born. The same sinking dread came back to me. I looked up over the roof-tops of brick buildings reaching three and four stories high, but I only saw a scattering of stars. Never had I felt so small and frail in all my life.

Josephine spoke a few words to the driver, then settled in beside me.

"Are you well, Miss Jane? You look pale."

"I'm well enough, thank you." I knew my voice sounded a little too shaky to fool the sharp-eyed agent. "Just weary from travel, I suppose."

"You needn't fear," she said, perceiving at once the real source of my paleness. The carriage began to roll; the hiss of steam from the trains faded behind us. "Minneapolis must seem a jungle to you, after the life you've grown used to. But this isn't so very large a city. New York is far larger. Boston, too. Why, Paris puts them both to shame."

"Have you been all the way to Paris?"

"Once." She smiled, and it made her look less icy and severe. I even found a hint of sympathy in her face. "Disorienting though a city may be, you've no cause for concern—as long as you listen carefully to my instructions, and always do as I bid."

"I will do that, mam; I can assure you." For Jessie's sake, if not my own.

"Very well. We shall board at the Christopher Columbus, one of this city's finest hotels. They've an excellent restaurant. We'll take a late supper as soon as we arrive. I'm famished; are you?"

Josephine was as good as her word. When our buggy rolled to a stop outside the Christopher Columbus—the finest place I'd ever laid eyes on, all pale limestone and leaf-carved cornices along the line of its third story—a soft-spoken young Negro man took our bags and promised to take them directly to our rooms. Then Josephine led me to the restaurant, which smelled as rich as Heaven itself. My stomach ached so badly from hunger, the sensation made me sick. I was certain I couldn't eat a bite, till a waiter in a fine black coat set before me a steaming plate of roast beef and stewed carrots. Then I found I couldn't slow myself, and I'm afraid I made a spectacle, digging so enthusiastically into my supper. I will be honest with you, Short Pants: more than once I wanted to ask for a whiskey, a glass full to the brim. But I didn't like to displease Josephine. I perceived that she would tolerate very little of my whooping up—and what she did tolerate had best be confined to Buffalo Bill's stage.

Josephine led me up two flights of stairs to my room. I was to have my own accommodations, a fact which filled me with shuddering relief. I didn't think I could maintain my best behavior indefinitely; it would be a mercy to close a door between myself and Josephine Brake.

My room was across the carpeted hallway from Josephine's. She handed me a key on a wooden tag. Then she glanced this way and that, making certain the hall was empty before she leaned close and murmured, "Now, Jane. You must take care not to do anything that would start ill rumors about the show. Mr. Cody won't stand for it—and, I must tell you, neither shall I. That means no roaming about without accompaniment. That's not what respectable ladies do in a city like Minneapolis."

I nodded. I had suspected Josephine might impose such limitations upon me. I didn't mind staying confined to my room—the city beyond the walls of the Christopher Columbus plum scared me right out of my trousers, and I ain't afraid to admit it. But I had darker suspicions about the checks she would set on my behavior. I said, "No smoking cigars, either, I guess. Nor drinking whiskey."

Josephine went pale. "Certainly not. Neither smoking nor

drinking can be considered acceptable behavior. I will thank you to remember as much."

I solemnly vowed to behave myself. In that moment, I earnestly thought it would be easy to do so—for not only was I determined to provide well for Jessie, but I felt rather sick at the thought of Minneapolis itself. The starless sky and the constant din made me feel as if I'd stepped from that train into a different world entirely—the fairy realm of children's tales, where nothing was as it seemed, where a lifetime could pass in the blink of an eye or an hour moved slow as a hundred years. A trap for ordinary men—a comfortable damnation, where those caught in the snare sank into complacent sleep while the world they had known died slowly around them. I craved whiskey something awful—the usual craving, but sharpened and made more urgent by my fear and sorrow. A stiff drink would have soothed my fears and eased me into sleep, but I couldn't give Josephine or Buffalo Bill cause to send me packing yet.

I let myself into my small room and made ready for bed. By the time I slipped beneath the velvet covers and settled into the feather mattress, I found I had no need for whiskey, after all. Worn out by awe—and by the pain of parting with Jessie—I fell into the deepest sleep I've ever known. I'm glad to report that I dreamed no dreams.

I DIDN'T MEET Bill Cody the following day, but I did meet another of his agents, a man who called himself by only one name: Farley, which I took to be his surname, though who can rightly say?

Josephine sent me to stand outside the Christopher Columbus, directly under one of the street lamps. I was garbed in an unfamiliar dress of plainest cut, all grayish-blue without pattern or pintuck. I imagined the nuns at Jessie's new school likely dressed the same way. But the simple clothing drew no attention from the swarms of men and women who passed in carriages or astride their horses, or on foot, tramping up and down the streets of Minneapolis. I was invisible again, just as I'd been in Salt Lake City so many years before. This time, I didn't mind—for I knew myself to be ill-fitted for city life; I wanted no part of it. I hadn't yet done my sworn duty to the Wild West Show, but I already longed for the end of the touring season when I could return to Deadwood and put the whole mad experience at my back.

Anyway—there I stood, Short Pants. Picture me, gray-blue and unadorned, my bullwhacker's build draped in the vestments of a near-nun. I would have looked ridiculous to any soul who cared to pause and observe me. None did, except for Farley. When another carriage just like the first halted in front of my lamp post, I knew Farley must be inside before he even opened the door.

Like Josephine, Farley was all city, from his John Bull hat to the shine on his shoes. He stepped down into the street and offered his hand as if to help me into the carriage. I didn't take it. I've never needed any assistance clambering in and out of rigs. To be frank with you, I've always looked askance at ladies who can't manage a few steps up or down on their own.

Farley seemed put out by my independence, but only for a moment. He followed me back inside the carriage and shut the door. Then he rapped on the ceiling with his knuckles and the buggy began to roll.

"Miss Jane," he said, tipping his hat, "it's an honor to meet you."

I wasn't sure how I ought to respond—what would a proper city woman say? I had no desire to ruffle Josephine's feathers with unladylike behavior. I set and stared at Farley while he waited for me to speak. Finally he tugged on the lapels of his jacket and went on with his business.

"We are all so glad you've agreed to join the Wild West Show, Miss Jane. Our company performs at the Star Theater in the heart of the city. We are on our way there now."

"Will Mr. Cody be there?" I asked.

Farley smiled. "Many people are eager to meet Bill Cody—naturally, of course. He has made quite a name for himself, and now you will take part in his fame."

I wasn't starstruck by Cody's name, as Farley imagined me to be. I merely wanted to get a good look at the man. Who was this fella, cobbling together a vision of the West and selling it to tenderfeet on their own turf? Cody had earned enough jingle from his gig that he never hesitated to send me that fat advance. The Wild West Show must be a lucrative business. I was curious about the man himself—his character, his presence. How well did he understand the goods he sold to his audiences? And was he the sort of fella a body could trust?

"I'm afraid Mr. Cody is unlikely to appear at the matinee," Farley said, "but he may grace the evening performance. We shall see. Bill Cody is a busy man. Now attend, if you please, Miss Jane. We haven't much time to speak, and it's my job to tell you everything you'll need to know before your first appearance on the stage."

I tried to focus on Farley's words as he described the show, the stage, the Star Theater itself. He spoke of the other performers the way I'd oft heard ranchers speak of their cattle. I scolded myself to pay attention, to remember every word he said. But his instructions came so fast and thick, I knew I was bound to forget something important, and I didn't like to make myself a fool by asking the agent to repeat himself.

"We've nearly arrived at the Star now." Farley peered out the buggy's window into the bustle of Minneapolis. "Straight away, you must report to Lucy Greaves, our costumer. You'll find her most congenial and talented."

"Costumer?" I said.

"Of course. You're our wild lady of the West. You must look the part."

"I could have met you looking the part already, sir, if I'd only known. Josephine Brake instructed me specially to wear this dress, but I most usually wear trousers and a shirt."

"Ah," Farley said with a small laugh, "Lucy will do better than that. Here we are now. I'll show you the performers' entrance. It's around the back."

The theater was unlike anything I had seen in my life—unlike anything I had imagined. High above the banks of wooden seats, gilded arches held up a domed ceiling painted deepest blue, adorned with silvery stars. The stage was even wider than the one I had used for my first shooting demonstrations at McDaniels' back in Cheyenne.

"Am I to shoot here?" I asked of Farley.

"Shoot? Heavens, no. Such a display would be far too dangerous, I'm afraid."

"I don't understand, Mr. Farley. If I ain't here for trick-shooting, what am I here for? What does Mr. Cody expect of me?"

The agent turned to me with a smile that felt a mite too condescending for my liking. "You are Calamity Jane, madam. You need do nothing but stand before the crowd. I believe that will be sufficient."

Next, I was conveyed to a large room somewheres behind the stage. The place smelled of sweat and a singed undertone of hot irons and well-pressed cotton—odors which had become all too familiar to me in my laundry days. The room was so crowded with racks of clothing and with can-can girls in various stages of undress that I could scarce navigate my way to the gray-haired, pinch-faced dame at the heart of the chaos. She was Buffalo Bill's costumer, and she needed only one glance at my big frame and blunt face to identify me.

"Calamity Jane," she said, even while she yanked on a dancer's corset strings with one hand. With the other, she swept a bundle of clothing from a rack and thrust the whole lot into my arms. "Your costume. Be quick, now, Miss; curtain is in one hour, and I must have time to make any needed alterations."

The can-can girls had no compunction about dressing right there in the costumer's room, so I did the same. It was a relief to shed that dress, for I never felt entirely comfortable in dresses, as I guess you've surmised by now. I slid myself into a fine set of twill trousers decorated with Indian beads along the cuffs and up the outer seams. A shirt of bright plaid followed, then a vest cut like a man's shooting jacket, but embroidered all over with flowers— which was, I assumed, an attempt by Lucy the costumer to make me seem more girlish.

Lucy paused in her ministrations to the can-can girls just long enough to look me over. She took a bit of chalk from the pocket of her apron, marked my shirt here and there, then placed a few pins and a few deft stitches. Then she declared me good enough for a matinee and thrust a buckskin jacket, a pair of boots, and a sugarloaf hat into my arms. She pulled a rifle from beneath one of her clothing racks and handed it to me, as well.

"Put these on," she told me. "Then you may go backstage and await your cue.

I did as I was told. Some fool had painted the boots with bright designs of red and blue. I had never seen a bullwhacker or a ranch hand with painted boots before. They was too big for my feet, besides, but I figured too big was a damn sight preferable over too small. The jacket's sleeves trailed heavy fringes that put me in mind of Wild Bill. A lump rose in my throat when I donned it. I could remember the sight of him, stark against a twilight sky, the light of emerging stars picking out the beads along his sleeves. Bill had loved a fancy jacket, to be sure—but he had never dressed as gaudily as that costumer dressed me. I found a looking glass standing in a corner and assessed myself. I wasn't best pleased by my own reflection. They had made me a scout of sorts—mine was a version of Wild Bill's beloved get-up. But the colors was garish and far too gay. No true scout would ever have dressed so fool-ishly—no scout would have survived long decked in scarlet and royal blue, with a flowery vest and glimmering beads everyplace a bead could be sewn. A body might as well have worn a sign reading Indians Shoot Here. I could swear I heard Wild Bill's ghost chuckling at sight of me. But I did feel closer to my dear Bill, sudden and unexpected, while I wore that buckskin coat. And so I wound my hair into a small knot at the nape of my neck and settled the oversized hat upon my head, and told myself I was ready for my first appearance in Buffalo Bill's Wild West Show.

I pressed myself against a wall backstage, grateful for the darkness, keeping as far from the curtain and the stage itself as I could manage. Fellas in workman's cover-all bibs scuttled here and there, faces and hands barely lit by the tiny, single-candle lanterns they carried. Their spots of ruddy glow drifted through the backstage darkness like ghost lights in a midnight cemetery. I could hear the crowd assembling in the theater, a constant murmur of voices and rustling activity that increased with each passing minute. Then a small brass band began tuning its instruments, somewhere out there under the painted stars where I couldn't see.

"You're new, aren't you?" said a girl in the shadows to my right-hand side.

I turned towards the voice, squinting in the darkness. I could just make out one of the can-can girls standing beside me. Her pale, round face and her flounces of ostrich feathers looked gray in the dim space, the feathers touched here and there along their edges by dim light thrown from the workmen's lanterns.

"Yes mam, I am quite new," I said.

"You look just about sick from nerves. But there's no need to worry about a thing. It's easy as can be; you only need to put on a little show, make them believe it's all real."

"What's all real?" I said.

"Why the Western hoopla, of course. That's what they've paid to see."

At that moment, the brass band struck up a wild fanfare and the crowd made a strange sound all together, a kind of "Ah!" of anticipation. The can-can girls filed past me, brushed through the swinging velvet drapes, and took their places on the stage just as the cymbals crashed with a triumphant ring. The audience applauded—whistled—shouted. And through the noise and rush, through the fever of my confusion, I struggled to recall Farley's words in the carriage that morning. I hadn't the first idea what I ought to do.

But the matinee moved easily from one act to the next—the can-can girls, the slim young fella who twirled his lasso and leaped in and out of its ring. The kindly old grandfather who draped himself in a bear skin and pretended to be a fearsome French trapper; the Japanese man who donned a bonnet of eagle feathers and made believe he was an Indian chief. I studied each performer's face as they came off the stage, leaving behind the audience's eager applause—and sometimes scattered jeers. Each time the curtain swung, the stage lights illuminated the perform-ers' faces. Whether they received acclaim or mockery, the result was always the same. Every one of them left the stage calm and easy, looking as if they'd just done a thing as routine as emptying their bowels, and so I told myself there was nothing to fear.

The announcer called out, "And now we present, the one, the only, heroine of the West and subject of more than a dozen popular novels, Calamity Jane!"

The brass band played my fanfare. I sucked in a deep breath, tugged on my buckskin jacket to be sure it was straight, and walked out onto the stage, holding my gun before me. The crowd cheered at sight of me, which made my blood pound in my cheeks. Then—as I stood there, smack in the center of the stage and half blinded by the lights of a dozen lamps—the crowd fell silent. I could feel the tension of their expectation filling the theater like a flood, creeping up its walls foot by treacherous foot.

The silence turned to shuffling. Then to murmurs. And then, to my outrage and mortification, a ripple of quiet laughter moved through the audience. I heard somebody from the wing of the stage clear their throat—trying to gain my attention. I thought it must have been the can-can girl who had spoken to me kindly some time before. But I couldn't see her, for she was shrouded in darkness, and besides, I didn't feel as if I could safely turn away from that audience. Their laughter held a feral note, an eagerness for my humiliation.

Somebody shouted from the back of the theater, "That's not Calamity Jane!"

A few more hecklers joined in. "The Belle of the Plains!" "It's the Hellcat in Leather, in the very flesh!"

I hefted my rifle, held it athwart my chest as if it was a shield to defend me. "I am too Calamity Jane!"

At my protest, some of the laughter died away, but not all of it. Somebody called out, "Calamity Jane is a beauty!"

The crowd murmured their agreement.

"Well," I said, "beauty is in the eye of the beholder. That's in the Bible. Or if it ain't in the Bible exactly, then your mas should have told you as much."

"Prove it!" a man cried, and applause bounced around the theater.

I swallowed hard, hoping the audience couldn't see my fear, praying the fringe of my sleeves didn't swing wildly with my shivers. How could I prove my identity? My face was growing hot under the glare of the lamps—burning with embarrassment and anger. I didn't like the thought of that pack of fools winning the day. Even less did I like the thought that Bill Cody might account me a poor investment if I didn't please his matinee audience. I knew I must give a performance convincing enough to appease those damnable fools.

Without the least warning, I lifted the rifle to my shoulder and sighted down its barrel, straight out into the crowd, as if I intended to fire upon them.

All laughter died on the instant. The crowd shrank back in their seats. Women screamed; men hollered in protest. A few people leaped up and ran for the doors.

"You dare to question me, the Hellcat in Britches!" I hollered. "Why, you know I can shoot the hat clean off a man's head. Who's man enough to come up and let me try it?"

I pointed my rifle this way and that, always aiming into the theater. No one volunteered, but as I stood there squinting down my sights, I could sense the mood of the crowd turning from fear to amusement. Chuckles sprouted here and there, tentative and small like mushrooms after an autumn rain. Men shoved each other towards the stage, but none of them climbed up to join me. They milled in the aisles between their banks of seats, slapping each other on the back and grinning up at me.

"It's me," I cried, "Calamity Jane, the true one and only, the White Devil of the Yellowstone. If you don't believe me, you can..." I searched my head for something suitably Calamitous to say, something that wouldn't upset Josephine Baker or anger Buffalo Bill. "You can sit on a hot poker!"

Genuine laughter rippled around the room—no longer tentative, but full and hearty. The announcer left his place beside the brass band. He climbed a few steps to stand beside me while the band played another triumphant chord, a flourish of finality. The announcer raised his hands to the crowd, but to me he gave a subtle jerk of his head—commanding me to high-tail off the stage. "Calamity Jane," he called out again. Tepid cheers followed me.

I cringed in the darkness, brooding over the humiliating affair, till the show had ended and the last performer made his way offstage. If I hoped to bring in more money, I would have to devise a new and better act. It wasn't enough merely to stand before the crowd—not for me. Those damned novels had made such a legend of my supposed beauty that no paying customer would ever take me for the real Calamity. If I hoped to win their hearts and bring in their cash, I must present myself in my element.

As the audience filed out of the Star Theater, somebody lit more lamps backstage. Light returned to the world, and I found

Josephine standing beside me. She eyed me with a sober, appraising air, from my sugarloaf hat to my painted boots. "You certainly look the part."

I couldn't help scowling at the woman, even if she was an agent, permitted to speak on Cody's behalf. "I look like a damnable fool."

"Nonsense. You look perfect."

"No one dresses like this in the West. If any scout rode out into the hills this way—" I plucked at the flowery vest— "like some kind of prancing peacock, he'd never make it half a mile. He'd be shot full of Sioux arrows before he could say boo."

"I don't doubt your... expertise," Josephine said while the can-can girls passed us in a herd and the false Indian chief shook out the feathers of his bonnet. "But our audiences haven't come to see a real scout of the Black Hills. They've come for a fantasy, Jane, and you must deliver it."

"I can't deliver much, standing about like I mislaid my wits and letting them jeer at me. Let me shoot a pistol if you want me to put on a good show. I shot on stages like this one before."

Josephine shook her head. "We would never obtain permission for such a thing here, in the theaters—in a city."

"Then you won't make good money off me. I ain't interesting to no one, standing there holding a rifle and shuffling my feet."

"The spectators have already paid their fee by the time they've taken their seats. It matters very little, whether they love your or hate you."

"Buffalo Bill could double his tickets sold if the audience loved me—if they told their friends to come down and see the famous Calamity Jane in the flesh. Why don't we give them something to talk about, Miss Brake? I can do much more than kick up my legs like those can-can girls. I can give your audience a spectacle they never seen before, and ain't like to see again. Think of the money to be made. I'm wasted, standing like a fence post. And Cody's money is wasted, too."

Josephine sighed. "You make a compelling argument. I will speak to Mr. Cody the first chance I get, but I must caution you, Jane: don't expect a miracle. Mr. Cody has been running the most successful Wild West show in the United States for years now. He knows the business well. Now, don't frown. I will present your case to him—you have my word on that count. You should come back to the hotel with me. You've an evening performance ahead. You must take your rest while you can."

Josephine Brake was a damned prickly bitch, but she was as good as her word. I endured only three more days at the Star Theater. Then, without the least warning, Buffalo Bill's Wild West Show up and transported itself to the outer limits of Minneapolis. Cody had leased a disused hay field not far from the train depot and had it mowed down; when I arrived with the rest of his performers (all of us climbing dazed and wide-eyed from our carriages to look upon our new venue) I found a crew of builders erecting a grand outdoor stage, complete with long red curtains shielding the wings from view and a fancy painted backdrop, all made up with cactuses and buttes under a sunset sky. Rows of empty benches waited for that night's audience to arrive. The smell of fresh-cut grass hung over the field.

To the right of the new stage I found an arena all my own: a trick-riding circuit marked out with stakes and simple cloth flags, and a stack of straw bales to catch my bullets. The workers had raised a fancy painted sign between two poles:

THE AUTHENTIC
CALAMITY JANE
MOST BRAZEN GUN OF THE WEST

The sign put me so much in mind of the old hotel back in Billings—and of Clinton Burke's kindly ways—that a great lump came to my throat and for a moment I could not speak. I could only swallow, blinking back tears of gratitude or nostalgia; I knew not which.

"Well," I said at length, turning to Josephine.

"Mr. Cody took your suggestion to heart, Jane. I suspect he wishes to recoup your advance as quickly as possible."

I thought that might mean Cody was somewhat less than pleased with my performance, but now that I could ride and shoot for him, I felt certain he'd come to regard me as a wise investment.

"I'll need a pistol," I said. "Two would be better. And I'll need a few hours to practice. Can't shoot straight with an unfamiliar gun."

"Lucy has a selection of pistols. You may choose any that appeal to you. And Mr. Cody has procured a few horses and saddles. They're waiting behind the stage—the horses and Lucy, alike. You'll find army tents back there, as well, serving as your new costuming rooms. Not as comfortable or convenient as the Star Theater, alas—but if you can double Mr. Cody's ticket sales, I believe both he and the other performers will forgive you for taking them away from the Star."

"I didn't intend to put anyone out," I said quietly. "Are they cross with me now—the can-can girls and the Indian chief?"

"No one wishes to abandon the luxury of a theater for a field, Jane. But we are all here for the same reason: to earn money. The more, the better. Now you had best go and choose your pistols. Tonight's show begins in four hours."

The pistols proved serviceable enough, though nowhere near as dandy as the two guns I had loved and lost so many years before. As for the horses, Cody had procured sweet-tempered old nags, but as trick-riding ponies they left much to be desired. In the end, I settled on a fat pinto with a flashy coat but lazy bones. The pinto was grudging and slow, but I could coax him to rear up on his hind legs when the occasion called for it, and I could make him lope around my shooting circuit if I kicked him with sufficient insistence. He would have to do for the time being, but I resolved to ask Cody for a younger, more spirited mount—one freshly broke to the saddle so's I could train it proper, for my special purpose. I reasoned if I impressed Cody's audiences enough—and made good on my boast to double his sales—then I could ask for damn near anything I pleased, and expect to get it, too.

Just before our first outdoor audience arrived, I rode one last circuit on my sluggish pinto, pinging tin cans off their posts. I reined in beneath my sign and made my resentful mount rise up on his hind legs to the applause of the can-can dancers, who had gathered to watch me rehearse.

"The show will never be the same," one of the girls declared.

Another admitted, "We were all sore when we learned we must to perform outdoors from now on. But it's plain to see we'll make more money this way."

"We're glad you've come, Calamity Jane—or whoever you are."

WELL, I guess I don't need to tell you that the first outdoor performance was a success. Minneapolis buzzed like nest of bees; every paper proclaimed that the great girl-hero of the West had come, and our rented field filled with such large and eager audiences that Cody set his workers to building more benches to accommodate the crowds. I earned back my advance in six short weeks, and began sending money to the convent school for Jessie's care and necessities. I was far from my daughter and missed her more terribly with each passing day, but I felt like a proper mother at last, for the first time since Jessie's birth. I had some hope of giving her the life she deserved—a life of comfort and safety. It had been too long coming, but the hour was finally at hand.

I toured with Buffalo Bill's Wild West Show for the better part of two years. We went from Minneapolis to Philadelphia, from

Chicago to Atlanta and every city in between. My shooting demonstrations drew bigger crowds in each new town, but I never grew used to the life, despite my hope and my fierce determination.

To tell you the truth, the Wild West Show weighed heavier on my heart with each passing day—as did the cities themselves. I longed for the open plains and the quiet red shadows of slot canyons so desperately that a permanent cloud of melancholy settled over my heart. Whiskey would have alleviated my sorrow, to be sure, but the thought of my girl in her fancy school—safe, well fed, and warm; getting smarter every day—kept me from my vice. But without the whiskey to bolster me, I grew pensive and heartsick. Josephine had instructed me to give our audiences the fantasy they craved. Meanwhile, I longed for the real West, not Bill Cody's fanciful construction of outrageous lies. I missed the singing of wind through prairie grasses, the creak of saddle leather on a lonesome trail. I missed the larks rising in the morning, and the slope of a mountain foothill blue with lupine flowers, and buffalo herds blackening the horizon between two widely separated buttes of ochre-red. I missed the stars. You never know how small and insignificant a body can feel till you look up at the night sky and find nothing looking back at you—nothing but black like an unwritten slate, unrelieved emptiness, the jewels of Nature Herself dimmed to insignificance by the thousand clamoring lights of a city.

The dime novelists had done their work, and no mistake: I was the biggest draw Buffalo Bill had ever exhibited. Cody made a generous profit from my appearances, but he was always fair in giving me my cut (delivered via Josephine, who skimmed her due share off the top, I dare say.) By the time we reached Chicago, I reasoned I ought to profit from my own name at least as much as Cody did. During our long engagement in Illinois's greatest city, I asked Josephine to locate a writer-for-hire. I met with that fellow every morning in a little café, and I paid for his cups of coffee and poured my tales into his ear, just as I'm doing to you now. His pen moved as fast as I could talk. Long before the Wild West Show was set to depart from Chicago, he presented me with a manuscript, some fifty pages long: my life and adventures, recounted in my own words. Well—they was more or less my own words. That writer-fella was far more eloquent than I ever could be. I hope you're half as good as he is, Short Pants.

I took that manuscript to a printer; had two hundred and fifty copies made. The biography was a type of insurance, you see— something to cushion my fall if the Wild West Show ever folded, or if Bill Cody grew tired of me. Something to fall back on, should the whiskey begin calling again, too strong to resist—or if I found I could no longer live without stars in the night-time sky. I could sell the biographies myself and keep every penny. After all, it was my own story. Why should anyone else profit from my life?

You've heard my story thus far. You know that most of what I told that Chicago writer was a pack of lies. I told him I was the hero of half a dozen scouting parties. I saved the life of a general, a colonel, a runaway stagecoach full of women and children. I told him I could ride for miles standing up in the saddle and light a cigar at full motion. I had rescued men from wild cats and made peace with Indians and I was the beloved daughter of two good and caring people.

And I told him Wild Bill Hickock had loved me. That Bill's heart and mine beat as one.

I still hoped I could make it so. I still hoped I could make myself believe, if only I repeated the tale often enough.

As the months dragged on—as Cody hauled his spectacle from one city to the next—the show routine wearied me ever more. I found it harder to rouse myself from my bed with each passing morning. The pains of whiskey sickness had long since left me in peace, but the slow, dreary dullness that replaced them felt somehow harder to bear.

The other performers was jolly company (the lively can-can girls in particular) and they had all taken a shine to me, for true to my promise, I had doubled the size of our crowds and the money poured in, steady and strong as a springtime river. I missed Jessie, of course, but it wasn't loneliness that plagued me and made me long for the quiet seclusion of my hotel room. What pained me most was the falsity of what we did—the can-can girls, the Indian chief, Buffalo Bill himself. And me. Oh, we gave our audiences exactly what they'd come seeking. In no time a-tall, I was a plum expert in portraying the Hellcat in Leather Britches; I could shout and whoop and fire my pistol good enough to bring an audience to its feet. But every night when the show was finished, and we gathered in Lucy's tent to strip away our false pretenses, my heart weighed so heavy, I half expected it to trip me right off my feet.

None of us bore the least resemblance to the West—the real West as I had known it, the land I fell in love with under skies swept with purple cloud. In fact, I will confide this truth in you: aside from Cody, who had honestly been a scout for a spell during the Indian Wars, I was the only performer who had ventured farther west than Kansas. The rest of the cast all hailed from the riverlands, the valleys of the Mississippi and the broad brown Ohio. And one of the dancing girls came from Carolina, if I rightly recall. Together, we was nothing more than a dime novel brought to jarring life, all loud music and bright color—our carefully practiced steps, our scripted words. Even my horses was fat with grain, having never run free on the open prairie.

And, Short Pants—I know you've set here beside me, at this Deadwood bar, and listened while I admitted to the hundred lies I told throughout my shameful life. You know by now that dishonesty don't agonize me especially, under ordinary circumstances (if any of my circumstances can be called ordinary.) But when it came to the West I portrayed, that routine of practiced falsehood pained me something awful. For since that day when (at a soft and tender age) I had fallen in love with Bill Hickock, he and the West were the same to me. They had been the same all along; I still feel the West as it once was, fighting against the confines of my heart, just as the ache of Bill's death strikes me in the center of my chest and floods me with trembling and tears, a dozen times a day or more. Each time I rode to my triumphant finish and reared my horse back on its hind legs, and brandished my pistols above my head with a hearty cry, I felt as if I danced upon Wild Bill's grave —made a joke of his memory, and all for the sake of a little pay. I needed that pay bad enough that I couldn't stop. But I didn't know whether I could go on living with myself for the dishonor I'd brought to Bill's memory.

I can see the doubt in your eyes. I know you didn't believe me when I told you I stayed dead sober that whole time, almost two full years. Not one drop of liquor passed my lips, for I believed the steely-eyed Josephine when she told me neither she nor Cody would tolerate whooping up. I knew drinking and carrying on would only strip me of my place and my income, and then my Jessie would suffer, just when I had finally found my way to a proper sort of motherhood and provided that precious child with everything she needed. So I guarded myself against the Devil Whiskey, kept myself away from his sweet and comforting grip, no matter how desperately I longed for an escape, no matter how powerful the sickness struck me—that deep and wretched craving. I never knew I had the strength to truly defy Whiskey's command, but I found the strength inside me, out there on the show circuit. Fortitude was the one good thing the Wild West Show gave me—though still I believe that I could have kept going much longer, and made far more money for Jessie's education, if Josephine hadn't been so hard, if I'd been allowed to wet my lips now and then.

Whiskey aside, I did long for some small portion of whoop-up. My wild cries and boasts before a paying audience couldn't bring the same rush of relief I found back West, where I was untethered, where I was free. Wors't, there was moments (just after waking, when the fog of sleep and half-remembered dreams still hung gray and thick inside my mind) when I couldn't recall who was the real, the One and Only, the Authentic Calamity Jane and who was the invention of the novelists, scratching out tall tales for their pay, just as desperate to keep a crust of bread on their tables as I was. I had worn the mask of the Frontier Belle for so many months, I could no longer say when I had taken it off and when I had donned it. Many a night have I set here at this very bar, on this exact seat, and listened to the women around me confide to one another, *I come all this way to find myself.* There was a time when I would have laughed at such foolishness. Who mislays her own self? Was a time when such a thing would have seemed impossible to me. But that was precisely how I felt then, at the tail end of my tenure with Buffalo Bill's Wild West Show. My very identity up and ran away, and the faster I chased her, the easier she found it to slip beyond my reach.

I don't know how I cooked up the damned-fool idea that came to me in Kansas City. I had picked up another novel about Calamity Jane back in Nashville (I never broke myself of the ill-advised habit of reading about my own alleged exploits) and I read that scurrilous trash on the train ride from one city to another. I can't recall the title of that book. It might have been *The Girl Scout's Great Triumph* or *The Rival Indian Slayers of Redwood Canyon.* I guess it don't make a lick of difference which one it was. But that particular book showed me as a fearless tamer of wild horses, even though I was a willow-slim girl. I trained my share of horses and mules, as you know, Short Pants. But never in my life had I tamed a wild mustang.

At first, I found the story amusing. I even chuckled over it in the close, stinking heat of the train car, and I was grateful to have my spirits lifted after so long and trying a spell. But that accursed story worked its way under my skin, just like a cactus spine or a porcupine quill, and all too soon, I found I couldn't let the idea alone—the sharp pain of a relentless goading, the drive to bring that vivid yellow tale to life.

By the time we reached Kansas City, I was fair consumed with the idea of riding a wild horse—taming its fearsome spirit, bringing it to heel. Maybe I felt the show had tamed me—broken my wildness, stripped away my liberty—but if I could pass along the favor to another creature, the strictures that bound my heart would lift, and I would be free and wild again. Or maybe it was just a lack of whiskey that addled my wits. All I know for certain was that my sleep was restless, haunted by dreams of bucking horses with me atop them, setting easy in the saddle, riding like I was born to the task. And the words I'd read about myself—lies, every one—colored the landscape of my dreams.

That was how I found myself (one starless night, after three back-to-back runs of our show) leaning on the top rail of the makeshift corral, watching my horses milling in the darkness. Cody had recently procured for me two new mounts, both young and fresh as new-sprouted grass. He said he wanted to see a little more pep in my rides, more drama and danger—and I told him I had to have horses trained special for the work if he wanted a real dandy of a show. No one had so much as saddled the two new ponies yet. They was skittish, mistrustful; I could see the big sorrel filly with a bald face and blue eyes staring at me above the backs of her lazier, more jaded herd-mates.

I though, *She's the one.*

I was tired that night, as I was every night. I wasn't right in the head. The desire to be what I claimed to be—what all the stories said I had been all along—came upon me so powerfully that I let go of all common sense (what little I'd possessed in the first place.) The rest of the performers busied themselves in the costuming tent, shaking out their cloaks of camouflage, donning their real and true selves. I still wore my beaded trousers and the jacket with the buckskin fringe. I could still feel the grease from my polished gun slick across't my palm, still felt its cold weight in my hand. And I could hear the audience clapping for me, shouting my name, though I knew the field was silent and empty around me.

I fixed my stare on that bald-faced sorrel filly. She stared back at me and switched her tail and gave a low grunt that sounded like a mountain lion's growl. And I knew I must prove to myself that very night the one thing I still felt I had failed to prove to the whole damn world: that I was Calamity.

The can-can girls and the French trapper and Lucy the costumer, and Josephine and Bill Cody—all would emerge from the lamp-lit tent any minute. Time for proving was woefully short. I slipped between the rails of the corral and took my lasso from a fence post. I walked after the herd, talking low and sweet while they shied and trotted away, till finally they settled around me and even the unbroke sorrel deigned to come near. It was a simple thing, to slide my rope gently over her head and lead her to the fence.

Saddling that filly didn't come near as easy. She tensed and snorted and kicked out with her hind feet, first one, then the other, warning me that that she wouldn't cooperate like the lazy pinto I most often rode. But I kept up my sweet talk and moved slow as molasses on a cold day, and by and by I buckled the cinch around her belly.

She wouldn't accept a bridle—not yet—so I twisted the rope into a halter of sorts. Then I led my new mount to the center of the corral and I leaped up into the saddle, sudden and sure, before the sorrel could crow-hop away from me.

I guess by the look of you that you ain't never rode a bucking bronc. Don't take it for an insult, Short Pants; tenderfeet seldom have occasion to launch themselves onto the back of a furious wild animal. How can I describe the sensation to a fella who has never felt it for himself? Hell, even I hadn't the least idea what to expect, for those dime novels had made the whole business sound simple—downright romantical. Calamity Jane, She-Scout of the

Great Frontier, setting her saddle with ease while the horse bucked and kicked beneath her. She laughed as her dark tresses swayed in the dusty breeze. And when her horse had tired itself and landed on all four feet, she swung down from the saddle and patted its neck, and kissed its velvet nose, and the horse lost its heart to the girl beauty, and followed her loyal as a puppy from that day on.

If only it had been so easy. The sorrel filly surged beneath me, springing high into the air. I felt the weight of the earth drag at my back; I grabbed white-knuckled for my saddle horn and clamped my legs around the filly's sides. I'd been riding all my life; I was as strong as I was ugly. But still I slid backward in that terrible moment, when the horse shot up from solid ground faster and more powerful than the firing of a cannonball. Then she reached the peak of her arc and she flung both heels out behind. I jolted forward; my nose collided with the crest of her neck and my vision flashed from the dark of night to a blinding white pain. I came down hard in the saddle; my feet left the stirrups; the violence of the moment knocked the breath from my body. All I could do was cling to the horn in terror. I had long since dropped the rope; it dragged under the filly's feet, and I prayed in dazed terror that she wouldn't step on it and flip end-over-end, crushing me in the dirt.

The filly rose in another raging leap and kicked out again; once more I was flung and battered like a rag doll. The muscles in my legs and arms went weak and trembly. I could feel my heart racing in my throat, choking off my breath. Seconds had passed, yet it seemed to me I had never done a thing in my life but hold in desperate fear to that saddle while the horse kicked and whirled and screamed beneath me. Nothing had ever frightened me so completely—not even facing down Wild Bill's killer in that butcher shop in Deadwood.

Well, I can't say to this day whether the horse threw me on its third leap, or whether I jumped, finding the hard ground a friendlier prospect than the wild upheaval of my saddle. As I sailed through the darkness, time paused expressly for me, giving me ample chance to examine all the foolish feats of a long and exceptionally idiotic life. Then I hit the ground. Pain crashed in upon me. I *heard* the pain, ringing high and sharp like the cymbals in Cody's band, punctuating my failure. The pain was particularly fierce in my neck and shoulder. I lay as still as I could manage, thinking myself killed (or near enough as made no real difference.) The sorrel filly's hooves thundered around my breakable body. I could hear her blowing and grunting, cursing me in the language of the mustang.

Then I heard the can-can girls shouting, "Jane! Jane, are you killed?" and folks running from the direction of the costumer's tent. A minute later, there they all stood around me, my fellow performers and Josephine Brake and even Cody himself, who snapped at the Indian Chief to bring a lantern so's he could see my face.

Cody bent over me. The night was dark, but I could see him clear as midday, for either my terror or his anger had turned the whole scene bright and significant.

"God's sake, Jane," Cody said, speaking through his extravagant mustache. "What fool thing have you gone and done?"

Josephine crouched on her heels beside him. "Her nose is bleeding badly. She must have broken it." She reached out and took me by the shoulder as if to shake me out of my stupefaction, but the moment she touched me, I cried out with renewed pain.

"Don't move," Cody said.

The Indian Chief had arrived with a lantern. Cody brought it close to my face; it blinded me with searing yellow light. I squeezed my eyes shut and tried my damndest not to whimper, but I was dreadful afraid I had broken my neck and wouldn't be no good to anybody no more.

"It's her collarbone," Cody finally said. "Look here; you can see how it's all popped up under her shirt."

The can-can girls made tiny sounds of faintness and disgust.

"Has the bone punched through the skin?" Cody said.

Josephine soothed me with a murmur, then unbuttoned my embroidered shirt, doing her best not to touch the fracture. I squeezed my eyes tighter still, fearing what Josephine would say. But a moment later she sighed in relief. "No, not through the skin —thank God. But it looks a dreadful break, all the same."

I hadn't killed myself after all, but my injury was terrible enough that I couldn't perform for six weeks while the fracture healed. Cody was sore as Hell. The moment I was installed in my hotel bed (left arm freshly tied up in a sling by the doctor Cody sent to me, plugs of cotton stuffed up my nose to stop the bleeding) Cody gave me a lecture for my get-well-soon present, delivered by Josephine Brake. She, after all, was his agent—designated to speak on his behalf. I had no choice but to set up against my headboard, blushing and shame-faced, listening while Josephine excoriated me for my foolishness. I dare say I deserved every word of that vicious chewing-out, for I had been the star attraction for many a month now. Without me, ticket sales would surely dwindle, and every member of the cast and crew would suffer.

The six weeks of my convalescence proved a dreadful trial. Even after I'd begun to feel somewhat stronger and had learned how to take the pain, Josephine seldom let me out of my bed. I did grow a mite better at reading during those miserable weeks, for I hadn't any other means to while away the hours. But I never touched a novel about Calamity Jane again.

One day, though—it was at least a month after my mishap with the sorrel filly—Josephine was called away to attend to more business on Cody's behalf. I was in the finest fettle that could be expected, all things considered, so I left my bed and peeked out the window, watching Josephine climb into a carriage and trundle away up the streets of Kansas City. The rest of the performers had gone, readying for the evening show. I strolled out of my hotel room, nonchalant as you please despite my bound-up arm, determined to stretch my legs and relieve my boredom for a few minutes. Then I would hasten back to my bed before Josephine could learn of my deception.

I descended the stairs on legs grown weak from inactivity and sauntered into the hotel's bar. I had no intention of drinking—I would only carry the deception so far. I wanted nothing more than to look at something other than the walls of my room (for I had counted every gilded fleur-de-lis on the paper by then) and hear a human voice that didn't belong to the stodgy Miss Josephine Brake.

Oh, Short Pants. To this day, I regret that decision. I wish I had never gone to that bar; bitterly do I regret my plan to leave the room a-tall. For I walked right in to a scene that cut me to my heart. A young man with a very inadequate mustache had climbed up onto the bar-top. He held forth to a crowd of laughing, jeering Missourians—city folk, to a one. The man on the bar wore a wig of long, braided locks, somewhat resembling the head of a mop but stained black with coal dust. He had painted two bright-pink circles on his cheeks in imitation of a girl's rosy complexion, and had drawn the long spikes of false lashes around his eyes. And he had decked himself out in a fringed jacket and beaded trousers, and held a rifle across his chest, and he fluttered his eyelids and spoke in a high, straining voice while he pranced to and fro down the length of the bar.

"It's I," he said, "the one and only Calamity Jane, the Beauty of the West, the Brave Girl Scout of the Untamed Plains!"

The men in that bar hooted and laughed and shouted up at him, urging him on.

"You aren't any kind of beauty," somebody hollered. "Why, I saw you last month at the Wild West Show. You are just about the ugliest cow of a woman I've ever seen!"

I turned on my heel and left that bar. I shut myself in the confines of my room and I wept for hours, till Josephine returned. I ain't ashamed to tell you that, Short Pants—that I cried the bitterest tears of my life, sobbing till I could scarce catch my breath, weeping till my stomach turned sick with my unrelieved sorrow.

I didn't weep because those men had mocked me. Goodness knows, I heard such insultations plenty times before. What broke my heart that day—what sullied my very spirit—was knowing that those men believed the West, my home country, the land I loved, was a thing to be laughed at and dismissed. A place inferior, a joke to be played, a picture to be viewed like a postcard, then tucked away again and forgotten while the real world—the city world—went on turning.

And as I sniffled and choked and waited for Josephine to return, I wondered if it really was so. I couldn't shake a sinking certainty that Braddick's prediction had come to pass. The West was dead. I had helped kill it by taking up with Bill Cody—by selling the life I loved to a crowd that jeered and then departed.

SOMETIMES I POP OVER A ROUGH, JEST TO KEEP MY HAND IN

THE NEXT WINTER CAME, SO HARSH AND DEEP WITH SNOW THAT Buffalo Bill's Wild West Show was obliged to halt its travels. Calamity Jane had become essential to Cody's profits; the man could no longer justify his show without my riding and trick-shooting (those six weeks I spent penned up in my room with one arm in a sling proved trying weeks for us all.) With every city buried under winter, there wasn't no sense in continuing through the darkest and coldest months of the year, for I couldn't ride like a wild thing in knee-deep snow, even if the audiences would deign to sit shivering in a field or a train yard watching me shoot and holler.

Happily, the work we did in milder seasons set us up proper. Each of us declared ourselves fit to make it through the winter—and none fitter than Cody, whose coffers had grown fat since I took up with his spectacle. The lot of us parted ways in Minneapolis, the very place where I had joined—the Indian Chief and the Fur Trapper shaking my hand, the can-can girls kissing my cheek, each of them teary-eyed over parting.

"Swear you'll come back to us in the spring," one of the dancers said. "It wouldn't be the same show without you."

I gave my promise, but I knew I spoke a lie. I was already itching to climb aboard my train and put the grand cities of the East at my back—forever, if fate would allow. I yearned for my own world—the real West—wors't than any hunger that had afflicted me as a child. The falsehood I made alongside Bill Cody, the bright and musical lie of the Wild West tamed and trotted out upon a stage... that was a poor imitation at the best of times. Certainly, Cody's show couldn't fill the void inside my heart, nor fool me into believing I had found the place where I belonged.

So I boarded that train with a trunk stuffed full of my books (the biographies of Calamity I had printed, as my surety against poverty.) I waved to the can-can girls and nodded my thanks to Cody and Josephine Brake, who stood frowning up at me from the platform. And as the train began to roll westward, carrying me home towards Deadwood, I settled in my seat with the longest sigh I ever breathed, and I promised myself I would never do such folly again. If I was careful with the money I had made, and diligent in selling my trunkful of books, I would have no further need for the Wild West Show in any case.

I WOULD ASK you to pour another whiskey, Short Pants, for now I've come to the last stretch of my sorry tale, the place where the road of my history bends sharp and sudden toward shame. But I swear you look as if you can't take another drop—and anyway, more whiskey now, at this dark juncture, would only redouble my misery. If I was still the type who could pray—the type who could hold some belief in a Grand Overseer—I'd wish you was a priest in a confessional. That seems a fitting man to hear the remainder of my story. But you ain't a priest. You're another writer come seeking my history. Like the dozen that came before you.

The hundred, the thousand.

Fuck it, Short Pants. Fill up the glass. What's one more drink in the final reckoning?

———

THE TRAIN CARRIED me toward Deadwood, but when it pulled into the familiar station and stopped at the platform with a shudder and a hiss of steam, I couldn't make myself rise from my seat. Despite my resolve to never again pedal the false flash of a fictitious West, I found I hadn't left that sinking guilt and self-loathing in Minneapolis after all. Regret had followed me all down the tracks, mile after snow-muffled mile. It gnawed at my conscience all the worse as the Black Hills appeared on the horizon, advancing in their pale winter shrouds till they stood gathered all around the tracks—around me—watching in silent judgment. I took one look at Deadwood out the window of my train car. Bigger than when I'd seen it last, growing like a child in sudden leaps—unexpected stretching toward a grim and inevitable maturity. The streets was boggy and slick with mud; deep snow lay heaped against the sides of buildings and the snow was crusted with grime like the coal dust of the cities, the ever-present filth. And though the snow was deep and the roads a morass, still the sidewalks of Deadwood hummed with activity. Men and women hurrying about their business. Men and women cultivating the place, nurturing it, tending to its growth.

I wanted no part of Deadwood. Not that day. Too many women wore the flounces and bustles of Josephine Brake. Too many fellas had grown out their mustaches in exactly the same style as Bill Cody's. The town was still small, but it wouldn't remain so for much longer. So I reached into my little beaded purse and extracted enough coins to carry me farther—into the heart of the West. All the way to the end of the line, wherever that end may be.

That's how I found myself in Gilt Edge, Montana that particularly cold and lonesome winter. Gilt Edge was a town like the ones I had known in my younger days: not much more than a hardgoods store and a couple of watering holes, one or two shabby boarding houses and a livery. It was sunk deep, like a post-hole or a prairie dog's burrow, straight down in the flatness of the prairie. Blue granite crags reared up to the west of town, sheltering and sharp. The mountains put me in mind of the palisade at Cuny and Coffey's. Of a certainty, between the mountains to the west and the abandoned prairie to the east, I couldn't see the rest of the world from Gilt Edge. The arch of the sky was interrupted, spilling from the teeth of the mountains, and no dark smut of city or industry fouled the broad sweep of grassland. Privately, I declared Gilt Edge the most perfect roost an old hen like me could hope for; straight away I found myself a room to let and I went about the business of settling in for the winter.

My first order of business was to write a letter to Josephine Brake. *I can't do it no more*, I said. *The show life ain't for me. Tell all the can-can girls and the rest of my friends I'm awful sorry to let them down. But Mr. Cody can hire some other woman to be his Calamity Jane. It won't make no difference to the crowd, and if they find a pretty girl to take my place, the audience will pay even more to watch her strut and holler.*

The money I made from Bill Cody kept me in comfort all winter long. My room was spacious, boasting of a feather bed—not as fine or well-made as the beds I'd enjoyed in the cities Back East, but a damn sight finer than any other bed in Gilt Edge. I would have wagered every penny I had on that. The boarding house was elegant and gracious, considering it stood at the end of an insignificant rail line in the middle of nowhere. Gilt Edge was a small enough place that I convinced myself for a good many weeks that my money would never dry up. I treated myself to such extravagances as I had never known before. I had a fancy suit made by the local seamstress—a proper woman's suit with a brocade skirt and a matching jacket, even prettier than the green dress I had worn at Madam Robair's place. What in God's name I thought to do with that suit is beyond my powers to comprehend. There wasn't no society to speak of in Gilt Edge, and if there was, it's a sure bet I would never have found myself on the receiving end of any gracious invitations. Guess I hankered after something pretty. I had lived a life of sore deprivation, but there was no reason to deny myself any longer. When the seamstress finished her work, I donned that new suit and stared at myself in the mirror. Martha Canary, arrayed in wine-red brocade, tucked and trimmed and looking as much like a lady as she ever was like to seem. I found if I held my back very straight and lifted my chin, I came perilous-close to looking like a respectable woman. I thought, *If Wild Bill had seen me this way, maybe my life wouldn't have been so hopeless.*

I had a picture made in that dress, standing straight and proud —but I only made one copy. I couldn't sell that image, you see. No tenderfoot would have parted with his money for the Beautiful White Devil of the Yellowstone looking decidedly un-devilish. No, it was not a picture of Calamity Jane. It was Martha Canary— me, given back to myself, returned to my own keeping and transformed at last into the woman I had always longed to be.

This story would be grim enough if my carelessness went no farther than my purse. But I'm afraid my attitude toward liquor— so strictly minded during the Cody days—loosened every bit as fast. For all I appreciated Gilt Edge's smallness and seclusion, still the weight of my lonesome heart began to drag at me within a few short weeks of my arrival.

Maybe it was more than lonesomeness, too. Maybe something yet more dire drove me back towards the whiskey. Day and night, dreaming and waking, my knowledge of the cities was a torment. That first startled sight of Minneapolis had burned itself into my memory, still smoking and stinking like a fresh brand on a panicked steer's hide. Nothing would allow me to forget it: the red, luminous sprawl of the city bleeding like a stain across the night. The lamps uncountable, more numerous than stars. A wound in the flesh of the prairie—a wound that wept and spread its infection, the human crowd increasing, the herd breeding and multiplying, the wide-open spaces crumbling little by little, falling to the encroachment of mankind.

And all those people in Minneapolis, in Boston, in Atlanta, in all the countless towns between—all hungering for the West, eager to see the land yet none of them knowing the land, none of them caring to learn the truth I knew. My world, my life, was naught but a fantasy to those countless crowds. A park through which to stroll; a wilderness to convert and tame, to bend to a city-man's will. I could see plainly what was coming. I knew what would be lost and forgotten, replaced by the costume of legend. I couldn't bear a future I had no power to change.

By the time the new year came—1899—I was back on the drink, hard as I had ever been before. In fact, I believe I may have fallen harder for the whiskey this time. I ain't proud of it now, looking back—nor was I proud of it then. A powerful shame consumed me, whether I was drunk or sober; even my dreams rebuked me, and if I couldn't remember the details of my nightmares, invariably I woke heavy and hot with embarrassment, and swearing another futile oath never to look at a bottle of whiskey again.

But in dreams—or in the moments just after waking, when my heart raced and the sweat soaked through my night-dress to dampen my feather bed—I could see the cities on the march, too. I could feel the reach of their long and countless arms. The nearness of those grasping hands frightened me. Whenever I shut my eyes, I saw the barrier around Wild Bill's grave, set in place to ward away the trampling masses. And I knew that even in death, we would be confined—fenced in.

In all my long and sordid life, never had I known what to do with fear or anguish, except to try to drown them both in liquor. But that's the trouble, I suppose. You can't hold yourself under long enough to do the job—long enough to make your fear succumb. Anguish is a resilient foe. It bobs to the surface the moment you release your grip, the second you let down your guard. And there it is again, where you can't ignore it: taunting you, patient as it always is, knowing you will try again to put your pain in its place.

You will try again, and you will fail.

There ain't no sense dwelling overmuch on Gilt Edge. They wasn't the proudest months of my life. I'd rather forget that whole winter, if I could—and the year that went before—but those lonesome stretches of time stick in my memory and repeat endlessly in my idle moments. Of late, I've had nothing but idle moments. Bitterly do I wish the past would leave me be.

Well, once the whiskey took hold of me again, I knew it was for keeps this time. That sly devil wouldn't let go, now that I had returned so willingly to its arms. And because I knew myself lost for good, I abandoned myself to the whiskey's cruelty; with hard and deliberate intent, I committed myself to its cause. I was a lost soul and I knew it. The West and me, we both was lost. But if Calamity Jane was destined to remain forever a half-truth, a legend (like the land in which she had dwelt) then at least I intended to have all the fun that legend would allow. I had done well enough with Cody's show—that much was true. But in the grand scheme, I had profited precious little from my own name. I reckoned I might as well wring some enjoyment from my identity while I still had enough wits and vitality to enjoy a wild time.

My God, Short Pants—if I could but describe the endless mischief I pursued in Gilt Edge! All the feats of reckless abandon, the delirious nights when I danced to the frantic cheer of a desperate piano. And the men I took to my bed, faceless and numberless in memory. The boasts, the lies, saloon lights blazing against encroaching dark. In my despair and folly, I gambled away some of Jessie's money, a sin for which I have longed to be damned as I deserve. But so far, divine justice hasn't caught up with me. I'm convinced by now that it never will. I drank to excess almost every night; I cussed where children could hear. I even fought, now and then—rough whores like the girl I used to be, and a few men who insulted me because of my looks, or who dared to scoff at the legend of my name.

Worst of all was one night early in the springtime, a night which smelled of honey and flowers for the first time since winter's passing. Intoxicated on the praise and goading of strangers (and on plain, dependable whiskey, or course) I rode through the streets of Gilt Edge on a borrowed horse, hollering at the top of my voice, brandishing my pistol to the cheers of a drunken crowd. I shot up the swinging sign of the Red Dog Saloon till it flipped end over end and wrapped itself in its own chains. I could have killed an innocent bystander with such reckless tomfoolery. Mercifully, no one was hurt—and I raised no objection when the sheriff locked me up for three days.

Disorderly conduct. Public drunkenness. I deserved it. I served my time.

And there was another night, Short Pants—one I can't forget. I stepped into my favorite tavern, the Flying Moon, itching for a game of faro to take my mind off my ghosts. Even an hour of peaceable distraction would have seemed a mercy just then. But the moment I entered the Flying Moon, my eyes went up to the bar—to the plaster wall behind it.

Tacked up there, high above the heads of patrons and revelers, I found a pair of my own bloomers. I can't tell you how or when I lost them, but I'm dead certain they was mine; I recognized the green silk ribbons at the cuffs.

No one noticed me when I entered the Flying Moon that night. All the fellas who had once drunk beside me or joined me in hands of faro now waited in a line, intent on the bar and what was nailed up there above it. I huddled beside the tavern door, watching as all those boys, every last one, paid a penny each to hop up on the bar and touch the cuff of my pants. For luck, they all said. And they laughed—every one.

I never returned to the Flying Moon again.

NOT LONG AFTER the incident with my stolen bloomers, I received a letter. Someone—the mistress of my boarding house or one of her maids—pushed it under my door, so I almost trod upon it when I made ready to leave my humble home and set out for the day's drinking.

I picked up the letter and settled with it on the edge of my bed. Caution sank like a brick of half-dried mud in my stomach. Instinctive dread squeezed my throat. The outside of the folio read: *Lena Bourner.*

Dear God, I thought, both sour and fearful, *whatever now?*

I broke the seal on the folio and read that letter slowly by the window, in the soft silvery light of a frosty morning.

Martha,

the letter began. No Dear Sister—just Martha.

Imagine my surprise to learn that you have a daughter. How do I know this? Because the headmistress of Jessie's school in Sturgis has written to me, seeking to collect on money owed for your daughter's room, board, and education. While I am pleased to hear that you have tried to give your child a proper upbringing—and relieved that she does not reside with you—I am not best pleased to be the one who must be held responsible for her bills.

Because Jessie is my blood—albeit a stranger to me—John and I have brought your accounts at Jessie's school up to balance. I implore you to

do the right thing and reimburse me for the cost. I have several children
of my own now and cannot spare a penny. I suspect, however, that you
never will return what I have paid. You must do the right thing and
support your daughter as is fitting for a mother. To be a proper mother
now is the only righteous thing you may do.

God alone knows how that school found me, and how they discerned
that I am your relation. I pray no one else knows.

Lena Bourner

I set for a long time beside the window, reading Lena's letter
over again, darkly musing on my sister's words. Lena was right,
and I knew it. Admitting her rightness stung, but no matter how
long I remained beside that window, staring out at the dismal
town while my breath frosted the pane, the sting of Lena's
righteousness never diminished. How had I forgotten to pay
Jessie's accounts? I asked myself that question a hundred times
at least, but I never discovered the answer. No, that ain't true; I
knew the answer all along. I hardly need to admit the truth to
you, for you understand already, don't you? After a long spell of
loathsome despair, I searched my purse and my travel trunk, but
I had no money left to repay Lena, and nothing to send on to
the convent school to keep Jessie's accounts from drying up
again.

Then what's to be done? I asked myself. I knew Lena was right; I
must behave like a proper mother now, setting aside my own pain,
sacrificing for my child. A headache had begun to pound behind
my eyes and the craving for liquor was mounting. But I kept
myself in that room, taking stock of my severely depleted
resources, examining each of my few remaining options.

I might pull Jessie out of Sturgis, I finally decided, and return
with her to Deadwood. That town drew enough tenderfeet that I
could hope to live off the sale of my little book, the biography I
had printed up Back East. But Jessie wouldn't thank me for
whisking her away from her sanctuary, back to the place she had

come to despise. I knew that much without having to write and ask her opinion.

No; what I needed was ready money, and the only way to get it was to sell something of real value—something of greater value than my story (which was mostly scurrilous in any case.) I still possessed two treasures of great worth: Wild Bill's pocket watch and his ruby-eyed snake ring. Both had accompanied me on the rail lines, traveling with me from city to city. In fact, I had seldom removed the ring from my thumb—only when necessity forced me. I set thinking of Jessie, two years older now than when I had seen her last with the crumbs of a sweet cake sticking to her chin. Two years older, and two years better off for having got rid of me. I twisted the ring on my thumb, watching dull light from the window glint in its small red eyes. The ring, I couldn't sell. That golden band was too much a part of me now; even to slip it off now and again caused a deep stab of agony. I do earnestly believe I would have found it easier to cut off the thumb that wore that ring than to sell what Wild Bill had trusted me to hold.

But his watch… I had kept that relic safe, treasuring it for many a year, but it seldom touched my skin. It hadn't grown into me, become a part of my body and my spirit the way the ring had done. I took the watch from my trunk and held it up beside the window, letting it swing from its chain, examining it, too, in the clear light of day. Yes. For Jessie's sake, I could sell Bill's watch. I wouldn't enjoy the task, and I never would have contemplated such blasphemy for any other person. But for Jessie… Gilt Edge still saw a few fellas who came prospecting for gold, venturing up into the mountains to pan in the icy streams. I might find a suitable buyer among the prospectors—one who could pay a good, fat price for a real relic of the West, the soon-to-be dead-and-buried world.

I had no sooner convinced myself to part with the watch than agony seized me by the throat, so hard I couldn't draw a breath. The watch fell from my hand and I lurched to my feet, swaying, loosening the buttons of my collar, gasping and willing myself to breathe. The watch and the ring was all I had left of the man I loved. I couldn't part with either one, after all.

I must find some other way. I convinced myself, poor gullible old Martha, that I could sell all two hundred and fifty copies of my biography—though I might have to roam from town to town to move them all. *Better that,* I told myself, *than parting with Bill's watch.* I would leave Gilt Edge the next morning. Take the train to the next town—any town. I would take up as a maid, as I once had done, to make my own way. I would peddle my books at the train depots, declaring myself the One and Only Calamity Jane, and every cent I earned from my biography, I would send along to Jessie.

Mind thusly made up, I packed my trunk and readied to leave Gilt Edge at the break of dawn. The firmness of my decision brought with it a pleasant peace, a stillness in my heart I hadn't felt for many a long and somber year. By the time sunset blushed the peaks of the Rockies, I was ready to bid farewell to the town. But I wanted to give Gilt Edge a private farewell—one from my heart, one born from my new determination to be Jessie's mother again. The occasion called for privacy and contemplation.

I slipped from my boarding house in the purple chill of twilight, then walked down to the river that ran through a stand of cottonwoods on the eastern edge of town. My thoughts was all for a long-ago night—a sweeter night, when I had been young and fearless. Young and full of my foolish hopes. It was the night the wagon had overturned on the Black Hills expedition. The night when Bill Hickock had been so fine and bold, so dashing in his buckskin coat, and so alive. I stood below the whispering cotton-woods, watching bats flit along the silvery ribbon of the river. I remembered that night, allowed myself to bend and fold the fabric of memory so the moment lived again, so I lived the moment—the river water brightly cold against my naked skin, the stars clamoring above in a velvet sky. And my heart beating with all its brilliant expectation, my heart and my love and the cold of the water.

All at once, I wanted nothing more than to slip naked into that river, though the night was chilly even while I stood fully clothed upon the bank. I guess I thought I could actually bring the treasured memory back if I acted out that wild impulse—resurrect everything that had died along with Bill. Or maybe I only hoped I would catch pneumonia and all my damn-blind foolishness would finally come to an end. Whatever my motivation, I found myself hopping up to a low, flat stone that reached partway out into the river. There I peeled off my off my trousers and my shirt, making ready to wade into the icy current. But as I folded my trousers over my arm, Wild Bill's watch slipped from my pocket.

The moment I saw the flash of gold, I dropped everything else I held and scrabbled for the watch. Like a snake escaping into tall grass, the watch with its golden chain slithered beyond my reach. I cried out with wordless desperation as it evaded me, staring in horror as the watch bounced from the edge of the stone, tumbling down the steep side of the river bank. It landed in the water with a splash—a tiny sound, far too small and self-contained for such a wrenching tragedy.

I didn't hesitate. I leaped into the water after my treasure, my sacred relic. Even at its deepest point, out in the center of the river (where, I frantically told myself, the current might have swept Bill's watch) the water only came up to my hips. But it was cold—so bitterly cold, I couldn't decide whether I was numb straight through to my bones, or tormented by a knife-like pain that stabbed everywhere at once. At first, my breath came in short gasps, hard involuntary heaves while I waded and pawed and wept in frustration. Then the cold stole my breath entirely, so I couldn't even cry out against my pain. Cold and loss flayed at me, while I floundered in that river wearing nothing but my bloomers, searching with hands and feet, groping through silt and in the cryptic spaces between stones till I was sluggish and shivering.

Finally, when my teeth chattered so hard I feared I might bite through my tongue, I hauled myself out of the water. There I stood in the darkness, dripping and stunned, sobbing wide-eyed and open-mouthed.

I didn't even catch pneumonia and die. How's that for God's vaunted mercy? You see how my life has cheated me.

HELLCAT IN LEATHER BRITCHES

I LOST MORE THAN WILD BILL'S WATCH THAT NIGHT, WADING AND grappling in the river, struck numb from cold and tragedy. My soul slipped away from me, too, lost in the lightless current, battered over submerged stone, swept downstream beyond my reach where I would never find it again.

Guilt and shame assailed me; how could I have been so careless with that watch, a treasure my true love had held in such grand esteem? I dressed once more and staggered back to my room with my trousers and shirt clinging to my wet body, hugging myself tightly to still my awful shivering and the spasms of self-loathing that wracked me. By the time I reached the boarding house, my need for whiskey was more powerful than it had been at any point in my long and sorry existence. And I had no intention of checking my cravings any longer.

A black shadow of loss eclipsed all my thoughts—my senses, my memory. Even Jessie slipped far from my mind. With dreadful abandon, I gave myself over—laid myself upon the altar of the demon who had hunted for my ruin since that first taste of whiskey long ago. I fell so heavily into drink that I can't tell you how I got from Gilt Edge to Butte, Montana—nor can I tell you how I ended up in jail there. Time had ceased to matter; I perceived no difference between day and night, nor did I feel any change of season. I knew only drunkenness or despair—the wrenching knowledge of my shame, and no escape from that agony till I'd swallowed enough liquor to rob me of my senses, to snuff the dim light of memory and understanding. Only liquor could leave me to the mercy of darkness, where neither thought nor deed could penetrate. And so I cannot tell you how I landed behind the bars of the Butte, Montana jailhouse, but while cooped up in my cell, I sobered up just enough to realize I stayed for two straight weeks.

My blood must have been half whiskey by then. Deprived of my sustaining force—the liquor that burned hot along my veins— I suffered a terrible sickness in that jailhouse. The hours passed with a slowness that seemed to me deliberate cruelty. For days I shivered and wept on the floor of my cell, pleading for mercy from the guards, begging for a drop of whiskey to ease my pain. Many a time did I vomit up the thin, yellow foulness inside me— or I soiled myself in other ways, in ways less dignified still, and I was so weak and shaken I could scarce clean away the mess when the jailer brought me rags and a bucket of water.

But the shaking and puking and the shame of my soiled body was easier to bear than the visions that assailed me whenever I closed my eyes—and sometimes when my eyes remained wide open, staring into the cold, unrelieved flatness of the cell's rearmost wall. In those visions, the worst moments of my life returned to mock me, bright and pulsing with color, echoing with sound—with cries and accusations I alone could hear. I saw Jessie go into the tent, hand in hand with the pretty, dark-haired woman. I felt Lena as a little girl cradled in my arms, heard her plead with me to find her a new family. I saw myself pressing Baby Sara against a stranger's breast. And I saw the stars high above the trail, watched them turning in their silent courses while hands and other things prodded at my naked flesh, took from my body whatever was wanted, discarding the rest. Locked up as I was, with no bottle to reach for, I had no more hope of hiding from my past. The life I had lived stared back at me from within my pitiless cell. All the walls became mirrors, and I was forced to look into them—to see what I had become.

But when the sheriff of Butte finally set me free, I found another letter waiting. I cringed when the jailer handed it over, for I had no great desire to read Lena's angry words again—not after the ordeal I had faced in my cell. Yet that very same ordeal had humbled me some, as much as a woman of my type may ever be humbled. I staggered out of the jailhouse with the letter clutched in my trembling fist and sank down on the boards of the sidewalk. Men and women muttered curses as they stepped around me; dust rose from the sun-baked street, so thick I could taste its earthiness with every breath. I ignored those who cursed me; I opened the letter with timid care. Another scouring from Lena's sharp tongue seemed a fitting punishment, I told myself. Penance for a lifetime of… what? Not sins, exactly. Failings.

I slid the paper from its sleeve, grim and steeled against what would follow. But I didn't find Lena's handwriting, neat and tidy, evenly spaced across't the page. These words was big and shaky, loosely scrawled—the way I wrote, when I wrote a-tall. I turned the letter over and read the signature at the end, before I read another word. Elijah Canary—my brother, Lije.

Dearest Martha,

I hope this letter finds you well. I guess you are still in Butte for I read in the news paper that you was picked up by the law and thrown in to jail. I know you would rather get out soon but I hope for a long enough sentance that this letter finds you. You have been hard to locate and I must share some news.

First: Cilus has returned and he is well. He got himself married to a nice girl and he has set up a business in Boulder. I am going over to join him soon to help him run it. Prospecks look good. I guess Cilus and me turned out all right in the end, as I am a reformed man who does not take to rustling cattle or frauding insurers any longer.

Isabelle has two little girls and loves them dearly. She is a good mother. Has come to visit us with her husband and children and they all are happy and healthy. She tells you hello and said to tell you she hopes you are well.

Lena has five children now and they are all dandys. I think they will miss their uncle Lije when I go out to work with Cilus but it can't be helped. John is well too and his farm is thriving so much that Lena no longer is oblijed to wash cloas for anyone except her own children.

Now I come to the most important news. Martha, I had a good long talk with Lena some months back and set her straight about you. She says she guesses maybe she was too hard on you after all. Lena and John and Cilus and me have all put some money together and we have sent your daughter Jessie to a good school in Helena, Montana where she will learn more then what the nuns could teach her at that place in Sturgis. Akshully, Isabelle and her husband gave a little to our fund too. So all the Canary kids pitched in (tho we still have not found Sara but we have not given up on her eether.) The new school for Jessie is a real good one that all the papers talk about. Girls get real smart there and some have gone on to ladys colleges back east. We want Jessie to have a good future because you did us all so many kindnesses when we was children, Martha, and at least Cilus and me never forgot. We understood all along, what you did to keep us alive. I guess it has gone hard on you to live that kind of life, but Cilus and me, we don't want you to think we never knew what you sacrificed. We know how you lowered yourself so we could all get by. You was always a real good sister to us, and a better ma than the ma we had.

I think senss you are Jessie's mother, it is only fitting that you know where she lives and what she is up to. I don't want you to worry on her account. But I think it is best if you leave her be, Martha. Let her get on with her life and you get on with yours. Now that she is in that school, she has a shot at a real good future and none of us wants to see her *chances put in any sort of danger. I am sure you understand what I mean.*

Oh I love you so very much, my good and kind hearted sister. I wish you all the health and happyness in the world. Please come and visit Cilus and me in Boulder when you have a chance. Cilus's wife has a baby on the way and I know he would like to see you again.

With much affection,
Your brother
Elijah Canary

I DID NOT GO to Boulder to visit my brothers, though I would be lying to you if I said I didn't ache to see them again. A more poignant and powerful ache drew me west to Helena. I heeded Lije's warning well, and kept myself away from Jessie's school. The school was a big, fine place, in a beautiful red-brick building right at the center of town—and Helena was growing fast, poised to become the bustling sort of place that would soon convert to a real, proper city, like those I had visited in the Cody days. Not once did I resurrect the legend of Calamity Jane; I didn't even dare sell my biographies at the train station, where the tenderfeet came and went in their Back-East city dresses and fashionable hats. I called myself Margaret Bird again, and took up work in a laundry, and kept myself in humble anonymity, swearing with every pass of wet cloth across my wash-board that I would leave Jessie alone to live her life —to pursue her grand new future—and never trouble her with my shadow. But I needed to be close to my girl. I was her mother, after all, even if she never knew it. What if Jessie fell sick, or got herself hurt in some dreadful accident? I couldn't bear the thought of dwelling far away if she should ever need the tender care of one who loved her. And who could ever adore my Jessie more than me?

Week after week, month after month, I toiled at the laundry

and never raised my head from my wash tubs or my iron. I pinched every penny I earned, living smaller than I had since my show days. A new and thrilling goal hung before me now: I would save up enough money to send Jessie off to a fancy east-coast ladies' college, just as soon as she was old enough and smart enough. Wouldn't she be glad when I stepped out of the forgotten shadows of her past—the weathered old grandmam she had all but forgotten—and opened for her a new door, the passage to a bright and shining opportunity.

That was my intent, I mean—to save as assiduously as a miser. But more often than not, the whiskey came a-calling, and I was more susceptible than ever before to its sweetly whispering voice. I would save every cent for a week or two. Then I spent it all when sorrow overtook me—when I got to thinking of everything I had lost, all the ways I had lowered myself (as Lije had said in his letter.) In those dark hours, the need for a wild time came over me —a need to forget my ghosts. And though I knew it was folly, still I took the chance every time that cold, black lonesomeness came calling—for whiskey was my only relief from that particular suffering, the only friend who could ease the burden of my self-loathing.

Thanks to the whiskey, I was no closer to sending Jessie off to college—even after a year spent working in Helena. But month after month, I told myself I still had time. I always had more time. Jessie was twelve years old by then; she couldn't leave for a fancy Back East ladies' college till she was sixteen at least. No matter how much whiskey I drank, I could always earn more money the following day.

One autumn afternoon, alone in the steam-veiled confines of the laundry (and nursing a whiskey headache that pounded cruelly in my head) I lifted a man's jacket from a heap of washing yet to be done. Some unknown weight swung inside, bumping against my hip. I reached into the pocket and took out the book which the jacket's owner had forgotten. Wouldn't you know, it was *The Beautiful White Devil of the Yellowstone*, that mad collection of lies, the first story that had made me famous. I stood there for a long time, staring at the book in my chapped and weary hands. The worn spine, the thumbed pages, the creases along its tired cover. The year was 1899; folks still liked to read that scurrilous trash, the lies about me. They still hankered for adventure, the romance of my supposed life.

I tossed that ridiculous novel aside and returned to my work, but I recalled my trunk full of biographies. I hadn't yet sold them all—I hadn't even come close. Perhaps, I thought, it was time to leave Helena. Take to the road again, and this time, I would truly work at selling every last copy of my story. Perhaps I would have more printed, too, and sell those from Salt Lake City to Wichita. Save *that* money for Jessie's future, since the laundry money turned to whiskey almost as fast as I earned it.

A few days later, I told the woman who owned the laundry that I must travel for the sake of a sick relation. Then I headed for Livingstone, where I'd heard a good printing press could be found, newly brought in from the East. Alas, I never made it to Livingstone, for a terrible illness overtook me on the train. Not whiskey sickness, I'll have you know—this time it was a real illness, the kind any respectable person may catch if luck declines to favor them. As the train crept east and my stomach soured—as I huddled in upon myself, aching and wracked with shivers—I recalled my wish on the river bank (to expire from pneumonia) and I was gripped by fear, for I thought I might actually die then and there, on that stuffy, rattling train. Death itself didn't worry me overmuch, but I hadn't made good with Jessie—hadn't saved up for her schooling Back East. I was damn determined to pull off that miracle before the dark angel came for me and carried me off to my grave.

I had been leaning my throbbing head against the pane of a window, but a queasy wave rose in my gut and I sat up, then tried to stand, thinking I ought to make my way back to the little toilet closet and heave up all the sickness inside me in the privacy of that stinking cell. But when I moved, a few women glanced my way. One of them let out a shriek at the sight of me—my sweating face, my pallor.

"God preserve us," said another woman, pressing a kerchief to her mouth and nose. "That woman is dreadfully ill."

"I ain't," I said—and thought to say more in my own defense, but my arms lost all their strength as I fought to pull myself to my feet. I collapsed back onto the bench seat and hunched there, head swimming, breath rasping in my throat.

"Go and fetch the usher," somebody said. "Her illness may be catching."

My feeble protests went unheeded, and after the usher took a long look at me (he too held a kerchief across his mouth and nose), the train made an unscheduled stop at a town of no consequence called White Sulphur Springs. The conductor himself came to my car and spoke to me, gently but without any possibility for argument.

"You are seriously ill, madam. You need the ministrations of a doctor."

"I can continue on. I won't give nobody the sickness. It's just a head cold, besides." I knew it wasn't. Even the worst of my whiskey fevers had never left me so weak or listless.

"I'm afraid you haven't any choice in the matter. For the safety of the rest of my passengers, I must insist that you get off here and seek a doctor at once."

There was nothing I could say to convince the conductor to keep me on board. I had no strength for arguments, anyhow. I left my trunk in the care of the station master and staggered my way to the only doctor White Sulphur Springs had. To be honest, I counted it a minor miracle that town had any learned man to boast of, but I will admit that he looked me over as carefully as any physician I encountered Back East. He pronounced me sick with pneumonia (my wish had come true, after all) and ordered me to check into a tiny, ramshackle hospital on the edge of town. But I hadn't any money to pay for a bed, and the hospital wouldn't accept copies of my biography as compensation. A squint-eyed, hard-mouthed nurse sent me to a poor house instead—a thoroughly inadequate, depressing sort of place, all gray planks and shadows, its corners hung with cobwebs that had caught only dust for years. The poor house was maintained, after a fashion, by stodgy women of the far-too-Christian breed, each dressed in bleak gray with starched white pinafores (upon which, if you looked closely in a fleeting slide of candlelight, you could make out the faint spatters and spots of old blood stains.) My new keepers was a grim pack indeed, but I was grateful for their ministrations. After all, I had nowhere else to go.

WELL, I had thought the days of my legend truly behind me. Certainly, a body doesn't feel especially legendary while convalescing—coughing and shivering—in a lightless poorhouse somewheres in the featureless expanse of the prairie. But word got out that the great Calamity Jane had landed under the roof of Christian charity in White Sulphur Springs, and before I could realize what was happening, every newspaper from Oregon to New York carried the story. Day after day, as I slowly recuperated under the scowls of my caretakers, letters began to arrive. First one, then a pair, and all too soon I found myself with a new stack of letters every day.

Never in my life had I imagined I had so many admirers—nor had I believed a name could spread to those far-flung places. Propped up in my hard bed, shaking my head in awe, I pawed through each new delivery, wondering over the names of towns and cities from whence my well-wishers hailed. Boston. Philadelphia. Ottawa. San Francisco. Seattle. Towns I'd never heard of in Tennessee, Carolina, Kansas and Delaware. My mind fairly reeled at the spread of my news—and the well-wishes contained in those letters did me a world of good. I will grant you, if each of those folks had sent me a dollar instead of a note telling me how much they liked the stories about my life, I could have set Jessie up for life and died in peace, right there in the poor house. But I appreciated their encouragement almost as much as I would have appreciated their money. I knew I was loved, you see—I knew that somebody out there, in the vast, impersonal world, feared for my health and wished me no ill luck. Maybe it sounds foolish to you, but knowing some folks still remembered Calamity Jane eased some of the pain in my heart.

I convalesced in that charity house for more than a month, till at last my lungs lost their terrible rattle and most of my strength returned. The white-pinafored old hags who looked after me sent for the lone doctor, and he pronounced me healthy enough to walk around some, so my caretakers wrapped me in a good woolen shawl and turned me out-of-doors to ambulate and take in the fresh air.

Oh, I ambulated, all right—directly to the nearest saloon. Nothing will make you long to forget your troubles like lying in the same damn bed in a gray tomb of a creaking house for nigh-on six weeks. I needed a little fun, just as bad as I needed the fresh air. And I tell you what: that was one drink I never regretted.

But I did get so addled—as you know—that I lost my way back to the poor house. It was a kindly young gentleman, scarce more than a boy, who took me by my arm and guided me back to my keepers. And it was that same jolly, sweet-tempered fella who helped the Christian ladies tuck me into my bed.

That's how I met you, Short Pants. And here we are.

No. That ain't right. My recollection has slipped—skewed itself, as it does now, sometimes. Year after year, I find it grows harder to keep my memories in order, to sort through the lies and the legends, and find the truth. I have folded the velvet so many times. I have walked this way and that, in search of the few sweet remembrances that still remain. I have sucked the nectar from the faded flowers of my past, and those blossoms have yielded the last of their sweetness. The petals are falling now.

But I got it wrong. I'm sure of that. You ain't Short Pants, after all. All this time, I had myself convinced that you was him. My God—how old is that boy now, assuming he still lives? He's long dead and in his grave, for all I can tell.

You ain't Short Pants. But if my life has taught me one firm truth, it's this: one writer is very much like another. As long as you aim to tell my story and tell it true, you'll serve just as well.

Don't fidget, now, my friend—whoever you are, whatever your real name might be. The story's almost over, and then you can get back to your notebook and pen. Your typewriter. What does your breed use, nowadays, to write? How do you spread the germ of your lies, the clinging burrs of legend?

Hell; it hardly matters to me. Top up that glass, you stranger— you friend—and then I'll go on talking.

―――――――――

NEXT MORNING, that same smiling young man arrived at the poor house, tapping on the door just as the sun came up. The stodgy Christian frowners had already carried in my breakfast tray; they was seeing to their own morning sup. They didn't seem best pleased to have a visitor, but I could hear the boy out there in the hall, asking to speak with me.

"Miss Canary is not well enough for visitors," one of the care-takers said.

"Please, ma'am; I'm the fellow who helped bring her home last night."

I heard only a sharp sniff in reply.

The young man said, "I have business with Miss Jane—or I hope to have business with her. If I cannot speak with her today, please tell me when I may return."

The prospect of business perked me up, and no mistake. I hastily set my tray aside and wobbled up out of my bed, dressed in a flannel nightgown, trembling a little at the knees—whether from the dregs of my pneumonia or from the whiskey haze, I couldn't say. I marched out into the hall and nodded to the scowling lady in her white pinafore, and when she had gone off in a huff, I clapped the young fella on the shoulder and welcomed him to my humble abode.

"My name is Lewis Ransome Freeman," he said.

He was such a colt of a man—so gangly and young—I laughed at the bigness of his name. "Your name is Short Pants, son. What do you want from me?"

"I'm a writer, Miss Canary. I've traveled all the way from Boston to White Sulphur Springs to find you. I read about your plight in the papers, and I felt inspired."

"Inspired?" I wrapped my arms around myself, suddenly conscious of the shapeless flannel I wore, of the smell of sickness that still clung to me—hung all about the poor house. Nothing could be less of an inspiration. But Short Pants seemed undaunted.

"I want to write about you." He took an eager step toward me. "I want to tell your real story—the true life of Calamity Jane. Not another silly, make-believe flight—the kind you can find in any dime novel."

I shook my head, rather dazed by his enthusiasm. "Ain't nobody out there who wants to know my real story. My history is a very sad and sorry one, I'm afraid. Take it from me, Short Pants: folks prefer the lies in the dime novels. They can eat those up like whipped cream, a spoonful at a time."

"It can't be true, that your admirers prefer falsehood to truth. Miss Canary, don't you know how many admirers you have?

You're a celebrity Back East. And I've come all this way to find you, and speak with you, and learn who you truly are. Won't you please agree? Allow me to interview you. I am young, I know—but I am a skilled writer, despite my youth. I can bring the truth to life for the benefit of your admirers. They will finally know your history—and however bleak that history may seem to you, I assure you, it will thrill and inspire the countless readers who already have come to adore your name."

It wasn't so much the flattery, but the earnest excitement that won me over. Short Pants Freeman seemed about as dumbfounded by my celebrity as he thought every reader in America would be, and I suppose his buoyant energy drew me in. I agreed to meet with him two days hence, just after the breakfast hour, and swore I would regale him with my adventures—my true and honest adventures, laid bare for the first time in my lengthy history of entertaining writers.

And I did honestly mean to go through with it: spill my guts to Short Pants, let him pen the mess of my life and expose it before my admirers—the whole, ugly truth. But that night I lay awake remembering it all—the trading on the trail, the whorehouses, the drinking, the many days spent languishing and suffering in a jail cell. I thought of all those letters I received—how those folks could have made me rich if they sent money instead of well-wishes. Maybe legend was preferable, after all. If the real Calamity Jane was exposed—if the mask of myth was ripped away and my shame revealed, sweating and pale—no one would admire me any longer. The most outrageous fiction of my life—the most impossible, wildest flight of fevered fancy—was a damn sight more appealing than any truth.

And my thoughts turned to Jessie, and lingered there far longer than I dwelt on my own shame and humiliation. My girl had a chance now to build a real life—a future unclouded by Calamity's notoriety. If I let the truth out—raised it up from an unmarked grave—my shame would follow Jessie everywhere she went. For I couldn't tell my life story without confessing that I was her mother. I couldn't say a single true word about my life without speaking Jessie's name. She was the whole of my life, my sun and my moon, even if I was obliged to love her from afar. If the truth was revealed, Jessie would lose whatever place she could carve among better society. Her future would be eclipsed by my long shadow. The daughter of a whore has no future—not in the West, not Back East. Nowhere.

That's why I boarded a train and put White Sulphur Springs behind me. It was dawn—a rosy flush on the eastern edge of the prairie—and it was the day I had promised to meet with Short Pants Freeman and tell him everything.

I couldn't face the truth back then. It ain't much easier to face it now.

DEADWOOD DICK'S DOOM, OR, CALAMITY JANE'S LAST ADVENTURE

BY AND BY, I FOUND MY WAY BACK TO BILLINGS, AND THERE I languished for some long while. With each slow-passing day, I felt a deep shadow encroaching—a patch of darkness stealing overhead, blotting out the sky. My life, the world I knew—the only world that truly existed, far as I was concerned—was vanishing around me. Billings sprouted new houses like toadstools popping up after an autumn rain. Faster and faster they came, till the long, lazy stretches of peaceful silence was replaced by the ringing of hammers and the rasping of saws. Mud roads gave way to streets paved with stone. The shops towered like a forest of pines—one story growing to two; two stories reaching upwards to three, to four. The bland, dry smell of brick dust and mortar replaced the sharp perfume of sage. Billings sighed and sank into itself, calm and resolute—a horse broke to the saddle, already forgetting the smell of wind on the open prairie and the freedom of flight beneath an unrestricted sky.

I watched Billings spreading, unfurling, eating the land. I wondered how large Salt Lake City had grown. And Cheyenne, and Laramie, and sour old Corinne. Boulder—had that town matured to a city? Had Boulder, in its hungry need, already consumed the house where I had lived, the pasture where my ox teams had grazed? What stood now in place of my first child's grave? A dry goods store or a fancy new boarding house, an impossible weight bearing down on those small and delicate, forgotten bones, my dead son slumbering alone in the dark.

I knew what was coming for me. I had seen it Back East. And I knew my only hope was to stay drunk, so I couldn't feel the worst of the pain, nor the sharpest pangs of despair. And so I did: I drank up every drop I could buy, and when my money ran short, I sold what few possessions I had—the biographies, and photographs of myself, the Hellcat in Leather Britches, posing as Western as you please with a rifle and a buckskin fringe and a lost expression on my broad, bewildered face.

When I had nothing left to sell, I begged for money or whiskey —either one would do. Many griefs and sorrows visited me during those times—and all of them due to my taste for liquor. But though I kept myself as drunk as my fortunes would allow, I never managed to convince myself that the end wasn't coming. No hurdy-gurdy or jangling piano, no frantic tapping of the dancing girls' feet, could drown out the voice that whispered in my mind. We are already gone, the voice said. They have fenced us in and cut a path to our grave—all of us, the West—who we was and the truths we knew. We been written over by pretty lies, our truth muted by the blaring bullhorn of show promoters, by the whistle of relentless trains.

My last great loss struck me Billings, and struck me so hard I felt sure my heart would wither and abandon me at last to Death's bleak mercy. I had stayed on the whiskey most doggedly for many a day. I can't tell you how many days exactly—I never knew the count then, for day and night had long since blended into one another, and nothing mattered to me except finding another glass and convincing the barkeep to fill it. All I know for certain is that the last amiable barkeep in Billings finally had enough of me, and turned me out onto the street. I stumbled past the post office and the remains of a disused livery. A small park lay beyond, a pretty place fenced in by white palings, dappled with the gentle blue shadows of cottonwood and aspen. Ladies liked to bring their children to the park so's they could play, but no children frolicked on the grass that afternoon. The place was empty and silent, but for the ceaseless noise of expansion echoing along every street. So I eased myself down onto the grass, under the whispering trees. I fell into a deep sleep, dreaming of my mulewhacking days—picking the ice from my animals' hooves, their comfortable nearness, the way they drew close to my small fire in the winter night, stamping and sighing, with the world spreading broad and free all around us.

I woke—who can say when; hours later? A day later?—groggy and aching, my mouth tasting both bitter and sour. I set up slowly, groaning at the pain as it throbbed in my head and my heart. I realized what I had done—what I had become—falling asleep sprawled on the ground as if I thought myself worth nothing more than the dirt beneath my feet, and I was sore ashamed. What was my legend or my name worth, if I laid like a bloated carcass under the public eye?

Even as I patted and brushed at my body, trying to clean away the grass and dust that clung to me—and trying to reassure myself that I was still whole—I felt a slow, creeping dread, a certainty that something had gone terribly wrong. Something was missing. My small purse still hung from my belt, light and empty as it had been when the barkeep had thrown me out. My boots was still on my feet. I hadn't worn a hat out of my boarding room that morning—or whenever I had left the room last—so my uncovered, tangled hair was no great surprise.

Then I caught sight of my hand as it moved down my stained and rumpled skirt, straightening my clothing, putting myself back into some kind of order. I stared at my hand for a terrible long time before I knew the worst was true. Before I realized my heart had broken.

Wild Bill's snake ring was gone.

Frantic, I pawed through the short grass around me, already certain my effort was useless. That ring had resided on my thumb for damn near thirty years. Only a witless fool would believe it could up and slip off after so long a spell. Even while I searched, I knew the truth. I saw it plain, though I could see little else through the tears that half-blinded me. Someone had stolen my ring. Come across me laid out flat, and taken that ring right off my hand. Robbed the half-dead corpse of a drunkard, Calamity Jane, the shame of Billings.

I could bear none of it—not the insult of the theft, and not the wrenching, sickening lurch of my disgrace. I let the tears spill down my cheeks as I left the park and prowled back down the road, into the heart of Billings. But by the time I reached the first saloon, fury had burned my tears away. I threw open the door and burst into that bar, raging like a gullywasher.

"Who took it?" I shouted.

My outraged bellow was so loud, the piano plunked into silence and every man in the place turned to stare at me.

"Who took my ring?"

The fellas in the bar cast looks at one another—wary or amused. Those who thought to laugh at my expense only made me all the hotter.

"What peckerless son of a poxy whore robbed me? I want to know!"

The barkeep held up his hands as if he could soothe away my anger, as if he could brush off my hurt like dust from his trousers. "Now, Jane—"

I didn't wait to hear what useless, mealy-mouthed excuse he would make. I reached towards the nearest man's hip and ripped his pistol from its holster before anyone could stop me—before anyone knew what I intended. As I brandished the gun, every fella in the place leaped to his feet. The whores went running for cover, shrilling their fear.

"Put down the gun, Jane," somebody shouted. Another man yelled, "She's gone mad at last! Run for the sheriff!"

But if anyone thought to escape that saloon, they would have to bull past me. And I was armed, and furious.

Again I hollered, "I want my ring back. And I want to know which of you dirty, shit-eating fucks took it!"

The man whose gun I'd stolen rose slowly to his feet. "Easy now, Jane," he said, all smooth and conciliating. "I don't think anybody here knows jest what you're talking about. Why don't you tell us more, and we'll see if we can't help you find what's missing?"

"Missing?" I cried. "Ain't nothing missing! It was stolen! I been robbed!" The injustice of it all—my whole damnable life—expanded in my chest with a force and suddenness that should have stopped my heart, by rights. I thrust the gun out before me and pointed it this way and that, and shouted at the whole blind lot of them. "What's missing? The fuck can't you tell what's missing? Look around you! Look at this world! Look at your lives, you liars, you frauds! Don't you see what you're bringing in?"

"Jane—poor old girl. Give me back my gun. Ain't nobody here gonna hurt you; you know that."

"The hurt's already done! I'm already dead, and so's the lot of you! So's the world all around you, the mountains and the rivers and the sky. The prairie, the Hills, every damn place and every damn thing! Dead on our feet—that's what we are. 'Cause none of you could get enough. Not enough gold, not enough of the trains, not enough of those spineless tenderfeet that come invading like a plague of locusts to eat us up and eat up all our land before they leave again. And what are we when they've gone? Gnawed and barren—that's what. They come to consume us, like we did to the Indians. By God, maybe we deserve it."

At that point in my raving, I scarce knew what I was saying, myself. The pistol trembled in my hand; it felt heavier than a load of bricks. My arm and my heart lost their resolve. The gun lowered to my side.

The man I had taken it from stepped closer and reached for his pistol, but in that moment, I jerked it up again.

"I want my ring back. I want it now. I'm willing to kill for it. Who doubts me?"

The barkeep said, "No one doubts you, Jane. But this is—"

The pistol bucked in my hand. That was the first I knew that I'd fired. The deafening report barely registered, for my head was already pounding, my ears already roaring with rage and the desperate certainty that I was lost. Again and again I fired—at the floor, just in front of fellas' feet, making them skip and dance and stumble to get away from me. They scattered around me like quail evading a hunter—small things, weak, easy prey for the strong and the powerful. I went on firing till the pistol clicked dry and silence crowded in.

Then a burst of pain exploded at the back of my skull. I remember the sound of shattering glass, the smell and sting of ale spilling down the back of me, soaking through my dress. I remember the floor rushing up to meet me, and a steep plunge into darkness that sheltered me from my rage.

It seems to me now as if I stayed in that merciful darkness for years. A new century came; a few years ticked by. Somehow, I eked out the same miserable existence in Billings, which became a city, all right—not as big as Minneapolis, but the outward spread of its stain couldn't be stemmed or contained. Sooner or later, it would swell to the size of any city Back East—bloated by a cancer that could never be excised.

Now and then, during the gray stretch of years, I ventured down to Helena, and there I orbited Jessie's school. Never had I ceased to ache for my daughter—for one word from her, for a single glance to reassure me that she was well and whole, that she had a future in this mad, unrecognizable world, even if I did not.

By 1903, Jessie was sixteen years old—old enough to make her own way. And she did intend to make her way, I knew, for Lije had written me once in Billings to tell me what he had learned of Jessie's life. She had done well in her fancy school, but though she was bright and hard-working, she decided not to venture to the east-coast colleges, after all. Rather, Jessie chose to stay on in Helena, and take up as apprentice to a well-to-do seamstress. She had developed a knack for the needle and had taken a shine to fashion and style—she told her uncle Lije all about it in a letter. She would not go Back East (she wrote to Lije) because she had seen a postcard of New York City and it looked a grim and heart-less place. That was the words she used: *It looks a grim and heartless place; I've no desire to leave behind this beautiful country where I feel quite at home.* Those words was so pretty to me, when I read them in Lije's letter. I thought my girl could write as well as any fancy novelist whose lies I ever read.

Jessie told Lije, too, that she never intended to marry. She preferred to work and make her own way. She had read the writ-ings of some high-minded Back-East lady in that school of hers, one of the white-clad suffragists who exhorted girls not to marry, but to heed a special call for special work. When I read Lije's report of my Jessie's heart, I swear I never felt prouder of that girl —and that's a heap of praise, for nothing in this miserable life ever made me proud except for my good girl Jessie.

Those long years, those gray years, when I drifted (half-sense-less) between Billings and Helena. I should have given up my wild ways, for they was awful unbecoming of a woman past fifty years. But I no longer cared to maintain a pretense of dignity. What was the use? Legend I might have been, but my fame never saved me from penury. What would dignity have brought me, other than sympathetic smiles from the folks who saw my outstretched hand and walked by without dropping a penny in my palm?

So my wildness continued. Mine was the lashing out of a creature caught in a trap—one who knows its fate is sealed, one who clashes its teeth against a foe it knows it can't subdue. I raised Hell in saloons and taverns. I made a nuisance of myself on city streets. Tales of my exploits still made the papers, though even in my drunken state, I could tell that reports of my legendary self had changed in tone from fondness to grim disapproval. Whenever I could get my hands on a paper, I scanned the damn thing, sheepish and cringing, for Calamity's name. In that way, I learned what dreadful things I had said or done while I bobbed and floundered in the whiskey, for I had little memory of my own exploits by then.

Now and again, the newspaper reports of Calamity Jane took a different shape altogether. Columnists hashed endlessly over my reported adventures, all the while opining on the uncivilized nature of the West, bemoaning the need for good people of clean conscience and respectable living to go and tame the wild women and men. *How can we call this America?* the writers asked. *Are we not more civil than this?*

Once, while I huddled across't the street from Jessie's school, pining for a glance of my dear child, I happened across't a column written by none other than Buffalo Bill Cody himself. *Calamity Jane does not deserve the scorn heaped upon her by so-called reporters,* Cody said, *who have never met the woman herself, but who merely recirculate sordid rumors of that good lady's doings for the sake of titillation. I knew Miss Jane personally,* Cody said, *while she toured with my Wild West Show. I can vouch for her character, and the editor of this paper should cease to besmirch a good woman's name.*

Cody's words was true enough. While I toured with his show, I held myself more rigidly upright than at any point in my life. But I knew how disgracefully I had fallen since the Buffalo Bill days. I knew—and that's why I never responded the following week, when that same paper ran a notice placed by none other than Josephine Brake. She had secured a pension for me (Josephine claimed) from Buffalo Bill Cody, in thanks for the good works I performed while traveling with his exhibition. She would send every penny to me if I would come out to see her, and prove that I was sober.

I was not sober, so I did not write.

YOU'RE WONDERING, ain't you, how I ended up back here in Deadwood. It's a reasonable curiosity, for you will remember that once I left Bill Cody's exhibition, I swore never to return to this place. And anyhow, Jessie was all growed up and putting down roots in Helena. There seems little sense in my being here now, yet here I am, undeniable, the One and Only In the Flesh, setting on this bar stool beside you.

It ain't a chapter I much like to discuss, but I promised I'd tell you the truth, my friend, and hold nothing back.

The truth is, I fell into some fool argument with a shopkeep up in Helena. I can't remember what the argument was all about now. I guess it don't matter, anyway. The end result was this: I took a hatchet to his store and busted the place up—broke his shelving, ruined much of his stock—scared the piss right out of him, too. Don't laugh, for it ain't funny—and I ain't one speck proud about my actions. What I done to that shopkeep was cruel and stupid—behavior better fitting Frank Lacy or Bill Steers than the legendary Calamity Jane. I was promptly arrested, which came as no great shock to me... but what happened in that jail was a real surprise, and no mistake.

By the time they tossed me in the pen and locked the bars behind me, I looked so ill that the jailer called in a doctor. That kindly old fella looked me over and asked me questions about my habits and my health, which I answered amiably enough. Then he excused himself. The jailer let him out of my cell, and both men stepped through a nearby door into the dim little hall that adjoined the jailhouse proper. But the door to the hallway didn't close all the way; it hung ajar by a hand's breadth, and so I could hear their conversation.

"She has rheumatism," the doctor said. "Unsurprising in a woman of sixty or seventy—and she certainly appears to be sixty-five at least, if one trusts one's eyes. But she insists that she is fifty-one years of age."

"Rheumatism never made anyone look so sickly," the jailer said.

"No—certainly not. I'm afraid she has fallen under the grip of a far more serious illness. She is terribly jaundiced; I suspect disorder of the bile. Perhaps a liver malady. Whichever the case, the disease is well advanced. I'm afraid the poor woman doesn't have long to live."

Not long to live.

I huddled on the narrow cot in a corner of my cell, stunned and shivering in the silence. Whatever the jailer and the doctor said after that, I cannot say, for I had ceased to listen. All my thoughts turned inward, squarely facing the fact of my imminent demise. And you know, after the first few minutes of panic and denial, that doctor's certainty settled over me like a loving embrace, warm and calming. No one can dodge death forever. At least I knew the hour—or had some vague idea of the hour. I could make my preparations—set to rights whatever could be righted, and meet death with a wink and a slap of my palm. How many folks could claim such good fortune?

That very day, I made up my mind that when my end came, I would be close to Wild Bill. I hoped that the proximity of our respective deaths would make it easier for me to find him—pave a path of sorts down which I could walk, a free-striding spirit, and find him there at the end of my trail with the red sunset a-glowing on his long red hair. And so I would return to Deadwood, where my heart had died so many years before. Let my body fall where it would; my spirit would remain in Deadwood forever.

Before I could reach the mercy of forever, I must part with Jessie for good. I had left her well alone, all those many years since I sent her off to Sturgis, and she seemed better off without me— thriving as no Canary had done before. I couldn't bring myself to break that habit now, and give her my farewell face to face. She would ask questions I couldn't answer, and the look in her eyes would surely kill me long before I reached Wild Bill's grave. But as soon as the sheriff released me, I disguised myself in a dark dress and wrapped a shawl around my head, so I looked like a bent old grandmother. Then I sought out the finest seamstress's shop in all of Helena and I set upon the sidewalk across the street. There I found Jessie at her work.

For hours, pinned to my place by love and awe, I watched my girl from the shelter of my disguise. She was lively and slim, dressed in a beautiful frock of rose pink, and I smiled at the sight of her, tucking and pinning the dresses she had made for her customers, frowning in concentration over her work, laughing with the grand old dame to whom she had sworn her apprentice-ship. Jessie looked plum happy—something I had never been. She had flourished into womanhood—beautiful and strong, untroubled by the misdeeds of her infamous relation. I was glad of it.

All that day, I set upon the sidewalk and watched my girl through the shop window, for whenever she was near the glass, I couldn't tear my eyes away. But whenever her duties carried her out of sight, into the bowels of the seamstress's workshop, I scribbled and scratched at a letter to Lije.

I'm dying, I told him. *And I aim to be in Deadwood when death comes for me. You was always a good brother to me—you and Cilus. Tell the girls I love them, too, and kiss their children for me. Tell them everything I ever done, I done for their sake.*

When the sun set, just before the seamstress closed up her shop, I watched Jessie sweep the floor, radiant in her rose-pink dress with her blackbird curls spilling down her back. Then she turned away to blow out the lamp, and I kissed my fingers in her direction. I rose from the sidewalk and made my way to the train station. I boarded a train bound for Deadwood, and never looked back.

PROPER SICKNESS HAD SET in by the time the train reached its destination. My stomach churned so bad, I could scarce make myself swallow my own spit, and my eyes was bleary, stinging from a terrible dryness. I felt unaccountably weak—wobbly and frail, like a kitten that ain't had time enough to open its eyes. It was all I could do to haul myself off that train. I carried one small carpet bag stuffed with my few insignificant possessions—among them, a battered old copy of *The Beautiful White Devil of the Yellowstone*, for with the snake ring long since departed, that damn-fool book was the last reminder I had of Wild Bill and the life we had shared. I leaned against a lamp post on the platform, wheezing for my breath, wondering where I ought to stay. I had almost no money left, nothing to my name.

When I felt steady enough to walk, I inquired here and there and found a room in a very inadequate boarding house, which I could afford for two weeks—no longer. I reasoned Death had better step lively if he wanted to take me in my bed. If he was delinquent in making his appearance, he would have to claim me in a gutter or an alley. I didn't mind, so long as I was near Wild Bill's grave when the call came—but I reasoned Death might prefer a more dignified state of affairs.

Well, I set myself up in that mildewed boarding house to wait my ending. That strange weakness crept back over me, so even setting up in my bed took a great deal of effort, a fixity of will I never knew I possessed. I did my best to sip at the broth the mistress of the house brought, but my stomach roiled with sickness no matter what I contrived to put in it. It was no great surprise when I began coughing up blood. I took it calmly, dabbing at my mouth with a dirty old kerchief, and in between my bouts of coughing, reading from that tattered book, remembering a time when I was young and free, when the mountains sang their hymns for me and the sky threw wide its arms in welcome.

The second week of my habitation dawned. Death still hadn't made his appearance, and I was growing impatient, but there did come a tap upon the boarding-house door. Because I had nothing else to do, I strained to listen in on the conversation. I heard the mistress's low, melodious voice, and then the higher strains of a younger woman. I could just hear their words over the sounds of Deadwood growing, Deadwood eating my memories.

"I've come to see Calamity Jane. She is boarding here, is she not?"

"Yes, but I don't think she's in a fit state for visitors."

I sighed and sank back on my pillow. Just another writer, come to observe the spectacle of my death—come to pen another scurrilous column about my life.

"Please, ma'am," the younger woman said. "If she's ill, then it's all the more urgent that I see her. She is my grandmother."

A few moments later, a timid rap sounded at my bedroom door. I tried to push myself up again, but my arms quivered too much to hold me. I whispered, "Come in," and she heard me despite the frailty of my voice. The door swung open—there she was, standing in its narrow frame, looking down at me with her girlish brow furrowed and her dark eyes brimming with unshed tears.

I couldn't speak a word. She was tall and beautiful—so beautiful, like my mother had been, and for one dizzy moment I even thought she was my mother, come back to guide me to the end of my road. But my ma had never stood so straight and determined. Ma's face, pretty as it was, had never held Jessie's radiance, that surety of purpose. Jessie was a woman now, confident and strong, proudly upright. She could look any man or woman directly in the eye.

"I found you," she said.

I nodded.

She glanced around the small, dim bedroom, sniffed the air—heavy with the odors of mildew and dust, the odors of my sickness. "You can't stay in this place," Jessie said. "Look at it."

"Don't matter none. It's all I can afford, anyhow."

She came to me. She sat on the edge of my bed and took my hand, held it in both of her own. She was warm and alive; I could feel a great current of passion running through her, the energetic trembling of her hands.

"Uncle Lije wrote to me," she said. "He told me you weren't well, and had gone to Deadwood. I came to find you, for he said you…" She swallowed hard, took a deep breath to steady herself. "He said you might not have much longer on this earth."

Again I nodded. I squeezed her hand, though even I could tell my grip was feeble.

Jessie sniffed, but she wouldn't allow a tear to fall. She couldn't look at my face, and I don't blame her for that. I must have looked a wreck by then, sallow and thin, ravaged by the long years. But she said, "I can't allow you to do this alone. To die alone. You're… you're my mother. Aren't you?"

The moment hung between us, silent, heavy with all the words I had longed to say to her from the moment of her birth till now. How heavy and how beloved was that burden—everything I had left unsaid. It leaned its cruel and beautiful weight upon my chest till I could scarcely breathe.

At last I managed, "How did you know? Lije told you, didn't he?"

"No. He kept your secret, though God alone knows why you wanted it to remain a secret, all these years. All my life." She shook her head; those black curls swayed, just like my beautiful ma's had done, long, long ago. "Lije wrote and told me, 'Your grandmother is dying down in Deadwood. You had best get down to see her, and make your final good-bye.' And I knew in that moment—I can't say how—I just *knew* the truth. I saw it all plainly. I suppose some part of me has always known—ever since you sent me off to that boarding school in Sturgis. But it doesn't matter now. Nothing matters. I don't mind that you kept it a secret. You had your reasons; that's good enough for me."

Poor Jessie—she couldn't remain mistress of her tears any longer. They broke like a river in flood, breaching its banks, washing her smooth cheeks. The tears ran faster than she could wipe them way.

"But I would have liked to have known sooner," she said, weeping, holding tight to my hand. "I would have liked to have called you Mother."

I raised my trembling arm, though it cost me a reserve of my fading strength. Jessie lay down beside me, tucking herself into my embrace. She rested her head on my shoulder, and I laid my cheek against her warmth—my daughter, my child, the hope of my life.

"You were always good to me, in your way," Jessie said. "Life was never easy for you, I know. But you were always good to me. You always kept me safe." Her body shook with a brief laugh, bittersweet. "Do you remember that terrible night in Billings? At the hotel, when those bad men kept shooting at one another? I thought the gunfire would never stop. But I wasn't as afraid as I might have been, because you were there, protecting me. I always felt safe when your arms were around me… Mother."

She sobbed and pressed herself closer, and I rocked my baby girl as much as I was able, laid out as I was, with her all growed up beside me.

"I remember how we used to ride," Jessie said, calmer now, with a fond smile in her voice. "I loved to ride with you, because you told such wonderful stories and you sang to me. Do you remember the song?"

I nodded, but my heart was too constricted by love for me to speak, let alone sing in my cracked, inadequate voice.

My girl sang instead, high and sweet. "She's a big lass, and a bonny lass, oh and she likes her beer. And her name is Cushie Butterfield, and I wish she were here."

I closed my eyes and listened till the song was done.

———

JESSIE TOOK an adjoining room in that miserable house, and paid my way for another two weeks just in case I needed them. She tended to my every need, no matter how foul and futile my situation became, as if she was the mother and I the helpless child. She never complained once, nor showed the least sign of resentment, and every day was blessed by her hand, warm and soft upon my brow.

I grew weaker, as you might expect. But with my girl beside me, singing the old songs and reciting my old tales, I found that every few days my strength would rally. On those days I took myself out walking—sometimes with Jessie holding my elbow, fearful I would fall, and sometimes (when Jessie fell exhausted into sleep) with only a walking stick to support me. I was obliged to move slow, to set my feet with greatest care, but the sun was warmer on my face than it ever had been, and above the heavy stink of coal smoke and brick dust, I could catch the smell of sagebrush on a hot breeze.

I'm sure you know where I ventured on those walks—every walk, for I had but one destination. I followed the well-trodden path to my true love's grave. Bill no longer rested behind that little white church with the crick and the cottonwoods behind. They had dug him up and moved him to a grander new cemetery, and they fenced him in with wrought iron bars. But every day I was strong enough to walk, I went to him and leaned upon that fence, and read the words engraved upon his stone. *We will meet again in the happy hunting ground to part no more.* I read the words, and I whispered to his shade all the memories I held of his goodness and his beauty. I told him all the legends the writers had spun about us—Wild Bill and Calamity Jane. I promised I would come to find him soon—very soon—and we would part no more.

One day, when a train whistle died away and I heard a meadow lark trilling in the fleeting quiet, a famous photographer came wandering into the grand new cemetery with the black box of his camera resting on his shoulder.

"Land sakes," he said, fairly dancing with excitement, "aren't you Calamity Jane?"

I told him that I was indeed, the very same—though I wondered that he should recognize me, sick and wasted as I was.

"How fortunate that I should find you here, at Bill Hickock's grave. Please, ma'am—won't you allow me to make your picture? A moment like this oughtn't to be forgotten."

At first, I thought to cuss the man out and scare him away, for he had intruded most ungraciously on my private ruminations. But then I reasoned a photograph couldn't hurt nobody, least of all me—not now, with the end so thoroughly nigh. Something of the old fun returned to me—those days when I still had admirers, when Calamity's name hadn't yet fallen under the shadow of complete and absolute iniquity. So I agreed, and I mustered the strength to stand up straight beside the wrought-iron fence and my true love's grave. I even managed to smile for the camera.

But the photographer frowned as he bent over his apparatus. He straightened again with the flash unfired.

"No, no—it's not quite right," he muttered. "Not the right image—not yet. Something is missing. Ah!" He reached into the pocket of his well-tailored jacket and took out a silk flower. Then he came to me and pressed the flower in my hand. The petals was blue, sky-blue; I remembered the forget-me-nots growing beneath the willows, remembered the smell of their green weeping sap when I tore them up and gathered them in my hands.

"There, now," the photographer said. "Lean over the fence, if you would, Miss Jane, and lay the flower on his stone."

An artificial flower. An artificial world. Ain't that just about right?

———————

I'VE WATCHED from these hills while the city has grown. I've paced the old trails, even as they've vanished, fading under prairie grass or dug up and erased, paved over by the endless spread of asphalt. Vanished or erased, but my feet still know the way; a memory can't be discarded, easy as that.

The West falls in upon itself. It thickens itself to legend. The people come in greater numbers, searching for me, searching for Bill, hungry for what we left behind. I watched the stage coaches turn to auto cars. I seen the birds in the sky replaced by roaring jets, the crisscross of persistent white smoke like the bars of a jail cell across't the sky. You're one of them, Short Pants—whatever your name is, whatever I should call you now. You're just like the rest, all the ravenous souls who came here searching for me. Tenderfeet, the lot of you—you, the outsider, and all those who was born and bred here in Deadwood, too, these many years since my death. But the soles of my feet grow harder with every step along the invisible trails. I am firm like the stones beneath the Black Hills dirt—my soul, hard and hidden, the bones of this place.

They found me lying face down across a table in my favorite saloon, surrounded by dancing girls, my last breath accompanied by the purr of an old hurdy-gurdy. The whiskey glass beside me was only half-drunk.

You know, it's a strange thing, but it takes some time to get used to being a specter. It don't happen all at once, as you might imagine. You must be willed back into existence—brought back by memory, by the senses of those you left alive in this strange and deep-stained world. That's the only way to find the path through the nap of your velvet. You follow the trails others have made, and you find yourself there—the real self, original and unchanged.

Because no one had yet folded the fabric of Calamity Jane and allowed me to find my path, I didn't see my own funeral. I was blinded to it, unawares—but I saw a night sky arching high above the river. I felt the water on my bare skin. Silt ran smooth between my toes, and when I bent and reached into that cold current, I brought up a golden watch hanging from a chain. It dripped water dark as whiskey. But no matter how long I stared into the watch's shining face, I never saw Wild Bill again.

They buried me next to him—right by his side. I expect Jessie saw to that; it was her last act of kindness towards me—her poor and broken, her inadequate mother—before she returned to her good life, her ready future. They buried me there, at Wild Bill's side, and I lie beside him still. And yet I don't. Here I am, talking to you, watching that whiskey slide down your throat, wishing it was my throat, my harsh burn to feel, my life to live again.

And now you know the truth of it, the life I lived.

I could walk outside and show you, if you please, the world I knew, the world that still lives. It vanishes a little more, day by day, but its trace is pressed into the hard, yellow earth. My feet know the way. You can find it with your fingers, like the cut of an arrowhead scored into old, dry bone. Walk with me out into Deadwood—the place that is Deadwood now. Stand just there, at the edge of the tavern's parking lot, where pavement crumbles into ochre dust. Shut your eyes. See beyond the glare of head-lights; listen past the moan of the interstate. You will find me in the silence. I stand at the end of the last stage line. Before me, ordered and straight and black-metal clean, the railway births itself, sleepers falling smack against the earth in a perfect rhythm. The line goes on toward an endless future. Behind me, a sage wind is rising. A drift of trail dust moves through Deadwood. It shines in the setting sun.

HISTORICAL NOTE AND AUTHOR'S
REMARKS

There's something about the West that gets under your skin. Like a porcupine's quills, the West embeds itself in the heart with a sharp stab, and little by little it works its way in, until its hooks are set deep and it can't be removed—not without greater pain and trauma.

I was born in 1980 in Rexburg, a tiny college town in southeast Idaho, a place surrounded by mountains and buttes, green river valleys and cold ravines of black lava stone. Idaho, like most of the West, is a place of contradictions: A land both severe and poetic; tamed by agriculture yet owned by wild things; a place that is both hard and home. For all its flat brown nothingness and its isolation, its long stretches of monotony, I can't ever think of the region of my birth without a lump rising to my throat and tears burning my eyes. I was born with the quill inside my heart. I may be a Northwesterner in the practical sense, but my soul is all West.

In 2010 I was going through a divorce. My plan was to leave Seattle and move back to the Rocky Mountains the moment the proceedings had concluded—back to my place of origin, somewhere in the vicinity of the Grand Teton mountain range, and there seclude myself in some deep, dark-green, snow-scented valley. In the shadow of the mountains I love, and gloriously alone (only in the Rockies can one appreciate such a vast, towering lonesomeness) I would get on with living and write a brand-new chapter of my life.

That didn't happen. Before I could make the necessary arrangements to take myself back home, I fell crazy in love with Paul, who would become, three years later, my second husband. At the time, Paul was dedicated to a career that required him to live close to maritime ports, so the Rocky Mountains were out of the question if I wanted to keep this man in my life. As much as I loved Paul (still do) it was difficult for me to let go of my dream a homecoming and a resettling in the West (still is.) Even now, almost a decade after meeting Paul, I can feel those quill-hooks tearing at me, drawing me toward the landscape I love with a fierce and poignant pain.

In 2015 the Historical Novel Society conference was held in Denver, Colorado, and I was not about to miss three days of partying with my fellow authors of historical fiction. (In case you're wondering how historical novelists "party," it mostly involves sipping coffee or tea while discussing the most minute details of one's favorite slice of history. Also, we wear a lot of period costumes, which are made with fanatical accuracy. This is all very thrilling, I assure you.) It would have been cheaper and quicker to fly from Seattle to Denver, but the conference was just the excuse I needed to make a leisurely trip across the Intermountain West. I planned plenty of cushion time on either side of the conference, including three whole days to mope around the Grand Tetons, and set off for my big vacation.

Although I've traveled through the West several times in my life, I'd never before made the trip alone. All that time with just my thoughts and the vast, heart-rending landscape did curious things to my mind. Everywhere I looked I saw the ghosts of my past, slender and pale, moving like mist among the sagebrush. I saw the life I might have had if I hadn't met Paul—or hadn't chosen to stay with him—but other specters haunted me, too.

There are things we cannot change about our lives, things over which we have no control. Where we come from, who our parents are—that's one of those factors beyond our power. Our origins are a toss of the dice, a flick of the card boss's wrist. Sometimes fate deals a bad hand.

My dad shaped and influenced me more than any other person in my life, more than anything—a work of art, a force of nature, a blind, crazy faith. What's odd to me is that his influence was in his absence. We were close when I was a tiny kid—I have a few brief, cherished memories that remind me he was once a loving and very present father—but by the time I was six or seven years, old he was in the grip of severe mental illness. The only respite he could find from his illness was in the substances he came to abuse —alcohol first, then prescription narcotics, and finally heroin.

Addiction is a monstrous thing. It strips away its victim's dignity—sometimes their humanity, too. And it reaches beyond its victims to wound many other lives. Those who love the addicted must decide whether they'll stay and watch their father or mother, their spouse or friend deteriorate and vanish—or whether they'll leave their loved one behind with the hope that they will someday find recovery and peace. It was a hard choice, to separate myself from my father—and all the more difficult because I made that decision at a very young age, when I was just fifteen.

By then, my father had been a sporadic and unpredictable presence in my life for nearly a decade. But he was still my father, and I loved him. He was—and will always be—so much more to me than his mental illness or his addiction. He was creative, bright, funny, with an enthusiasm for storytelling that I think I must have inherited from him. He was a brilliant artist whose stirring, light-filled paintings of the American West are still sought out by serious collectors to this day. My dad felt the West like a pulse under his skin, and his talent for depicting the land-scape in his preferred medium—oil paint—fairly stops my heart whenever I think about it. I'm objective enough about my writing to feel confidence in my abilities. But when I consider how easily, how naturally my father expressed his love for the West with his brushes and pigments, I feel that my efforts in my chosen medium —words—can never compare.

His ability to carve out a career in the arts made me realize that I could be a writer when I grew up, if I just wanted it badly enough—if I poured my passion into my art. His expression of his own loves—his dreams and his misted, light-filled longings—made me hope for his recovery, so that I could admire him without restraint. I know my love for the West, which is the sharp-hooked center of my very heart, comes from my love for my dad. He was undeniably a mess—a brilliant, tragic, beautiful, infuriating calamity. He died in his sleep when I was 23 and he was 49. He'd been in recovery for about two years, and as far as I know, he died sober. The knowledge that he spent his last days beyond the grip of addiction has remained a great comfort to me all these years later.

I never realized how closely my experience of the West is tied up with the memory of my father until I made that drive out to Colorado in the summer of 2015. Every isolated town I passed reminded me of the summers I'd spent with my strange, distant dad in the canal-crossed farmlands between Rigby and Ririe, Idaho. Roadside convenience stores, their sides patinated with dust and age, brought back the taste of Reese's peanut butter cups and blackberry soda, which Dad would buy me almost daily on those court-ordered visits. Buttes touched by fading red light held the contours of his face. And everywhere—in the long, ochre yellow of a dry plain touching a thunder-blue horizon, in a purple curve of the Snake River, in the umber crags of the lava heaves—I saw the colors of his palette.

By the time I reached Denver I was wrung out and haunted.

The quills in my raw heart ached. The fact that I arrived in the city at exactly the same time as a freak tornado seemed too significant for coincidence. I was ready to have a good time at the conference, but a persistent irritation had settled inside me, an itch I couldn't scratch. After days of solitude in the Western landscape, I knew I wanted to write about my dad—not his biography, and not a family history, but something broader, something more accessible. Something that could touch more hearts than just my own. I wanted to write about emotion and addiction, love and loss, striving and failure—a brilliant, beautiful mess. But I couldn't write such a book until I found the right subject. Who, in all the history of the West, could carry such a theme?

A more practical problem weighed on me, too. I'd recently sold a novel to Lake Union Publishing—*Mercer Girls*—and I knew that fairly soon my editor would wonder what I'd have to offer next. I needed a very particular subject for my next historical novel if *Mercer Girls* was to work optimally within the framework of my business. I had to identify a historical figure whom fans of *Mercer Girls* would be likely to enjoy. She had to be female, had to exist in the late nineteenth century, and had to promise enough humor and fun to keep fans of *Mercer Girls* turning pages.

It wasn't until the second day of the conference that I ran into Calamity Jane, face-first in the midst of a panel about wild women of the West. One of the authors on the panel casually tossed out a remark about Calamity—something along the lines of, "Everybody thinks she was a famous scout and even a soldier, but the truth is that she was just a terribly afflicted alcoholic." Just like that, the itch was scratched. Inspiration—even conviction—dawned like the sun on the Tetons, and I fumbled my phone out of my purse and excitedly tapped out an email to my editor: *I'm doing my next book about Calamity Jane and it's going to be really, really awesome.* At that point, all I knew about Calamity was that hers was a famous name in the West and that she apparently struggled with addiction. But that was all I needed to know; I'd found the perfect vehicle for the story I wanted to tell.

I began researching Calamity that very evening. While waiting for a fellow novelist to join me for dinner, I bought *Calamity Jane: The Woman and the Legend* by James D. McLaird and began reading it on the Kindle app on my phone. By the time my friend arrived I'd already highlighted so many passages that my wrist was getting sore, and my phone's battery was almost dead. The more I read about Calamity—the real Calamity, not the towering legend she created to mask her true and tragic self—the more certain I became that I'd found the perfect subject for my novel. To my immense pleasure (and relief), I could recount a moving story of addiction, love, and loss without stretching the facts too far. Calamity Jane's history was complicated and heavy enough to bring a tear to any reader's eye. It needed virtually no embellishment to suit my purposes.

Her real name was Martha Canary, and she was most likely born in the spring of 1856, though historians have had a hard time discerning her exact date of birth. Late in her life, Calamity's only living came from the propagation of her own legend. In order to maintain her dazzling reputation, she had to prevent newspaper reporters and other interested parties from discovering too much about her, for the ugly truth never lurked very far beneath Calamity's surface. Her early life was very much as I presented it in this novel—the most important exception being the timing of her mother's death. Charlotte Burch Canary actually died in the Montana gold fields—I tinkered with the place and circumstances just to kick the story off faster—but otherwise, Martha/Calamity Jane's childhood and family were as I depicted them. The exact cause of her father's death is unrecorded, but he died while he was en route to Salt Lake City, freshly made a widower with his children in tow.

As an orphan, it fell to Martha—who was between twelve and fourteen years old—to support her siblings. She took to sex work straight away, having few other options, and certainly no options that would pay as well. She really did place her siblings with other families, one by one, as the weight of so much responsibility proved too much for her young body and spirit to bear. I believe it must have been these early traumas that set her on her notorious life path and saddled her with the burden of alcoholism. I can hardly blame her. If I'd found myself in her situation, forced to take up sex work as a young girl merely to keep my brothers and sisters alive—and failing at that—I'm sure I would have ended up far more bitter and afflicted than Jane ever was.

I read more about Calamity Jane, I was struck by her buoyant spirit. True, her character and her legacy were forged in loss and pain. But though her alcoholism often caused trouble, leading her to indulge in destructive behaviors, she was without question a kind-hearted and generous person, quick to laugh, eager to make friends, and with an overall enthusiasm for life.

Her great tenderness for animals led her to mule- and bull-whacking careers, which she was able to maintain for a number of years. Her skill as a driver of animal teams almost kept her out of the dangerous world of sex work for good. And the fact that she nursed people who suffered from smallpox is well attested in several different sources, though the precise dates and locations of these stints as a nurse are difficult to verify. It's possible that she acted as nurse to smallpox sufferers multiple times throughout her life. (Why she never caught the terrible disease herself isn't known. Some who were exposed to smallpox in those days ate or drank preparations made from the scabs of smallpox wounds, which may have acted as a vaccination of sorts. There is also a genetic variation in the CCR5 gene that appears to provide natural immunity against certain viral diseases, smallpox included, and is present in about 10% of people of European descent.)

I really began to *like* Calam on a personal level as I put in the work of researching and planning this novel. How could anyone fail to like her? More than a hundred years after her death, her personality still shines through every letter, journal entry, and newspaper article that was written about her true exploits.

I say her *true* exploits because there's a whole heap of fiction about Calamity Jane. That has been the case since Calam's own time. I was never able to discern exactly how or why her fame began to spread, but spread it certainly did. She quickly became a fixture of the adventure novels that helped sell the idea of westward expansion to Americans living on the eastern side of the continent. She witnessed the birth of her own legend and watched it take shape, saw her name take on a personality of its own. The legend, alas, bore no resemblance to the truth Calamity Jane lived.

Aside from altering the circumstances of her mother's death, guessing on the smallpox incident, and shortening her stint with Buffalo Bill's Wild West Show (she really toured with Buffalo Bill for at least three years), all the other events depicted in this novel occurred how and as I portrayed them. Sources seem to agree that she had one daughter for certain, named Jessie and fathered by the ill-tempered and abusive Bill Steers, one of Calamity's many common-law husbands. Calamity really did try to pass Jessie off as her granddaughter for reasons unknown. She also had at least one still birth while running her bullwhacking business. She may have had other children—the sources couldn't seem to agree. I have invented accessory characters here and there for the sake of narrative color (Billy Voss, Red Nancy), or have inserted other notorious Western personages into Calamity Jane's story (such as Molly B'Damn), but by and large, if I wrote a scene where something important happened to Calamity, it truly happened when and how I portrayed it—according to the available sources, that is, which I had to approach with caution. When you're writing about a subject whose very livelihood depended on inflating the glamour of her own name, you must take certain accounts with a grain of salt. But I worked hard to faithfully depict as many parts of the verifiable historical record as I could. The result is a novel that cleaves as closely to truth as I believe any novel of Calamity Jane's life may aspire to do. It was a project three and a half years in the making—my longest writing jag yet.

Speaking of the countless fictions that surround this enigmatic subject, it may interest the reader to learn that I took the chapter titles from novels and newspaper accounts written about Calamity Jane and published during her time. The chapter titles were intended to contrast the vibrancy of her legend with the harsh realities of Calam's actual life. It was a bittersweet process, combing through 19th-century writings about Calamity Jane and pulling out lines that might work as titles for the chapters I had already written. Hers was a life of struggle and heartbreak, patiently endured under the shadow of her fictionalized brilliance.

Most affecting of all were the many novels and stories written about Wild Bill Hickock and Calamity Jane. Calam seemed to have loved Wild Bill—passionately, completely, and hopelessly. Even after his death—which she truly did witness, as depicted in this book—she went on carrying his torch. She told some people that her daughter Jessie was fathered by Wild Bill in what I can only assume was a case of wistful longing. She really did keep his pocket watch and a golden, ruby-eyed snake ring throughout most of her life—and the ring truly was stolen while she lay in the grips of an alcoholic black-out. And the last photo of Calam was taken at Bill's grave, holding a silk flower. When she died only a few days later in a Deadwood saloon, she was laid to rest at Bill's side.

I can't tell you what inspired me to end this novel in modern times, with the revelation that "Short Pants" is actually the reader him- or herself, listening to the ghost of Calamity Jane spill out her true story in present-day Deadwood. The thought simply came to me and stuck in my head, with that peculiar, quiet persistence I've come to recognize as the flourishing of a Good Idea. But I knew I'd made the right decision when I gave the manuscript to a friend to read. This particular friend has struggled with addiction herself, and after reading the book, she said to me, "Thank you for making Calamity Jane more than just an alcoholic. You gave her dimension and life beyond her addiction. You made her addiction understandable. And somehow having it end in the present day makes it feel that much more real—like you aren't just writing about an addict from history; you're writing about addiction itself, as a contemporary problem that affects real people."

Of course, that was what I'd set out to do all along. I was gratified to hear that I had found my mark.

I have many people to thank, whose support, help, and enthusiasm for this project kept me working on it for nearly four years.

The team at Lake Union Publishing ultimately decided not to publish this book because I wouldn't agree to trim down its size. I simply couldn't—there was too much story to tell, and all of it was critical. In the end, I self-published *Calamity*, but Lake Union's interest in the book kept me working steadily.

Thanks to the Historical Novel Society and all its volunteers for throwing the best conference in the genre—a conference that can inspire the creation of new novels.

To my family—especially my mom, Cheryl Grant (who is of the opinion that this is the best book I've written so far) and my sister, Georgia Schlegel—for being this book's greatest cheerleaders: thank you.

My biggest thanks to Jackie Zebrowski, whose peerless performance of the audiobook edition left me speechless. She is the true voice of Calamity Jane; she understood this character as even I couldn't and brought Calam to life in ways no writer ever could. I will forever regard the audiobook edition of *Calamity* as one of the finest products of my career as a novelist.

Thanks to my dad for being who and what he was—for shaping my life, for making me who and what I am, for better and worse. There's a star on the horizon. I still remember. I always will.

And thank you to Paul, for everything.

-Libbie Hawker
2019, San Juan Island, WA

ABOUT THE AUTHOR

Libbie Hawker writes historical and literary fiction featuring complex characters and rich details of time and place. She is the author of more than twenty books, including the Washington Post and two-time Amazon #1 bestseller *The Ragged Edge of Night* (written under her pen name, Olivia Hawker.)

She lives in the beautiful San Juan Islands of Washington State with her husband and several naughty cats. When she's not writing, she enjoys gardening, spinning wool, and knitting sweaters.

Follow Libbie on Instagram for more pictures of cats and flowers than you could ever desire.

CPSIA information can be obtained
at www.ICGtesting.com
Printed in the USA
LVHW051210230920
666818LV00001B/19

9 781947 174221